"It's the
drive...

Brock continued his discourse. "It ignites their internal fires beyond all reason. The male catches her scent, takes it into him and knows he must possess her. Once he's gotten her scent, he'll never give up until he has her."

Brock's warm, enticing breath fell across Shana's forehead and then angled down toward her cheek causing tiny quivers to dance down her spine.

"The teasing of their courtship prepares both male and female for mating. All the senses come into play—sound, sight, smell, touch. He calls to her. She darts away. He follows. Circling, watching, exciting her until she wants him as much as he wants her. She no longer runs away. His desire pulses hard in his loins until it cannot be denied. She aches to be filled. She..."

Shana's heart pounded like a frenzied bass drum in her chest. She closed her eyes, tried not to listen, but she couldn't shut out the clean, masculine smell of Brock, the mesmerizing tone of his deep silky voice, the steamy images his words evoked.

That's when Shana knew Brock was no longer talking about horses.

ABOUT THE AUTHOR

A seasoned Intrigue author, M.J. Rodgers is thrilled to publish her first American Romance novel. When asked to describe the ideal man, M.J. replied, "He knows real strength comes from character and is displayed at its best with gentleness. He understands a man and a woman really give of themselves when they share their time, thoughts and feelings with each other." M.J. makes her home in Washington State with her husband and son.

Books by M.J. Rodgers

HARLEQUIN INTRIGUE

M.J. RODGERS

FIRE MAGIC

Harlequin Books

TORONTO • NEW YORK • LONDON
AMSTERDAM • PARIS • SYDNEY • HAMBURG
STOCKHOLM • ATHENS • TOKYO • MILAN
MADRID • WARSAW • BUDAPEST • AUCKLAND

This book is for the warm, wonderful people of Tonopah, Nevada, and for those special women and men who serve in the U.S. Forest Service.

Published June 1993

ISBN 0-373-16492-0

FIRE MAGIC

Chapter One

Shana O'Shea's heart swelled into her throat as Fire Magic, the magnificent wild stallion, galloped headlong toward the dangerous precipice and certain death.

His hooves pounded the dry Nevada Mountain dust into a silver cloud beneath his long swift legs. The rays of the high-desert sun struck his red coat, turning it into iridescent fire, his flying mane and tail into leaping flames. He did not slow but rather increased his speed as he charged toward the chasm that ended in a two-hundred-foot drop onto the jagged rocks below.

No! Shana's heart cried.

She urged Mickey Finn, her mustang mount, faster, desperate to head Fire Magic off. She could feel the steam of Mickey's sweat, hear his labored breathing as he gave her his all. She leaned against his neck, strained with every ounce of her being to will him more speed.

To no avail.

Fire Magic got to the cliff first. And jumped.

Shana's heart stopped as she stared in shock and horror.

Then her mouth dropped open. She couldn't believe her eyes! The stallion wasn't falling. He was sailing across the thirty-foot expanse to land on the other side!

She reined Mickey in and peered through the settling dust. The stallion pranced on the other side of the chasm, his thick majestic neck and tail both arched in defiance as he seemed to give her a good old-fashioned horse laugh. She would have wagered anything that no horse could make that jump. She would have lost.

Relief and exultation filled her heart.

"Half fire. Half magic. He is well named, is he not, Shana?" Tommy Windway, her Paiute Indian helper and friend called as he reined in next to her, the perspiration rolling off his young dark brow.

Shana's eyes glistened, her voice almost breathless in response. "Did you see him, Tommy? He flew across that chasm!"

John Cloud, her second Paiute Indian rider, nodded his ancient silver head as he also drew alongside. His wise black eyes appraised the prancing stallion. "He is a creature of wind and fire and magic, Shana. That one carries the true wild spirit in his heart. Such a horse is not meant for the touch of man."

Or woman, either, it appears, Shana thought as she sighed deeply and audibly. "John, it's my job to keep trying. He's proving quite an expensive pest, you know."

"What I know," Tommy Windway warned, "is that if you don't get a rope around Lady Blue, Fire Magic might just persuade her to make that leap after him."

Shana quickly reached for her lasso as she heard Fire Magic's call to the roan filly on their side of the chasm. Sure enough, Lady Blue was beginning to dance around as though she was mustering up her courage to follow the impetuous stallion across the impossible leap. After several twirls above her head, Shana's rope sailed expertly around the mare's neck, and she gave her a dissuading tug away from the edge. Reluctantly, Lady Blue came.

Shana pulled her alongside and gave her hot neck a reassuring pat. Fire Magic had run her hard since stealing her from Amy Edel's breeding ranch several hours ago. But the young mare was strong and in good shape. She was none the worse for wear. Still, Shana knew if Amy hadn't called her right away and she hadn't spotted the horse by helicopter, she never would have had a prayer of getting the mare back. This time, she'd been lucky.

The Thoroughbred mare's black coat shimmered blue in the hot rays of the late spring sunshine as she whinnied plaintively in response to Fire Magic's continuing shrill mating call. Shana held the restraining rope snugly, soothing the mare's matted mane.

"Settle down, Lady. I admit he's a handsome devil, all right. But no reason to break your neck over him. There are plenty more for you back on the breeding ranch."

Lady Blue shook her head to discourage the biting flies that had attacked her sweating neck. At least that's what Shana imagined she was shaking her head about.

"You don't need our help now that you've got a rope around her," John announced as he turned his horse away in one of his typical quick goodbyes.

"Call us again when Fire Magic steals the next one," Tommy chorused with a friendly grin and wave.

Shana turned in her saddle to send a thank-you toward their disappearing backs as they rode up the trail. Although not officially employed by the U.S. Forest Service, as she was, John and Tommy never hesitated to lend her a hand when duty took her into the Toiyabe

National Forest of central Nevada. They were her riding companions. And her friends.

Her fingers automatically caressed the leather pouch she wore around her neck—the contents of which John Cloud had given her many years before. And she carried with her always.

Fire Magic called again, breaking into her thoughts. She looked across the wide chasm at him snorting and prancing on the other side, feeling transfixed by his wild beauty and strength. Tommy was right, of course. Fire Magic wouldn't give up.

She leaned back in her saddle and let her eyes feast on his beauty. Every inch of his red coat, mane and tail glistened with fire. His lightning-swift silver hooves seemed to set off sparks beneath him. She had never seen anything like him. This time they'd been chasing him for two hours straight, and he didn't even look winded.

Still, it wasn't just his beauty, his larger-than-life size, his swiftness or his stamina that held her in awe—it was the way he had outfoxed her no matter what kind of a trap she had set for him.

Fire Magic was no ordinary wild stallion.

She watched him rearing up, pawing the air—in freedom, in challenge. Brazenly, he called to the mare again and Lady Blue's head rose as she whinnied back and strained on the rope. Shana knew she shouldn't be tempting fate. She knew she should turn her mount and the mare away and ride back down the trail. But as always when she got this close to Fire Magic, she felt awed, mesmerized by the sheer power and splendor of him.

"He's like a red Pegasus—straight out of a mythology book."

The deep masculine voice drummed in Shana's ears. She whirled around to see its possessor, directly behind her, sitting on a beautifully proportioned buckskin. Normally such a horse would have immediately claimed Shana's full attention. But this time it was the man on his back at whom she stared.

He was a blond, bronzed giant with long hair resting on a set of shoulders that went on forever. His shirt was open to his waist, revealing an imposing wall of smooth, rippling muscles. His equally impressive forearms corded out of his short-sleeved shirt as he wrapped the reins around his saddle's horn. Jeans—designer if Shana was any judge—hugged legs as thick and hard as tree trunks. Above the high cheekbones of his hand-somely rugged face, his eyes were a gleaming, assessing gray. He wore a smile that said he knew what his looks did to women.

Shana shivered a little. Behind her the sound of Fire Magic's hooves made her swing back just in time to see the majestic stallion gallop away in a cloud of silver dust.

She sighed, understanding the plaintive whinny of Lady Blue beside her. She was already missing him, too. Somehow she could never get her fill of the awesome perfection of that stallion. Her head angled back to the intruder.

He was smiling. "Sorry if I startled you. Or the horse."

He looked smug, contented—anything but sorry— and all male. His eyes raked her boots, then her long, dark-green-uniform-clad legs and presumptuously traveled farther up her anatomy to take in her short-sleeved forest-ranger shirt. He grinned in blatant enjoyment of the process. Shana found herself fighting a very sudden and uncharacteristic nervousness.

She imbued her tone with the authority of her position. "I'm sorry, but you shouldn't be here in this wilderness area."

His smile never faltered. "It's Toiyabe National Forest, isn't it? Open to the public? Well, I'm the public. Brock Trulock by name."

He nudged his beautiful buckskin to move toward her as he held out his hand. Shana didn't take it. For one, she still held her reins and the rope that kept Lady Blue in check. For two, she had the disturbing suspicion that to take this man's hand would be dangerous.

She stared straight into those assessing gray eyes, trying to ignore the continuing and quite annoying flutter in her stomach. "Well, Mr. Trulock, you are only partially right. Yes, this is Toiyabe National Forest, but the signs are clearly posted around this section. It's closed to campers and hikers."

His smile remained unperturbed. "Glad I'm not either, then. Don't call me Mr. Trulock. Call me Brock. And you are?"

Deliberately, he wasn't letting her message get through. She straightened in the saddle, feeling herself bristle as she pointed to the restricted signs not twenty feet from them. "I'm an employee of the National Forest Service here in Nevada, *Mr. Trulock*. And whatever you are, you are also a trespasser. Those signs say this section is not open to the public. Period."

His mouth twisted in amusement. "You're a ranger?"

Shana didn't like the quick sweep of his eyes over her tanned bare arms or the light lilt to his tone, as though he understood some joke she wasn't getting. Her spine stiffened. "Actually, my title is Supervisory Range Conservationist, but ranger will do. My boss is the Tonopah District ranger. It's our job to protect the land and wildlife here in Toiyabe National Forest."

"Wildlife? Like the wild mustangs?"

"Some make their home on National Forest Range, yes. There are also other protected wildlife here. And vegetation. As I said before, you're trespassing. I'll show you the trail out."

Shana urged her mount forward.

Out of the corner of her eye, she saw Brock Trulock move his horse alongside Lady Blue. "So this is the latest mare Fire Magic stole. She's a beauty."

Shana looked over to see him eyeing Lady Blue appreciatively and tried to keep the surprise out of her voice. "What do you know about Fire Magic?"

He leaned back in his saddle as though he were a part of it, that damn knowing smile still on his lips. "You're Shana O'Shea, aren't you? The one who took that picture of the red stallion fighting off the mountain lion?"

"Yes, but how did you—?"

"I read the piece on it in the Las Vegas paper and all about his penchant for fine-bred mares. Your picture of the stallion intrigued me. I decided I had to take a look for myself."

Shana clenched her teeth. She knew nothing good would come of her boss's insistence on giving that story to the newspapers. She had begged him not to. But as usual he'd ignored her and gone ahead and done it anyway. Now she had to deal with tourists! "So you rode out here just to see Fire Magic?"

"He was worth the ride."

New suspicions rose in Shana's mind. "This section of Toiyabe Forest is more than a million acres. How did you just happen to ride in the right direction?"

"I didn't just happen to. I overheard the report of Fire Magic stealing a prime Thoroughbred mare, and I was on hand at the Tonopah Ranger Station when you came back to collect your gear after landing the helicopter. I decided to tag along—at a discreet distance from you and your companions, of course. Didn't know how warm my welcome would be, and I was determined to stick with you until you found the horse. And what a horse he proved to be. That jump was nothing less than spectacular."

Again the charming smile. Except Shana was determined not to be charmed. "Fire Magic is not a tourist attraction, Mr. Trulock."

"Never thought he was. I'm a breeder of horses. I could see right away Fire Magic is not the typical wild Nevada mustang."

Shana bit her lip. A breeder? Interested in Fire Magic? She didn't have a good feeling about this. She tried to sound nonchalant. "Nevada mustangs represent a wide variation. A lot of different horses have infused the herds with their blood."

"But you'll have to admit that most look like the gelding you're riding, don't they?"

Mickey Finn pricked his long ears back as though he knew he was being discussed. He was a sturdy, large-headed, shaggy little horse that would win no beauty contests but had a disposition as sweet as a saint's, and twice the stamina of any "well-bred" horse Shana had ridden. She gave his short neck a reassuring pat.

"Yes, Mickey Finn used to run with a wild herd. I adopted him out of a roundup we did with the Bureau of Land Management a couple of years ago. He's an unbeatable mount for the rough hills. Surefooted, rugged, a real trooper.''

"And nothing like Fire Magic," Brock added.

"No, nothing like Fire Magic," Shana conceded.

"How long has the red stallion been in Toiyabe?"

Shana nudged Mickey Finn forward. Now that Fire Magic wasn't around to distract her, Lady Blue picked up her delicate hooves without protest and followed. "Probably since he was born."

Brock eased his buckskin into a comfortable lope beside them. "You think he was born wild, then?"

"Yes. I'm sure if someone had lost a horse like him, they would have put out a bulletin and offered a reward. He's quite distinctive."

"Yes, quite. He's enormous. Probably eighteen hands at the shoulder. With a broad forehead and dish-shaped face like an Arabian and their iridescent coat, a high rump like a Thoroughbred, a massive chest, a short back and long, swift legs."

His words brought her eyes to his face. "You seem to have studied Fire Magic's conformation quite thoroughly. Why?"

His eyes gleamed at her like cool steel. "Because I intend to capture him, Shana O'Shea."

Shana's protest tumbled out before she could check it with her normal cool reason. "You can't do that!"

Brock gave her one of his charming smiles. His deep voice carried no inflection, which should have made his words bland but instead underlined them with a chilling determination. "Yes, I can."

Shana couldn't believe the arrogance of the man. She controlled her voice with difficulty. "You obviously don't understand. Fire Magic and all the other wild horses within Toiyabe National Forest are under my protection. I will not tolerate you or anyone trespassing onto their grazing areas and annoying them."

"Seems to me that it's Fire Magic who's been doing the trespassing and annoying lately. No doubt when I catch him the local breeders and ranchers will exhale a sigh of relief."

Shana drew Mickey Finn up short and twisted in the saddle to glare at Brock. She was blazingly mad and only just keeping it under control. Her words came out through clenched teeth. "Mr. Trulock, you will ride your horse out of this restricted wilderness area of Toiyabe National Forest this instant, and you will not return, or I promise you I will put you in handcuffs. Now have I made myself clear?"

A flash of new speculation entered his gleaming gray eyes before they took a leisurely run up and down her body, as though he had just decided she deserved closer inspection. Everywhere his eyes touched, her skin burned. Shana felt her lungs laboring to suck in enough air as he flashed her another charming smile.

"Our getting better acquainted while my hands are tied conjures up all sorts of interesting images, Shana O'Shea. Too bad I don't have time now to take you up on that very intriguing offer. But I'm afraid I'm late for an appointment, so it will have to be later. But don't worry. I'll get back to you. Keep the handcuffs handy."

And with those parting words he gave his beautiful buckskin a nudge with his tree-trunk thighs and trotted off.

Shana stared wild-eyed at his broad retreating back, nearly bursting with a million angry retorts but mute from choked rage.

BROCK SAT in the close confines of the Las Vegas table, ignoring the nearly nude dancers strutting their stuff on the stage above him as he focused on the man sitting next to him. Tonopah District Ranger Phil Hudson was short, bald, fiftyish, with dark eyes and freckled-spotted fists that pounded excitedly on the tabletop.

"To think I'm finally sitting across from Brock Trulock! Damn, this is sensational. You'll never know how much I've admired your work. The falls you've done off cliffs, the incredible rides you've made on horseback—well, they're nothing short of spectacular. You're already a legend. Everybody says so."

A scantly clad waitress literally falling out of her low-cut dress leaned over their table. Phil Hudson stopped talking long enough to salivate and ask her to bring him a double Scotch. Brock didn't even glance in her direction as he ordered a straight vodka on the rocks.

Phil's dark eyes hazed over dreamily as soon as the waitress left. "You know, I once wanted to be a stuntman. Used to watch all the Westerns. Learned how to rope and ride. Even traveled out to Hollywood for a tryout."

Brock heard Phil sigh as he hoisted a hand over his bald head. "So what happened?" Brock asked, pretty sure what Phil would say but knowing Phil would have to be the one to say it.

The dreamy haze faded in the other man's eyes. "Oh, hell, I was kidding myself. Hollywood didn't want a pudgy, five-foot-eight guy who was already losing his hair taking a fall for Clint Eastwood."

Phil chuckled as he took some peanuts out of the condiment dish and dropped them into his mouth, munching noisily. "Anyhow, it's just as well. Probably would have broken every bone in my body. Still, you'll never know how great it is to meet somebody who's living the Hollywood dream.''

Brock shifted uncomfortably in his chair. At least he was living *somebody's* dream. "I hope you understand my need for keeping this little endeavor I'm planning under wraps?"

Phil leaned forward and lowered his voice. "Oh, yes. Certainly. And contacting me while I'm on vacation down here in Vegas will help to keep it all confidential. Tonopah is a small town. Were we to have met up at the ranger station, the rumor mill would have already ground out heaps of speculation. They don't miss much there."

A shapely naked leg kicked up in Brock's peripheral vision. He didn't bat an eye. Phil leaned back again in his chair and let his eyes stray to the showgirls on the nearby stage. "Besides, the scenery here is so much better."

Brock shook his head. "I've had my fill of that kind of scenery. While we've still got some time, I'd like to know more about Shana O'Shea."

Phil shrugged somewhat disappointedly as he leaned forward and let his elbows find the tabletop. "I guess since you'll be working with her, it's only natural. Well, let's see. What do you want to know?"

"How long has she been with the National Forest Service?"

"Joined right after getting her Associate in Arts degree in Wildlife Management. Must be eight or nine years ago. Knew exactly what she wanted to do."

"Is she married?"

"Naw. Too independent. She's almost thirty, and I've yet to see her with a man. Except Cort Donner. But it's hard to tell what they've got going."

Brock's eyes narrowed. "Who's this Cort Donnor?"

"Local guy. Bit of a hothead. Son of the richest rancher in Nevada. He and Shana have known each other since grade school."

Brock eased back in his chair. If Donner hadn't corralled Shana O'Shea after knowing her since grade school, he wasn't likely to. "You know why she decided to join the U.S. Forest Service?"

"Just followed in her mother's footsteps, I suppose. Patricia O'Shea was one of our first archaeologists with the Forest Service here in Nevada. She located and recorded hundreds of archaeological sites of prehistoric Indians in the Toiyabe wilderness. She's still working vigorously with the American Museum of Natural History in researching and categorizing them. Patricia's strong and ornery and as tough as any man. Shana's a chip."

"What about Shana's father?"

"Oh, he was a photographer up at the digs. Ran out on Patricia when Shana was just a baby. A black Irishman with lots of easy charm and a wanderlust spirit. I met him once, long time ago. Shana favors him in her looks. But she's got her mother's feisty temperament. She's great at protecting the terrain and the wildlife, though. Couldn't ask for better. And she knows the forest and this wild stallion like no one else alive. You and she will make a good team. Of course, in all fairness, I should warn you about Shana's—"

Brock sensed the shadow across his shoulders before it hit the table. "About Shana's what?" Shana demanded from behind him.

Brock turned around slowly. Her gaze flew to him immediately, and he saw recognition solidify in her glinting gold-flecked brown eyes, and something else that he'd noticed from the first moment he'd met her. Something contained. Something untouched. Something wild.

She had on a simple ice blue dress with a wide belt around her waist, accentuating her height and slimness. Her only accessory was the small leather pouch she wore around her neck that he had also noticed on the previous day. Her shoes were flat pumps. Her long black hair was free and flowing over those firm, golden-tanned arms. No makeup was necessary to emphasize the strong bones and smooth skin of her exquisite face.

Brock was vaguely aware of the sequined, nearly naked bodies of the performing showgirls behind her. But only vaguely. He didn't take his eyes from Shana O'Shea as he stood and held out a chair. He gave her his most charming smile. "How nice you could join us."

Shana remained standing. She, too, did not take her eyes from Brock, although her words were clearly for Phil. "What's this all about? Why did you insist I meet you here and what does *his* presence mean?"

Phil glanced around nervously. "Please, Shana. Sit. You'll draw attention to us. This business is confidential."

She looked away from Brock to find a chair other than the one he was holding out for her. She scooted it up to the table and sat as far away from Brock as she could manage. He deliberately bumped her knee with his as he reseated himself. She showed no sign she was even aware of it.

Everything in her cool look and actions dismissed him. He felt a sudden primitive heat coursing in his veins and thought he might be understanding for the first time why prehistoric man had ignored all the willing females and insisted on dragging into his cave the one prehistoric woman he had to hit over the head first.

Shana turned to Phil, her voice deadly calm. "All right, I'm sitting. Now how about those answers, Phil."

Brock watched Phil squirm in his seat, looking thankful for the interruption as the waitress arrived with their drinks. Phil took a large swig of Scotch before hesitantly inquiring if he could order something for Shana. His voice was barely audible. She shook her head in a controlled, purposeful movement. And waited.

Phil gulped, then straightened, as though attempting to remind himself that Shana reported to him and not the other way around. He coughed, trying to lower his voice into a more commanding tone. It came out as a high squeak. "Brock mentioned you met on the trail. Told me he was impressed with the way you retrieved Lady Blue from Fire Magic, didn't you, Brock?"

Phil looked hopefully to Brock for support. Aware Shana O'Shea did not like his charming smiles, Brock gave her another one. "Too bad the red stallion has stolen her again."

Shana's spine stiffened. "Stolen her again? How could he? I only returned Lady Blue to Amy Edel yesterday evening!"

Phil's shoulders twitched. "Yeah, I know, Shana. But Fire Magic came after the mare again last night. Demolished the stall Amy had locked her in. Amy's manager found Lady Blue gone and the unshod stallion's hoof prints everywhere this morning when he showed up with Lady Blue's feed."

"Why didn't Amy call me?"

"She said she did, Shana. Early. Got no answer."

Brock watched for a sign from Shana that would explain why she wasn't available to receive the call. Her expression gave nothing away. She offered no explanation.

Phil continued. "But even if Amy had gotten hold of you, what good would it have done? Fire Magic had too much of a head start."

Brock watched as a tiny frown worked its way between Shana's dark eyebrows. "Still, Amy contacted you. Why? Everyone knew you were on vacation here in Vegas. What could you do from more than two hundred miles away?"

"Get you some help, Shana. Catching that wild stallion is not a job for one person."

Her chin rose. "You know perfectly well that John and Tommy are always available to assist."

"Now I'm not saying John Cloud and Tommy Windway aren't good trackers, Shana. But they're not horsemen. You need a trained professional. Like Brock here."

Brock felt her eyes cut through him like sharpened daggers. "Oh? And how is *he* a trained professional?"

Phil's eyes bulged. "How is he a trained professional? Don't you go to the movies? Don't you watch television? This is Brock Trulock. *The* Brock Trulock. A living legend! He's done nearly every stunt on a horse that you can imagine. And he's the best all-round stuntman Hollywood has ever known!"

A *Hollywood stuntman?* Terrific. Just what she needed.

Shana turned deprecating eyes to the handsome face next to her. "I thought you said you were a horse breeder."

He smiled his charming smile again. "Obviously I'm a man of many talents. Some you'll find quite stimulating, Shana."

The way he said her name and the look in his eyes raised the tiny hairs on the back of her neck—almost as if he'd run a warm caressing finger across her. Shana felt a jolt that she hid for all she was worth. She was sure he was doing this deliberately to get a rise out of her—just as he had done on the trail the day before and earlier when he'd bumped her knee under the table.

Well, she wasn't going to rise to any of this man's bait. She turned back resolutely to her boss. "Look, Phil. I've got all the help I need. No reason to make a Hollywood production out of it."

"Isn't there?" Phil asked. "Since Fire Magic appeared last spring, he's inflamed not just the breeders like Amy, but also the ranchers who are trying to use the range for their livestock. And no matter how many times you've gone after him with your Paiute friends, you've come back empty-handed. Something is not working."

It was an uncomfortable truth that Shana swallowed in stoic silence. Phil sat forward, rattling the ice in his Scotch against the sides of the glass. "Look, I'm being pushed up against a wall here. Amy Edel didn't just phone me after Lady Blue was stolen by the stallion last night. She arrived at my hotel room this morning before coffee and my newspaper to register her complaint."

Shana's voice rose in surprise. "She's here in Vegas?"

"Staying at the Excalibur with her trainer, Frank Panew. That's the reason I was so insistent about your coming down and booking a room there. I want you and Brock to go see Amy this afternoon. Have a nice friendly talk. Tell her you're working together now. Smooth over her ruffled feathers. Let Brock tell her about his plan to capture the stallion and retrieve her horses."

Shana came out of her chair. "*His* plan?"

Phil waved her back down again. "Now, Shana, hear me out. It would be foolish for us not to accept Brock's help. He knows horses. And besides, the stallion is really his since he's officially adopting Fire Magic as soon as he's caught."

Shana swallowed hard as she looked from Phil's face to Brock's and back again. She tried to keep the anxious quaver out of her voice. "Adopting him? Since when?"

"Since this morning when I filled out the papers with the Bureau of Land Management according to the Wild Horse and Burro Adoption Act," Brock said, flashing her yet another charming smile. "Since Amy Edel's ranch is on BLM land, and Fire Magic has visited it so frequently, they consider the stallion's range within their territory. And since his range is under their jurisdiction, so is he. Phil looked over the documents and concurs with the adoption. All perfectly legal."

Shana wanted to pick up his drink and throw it at that damn smiling stuntman. So smug. So sure. Her heart sank. Damn him, he said he'd get Fire Magic, and he sure as hell wasn't wasting any time getting to it. What was she going to do?

She deliberately crossed her arms over her chest and leaned back in her chair. "So the Bureau of Land Management gave you approval to adopt the horse? Well, then they can just help you catch him."

Phil leaned toward her. "Except you know perfectly well that they've tried and failed. Fire Magic always retreats into Toiyabe and hides. Even their best have failed to locate him."

Yes, she did know. Perfectly well. "I'm not going to help in Fire Magic's capture. Since you've got a *plan*, Mr. Trulock, you can just go put your *plan* into effect and see where it gets you."

Phil downed the rest of his drink nervously. "Now, Shana. Let's try to be professional about this. Brock isn't familiar with the Toiyabe National Forest terrain. He's going to need a guide to locate the horse."

Shana's eyes glittered dangerously. "Maybe he can convince John Cloud or Tommy Windway to track for him."

Phil shook his head. "You know very well, Shana, that John and Tommy help you only out of friendship. They are not for hire. And even if they were, Brock's capture of Fire Magic has to be kept a secret—from everyone including your Paiute friends. If word got out that Hollywood stuntman Brock Trulock were here on a wild-horse hunt, well you can just imagine the flock of folks who would descend on Toiyabe wanting to watch or be in on the action. Then we really would end up with a Hollywood extravaganza, and who knows how the Toiyabe wildlife and vegetation would be affected."

Grudgingly, Shana saw the wisdom behind Phil's words. Not that she felt inclined to admit it. She sensed Brock's eyes on her, smiling and sure. Her temper sizzled. She purposely kept her eyes on Phil. "If *Mr. Hollywood's* track of Fire Magic is supposed to be so secret, why is it you want him to accompany me when I talk with Amy Edel? Isn't that going to spill the beans?"

"Brock isn't going to tell Amy who he really is. You're going to introduce him just as an expert in catching horses."

"Oh, I am, am I?"

"Come on, Shana. I know you're proud and wouldn't dream of asking for help under normal circumstances, but there's no shame in seeking some assistance in catching this stallion. I mean, any horse who can buck a mountain lion off his back—"

"What's this? Did I just hear you say some horse bucked a mountain lion off his back?"

Shana whirled around in her seat to see Victor Badham, leaning over Phil like a vulture sniffing the air for decaying carrion. He was short and squat, with a froglike face and body. Turquoise-and-silver rings quivered on his fat, nervous fingers. His thick, musk cologne clogged Shana's nose and throat. Behind the froglike man stood his six-foot-two bodyguard, Jebb, with the lumpy shoulders and punched-in face of an ex-boxer.

"Yeah, Victor," Phil said. "This wild horse Shana's been chasing. She got a picture of him a couple of weeks ago duking it out with a mountain lion. Final score was stallion one, mountain lion zero. It was in all the Vegas papers. Can't believe you missed it."

Shana groaned internally. She wished someday Phil would learn to keep his mouth shut. Particularly in front of Badham. The man was a slimy lowlife. How many times had she warned Phil about him?

Tiny beads of light flickered in Badham's dark eyes as he hopped into the chair Brock had originally held out for Shana and then scooted it closer to Phil. His long, pointed tongue shot out to wet his thick lips. "That so? Must have missed it when I went to Phoenix to put together that rodeo. So tell me more about this stallion."

Phil had just begun to open his mouth again when Shana's palm came slapping down on the tabletop. Her voice was icy. "You were not invited to this table, Mr. Badham. But I am inviting you to leave it. Now."

Victor Badham swiveled his head in Shana's direction. His small dark eyes regarded her silently for several quiet seconds. "Ms. O'Shea, you can't *still* be carrying a grudge against me after our little misunderstanding? It was such a long time ago."

Shana enunciated through clenched teeth. "We've never had a *misunderstanding,* Mr. Badham. I understand you all too well. You tried to use the BLM adoption program to illegally secure mustangs for commercial exploitation."

Badham raised a cautionary, ringed finger. "Now, now. That was never proved. It was my misguided employee Jebb here who sought to make those unsavory arrangements, remember?"

Shana's tone dropped several more degrees as she glanced up at the stoic, broken-nosed bodyguard. "What I remember is who paid this so-called misguided employee's salary. And who still pays it."

Badham's smile was sinister. "Jebb was sorry. Repented. Surely you believe in giving a man a second chance, don't you, Ms. O'Shea?"

"What I believe in, Mr. Badham, is nothing you could begin to understand. Now, you have interrupted a private conversation. I've asked you to leave. Do it."

Shana felt Victor Badham's dark eyes trying to burn intimidating holes through her. She returned his scorching stare unflinchingly. The man thought he could bulldoze people with the weight of his wealth.

Well, he'd never bulldozed her and he wasn't going to now.

Badham finally left, his bodyguard shuffling after him.

Brock watched Shana O'Shea stare down Victor Badham with growing respect. He knew who Badham was—at least by reputation. A powerful man. But Shana gave him his walking papers, and he took them. This was one interesting lady.

"For pity's sake, Shana, couldn't you at least have been civil!" Phil exploded as soon as Badham was out of sight. "The man's a billionaire promoter!"

Shana's eyes flashed dangerously. "The man's a slimy crook who adopted mustangs so he could sell them illegally. And the damn BLM was letting him get away with it!"

Phil twisted his glass nervously. "Now, Shana. You know the guys at the BLM have their hands full. Can't always do the kind of follow-up checks on the adopted horses and burros that they want. Besides, they didn't charge Badham."

"Only because Jebb did his dirty work. Phil, you've got to stop blabbing to Badham so freely about Fire Magic."

Phil looked uncomfortable. "What's wrong with my talking to him about Fire Magic?"

Shana's eyes sought the ceiling. "Heaven give me strength!" Her eyes came back down to earth, precisely level with her boss's. "Phil, don't you understand that Badham is an exploiter? That anything that draws his interest he considers up for grabs?"

"You can't think that he—"

"I can and do think that the man is capable of anything if he saw a buck to be made. You've got to be more circumspect around him. Particularly about Fire Magic. You've simply got to. Please.''

Brock had a hunch that the world "please" did not flow easily through Shana O'Shea's lips and she only used it in desperation. From Phil's startled look, he decided his hunch was on the mark.

"Oh, all right, if you're that het up about it," Phil said. "But if I'm giving a concession, then I want one in return. No more lip about helping Brock capture Fire Magic."

"But—"

"That's the deal, Shana. The problem of Fire Magic has gone too long without resolution. His herd is far too large. It's decimating a lot of the high range that other species depend on. We've got to do whatever is necessary to catch that wild stallion. It's our job, you know."

Brock was sure she knew that, all right. It was crystal clear in the sudden fierce sadness in her eyes.

And seeing that sadness, Brock was sure of something else, too. Something he had suspected from the first moment he saw the ravishing forest ranger staring at the magnificent stallion.

Chapter Two

"After you," Brock said, as one of his large hands shot out to keep the door from closing, brushing Shana's shoulder.

Shana just bet that brush was deliberate as she stepped off the elevator onto Amy Edel's floor at Las Vegas's fabulous Excalibur Hotel, built in every way to resemble a gigantic medieval castle.

Such a robust setting certainly seemed to suit her companion. She'd been shocked to see him sitting with her boss in that casino dining room—not just by his presence but by her reaction to it. For no matter how strongly her mind fought to reject him, her body automatically responded to the overwhelming maleness he broadcasted so blatantly with his open white dress shirt exposing all those bronze, bulging muscles and that thick, romantic, wild blond hair flowing free to his shoulders. He looked like some incredibly sexy medieval Saxon warrior or Viking king.

Except he's nothing but a tinsel-town stuntman with an inflated ego, she reminded herself.

Still she sensed his body heat, his clean masculine scent, the force of his will all reaching out to her like tangible entities. And when once more the deep resonance of his voice vibrated through her, every one of her nerve endings bolted to attention. "I'm looking forward to riding back into the Toiyabe National Forest with you, Shana. And your handcuffs. I do hope you're a woman of your word. I'd hate to think you'd disappoint both of us."

Shana remembered his very suggestive comment about the handcuffs from the day before and felt her blood boil. Her eyes flew up to his face, her neck feeling strained. She was a respectable five nine, but he had almost seven inches on her. Still, it was time to cut this LaLa-land lothario down to size.

"Let's get a few things straight right now, Trulock. I'm being forced to act as your guide through the Toiyabe National Forest while you *attempt* to catch Fire Magic. But a guide is all I will be. I don't intend to lift a hand to help you catch that stallion or anything else. You're on your own, stuntman."

His gray eyes gleamed at her in amusement. "If that's so, Shana, then I think you'd best let me do the talking when I meet Amy Edel. I don't think she'll be too pleased to learn that not only aren't you bent on capturing Fire Magic, but you also aren't interested in reclaiming her stolen horses."

Shana's brow furrowed. "Now just a minute. I didn't mean to imply I didn't want to capture Fire Magic or reclaim the mares he's stolen. It's what I've been trying to do for nearly a year!"

Both his smile and words taunted. "Is that what you've *really* been trying to do?"

Shana bristled. "What kind of question is that?"

"A simple question, Shana. Have you *really* been trying to capture Fire Magic?"

They had reached Amy Edel's hotel door. Shana sent Brock a fierce glare. "I don't know what you're trying to imply, and I don't care to know. But hear this. Amy Edel is my friend and I know what to say to her. So when we get inside, *I'll* do the talking." She turned from him and rapped sharply on the door.

Almost instantly, a slight, sixtyish, quick-eyed man with long ears and a receding chin threw open the door and gestured them inside as though he'd been impatiently waiting for their arrival. He rubbed the fuzzy hair on his exposed forearms and hopped around them like a nervous skinny rabbit.

"Frank Panew, this is Brock—"

"Mr. Brock," her companion interrupted before Shana could get out the rest of his name. Somewhat tardily she remembered that she wasn't supposed to be revealing his identity. She snapped her mouth shut. Damn. He had a disturbing way of making her lose her concentration.

Brock extended a large hand and Frank Panew gave it a careful, almost hesitant shake as he took in the strength of the arm behind it. He even looked surprised when he got his hand back all in one piece. "Phil Hudson mentioned you'd be bringing a specialist, Shana. I'll get Amy. She's lying down. As I'm sure you can imagine, this whole business has been quite distressing for her."

Panew disappeared into a back room to reemerge a moment later with a silver-haired woman with faded blue eyes and wearing a wrinkled, pink two-piece pantsuit. Dangling from her limp left hand were her matching high-heeled shoes. She made no attempt to put them on as she advanced on Shana in stocking feet.

"It's too late. He's got her now. She's disappeared like all the rest. My poor Lady Blue!"

Shana stepped forward and put a consoling arm across Amy's slim, shaking shoulders as tears formed in the woman's eyes. If ever there was a time to sound encouraging, she knew this was it. "I'll get her back, Amy. I found her before. I'll find her again."

"I told Phil you would. Told him he needn't go scouring the hills for some wild-horse he-man. Of course, he wasn't listening. Men never do listen, do they? As much as I loved my Sam, he didn't listen, either. Told him the wooden stalls should be reinforced with steel. In case of earthquakes. I'm originally from Southern California and I think of these things. Sam told me I was crazy. But if he'd only listened, that damn stallion wouldn't have been able to kick down Lady Blue's stall!"

Amy's free hand stole into her pocket for a tissue to stop the ready flow of tears. Shana gave her shoulder another squeeze. "I'll get out there and track her right away. No matter how much time it takes, I'll find her."

Amy's voice cracked. "She was the best little mare I ever bred. Impeccable bloodlines. Descended from not one but all three of the original Oriental stallions!"

Brock's deep voice broke in from behind Shana in authoritative tones. "The Byerly Turk, the Darley Arabian and the Godolphin Arabian."

Shana heard Amy's breath sucked in anew as her head popped around Shana's shoulder. "You know about them?"

"About the desert stallions who mixed with the English pacers to produce the Thoroughbred—the fastest horse in the world? What horse lover does not?"

Shana turned reluctantly. She knew Brock had spoken the one introductory line guaranteed to ingratiate him with Amy Edel. The light in Amy's eyes as she stared at Brock was nothing short of blinding.

"This is Mr. Brock, Amy. The man Phil thought might be of some help in catching Fire Magic. Mr. Brock, Mrs. Amy Edel, breeder of the finest Thoroughbreds in the West."

Amy had already drifted across the several feet separating her from Brock and placed her hand in his outstretched one. Shana watched her assessing Brock's considerable height, muscular shoulders and arms appreciatively, much as she might the conformation of one of her prize stallions. Her voice lost all of its previously tragic tone. "Well, you certainly look quite capable of catching wild stallions, Mr. Brock. How nice Phil Hudson has finally gotten our Shana such...impressive-looking help."

Shana shook her head at Amy's changed tune. Less than a minute before, she'd been protesting that Shana didn't need any help!

Frank Panew looked on with jealous eyes as Amy not only let Brock continue to hold her hand but seemed to be insisting on it.

Shana knew that Amy and Frank had an understanding—had had one ever since the death of Amy's husband ten years before. But Frank had refused to marry Amy because her bank statements went into the high seven figures and his barely made the low fives. He didn't want people saying that he'd married her for her money.

From the look in Frank's too-bright eyes, Shana wondered if he might be regretting that decision. For a moment she indulged a satisfying image of Frank

Panew flying into a jealous rage, taking a swing at Brock and flattening him. But she knew it was too much to hope for. Even if Panew had the stuffing inside him, Brock didn't look like a man who would fall from a single blow. Or even a dozen. At least, not from Frank Panew.

Brock flashed Amy an engaging smile as he beckoned her to the room's sofa, knelt before her, took the shoes out of her hand and placed them on her feet one by one. There he was—Mr. Prince Charming, long, golden shoulder-length hair and all. Shana cringed as she watched Amy melting in his hands like pink peppermint ice cream under a hot sun.

Frank's voice rose vehemently as he began to hop around the room. "That damn wild stallion should have been shot last year when he raided the ranch the first time. He doesn't just have Lady Blue. He's got four other very carefully bred mares. If he hasn't run them into the ground by now."

"A master stallion takes good care of his herd," Shana insisted. "I seriously doubt any harm has come to the horses he's taken."

"But what about mountain lions?" Amy interjected. "They attack horses! You even got a picture of one attacking that red stallion!"

Shana shrugged. "True. But Fire Magic had lunged into the clearing to protect a mare from the mountain lion. And he managed to get the mountain lion off his back and give the cat a pretty good kick that sent it scurrying for the brush. No, I've got a feeling that as long as Fire Magic is looking after your horses, they're in safe hands."

"Safe hands?" Amy echoed two octaves too high. "Shana, what are you saying? It's Fire Magic who stole my horses!"

Shana swallowed, suddenly feeling about two inches tall. She had certainly expressed that badly. "I only meant—"

"What Shana meant, Mrs. Edel, is that she and I will be able to return your horses to you in good shape," Brock cut in smoothly. "As a breeder myself, I can understand how distraught you must feel to have lost such an exceptional roan mare. I got a chance to see Lady Blue yesterday when Shana reclaimed her, and I could tell immediately what excellent breeding she possesses."

"Impeccable," Amy reiterated, seeming a bit mollified by Brock's words of praise. "Four years old. Just turned from filly to mare. This is her first season. I plan to mate her only with the best."

"Of course," Brock said with another one of his charming smiles. Shana wondered if he ever ran out of them, and if he did, what expression he would then wear. "That's why I came here this afternoon to assure you that I have a foolproof plan to capture Fire Magic and reclaim all your stolen horses—not just Lady Blue. The only thing I ask in return is that you give me any foals the red stallion has sired through your stock."

Amy's eyes grew large. "You *want* that wild stallion's offspring? Whatever for?"

Shana's eyes widened also in surprise as Brock shrugged his massive shoulders. "Curiosity. Not all horses can be the beautiful pure Thoroughbreds you succeed so well in producing. Do we have an agreement that in exchange for the return of your Thoroughbreds, I can have the offspring?"

Amy didn't hesitate. "Of course, Mr. Brock. I have no use for a horse that doesn't have a pure Thoroughbred strain. Take them one and all!"

Brock reached into his jacket pocket. "I would like to make our agreement a bit more formal. Would you have an objection to having it in writing?"

Amy shook her head as she took the typed agreement Brock was holding out to her. Shana frowned. What was all this about?

Frank Panew immediately moved beside Amy and they both read the agreement Brock had prepared. When Frank nodded his approval, Amy signed without hesitation. Brock signed after her and insisted Shana and Frank sign as witnesses. When Shana did so, she quickly scanned the wording on the document. It seemed straightforward enough. Title to all weaned and unweaned foals sired by wild stock out of Amy's mares would be his when those mares were safely returned to Amy.

Once Amy had pocketed her copy, she turned back to Brock. "My Thoroughbreds are quite valuable, Mr. Brock. Are you sure that's the only payment you want for returning them?"

Brock wore that easy smile of his. "Quite sure, Mrs. Edel. Now I really must leave and make preparations for tomorrow when Shana and I will go after this troublesome stallion and put a stop once and for all to his raiding of your stock. Why don't you go back to your ranch and rebuild Lady Blue's stall? She'll be back in it soon. And if I were you, I'd use the reinforcing steel. Not that you'll have any more trouble from Fire Magic. But I happen to agree with you that you can never be too safe from earthquakes—even here in Nevada."

Shana watched Amy Edel look at Brock as though he were mounted on a white horse about to ride off in pursuit of the Holy Grail for her. Damn the man, but he knew how to handle women horse breeders. Oh, hell, Shana could admit it. That man obviously knew how to handle women, period.

Except for her, of course. She wasn't one to be taken in by some arrogant, albeit handsome, Hollywood stuntman on the make. And if he didn't already know that, he would find out soon enough.

"WHAT DO YOU WANT with Fire Magic's foals?" Shana shot at Brock the moment they were outside Amy's hotel room.

"Come to dinner and we'll discuss it," Brock responded easily.

He watched her look at him with unhidden suspicion. "Why can't you simply answer my question?"

"Because the answer isn't simple and I'm hungry. Aren't you hungry?"

Yeah, she was hungry. And curious. He'd bet she'd hold out a lot longer on satisfying her hunger than she would on satisfying her curiosity. That's what he was counting on. The suspicion in her eyes deepened. "Where?"

"There's a reenactment of a knightly joust and a hearty dinner with the show here at the Excalibur. You eat the food with your fingers while men in heavy mail riding valiant steeds get pitched into the dirt. Lots of fun. Takes you right back into medieval times where—"

She shook her head, her dark mane flashing like sheets of black silk under the hallway light. "The latter part of the twelfth century might suit you, Trulock, but

I'll take the latter part of the twentieth any day. A buffet dinner with a good selection is being served with knives and forks in the Round Table room down on the second level. If the line to get in isn't too long, we should be in and out in under an hour."

Brock met the self-contained certainty in her eyes. "You have another appointment this evening, or are you just a believer in our getting to bed early?"

He'd deliberately given a suggestive tone to his last words. As usual she ignored it. "Look, Trulock, I don't intend to draw out this meal with you. Now, do we go downstairs to the buffet to eat and talk, or just forget it?"

She wouldn't be persuaded any further. He could see that. He liked that. She wasn't going to be easy. He smiled graciously as though the buffet had been his first choice, knowing such a smile would annoy her. "By all means, let's try the Round Table buffet."

He'd managed to get her in a corner table of the large informal dining room. He wasn't surprised that she'd been right about the very good selection of the buffet. The more he learned about the lady, the more he realized she knew what she was talking about. Naturally, she'd insisted on paying for her meal.

Brock's plate was piled high. He was glad to see her plate was pretty full, too. He'd always hated to eat dinner with a woman who ordered only a salad and then picked at it. He liked a woman with a hearty appetite for food . . . and other things. And who could still surprise him.

Since the instant he'd met Shana O'Shea on that ledge in the Toiyabe Forest, Brock had been surprised. Even her beauty was nothing like the flashy Hollywood he knew. Hers had a wild, strong, elemental quality that went clear through to her very bones.

But her physical draw hadn't been the reason she'd remained on his mind.

No, it was the way she had so casually dismissed him—the shield of provocative unattainability that she wore so boldly—that challenged, taunted and lured him.

Women did not put up shields against him. On the contrary. Women—gorgeous, desirable ones—frequently threw themselves at him. Or at the very least, welcomed his advances.

But not Shana. Not this tall, sleek, black-haired, golden-eyed beauty with the lithe grace of a cat and a will as strong and wild as the stallion she sought.

"So what do you want with Fire Magic's foals?" Shana asked again as she sat across from him.

Brock noticed she had made a good dent in the food on her plate. As she brought a new forkful into her luscious, generous mouth, he found a new hunger growing inside him and had to forcibly put it aside to concentrate on her question.

"Do you know the origin of the Morgan horse?"

Shana chewed and swallowed her food. "He appeared in the 1790s in Vermont when a schoolteacher, Justin Morgan, acquired him. The horse was a two-year-old then, and nothing was known about his ancestry. He was small, weighed only 950 pounds. But he was well proportioned, with a dark bay coloring, and a lean and bony head. Some say that he trotted a mile in three minutes. At least twenty-five of his progeny could trot a mile in under two minutes and thirty seconds. That one stallion sired a trotting breed that is among the speediest, sturdiest and most versatile of horses. That the Morgan horse you mean?''

Brock smiled and he nodded. For a forest ranger, she knew her horses.

She reloaded her fork. "So what does the Morgan horse have to do with Fire Magic?''

"If what I suspect is true, Shana, Fire Magic has something very much in common with the Morgan horse."

She put down her fork. He had her attention now. He thought he would. "How do you mean?"

Brock reached inside his jacket pocket and pulled out a newspaper clipping of Fire Magic's confrontation with the mountain lion and Shana's photograph that captured the horse's successful bucking of the predatory cat. He watched surprise enter her eyes when he also produced two five-by-seven glossies—other pictures she had snapped of the fight and given to her boss that the newspaper hadn't used. Brock set all the pictures on the table between them, pointing to various parts of the red stallion as he explained.

"Fire Magic possesses a lean, clean head—like a Thoroughbred but with a broad forehead and deeply dished like an Arabian. See? And his magnificently arched neck—again with an Arabian conformation, but even thicker, more powerful. He's as tall as the tallest Thoroughbred, but his belly is thinner, his legs even longer. And in this shot you've captured his compact, high-rump back, but it's definitely shorter than a Thoroughbred's—again like the Arabian, who has one less vertebra."

Her eyes had followed his fast pointing fingers, taking it all in. Now her head rose. "Are you saying these conformation points mean that Fire Magic is a cross between a Thoroughbred and an Arabian?''

"I think his sire and dam could very well have been a Thoroughbred and an Arabian, yes. But I don't think Fire Magic is just the sum of his parents' genes."

Her eyes were focused, intent. "Then what is he?"

"Well, Shana, I think Fire Magic is one of those lucky and rare mutations of nature that have resulted in slightly different genes—superior genes residing in a superior horse. Like what happened with the Morgan horse. And if I'm right, Fire Magic is also the first of a new breed—a faster, stronger, superior one."

He watched her digesting his words, their meaning flashing excitement through her eyes. Almost passion. His stomach clenched in a very interesting way as he watched her study the pictures more closely.

"He's faster than anything I've seen," she said at last, an obvious tone of reverence in her voice Brock had come to realize was reserved for the stallion alone. "And that gorge he leaped yesterday—it had to have been thirty feet across. I've never known of any horse being able to make such a jump."

Her head came up then, and Brock looked into the raw excitement now in her eyes and felt a renewed tightening in his gut. Of its own volition, his hand sought to cover hers as he leaned across the table.

His fingers contacted with firm, incredibly soft, cool skin, but only for an instant before awareness flickered through her eyes and she leaned back, pulling her hand away.

A new emotion entered her eyes then—suspicion, strong and frosty. He leaned back unperturbed and smiled to disconcert her further. It was too late for her icy shield. He'd seen her fervor for Fire Magic. As he had suspected from the first, she was a woman of strong passion.

Her suspicious eyes still regarded him closely. "How are you going to be able to tell if you're right and Fire Magic does represent a new breed of horse?"

"The Morgan horse's genes were so dominant that all his foals resembled him much more than their dams. And that's what made him the father of a new breed of horses—those dominant genes that he passed on to make his progeny so recognizable as his."

"And that's why you want Fire Magic's foals? To see if they are carrying his characteristics?"

"Yes. They'll be the proof one way or another. If Fire Magic breeds true—passes on his outstanding characteristics—then I'll know he's a new breed of horse. And I'll have him and his progeny to begin what will someday be the most sought-after, spectacular horses in history."

"And if you find out he doesn't breed true?"

"Then I'll know he's just manifesting the best of the genes that were present in both his parents and he'll be the only valuable one of the bunch."

"What will you do with him then?"

"Tame him. He'll still be the most spectacular horse of this century. Maybe any century."

"And his progeny?"

"Give them some good pasture to roam. There won't be much else left to do with them."

He saw her considering his words—not quite convinced. He waited, knowing she had more questions. "Amy lost four mares last spring to Fire Magic. Assuming they all foaled this spring and the stallion impregnated them again, you could be responsible for eight of Fire Magic's offspring."

"Nine. Remember Lady Blue. Fire Magic wouldn't have come for her if she wasn't in season. If he hasn't done the deed yet, he no doubt will have by the time we reach them. It's a good chance we'll find Lady Blue carrying his foal, too."

Shana sighed as she shook her head. "Which of course will delight Amy no end. According to that contract you signed with her, you could be legally responsible for nine horses that might turn out to be worth very little monetarily. The care of nine horses—ten, in the unlikely event you caught Fire Magic—can be downright expensive. Have you considered that?"

"I've put away a few dollars for a rainy day."

The golden flecks in her brown eyes flickered uneasily. "The odds of Fire Magic being the kind of mutation you describe have got to be ten million to one."

"More like a hundred million to one," he said with a smile.

She frowned at him and his smile. He imagined kissing that frown and the corner of her full wary lips. He imagined what it would be like to coax those lips to open beneath his.

"I can take you into the Toiyabe Forest to where I know Fire Magic travels this time of year, but our chances of even sighting the stallion are pretty slim."

He took a deep breath as he refocused his thoughts. "We'll find him. I have a plan, remember?"

Her eyes narrowed. "What is this plan?"

"I'll let you know when we get into the Toiyabe Forest."

She eyed him some more. "Phil said you knew horses. How many wild-horse roundups like this have you been on before?"

"Including this one?"

"Yes."

"One."

He read the shock his answer brought to her eyes. It took all his control to keep the bland smile on his face.

She bolted upright in her chair. "This is going to be your first wild-horse roundup? You've got to be crazy! You have no idea what's ahead. We're going into rugged country after a rugged prey. These are not the docile, Hollywood-trained horses that mind their manners when you use them for your stunts. These are clever, unpredictable wild animals who will do anything they have to not to let themselves be caught!"

It was getting harder and harder for Brock to contain himself in the light of her agitation, but he managed a bland retort. "That so?"

She fell back into her chair. "I don't believe this. What could Phil have been thinking?"

"That I could do it, obviously. And I can."

She looked at him as though she was trying to decide something. He felt her eyes on his shoulders and arms, assessing him. His pulse quickened at her physical scrutiny. He engaged in his own scrutiny of her long, luscious neck, the perfect symmetry of her collarbones, and wondered how they would taste beneath his exploring tongue.

Her mouth twisted in annoyance, as though she couldn't decide what to believe. "Have you really thought this through?"

He leaned across the table, staring into her confused eyes. "You worried about me, Shana?"

She straightened at his words, the confusion fleeing. "I'm *only* worried about Fire Magic and his progeny. And maintaining the Toiyabe as a safe place for all the mustangs who make it their home."

She was dismissing him again. Her tone, her every gesture, shut him out. He wasn't the kind of man who could be dismissed. She hadn't learned that about him yet. He was looking forward to teaching her.

He had time and relaxed back into his seat. "You told me yesterday that Nevada mustangs represent many breeds. How did that happen?"

She hesitated before responding, as though first making sure in her own mind that what she told him would be of no use in catching Fire Magic. "Early Nevada ranching favored an open range. Horses as well as cattle were allowed to roam over the thousands of square miles to find their feed in the wild rye, wheat and bunchgrass. When it came time for the annual round-up, many of the horses escaped into the higher, less hospitable hills."

"They went wild?"

"Only the hardiest survived. Their offspring were wiry, fast and small—no more than fourteen hands. When ranchers needed more horses, they would often raid the wild herds and select colts or fillies that could be easily tamed by raising them with tame horses. After a while, ranchers deliberately let some of their prize studs loose to run with the wild mares to improve the stock. Shires, Percherons, Hambletonians, Morgans, French Coach, Thoroughbreds and even imported Irish stallions mixed their bloodlines with the mustangs."

"Any Arabians?"

"No. Few Arabians were in this country during those early days."

"And since?"

"No. They—well, now that I think about it, there was an Arabian stallion who got loose just about six years ago."

"Tell me about him."

She exhaled heavily. "It's not the kind of story that gladdens the heart."

"I'm tough. I can take it."

Her eyes flashed to his. She brought her coffee cup to her lips. She had lightened it with just a touch of cream, and the vibrant resultant color reminded Brock of the shade surrounding the golden flecks in her eyes. "The stallion was Silver Mist, a direct descendant of Golden Silver, one of the purest Arabian bloodlines ever shown at Ascot. He was being transported to his new California owner when the truck pulling his trailer overturned on the highway. The driver received only a few scratches. But when he went back to check on the stallion, he found the trailer busted open and the horse gone."

"Did they find him?"

"His new owner launched a thorough search of the surrounding desert. For months, jeeps, planes and helicopters combed the area, but no trace of Silver Mist was found. Then, about a year later, a couple of campers up on Table Mountain in the eastern section of the Toiyabe Forest, hundreds of miles away, came bursting into the ranger station. They told the story of how all the day and night before they had been kept awake by the sounds of a fierce wild-stallion fight. A couple of rangers went up Table Mountain to take a look and found Silver Mist's body and that of a huge black stallion beside him. The splendid horses were too evenly matched. Their fight for supremacy of a wild herd had left both of them dead."

Brock shook his head. "What a dreadful waste. No, your story certainly doesn't gladden the heart. Still, I suppose it's already occurred to you that if Silver Mist survived for a year, he could have crossed his blood-lines with the mustangs'?''

He could see it was only the tragic death of the horse that had really made an impression on her. "Yes, I suppose that's possible." Then the full import of the suggestion brought her to the edge of her chair. "Wait a minute, Trulock. Are you saying that you think Fire Magic might be an offspring of that Arabian?"

Brock smiled. "After seeing Fire Magic's conformation, I'd lay odds on it. Let's do the math. Silver Mist got loose six years ago. Right?"

"Yes."

"And Fire Magic emerges as a major stallion contender last year. Admittedly, four years is a bit young for a stallion to start taking over a range, but with the kind of bloodlines running through his wild veins, I wouldn't be surprised."

The possibilities had caught her imagination. She licked her lips, and Brock stared at the pink shine, wondering how such a simple act could be so provocative. Her voice was almost dreamy now. "I wonder if Fire Magic's dam was a mare of that black stallion? I didn't see the body myself, but the rangers who did said the horse Silver Mist challenged was a more mature stallion and had the distinctive markings of a Thoroughbred."

"Well, whatever she was, she must have been some mare, too. Fire Magic is kingsize, much taller than any Arabian I've seen. And even more beautiful. He's a miracle of nature. Owning and breeding him is the kind of opportunity that only comes once in a man's life."

Her previously open expression closed as she retreated into that self-contained coolness that was so much a part of her. "Not all opportunities are realized, Trulock."

His voice carried his assurance of many things. "Mine are. I'm going to catch Fire Magic. And his progeny. Believe me. I'm a man of my word. And I know I'll find him breeding true. I'm going to end up with at least ten horses that will each be worth their weight in gold. And all for the price of their transportation out of the wilderness."

She studied him then. An assessing look. Guarded. Curious. Brock watched the interesting planes of her face, formed by her strong bone structure and the shadows cast from the dim overhead light. Damn, she was beautiful.

She looked perfectly poised in some still, quiet, unattainable center. He yearned to rush in, grab hold of her, inflame every shred of her passion and bring it all to focus on him. The desire swept through him so strongly that he suddenly felt out of breath from the sheer energy it took. Without thinking, he clasped her hand.

She withdrew instantly and was on her feet before he'd even realized it was her intent to stand. "It's getting late. If we're going to get an early start tomorrow, I need to get back to my room. Good night."

He caught her arm as she started to leave.

"My mother taught me to escort a lady home after I've enjoyed the pleasure of her company."

Shana extricated her arm from his grasp. "A lady is a titled member of royalty. You won't find any such pretensions in my lineage."

Her eyes mocked him. Brock smiled. "It's all right, Shana. I'm prepared to take whatever I find."

She said nothing as they ascended in the elevator, but the considerable ice in her eyes told him just how angry she was at his insistence on seeing her to her room.

As they walked down the hall, she said, "I will meet you at the ranger station in Tonopah at nine. I'm not supplying you with provisions, Trulock, so be sure you bring all the food and water you'll need and sufficient feed for your mount. Because when your provisions are gone, so am I."

They approached her door and she had her magnetized card key out, slipping it into the lock and turning the handle in a quick, practiced arc that had the door open in a fraction of a second. "Good night," she called as she pressed the door open. But he was ready for her attempt at a quick getaway.

His arm shot out, grabbing the door, preventing it from fully opening. Her body ran into his restraining arm, bringing her to an abrupt halt. Before she had so much as a chance to take another breath, he buried his face in her clean, silky hair and brushed his lips against the back of her neck.

Immediately he heard the sharp intake of her breath, the press of her body against his restraining arm. Her natural scent was light and incredibly enticing to his brain and body.

He leaned close against her so that his breath would brand the back of her long, luscious neck. "Sleep well and think of me. Soon the dawn and I will both be on your doorstep."

Then he felt the sharp heel of her shoe scrapping painfully across his right shinbone.

SHANA LAY AWAKE in the early-morning hours thinking that there was nothing soon about this dawn's greeting. She had not slept well. She kept reliving Brock Trulock's kiss. Kept feeling his hot breath on the back of her neck and hearing those parting words.

"Sleep well and think of me."

Shana punched her pillow. Well, she had certainly followed one of his directions, like it or not. And she decided quite firmly that she didn't like it at all. Even her retaliatory kick that had succeeded in removing his arm hadn't wiped that smile from the arrogant stuntman's face.

Damn. Perhaps she should have just ignored his latest advance as she had ignored all the rest. Pretended she hadn't noticed.

But the trouble was, she couldn't pretend. And she couldn't ignore the quickening of her pulse at the memory of his strong arm restraining her body so effortlessly, at the liquid fire of his touch, at the curious melting of her spine and the sudden impulse she had had not to move away but rather to sink back against that powerful chest.

Damn. She gave the pillow another punch. The clock on the nightstand flashed four-thirty.

Oh, hell. It was no use. She might as well get up. She wouldn't be sleeping any more, anyway.

And tomorrow—correction, today—they would be riding off to spend what was probably going to be several nights alone together in the wilderness.

Shana sighed as her bare feet padded to the shower. She'd been over all this for hours and it still came down to this: As much as she hated to admit it, she was physically attracted to that overbearing oaf of a stuntman. But he didn't have to know it. And if she was smart about it, he wouldn't.

She stepped into the shower and endured the icy water spray before the hot water kicked in. Penance for her body's betrayal under that man's touch.

She turned under the spray, wetting her body all over, lathering herself with soap, vigorously rubbing the back of her neck, trying to wash away the lingering scent of him—the feel of his lips—the warmth of his breath.

No use. They were locked in a stubborn memory cell that wouldn't let go, no matter how hard she scrubbed. She sighed.

Still, if Brock Trulock thought he had an opportunity to take advantage of her because they would be alone together on the trail, then he had a surprise coming.

These good-looking Hollywood types just assumed every woman was ready to warm their bed when they blew into town. Well, maybe many women were. But she wasn't. She knew all about his type of man.

She'd get over these inappropriate physical responses to his presence. It was just a matter of time.

Chapter Three

"Cort, what in the hell are you doing here with half your ranch hands?"

Shana had called out the question even before she'd swung her legs out of the cab of her truck onto the desert dust in front of the Tonopah Ranger Station surrounded by cowboys and their cow ponies.

Big, bold and brash, Cort Donner strode up to her, as always a whip in his right hand. In his left he held the reins of his impressive pinto stallion, Heavy Metal, who for once looked cool and domesticated in contrast to the wildness in the black eyes and hair of the man who led him. "Damn it, Shana, where have you been? I've been waiting for you for over an hour!"

Shana bristled at the address and as always felt edgy at the presence of the whip. "It's only ten to nine. This ranger station is scheduled to open at nine and not before. Now I repeat, what in the hell are you doing here with all these men?"

Cort's mouth worked angrily. His eyes darted to his watching men. Then his voice suddenly dropped. "I stopped by your place on my way here. You weren't home. Where were you last night?"

Shana took his lead and dropped her voice, too, but not the anger from her tone. "Take that presumptive intonation out of your voice, Cort Donner. Where I was last night or any other night is none of your business. Now tie up Heavy Metal and come into the station if you have some real business to discuss. I'm not standing out here under the hot sun."

Shana didn't wait for a response. She charged up the steps of the ranger station, unlocked the door and went in. She heard Donner's footsteps behind her as she knew she would.

She went to the counter and plugged in the automatic coffee machine. She knew Joan, the support-services specialist, would be by in a few minutes to officially open the station and would be pleased to find the coffee ready. From the corner of Shana's eye, she could see Donner still held his horsewhip in his rough hand. She frowned in annoyance.

Donner paced, clearly agitated. Suddenly, he aimed his whip and lashed out angrily, the rawhide snapping around a chair leg behind the counter, only inches from Shana's leg. She jumped when the chair screeched across the wooden floor as Donner yanked back his whip.

Shana swallowed anger as her tone dripped sarcasm. "Feel better now that you've beaten up on my furniture?"

Donner righted the chair and shoved it back into place, not looking at her. He rarely did. Not square in the eyes. "It's that damn red stallion again, Shana."

Shana's chest tightened as the volume of her heartbeat began competing with the noisy percolator in the corner. She was almost afraid to ask. "What happened?"

Donner recoiled his whip, snapping it against his high boots as his eyes glanced across the Indian arrowhead display in the glass case against the wall. "We drove the cattle up to the spring range this morning. What was left of the range, that is. The damn horse had already led his herd across it. Gobbled up every damn blade of grass in sight!"

"Did you see him?"

"I didn't need to see him to know he'd been there."

"Still, if you didn't see him, how can you be sure it was Fire Magic? The wild antelope—"

"Oh, come off it, Shana. The ground was stamped with unshod horse hooves. A lot of unshod horse hooves. And a few shod ones. It was him and his herd, all right. I swear if I just knew where that sucker hid out, I'd—"

"Come tell me so I could catch him," Shana interrupted deliberately.

Donner's eyes glinted at her. "Catch him? What are you talking about, catching him? Alive, that stallion is no good to anyone and you know it."

Shana's eyes flashed. "I know nothing of the sort. Let me remind you, Cort. Fire Magic and every other wild horse on Toiyabe National Forest land are my responsibility. If you or any of your trigger-happy cowboys shoot at him or any of his herd—"

"Yeah, yeah. We'll get our hands slapped."

"You'll get your butts shoved in federal prison, Cort Donner. And I'm the one who's going to be doing the shoving. I'm here to protect those wild horses, and that's just what I intend to do."

Donner shot her a sour look before he resumed pacing. Once again he slapped the whip against his boot. "You're also here to control their numbers so ranchers like me can use the federal range to graze our cattle. What about protecting our rights for a change? Do you know what it's going to cost me for the extra feed this spring?''

Shana exhaled a heavy breath. "I know you count on using the government grazing lands, Cort. I know how expensive feed's become—"

''You also know Fire Magic has amassed a wild herd far in excess of the available grazing range and the U.S. Forest Service guidelines,'' Cort interrupted. "That herd's got to be thinned out, Shana. That's your job, too, in case you've forgotten.''

Shana bristled. "Don't tell me what my job is.''

''Well, someone has to. You've obviously forgotten. Seems like you've forgotten a lot of things lately.''

Shana turned at the edge in his voice, irritated at his tone as well as the continued smacking of the whip against his boot. "What's that supposed to mean?''

''You were supposed to call me last night. I kept trying your number until 2:00 a.m. Where were you?''

Shana counted to ten as she took a deep steadying breath. "First of all, I did not promise to call you last night or any other night. And second, where I was and what I was doing are my business.''

''You didn't answer your phone the night before, either. I called until ten the next morning. I was worried.''

Shana exhaled, relenting slightly. "I got up early yesterday. Took a long walk. I had things on my mind. You've no reason to worry about me. I can and do take care of myself.''

Cort strode up to Shana, frustrated, almost angry. "Don't you remember our conversation two nights ago? Don't you remember what I asked you?''

"What you asked does not obligate me to anything, Cort. And my answer certainly didn't."

His expression darkened as he raised the whip in his hand and rested its curled rawhide at the back of Shana's head. "So change your answer. Tell me you'll marry me."

Shana could feel the pressure of the whip coaxing her head forward as for once Cort's eyes looked into hers. She smelled leather mixed with sweat as he leaned closer, the intensity of his look telling her he would kiss her soon if she didn't move.

She moved. "Look, I told you, Cort, the answer is no. Crowding me will not change it."

He followed her, his right hand holding the whip at his side. His left hand circled only her arm this time, but it was a hard grip. The passion turned hard in his dark eyes, too. "Who you waiting for, Shana? I'm the only real man around here with anything to offer a woman like you. I'm inheriting a big chunk of Nevada land and money. Don't tell me you're going to settle for one of my penniless cowhands outside? Or some cologne-splashed, soft-handed pansy from Vegas?"

Shana met his hard stare. "I'm neither waiting nor settling for any man, Cort. I don't need one and I don't want one. And that includes you. Now remove your hand."

Anger flickered through Cort's dark eyes, but Shana knew the icy determination in her returning stare matched any flash of temper he could produce. Still, even as he backed off, she didn't like the way his eyes dropped to her lips or the fact that he had yet to remove his hand. She was just debating whether a stomp on his toes or a knee in the groin would be necessary to cool his ardor when a deep, familiar voice vibrated into the room.

"Good morning! Great-looking day, isn't it?"

Shana started as Cort whirled around toward the door and the direction of the voice, the whip automatically uncoiling and snapping to attention at his side.

Brock eyed it unconcernedly as he casually closed the door behind him. "You did say nine o'clock, didn't you, Shana?"

"Who in the hell are you?" Cort barked.

Brock didn't say anything for a moment, but Shana thought she saw a flicker of irritation in those gleaming gray eyes. "Why, I'm a friend of Shana's, of course," he finally answered, in a deceptively even voice. "Name's Brock." He strolled nonchalantly up to them. Then he deliberately turned his back on Donner and his whip and gave all his attention to Shana.

Brock's voice descended into an intimate tone that sounded almost like a caress. "I can't tell you how much I enjoyed last night, Shana. And you look positively ravishing this morning. Don't you think so Mr. . . . ?"

He turned toward Donner then and held out his hand. Blood rushed into Donner's face. The whip was still in Donner's twitching right hand. In order to shake Brock's offered hand he would have to shift the whip to his left. The whip remained where it was.

"You were with this joker last night?" Donner demanded, not removing his eyes from Brock's.

Shana internally steamed at the demanding note in Cort's voice and the deliberately seductive tone of Brock's when he'd spoken to her. Like two wild stallions, these men were already emotionally rearing at each other.

She wanted to kick some sense into them both but knew it was no use. If she didn't do something soon, they might start getting physical. For the moment, saying what was necessary to defuse an escalating situation seemed to be the best course.

She purposely kept her voice cool and controlled. "Phil Hudson has asked Mr. Brock to help me capture Fire Magic. We'll be leaving in just a few minutes to do just that. Since capturing the stallion is what you've been just raving about, you should be happy to shake the hand of the man ready to help do it."

Shana could feel Cort's surprised and stormy stare. "You're letting *him* help you catch the stallion?"

She hated saying it, but she knew she had no choice. "Phil says Mr. Brock is an expert with horses. It would be foolish to turn down his help." She punctuated her words with an icy glare back at Donner that spoke volumes about what would happen if he didn't cool down. Shana watched him slowly shift the whip into his left hand as he took Brock's right with his.

"Donner," he spat out reluctantly. The two men eyed each other as their hands met. Cort was a good two inches shorter, but his chin stuck out far enough to raise his eyes sufficiently for his half of the glower. They seemed to shake hands forever. After more than a minute passed, Shana could see perspiration breaking out on Cort's forehead and above his lip. Brock's face, on the other hand, still had the healthy sheen he'd arrived with. When their hands finally parted, Cort's face was white.

Shana's stomach turned at the fury in Cort's black eyes as he immediately sought to transfer his whip back into his right hand. But his right hand no longer had the strength to hold the whip. The blood had been squeezed out of it during the handshake. The whip crashed harmlessly onto the floor. Cort swore an ugly oath as he dropped to the floor after it. Brock turned unconcerned eyes toward Shana with his ever-present smile, sounding as relaxed and unhurried as always. "Coffee smells good. Shall we sit and have a cup?"

Shana glared at him, finding it very hard to keep a civil tongue. "I'd like to leave right away."

"Whatever you say," Brock answered easily.

Shana snatched up the first-aid pack that she kept under her desk and then headed quickly for the door. She let her words trail behind her. "Do help yourself to a cup of coffee, Cort. Joan will be by in a minute to officially open up."

Cort didn't respond to her words. She could hear his angry cursing as Brock closed the door behind them.

"Damn it, why did you provoke him?" Shana demanded as soon as they were outside.

Brock's eyebrows raised in all innocence. "Me? Provoke him? Why, Shana, whatever are you talking about? My manners were so good that even Mother would have been proud."

Shana ground her teeth, trying to keep her temper. "Damn it, you know your tone and words gave him every indication that we spent last night together."

Brock said nothing, just smiled that damned charming smile of his.

Shana exhaled heavily as she gave up trying to get through and quickly sped toward her truck. She glanced sideways at Brock's vehicle. He had a shiny, brand-new, double horse trailer hitched to the back of his equally new and unblemished truck. It didn't give her confidence. She'd hoped he'd been kidding when he said he hadn't been on a wild-horse hunt before. Damn. She hated getting saddled with a novice. So many things could go wrong.

She headed for her well-worn cab and the attached flatbed, slatted truck where Mickey Finn waited patiently. "Follow me in your vehicle. We keep our pack animals at a range near Hunts Canyon. I'll have to pick up some mules to carry out supplies."

"Good. I'll need at least four."

"Four?"

"You told me to bring all the supplies I'd need."

Shana knew she didn't have time to argue. "After we get the mules, we'll head in the direction of the Toquima Range and drive as far as the road allows before switching to the horses. Which means we probably won't get there until afternoon. Use your horn if you need to stop for some reason."

Shana had expected Brock to head for his own vehicle, but he insisted on coming around to the driver's side of her vehicle first and holding the door open for her. She jumped in and dropped the first-aid kit on the passenger seat without ceremony, feeling irritated at his obvious denseness. "This is no time for chivalry," she whispered with an impatient breath.

Brock closed the cab door and leisurely rested his hands on its window frame, his eyes flicking momentarily to her side-view mirror. "My mother would disagree, Shana. She taught me that there is always time to give a lady the attention she deserves."

Shana shook her head in frustration. "Don't you understand? Any minute now, Cort will be getting the strength back in that whip hand of his you temporarily squeezed out of commission. Believe me, I know him. He's got a mean temper. We've got to get out of here before that temper starts wielding that whip."

Brock's expression looked totally unconcerned, although his gray eyes held a distinctive, almost anticipatory gleam as they once more flicked toward the side mirror. "On the contrary, Shana. While it was my mother who taught me my manners, it was my father who taught me that running from a man with a mean temper is always a mistake. Better to—"

He didn't finish whatever he was going to say. Instead he whirled around just as a crack as loud as thunder split the air.

Shana froze. The whip! Cort was using it on Brock! She grabbed for the rifle on the rack behind her seat and spun around with it in her hands.

She blinked at the blur of action before her, barely believing her eyes. Somehow, Brock had anticipated Donner's strike. As Brock whirled around, he snatched at the end of the whip that had been meant to slash open his back. Catching it in midair, he quickly laced it snugly around his right hand. The next instant, Brock yanked the whip toward him, tumbling Cort off his feet and dumping the rancher face first in some sagebrush.

Shana jumped from the cab and watched in appreciative awe as Brock calmly gathered the long whip into a curl over his powerful shoulder and advanced on Donner. The rancher raised his head, trying to cough the desert dust out of his lungs, trying to see through his dust-caked lids. Brock yanked the handle of the whip out of his outstretched hand, spewing more dust into Donner's gaping mouth and sending him into a new coughing fit.

Brock's deep voice and cutting words rang out to catch every ear of the man's listening ranch hands, who were standing like statues in a circle around their prone and coughing boss.

"Only a coward comes at a man's back, Donner. Particularly when the coward's armed and the man isn't. Get up. If you want a fight, stand and face me now."

Shana held her breath as the minutes ticked by, but much to her surprise Cort stayed prone. Since she had first witnessed Cort starting a fight in the second grade, she had never once seen him bested. Or seen him back down. Until now.

Brock finally turned and left Donner in the dust. But he kept the whip curled around his shoulder as he turned and walked up to Shana.

He gave her a charming smile as he handed her back into the cab of the truck. She ripped her arm away from his grip. The residue of fear still clogged Shana's throat. She wanted to strangle Brock for daring to look so calm and collected and unaffected by what had just happened. She wanted to kick him for having contributed to the escalation of that violence.

But she was so thankful that he was all right that she just climbed onto the driver's seat of the cab and replaced the rifle on the rack behind her. Then her eyes followed his confident walk to his truck, his powerful body fluid and graceful.

As she drove away with Brock keeping pace behind her, she glanced back at Cort in her side-view mirror. He was on his feet now, angrily pushing aside the cowhands who had extended a hand to help him up. She could almost see the steam curling out of his ears.

A curious stirring started in the pit of Shana's stomach. Brock might just be a tenderfoot from tinsel town, but at least he'd brought Cort Donner down a peg or two and all without spilling any blood. She smiled in her rearview mirror at the Hollywood stuntman on her tail.

But the smile quickly faded when, out of the corner of her eye, she saw the streak of red on the sleeve of her blouse where Brock's hand had just been.

BROCK WRAPPED some gauze around the open slash on his palm as he maneuvered his truck behind Shana's and drove out of the ranger station parking lot. After all the bones he'd broken and the deep gouges he'd sustained in his stunts, a little whip slash was nothing. The pain hardly bothered him at all.

Her kick of the night before didn't bother him, either. Lots of mares kicked at a stallion before welcoming him. All part of the courting process. He always thought such token resistance piqued a stallion's interest. He knew it piqued his. Especially when she'd leaned into his arm and he'd felt the hammer of her heart and heard the quickening of her breath.

Anger? Surely some. But beneath it he'd sensed the raw, hot passion behind her icy wall of unattainability. His stomach muscles tightened with the memory. No, Shana's resistance wasn't bothering him at all.

But what was bothering him was how close Cort Donner had been standing next to Shana when he'd walked into that ranger station. As if he was just about to kiss her.

Also bothering him was the proprietary tone Donner had used when he demanded answers from Shana about her whereabouts of the night before.

If he had tried to question Shana like that, she would have told him to go to hell. But she didn't tell Donner to go to hell. On the contrary. She had tried to explain Brock's presence in a decidedly conciliatory tone.

Brock didn't like Shana's using that tone. Nor the way she seemed to be protecting Donner from his own foolhardy actions. No, he didn't like this at all. What was Cort Donner to Shana O'Shea that she showed him such deference?

Phil Hudson's words came back to him then. *"I've yet to see her with a man. Except Cort Donner. But it's hard to tell what they've got going."*

Brock jammed his gearshift into second and released the clutch as they began to climb a hill. Well, whatever they might have had going, it was officially at an end. He wasn't planning on sharing Shana with anybody.

The sudden strength of his anger surrounding that resolve surprised even him.

CLIMBING OVER the circuitous Toiyabe mountain dirt roads into the higher grazing lands hauling horse trailers took quite a bit longer than covering the same roads by regular car. Shana was especially careful as she took the curves, knowing Mickey Finn and the pack mules she had picked up at Hunts Canyon could brace themselves fairly easily with forward acceleration or even quick stops, but had no defense against a jolt to the side. She would not risk injury to them.

It was therefore midafternoon when they arrived at the end of the road where their vehicles would have to be left. After the long journey, Shana felt good getting out and stretching her legs. She immediately went back to let her pack mules and Mickey Finn out so she could walk them around and let them stretch their legs, too. She noted with approval that Brock had also headed to his horse trailer to do the same.

Her eyes took in the gauze around his right palm as he undid the latch. She was heartened to see that he didn't seem to be favoring the hand. She'd had enough experience with men to know they didn't appreciate being fussed over, so she didn't offer to take a look at the wound. Besides, she wasn't sure how comfortable she'd be getting close enough to that man. She turned to attend to her animals.

But she couldn't help glancing back at Brock. He wore tight blue jeans and an open white shirt today, his sleeves rolled up, setting off the deep bronze of his tanned skin and the rippling muscles beneath it. She was staring and she knew it, but it was hard not to. Despite his overbearing arrogance, this was not the common, garden-variety male. Brock Trulock was what Shana thought of when the word "hunk" came to mind.

She was still watching when he brought out the beautiful buckskin she'd seen him on the first day. But when he led the second horse out of the trailer, her mouth dropped open.

It was a young, rose-dappled Arabian mare with perfect conformation—absolutely beautiful from her large dark eyes to her long silvery arched tail. She didn't walk, but pranced about on jet black hooves as light as air as Brock led her toward the minuscule shade of a few scrubby junipers where he had already tethered the buckskin and where they could drink from the trickle of water in the small creek.

Shana led Mickey Finn and the pack mules to the same small area of shade and just stood there and stared at the mare. The Arabian looked like some ethereal creature, her coat glistening silver and rose in the hot afternoon sun.

Shana came out of her trance when she suddenly sensed Brock behind her. She could feel the dangerous masculine heat radiating from him. Her pulse jumped most annoyingly.

"Like her?" his deep voice asked.

Shana swallowed. "Who wouldn't? She's exquisite. What's her name?"

"Roseblush."

"Suits her, all right. But you're mad to bring her on a rough ride such as this. She could so easily be injured. What could you have been thinking?"

"Of Fire Magic."

Shana turned away from the mare and toward the man, new speculation in her eyes. "Fire Magic?"

"You said it yourself. We might be in his range, but finding him is unlikely if the stallion is determined to hide. So we don't waste our time trying to find him."

He was smiling at her again. A brilliant, dazzling smile. She felt as though she were inhaling it along with the poignant scent of honeyed sagebrush, and both were whirling in her mind. "We don't?" Shana repeated.

Brock's gray eyes gleamed at her as he moved in closer. "It's breeding time, Shana. And Roseblush is coming into season. Our red stallion has a penchant for well-bred little mares like her. All we need to do is let Fire Magic get a whiff of Roseblush, and he'll come to us. As a matter of fact, I predict we won't be able to keep him away."

His massive chest seemed to be surrounding her as his deep voice vibrated slowly and silkily along her spine, releasing bubbles of warmth throughout her body. Shana snatched at her rapidly fleeing thoughts. "This is your plan to capture him? You're going to let Roseblush draw him to us?"

Brock's eyes caressed her face as he leaned closer, his powerful chest brushing lightly against her breasts. Shana inhaled sharply at the contact, stepping back, her heart suddenly beating wildly as the blood rushed through her chest into her neck and face.

"It's the overwhelming drive of nature, Shana, igniting their internal fires past all reason in the pursuit of procreation."

Once again he closed the distance between them, looming over her. His gleaming gray eyes held hers with their intensity. He was close but he didn't touch her. Shana knew all she had to do was move away. She tried to, but somehow she couldn't. Her hard, disciplined muscles mutinied into mush as his voice lowered seductively.

"It all starts with the gradual lengthening of the day in the spring months. Light stimulates the master endocrine gland, the pituitary. The same pituitary hormones stimulate increased sexual activity in the stallion."

His warm, enticing breath fell across her forehead and then down toward her cheek, causing tiny quivers to dance down her spine. "Then he catches her scent, takes it into him and knows he must possess her. Once he's gotten her scent, he'll never give up until he has her."

Shana knew Brock was no longer talking about horses. Her heart pounded like a frenzied base drum in her chest. She closed her eyes, tried not to listen, but she couldn't shut out the warm, clean, masculine smell of him, the mesmerizing tone of his deep silky voice, the steamy images his words evoked.

"The teasing of their courtship prepares both male and female physically and mentally for mating. All the senses come into play—sound, sight, smell, touch. He calls to her. She answers. She darts away. He follows. Circling, watching, sniffing, rubbing, exciting her until she wants him as much as he wants her. She no longer runs away. His desire pulses hard in his loins until it cannot be denied. She aches to be filled. Then—"

"Shana? Everything all right?"

Shana's eyes flew open, and she jumped back as Tommy Windway's voice pierced Brock's verbal mating spell like a well-placed arrow. She swung toward the approaching Indian, mounted on his domesticated mustang, thankfully sucking in air like a rescued woman who'd just been going down for the third time. It took her a moment before she could find the breath or collect her thoughts well enough to respond. By then Tommy was reining his horse in next to them.

Despite the best of her efforts, she knew her voice was a bit shaky. "Everything's fine, Tommy. We just got here. Your timing's good." He'd never know how good. "Where's John?"

Tommy slid off the bare back of his shaggy mustang with a practiced grace. He looked inquisitively from Brock to Shana, but didn't comment on the close proximity he'd just witnessed between them or Shana's still-flushed face.

"John sent me ahead to tell you he's picked up their trail. It's a half mile away. Probably about ten hours old, but it tells us the stallion definitely came this way with Lady Blue."

"Tommy, that's great news. Oh, by the way, this is the man I told you about over the phone. Mr. Brock, this is Tommy Windway, one of the two best trackers in the entire state of Nevada."

Tommy shook hands briefly, giving Brock another inquisitive look. Then he turned back to Shana. "You want to get mounted and go see those tracks?"

Shana nodded eagerly and headed toward Mickey Finn to saddle him. She would have cheerfully joined a harem on the way to Saudi Arabia about now to escape Brock Trulock's company.

Tommy followed her, stopping dead in his tracks when he got a look at their tethered animals. An appreciative whistle escaped his lips. "Outstanding Arabian you got there, Mr. Brock. Mind if I take a closer look?"

Shana watched Brock silently nod his okay. She noted he'd been unusually silent since Tommy's arrival.

As Tommy went to take a look at Roseblush, Shana felt Brock move up behind her. She tried to steel herself, but even his closeness caused her hands to slip with excessive moisture as she sought to tighten the cinch around Mickey Finn's belly.

Brock's deep whisper had none of its previously silky tone. He sounded definitely put out. "I thought your Paiute friends weren't to be told about this roundup?"

Shana kept her voice low, too. "I didn't tell them who you are. They just think you're a breeder determined to try your hand at catching Fire Magic. I can't think why you'd want to complain. By finding Fire Magic's tracks so quickly, they've probably just saved us several days of searching."

She turned to see Brock's face set in a scowl and was perversely pleased. Seemed the indomitable Brock Trulock did occasionally run out of those charming smiles.

"I don't want them along on this roundup, Shana."

She shot him a challenging look. "Oh, really? Why not?"

"Because Fire Magic could get spooked by too many trackers. With such a heavy human scent around Roseblush, even she may not be enough temptation to draw in the stallion."

Shana's voice turned low and sweet with sarcasm. "Oh, you mean his internal fire might not ignite past all reason in the all-important pursuit of procreation?"

For an instant thunder descended across Brock Trulock's brow, and Shana experienced a delicious thrill that was at once scary and sweet. Then, like lightning, the scowl Brock had been wearing faded into a faint smile. "Ah, now I see what you're up to."

Shana felt decidedly uncomfortable at this emotional change. She didn't want to ask the obvious, but she couldn't seem to help herself. "Oh, and what is it you think I'm up to?"

He crossed his arms across his powerful chest and stared at her very intensely for a moment. When he finally spoke, the silky tone was back. "You're afraid to be alone with me."

Shana was finding it curiously difficult to catch her breath, but she stood her ground. "I'm not afraid of you, Brock Trulock."

"Oh, I know you're not afraid of me. You're insisting on bringing Tommy and John along because you're afraid of yourself. You know the minute we're alone, you're going to want me in your bedroll. Why don't you just admit it?"

Shana felt rocked by the arrogance of his words and literally had to hold on to Mickey Finn's saddle horn to steady herself as anger shook through her.

She struggled to get her words out. "I suppose *Playboy* magazine assured you that line was a sure-fire winner to put any woman on the defensive. Well, welcome to the real world, Mr. Inflated Ego. I'm not one of your showbiz bimbos, and I'm not buying."

And with that, Shana swung herself onto Mickey Finn's back and nudged him into a trot. Startled she was leaving without him, Tommy leaped onto his horse's back and gave the rein a twist to catch up with her. "Shana! Hold up!"

But Shana wasn't reining in even for Tommy, and he had to give his mount an encouraging knee to try to catch her.

Brock smiled as he watched her gallop away.

Run as fast as you can, Shana O'Shea, he thought. *It will do you no good. Because when you get to where you're going, I will be there to greet you. You see, I've caught your scent. And I will not stop now until I have you. It's just a matter of time.*

Chapter Four

"See the markings there, Shana?" John Cloud asked as he pointed a long, leathery finger. "Fire Magic's distinctive, curved hooves and the shoes of Lady Blue. They went east toward the lower range. Last time he captured a mare he went almost due north. He never goes the same way twice."

Shana nodded. "He's smart. We'll start out tomorrow at first light. I've brought provisions for the roughest and longest of the wilderness trails. We could be gone a week or more."

"Can this Mr. Brock make such a ride?"

Shana turned back to John. "He sits a horse well enough. But I don't know whether he's got any endurance. You realize this is his show. I've only agreed to lead him to Fire Magic's range. He's supposed to capture Fire Magic."

John nodded in instant understanding. "You don't want him to."

Shana's lips twisted. "I want to see him fall flat on his face."

"What about Amy Edel's mares?"

"After I've disposed of Brock, I'll come back and stay up here until I find them. But I'm not lifting a finger to locate them on this trip. Not with that man along."

John watched her silently a moment. "You speak of this man with a depth of feeling I have not sensed in you before."

Shana's eyes flashed to her friend. "He's an extremely arrogant man, John. I'm only taking him to Fire Magic's range because Phil is forcing me to. But Phil can't force me to help him catch the horse. Or to make the searching easy. As a matter of fact, I'll make sure it won't be."

John's black eyes stared into hers like deep, dark, quiet pools. "I understand, Shana. I hope you do, too. Such strong feeling can be like drying rawhide. Changing shape. Wrap it around you and it will soon tighten and bind you in its grip before you know you have been snared. Or by what."

Shana frowned at his words, suddenly feeling on the defensive. "John, I have good cause to dislike this man. I told you why I asked you and Tommy to accompany me. He struts around acting like everything is his for the taking, including Fire Magic and me!"

"So he makes advances to you. So have others. Why do his advances make you bristle like a sharp sagebrush?"

Shana shrugged. "It's not the advances. It's the way he comes on to me, John. Like it's inevitable. Like I won't be able to refuse him."

"And Cort Donner does not also act this way?"

Shana inhaled a deep breath and shrugged as she let it out. "Well, of course, Cort is like that, too. But you know he's always been like that."

"Yes. I know. But I also know you do not have such strong feelings toward Cort Donner as you do toward this other man."

Shana looked away from John's penetrating eyes, tracing her fingers through Fire Magic's hoofprints in the dust. "I've known Cort since grade school. Been fighting off his propositions since high school. Now he thinks he's in love with me. I suspect the real reason for his proposals is that he can't understand why I haven't taken him up on the propositions. The man's a bully and a bore. But I'm used to his insolence. I can handle him."

"But you cannot handle this Brock?"

Shana removed her fingers from Fire Magic's hoofprint and wiped the dust on her slacks as she rose to her feet. Something about the quiet probing quality of John's questions was beginning to get on her nerves. "Of course I can handle him. What's all this about, John? Did you think I couldn't?"

John got to his feet to stand beside Shana, looking at her steadily. "I think you *can* handle him, Shana. But you have asked Tommy and me to come along. This makes me wonder *how* you might want to handle him."

Shana bit her lip, feeling trapped by her own words. "All right, John. I don't want to spend my time dodging the man's advances. I thought with you and Tommy along he'd be less inclined to make them. And now that Tommy says his prior commitment won't let him come tomorrow, I'm going to need you all the more."

John Cloud watched her silently a moment more before responding. "You have prepared your trip plan?"

"Yes. Here." She handed him a marked map, glad he had dropped the subject of Brock. "I drew it last night. We'll keep close to the crest trail. Some of the roughest terrain in the wilderness. We'll be mostly in piñon and juniper woodlands on the rising mountains. It will be nearly straight up to the higher elevations of the steep, dry range about here, with lots of rocky canyons dotted with limber pine and patches of aspen.''

Tommy emerged from some dense brush beside them in time to hear the itinerary and frown at Shana. ''Except Fire Magic didn't go toward the crest trail this time, Shana. He's hiding his hoofprints in the dense undergrowth, but it looks to me like he's moved his herd down to the lower elevations. Seems strange he'd do that for the summer months. You'd think he'd go higher into the alpine meadows. But his tracks definitely indicate he's down in the lower valleys.''

Shana smiled. ''Yes, when I got a look at his tracks, I figured that's where he went, too.''

It took a moment for the truth to dawn on Tommy. ''Oh, ho! So squaw lead big cowboy on even bigger wild-goose chase. Hmm. Squaw better hope big cowboy not find out.''

Shana's eyes twinkled. ''Squaw going to do her best. I just pray Fire Magic doesn't find out about Roseblush.''

''Roseblush?'' John repeated.

''Brock's Arabian mare. He hopes Fire Magic will scent her and come calling.''

Tommy turned to the older Indian. ''She's a perfect little lady with strong legs and back. Wait until you see her.'' Tommy's eyes danced back at Shana. ''I think if Fire Magic got a glimpse of Roseblush, he would have the same eyes for her that this Brock has for you, Shana.''

Shana frowned. ''Which is why I have no intention of letting Fire Magic anywhere near the mare. John, how far away do you think a stallion would have to be to sense a mare in season?"

John placed a hand on Shana's shoulder. "I think where Fire Magic is concerned, it would be safest to send the mare to Alaska. But since you are taking a trail many miles from where Fire Magic's tracks show he has headed, you should be able to avoid the stallion finding her. Now let us go eat supper together. I would like to meet this man Brock and see this Arabian mare."

Brock watched Shana riding toward their parked vehicles with both Indians beside her. Like them, she seemed a part of her horse, gliding in a fluid natural motion at once graceful and purposeful. Hers was real horsemanship. The kind that was instinctive.

He'd never seen a woman ride like that before. Of course, he'd never seen a woman like Shana before. He would have liked to have had her alone on this trek, but he was determined to have her no matter who she brought along.

All three dismounted next to the tethered animals. Tommy led the horses over to the tie line as Shana went to get them feed out of the back of her truck. The second, older Indian took a brief, appreciative look at Roseblush and then headed for Brock. His walk reminded Brock of Shana's—smooth, swift, silent.

"Mr. Brock, I am John Cloud," the older man announced in a voice deep with a natural authority when the distance between the two men had been closed. He held out his hand.

Brock took it, impressed by both the strength of the man's shake and the straight look from his eyes.

"Tommy mentioned you found Fire Magic's tracks."

"Yes. But the stallion is wily. His trail will not be easy to follow. Nor will he be easy to catch."

Brock dropped his hand from John Cloud's. The Indian's words had not voiced a question, but his black eyes certainly did. Brock crossed his arms over his chest. "I didn't think it would be easy. But then, I've found that a man finds the best of himself when he takes on the more difficult challenges."

His eyes glanced toward Shana as she affixed feed bags over the heads of the horses and mules. She was efficient yet gentle, giving each an affectionate pat and whispering an endearment. Her long black hair hung in two heavy braids today that swung seductively across her breasts as she leaned down to check Mickey Finn's hooves. His eyes followed the line of her slim waist to the exciting curve of her hips. The sun stroked the golden skin of her neck and arms with every supple movement of her body.

"Have you tracked in this wilderness before?" John's voice asked beside him.

Brock's eyes flashed in his direction only momentarily. "No. That's why I wanted Shana along."

John Cloud turned to face the tethered animals, following Brock's glance, allowing several seconds to pass before he responded in a voice already full with knowledge. "Is it?"

Brock knew the older Indian understood how he was looking at Shana. He saw no reason to deny his intentions. "Obviously that's not the only reason. She's quite a woman, isn't she?"

"Yes, I would say so, but perhaps our similar words do not carry the same meaning."

Brock heard the genuine affection in John's tone and felt a pang of discomfort. "I mean she's strong and stubborn, like that red stallion she chases but never intends to catch."

Brock felt John's eyes boring intently into his temple. "Your observation interests me, Mr. Brock. When did you learn this about Shana?"

"About her not intending to catch Fire Magic? That's easy. From the moment I saw her look at him. I see it comes as no surprise to you, either."

"No, but I think it would come as a surprise to Shana. You see, I have known her a long time. I am curious. Why do you think she does not intend to catch Fire Magic?"

"That I don't know, John Cloud. The lady is a bit of a puzzle. A very interesting puzzle."

"And what do you intend to do with the horse if you catch him?"

"Tame him. Breed him."

"And with Shana?"

Brock let his eyes travel over her ranger shirt to the soft curves of her breasts. He quickly subdued his various body parts reacting to those sights and cleared his throat. "The answer should be obvious. I'm a man. She's a woman."

"A woman with good friends," John's voice added quietly.

Brock wondered if he hadn't been too outspoken with John, considering the man's close relationship with Shana. He got the sudden impression of standing in the living room with the father of his teenage date, being questioned about his intentions.

He gave himself a mental shake to dispel the image and turned to the man next to him. He was well over twenty-one and so was Shana, and this man was not her father. He had no reason to be on the defensive.

"Look, John Cloud, I have never lied to a woman about what I wanted from her. Nor have I ever forced a woman to do anything she didn't want to do with me. That good enough for you?''

The black eyes stared unflinchingly into Brock's. "Has it been good enough for you?''

Brock was taken aback by the unexpectedness of the question, and the fact that he had no idea what John meant by it.

John's eyes switched to Shana as he continued. "What a man gives is what a man receives, Mr. Brock. All his growth and discovery of himself depend on that giving. And unless a man is ready to give everything to a woman, he gives nothing. You have read parts of Shana well. Perhaps Shana can help you to read parts of yourself equally well.''

Brock knew there was some message in John's words, but for the life of him he couldn't seem able to grasp it. Before he had any more time to consider it, Tommy strode over. "Your Arabian mare is something else, Mr. Brock. If it were me, I wouldn't be taking her into Fire Magic's territory for all the money in the world. That stallion lets nothing stand in his way when he wants a mare.''

Brock strode up to Roseblush where she shaded herself beneath a piñon pine. He stroked her arched neck. "That's what I'm counting on. Roseblush will bring him to me. And I'll be ready. And we'll both take him home with us, won't we, girl?''

Roseblush raised her head appreciatively as Brock's fingers gently rubbed her soft velvety muzzle.

"Do you have other mares you plan to breed?'' John asked as he moved alongside.

"No. Roseblush is it. My first. But I'm sure she won't be my—'' Brock cut off his response to John and froze in midsentence, as a sudden movement flickered out of the corner of his eye.

Tommy Windway read the changing expression on Brock's face and whirled around, his hand flying to the knife on his belt.

But Brock knew Tommy's knife would be too late as soon as he saw the snake curling back in preparation for its lunge and its deadly rattle filled the air. He had no gun or knife. There was only one thing to do.

He dived beneath the right hoof of Roseblush, grabbing for the striking snake with his bare hands, using reflexes honed lightning fast from years of unrelenting practice. He caught the diamondback's triangular-shaped head just above its forked-tipped purple tongue and plunged its venom-spewing fangs into the dirt.

Startled at Brock's unexpected movement and the commotion she could not see, Roseblush lunged against her restraining rope. John Cloud's calming hands were on her instantly, steadying her, talking to her, keeping her hooves wide of the man twisting beneath her belly. A crush from Brock's powerful hands and the diamondback rattlesnake's head lay limp in his palms.

Brock stared at the dead snake as his pulses raced with sickening speed. He had acted before he had even had time to think. As reaction began to set in, a sharp shiver knifed through him.

He felt more than saw Tommy Windway lean down next to him. The Indian gently removed the body of the snake from his clutching hands. "Shana," he called.

"Save your voice, Tommy. I'm right here."

Brock looked up to see her staring at him as he lay in the dust beneath Roseblush, an unreadable expression on her face as she folded her rifle into the crook of her arm.

"Mr. Brock just caught our dinner," Tommy said in an easy conversational tone as he rose to a standing position. "Shall I skin it or will you?"

Shana reached for the snake Tommy held out and lifted it, testing its bulk within her fingers. Brock couldn't believe how even and unemotional her tone was. Any other woman he knew would be recoiling in horror. "I'll skin it. Beautiful supple hide. An exquisite creature. Shame it had to die. There'll be more than enough meat for four."

Tommy flashed her a smile as he put the knife in his hand back into the pouch at his side. "You must have forgotten how much I can eat."

Shana grinned back at him before she walked away toward the back of her truck and reached for her skinning knife.

Brock slowly rolled to his knees, then got to his feet, brushing the dust from his shirt and jeans. He laid a hand against the flank of the mare. She was calm. John had steadied her like a rock. It was he who was still shaking inside.

"This terrain can present some difficulties," John said quite blandly, continuing their conversation as though it had never been uninterrupted. "Snakes like the cool shade of these trees just as much as the animals. And they're not too happy when they get awakened from an afternoon siesta."

Brock smiled and shook his head, rubbing his still-sweaty palms against his jeans. "So I see. You are certainly cool about it."

John's weathered face rose to Brock's. "I was not the one whose valuable Arabian mare was in danger. I was not the one to swoop down on the rattlesnake's back like a striking hawk."

Brock couldn't be sure from John Cloud's bland tone and expression, but he thought he detected a certain approval in the man's dark eyes.

"DINNER IS GREAT," Tommy said as he dug into yet another helping of hot rattlesnake meat dipped in corn meal, milk and egg and stir-fried in olive oil. Shana served it accompanied by some lightly sautéed carrots, onions, cauliflower and broccoli she'd brought along in her portable cooler and mixed together in the small versatile wok she'd cooked the snake in.

"Yes, excellent," Brock chimed in as he, too, scooped out more of the meat and vegetables. "First time I've had rattlesnake. Not bad at all."

Tommy gave him a sideways glance. "The skin will make a fine belt. If you know how to fashion one."

Shana watched Brock eyeing the snakeskin where she had it hanging over the back of her truck. "Well, since I don't, Tommy, why don't you take it and make one?"

From the grin on Tommy's face, Shana knew he'd gotten the precise answer he was hoping for after bringing up the snake belt.

"Do you want the rattlers?" she asked Brock.

He smiled at her, teeth dazzling white in the fading evening light. "Have no idea what I'd do with them. Do you want them, Shana?"

"I'd like to give them to a friend," she admitted quietly.

He smiled magnanimously. "Then they're yours. What will your friend do with them?"

"That's up to him," Shana responded.

Brock continued to look at her with a gleam of curiosity in his eyes, but he must have sensed her reluctance to pursue the matter because he didn't inquire further.

His sensitivity on the matter surprised her. So, too, did his easy comradeship with her Indian friends. Tommy didn't take to strangers, as a rule. And John also seemed to be treating the big, blond cowboy with an unusual warmth. Of course, both Tommy and John had seen Brock handle the snake. No doubt he'd gone up a notch in their estimation. Her friends were men who recognised and appreciated such bravery and skill.

Shana rather appreciated it, too. She would never get over how lightning fast Brock had lunged for the rattlesnake. Or how quickly he'd caught and overcome it with just his bare hands. She knew neither her rifle nor Tommy's knife would have been in time. She'd seen fast reflexes before, but she'd never seen anything like that. She had to admit the man could be impressive.

Not that she had any intention of letting him know it. Ever since she'd ridden back with Tommy and John that afternoon she could feel Brock's eyes on her, making their claim, grabbing for her attention, as strongly as his powerful hands had grabbed for the snake. She resented those visual advances. Most strongly.

"So what time will you leave tomorrow, Shana?" Tommy asked.

"At sunup. Weather report predicts it will be in the eighties and nineties until we get to the higher elevations. I'd like to find some shade, and rest the horses during the hottest part of the day."

"You're not coming?" Brock asked as he turned toward Tommy. Shana didn't miss the hopeful tone in his voice.

"No. I have a previous commitment to a lady. But John will keep you and Shana company."

Some of the enthusiasm left Brock's tone. "Oh."

"A storm will be passing by the end of the week," John Cloud said as Tommy got out a flask and motioned his intent to fill everyone's cup.

Tommy turned toward Brock first and Brock obligingly leaned forward to get his cup filled. "The weatherman didn't seem to think so, John. Said it would be fair for the next week and a half."

Shana's eyes set on John's silver head with a defiant pride. "But then, the *weatherman* isn't always right."

She felt Brock's assessing eyes back on her as she held her cup out for Tommy to fill. It took a bit of an effort to keep her hand steady. She noticed Tommy only gave her a quarter cup whereas he'd filled Brock's cup to the top. John refused any. She doubted Brock had noticed. He'd been too busy watching her every movement.

His continued deliberate scrutiny made her feel self-conscious and angry. She wanted to be able to just ignore him but she couldn't and that angered her further. He looked so damn smug and in control and confident as he leaned against the back of her truck, amicably conversing with Tommy on one side and John on the other. Bosom buddies. With *her* friends.

Brock sipped Tommy's brew and nodded appreciatively. "This tastes a little like a sweet tequila."

"They are both made from cactus," Tommy said serenely. He looked over at Shana and gave her a quick wink before turning the nozzle back in the direction of Brock's cup. "There's plenty more. Come. Drink up."

Shana smiled to herself. It seemed Brock Trulock hadn't completely won over her Indian friends, after all. A small attack of conscience got the better of her as she watched him downing the contents of his cup and holding it out to be refilled.

"You'd best be careful," she said. "It's not as mild as it seems."

His gleaming gray eyes looked amused as his voice caressed her in silky tones. "Worried about me again, Shana? No reason to be. I can handle *anything* that comes my way."

Shana felt the angry heat rising in her veins. Every caress of his look and suggestive inflection in his tone clearly indicated that she was one of those *anythings* that had come his way.

Brock grinned at her chagrin and downed another cupful of the cactus drink as though it were lemonade. "So, John, you think it's going to storm. Is there anything special that happens around here when it rains?"

"Things can get tricky," Tommy admitted. "John and Shana and I chased Fire Magic during a rainstorm last year. Gave us a pretty close call."

"Close call?" Brock repeated, as his eyes strayed only in short spurts from Shana's countenance to Tommy's as he refilled his cup.

Tommy nodded. "We'd been on Fire Magic's trail for two weeks. When we knew our horses were rested, we set up a relay to run him until he was so tired we could get a rope around him. We started out with our first three horses and then each of us changed horses twice more as we took turns chasing him. Then we drove him down this canyon and all hell broke loose."

Brock's eyes found her face again, caressed it. "What happened?"

"You tell him, Shana," Tommy urged.

Shana fought down the considerable heat of Brock's gleaming eyes across the glow of the camp stove. She clutched at her anger as she tried to ignore how the setting sun played along the light strands of his hair and the taut smooth muscles of his exposed chest.

She was thankful to resume the storytelling since it helped to distract her mind.

"While I was chasing Fire Magic I suddenly heard John calling urgently to me, and when I whirled around, there was this wall of water bearing down on us."

"A flash flood?" Brock asked.

"Yes. They can happen in an instant here in the desert. All three of us immediately rode our mounts quickly up either side of the canyon face to get to higher ground, just barely escaping being washed away. We expected that Fire Magic would do the same. But that big red stallion just continued to tear down the canyon, directly in the path of the rushing deluge."

Brock lifted a long leg and leaned a powerful arm across his knee, cradling an empty cup in his hand. Tommy refilled it automatically. Shana wondered what kind of a trick it was that let the man direct his presence at her so forcibly that she could feel its pressure against her skin.

"What happened?" Brock asked.

Shana reassembled her dismantled thoughts with renewed discipline. "Fire Magic did it. Somehow he outran that wall of water. After we had chased him at high speeds for close to an hour, he still had the swiftness and stamina to outrun that flood. It was incredible."

"It was also then we learned we'd never catch him by trying to run him into exhaustion," Tommy offered as he took another small sip of his drink. "Nor could we use any of the other ways that wild horses are generally caught."

"What other ways have you tried?" Brock asked as he gulped more cactus juice.

Despite the steadiness of his hand, Shana thought that she detected a little less crispness to his words this time.

"Oh, we tried them all," Tommy said. "We upturned the sagebrush around all the water holes except the one that we had built a corral around, but amazingly he seemed to realize there was no harm from upturned sagebrush and led his herd to water at the safe holes. Normally you can't get a stallion near a water hole surrounded by upturned sagebrush."

"That is where Fire Magic's real strength lies," John said. "This stallion reasons. And learns from experience. He is not spooked like other horses. He knows escape is not always achieved by running, so what he will do is totally unpredictable. He thinks he can do anything and so he does. He reminds me very much of our Shana."

Brock leaned closer to John. "He reminds you of *our* Shana?"

Shana didn't like Brock's referring to her as *our* Shana or the turn the conversation had just taken. Her spine straightened. "John doesn't mean—" she began.

"Let John say what he means," John interrupted as he raised his hand to halt her. "From the age of four, she played with my sons like one of them. When she was twelve she rode with us to round up the wild horses, as good a rider as any young brave."

Shana recognized the gleam of pride in John's eyes as they swept over her and then rested back again on Brock. "She would see a mustang she admired in the wild herd, and after we stampeded them, she'd race her mount until she caught up with the horse and then leap from the back of her mount onto that of the mustang. I'd ride behind her to pick up her dismounted horse while she'd slip a rope over the mustang's head and ride it until it wearied enough to let her lead it out of the herd."

Shana felt Brock's disapproving look volley between her and John. It finally alighted on her friend. "You allowed her to do this?"

John smiled. "I could not stop her. She was never hurt because it never occurred to her that she could be."

The smooth, nearly hundred-proof homemade alcohol slid down Shana's throat in a warm caress. For a moment she was again reliving those days of carefree abandon John had described.

She looked up to find Brock's eyes on her again, bringing her forcibly back to the present. He wasn't letting her forget for a second that he was there. She sucked in an irritated breath. Damn that arrogant man.

"More cactus juice?" Tommy asked Brock.

"Sure," Brock replied, holding out his cup. "So, our Shana was brought up riding wild mustangs and taming them to her will. Not exactly the normal childhood for any youngster, much less a girl. Is that why you enjoy a job that keeps you in the wilderness? So you can continue to tame the wild animals?"

Shana took a small sip of her drink. "I don't enjoy taming anything wild. Nor is it my function. On the contrary. My job is to preserve what is wild in its natural state. The only reason I've been part of any roundup of wild creatures is in an effort to control their numbers so that the available resources for their survival can be maintained. If man wasn't continually encroaching on the few wildernesses that are left, even that wouldn't be necessary."

Tommy grinned. "You have sat our Shana on her favorite cactus by opening up that subject, Mr. Brock."

Brock rested his powerful arms across his raised knee. "So you're one of those folks who think there should be fewer people and more animals?"

Shana's spine stiffened. "Don't put words in my mouth. What I'm saying is that we have finite resources that all living things must share. I'd like to see an understanding and appreciation for the other fascinating and wonderful species that populate our planet."

"And you think Mother Nature should be our guide?"

"Why not? Most animals interact with land and one another in a way that preserves them both."

He stared at her pointedly. "So if you saw a coyote getting ready to pounce on a helpless rabbit, you wouldn't interfere to try to save the rabbit?"

Shana eyed him steadily. He was testing her. It was a waste of time. She had already tested herself years before. "No. I wouldn't interfere. The coyote kills only when it is hungry and to feed its young. It, too, has a right to exist."

Brock didn't immediately respond, just stared at her with a new assessment in his eyes.

"More cactus juice, Mr. Brock?" Tommy asked.

Brock dropped his eyes to his empty cup and held it out. "Don't mind if I do. So tell me more about the wild-horse hunts you've been on."

Tommy was the one to oblige both with the filling of Brock's cup and a story of his first roundup at the age of eighteen that resulted in his being thrown and losing his own mount to the wild herd.

"Were you hurt?" Brock asked.

"Nothing but my pride," Tommy said with a grin "And my pocketbook. I never did get my horse back."

Shana got up to clear away the remnants of their dinner as she watched Tommy once again filling Brock's cup.

When she returned a few moments later after cleaning their utensils, she found Brock slumped heavily to one side, out cold.

Tommy was grinning up at her from his seat beside Brock, holding out a nearly empty bottle of his homemade brew. "Paleface with big eyes for Shana drink Indian cactus juice and bite dust."

Shana couldn't help smiling at Tommy as she leaned over Brock's partially supine form, seeing the steady rise and fall of his chest. She wrapped one of his arms around her shoulder and got ready to hoist. "Well, he can't say I didn't warn him. You want to help me get him into his truck so he can sleep it off?"

Both John and Tommy nodded as John took Brock's other arm and Tommy tackled his feet. But Brock was no lightweight, and they were all huffing by the time they laid him across the front seat of his truck.

Tommy wiped his brow. "Well, I dampened his fire for you tonight, Shana. Should make up a little for my not being able to come along. You want me to leave you a couple of bottles of this cactus juice for the rest of the trip?"

Shana smiled at her friend's mischievous grin. "Keep your home brew, Tommy. Doubt he'd fall for it a second time anyway."

Tommy gave her a wave as he retreated into the dark. Shana was just extricating Brock's leaden arm from her shoulder when he rolled over in his sleep, pinning her beneath him on the cab's seat. Shana fought down an exciting quiver as his arm cradled her breasts. His breath caressed her cheek, warm and sweet smelling from the drink.

He nestled his nose into her neck and let out a soft, satisfied sigh, almost as though he was aware of the tremors he'd just started throughout her body. Shana felt her temperature rising most disturbingly as the solid weight of him registered on every one of her feminine scales.

"John!" she called, feeling suddenly panicked.

John stepped forward and lifted Brock's arm so Shana could get herself free. As soon as she was out from under his weight, Brock rolled onto his back, his arms and legs falling away from his body as he snored loudly.

Shana stared at him, trying not to smile, thinking how different—how defenseless—he looked at the moment, sprawled every which way. Then she realized what she was doing and gave herself a determined mental kick. This man deserved no softer feelings for having gotten himself drunk. Besides, that powerful body was as solid as stone and so was the domineering will behind it. And as obstinate. Neither would be incapacitated for long.

But it was hard to tear her eyes away from those handsome features and from the splendid sinewy chest and the impressive concave stomach that exposed themselves so unconsciously from behind his open shirt.

"So this is the man who inflames my wild mustang rider?" John's voice asked quietly beside her.

Shana started. In her scrutiny of the unconscious Brock, she'd forgotten her friend. Carefully reclaiming a more controlled expression, she turned to John. "Infuriates is the better description. You see how he follows me with his eyes?''

"Yes, I saw. He is a man of strong emotion and will. He makes no secret of his desire for you. But I do not believe he would physically force himself on you.''

Her eyes glanced back to the powerful body of the sleeping man, to the sensuous curve of his mouth and the long romantic hair. "No, he's not into force. He's into charm. He thinks he's irresistible. Mr. Love 'Em And Leave 'Em. He has no idea who he's up against.''

John Cloud almost smiled. "I think neither of you have seen the other clearly yet. Or yourselves.''

Shana turned to him. "What's that supposed to mean?''

"You are a woman of strong emotion and will, too, Shana. A woman who needs a strong man. Could it be this Brock disturbs you because he is your match?''

"Match? Don't be ridiculous, John. I'm more than his match. I learned to be at my father's knee.''

"At your father's knee? But your father left before you even learned to crawl. His knee was never there.''

Shana's eyes flashed. "Exactly! His knee was never there! Men like my father are racers. Racing after a woman only until they've caught her. Then they race away.''

"You think this Brock could be such a racer?''

Shana looked down at the handsome face and superb body stretched out in front of her. Even she heard the bitterness in her tone. "I don't think he could be anything but.''

"Perhaps it is true he pursues you only for the challenge. But he does not know who you are yet. A man who has not yet spoken his heart can still have much to say. Maybe all he needs is to be sure that the right woman is listening.''

Shana sighed as she rested a hand on John's arm. ''More likely his heart doesn't speak because long ago he surrounded it with a thick, soundproof ego. But I like finding out you are a romantic, John. I never knew.''

John's hand patted hers where it rested on his arm. ''I do not like finding out you are such a cynic, Shana. Thank you for putting the rattlers in my saddlebags. Sleep well and be careful of that drying rawhide. Tommy and I will be gone tomorrow when you awake.''

Shana turned surprised eyes up to his. ''You're not going on this trip?''

''Not this time, Shana.''

''John, I don't understand. You said you were coming. Why have you changed your mind?''

''Because the only things you should ever take on a trip are the things you will need. Good night.''

And with that John Cloud turned and walked away into the dark desert night, leaving Shana frowning in confusion.

BROCK AWOKE with a headache that throbbed and a stomach that threatened to heave in revolt any minute. But worst of all was the bright, smiling face of Shana O'Shea bending over him, her dark braids wrapped around her head like a gleaming black halo. ''Sun's up, stuntman. Horses are watered and fed. Mules are packed. You've got ten minutes to get it together.''

Her face turned away, and in its place bright sunlight stabbed without mercy into his open eyes. Brock blinked, trying to focus in on his surroundings, feeling incredibly disoriented. He found himself spread across the seat of his truck, both the passenger and driver's doors open to accommodate his considerable length, but failing as his head and legs hung off both ends.

He groaned, straightening to a sitting position, head in his hands, as the night before came back in far-too-bright flashes. His stomach gave another turn as he discovered the roof of his mouth and found it tasted like the inside of his boots. Damn. What in the hell had been in that cactus juice?

"Nine minutes," he heard Shana call.

He gazed through bleary eyes to see she had packed four mules with the provisions and equipment he'd brought along in his truck. But his buckskin, Hamlet, still had to be saddled, and Roseblush needed a halter lead. And before he readied his animals, he needed some coffee, aspirin and a blood transfusion. He decided he'd settle for the first two, looking hopefully toward the side of her truck where she'd set up the portable stove the night before.

The stove had disappeared. He should have known. Already packed. There would be no coffee. Or aspirin.

And then what he hadn't seen finally hit him. Both of the Indians and their horses were gone. He straightened.

"Where's John?" he called, and then cursed himself as the sound of his voice reverberated in his ears like the inside of an base drum.

"John won't be coming with us, after all," Shana replied after a noticeable hesitation.

Her words opened Brock's eyes a bit wider and sent some blood to squeeze life past the clogs of his industrial-size hangover. Was he hearing right? He was alone with Shana O'Shea? There would be no chaperon on this little trip, after all? How . . . interesting.

With manly resolve he dropped his feet to the desert dust and made an almost successful attempt to stand. The beige landscape dotted with the thick sagebrush and scrubby pine undulated before his eyes. It was a long way over to his horses.

"Eight minutes," Shana warned.

Damn. This was a hard woman he was up against. Still, he was no cream puff. He could take whatever she could dish out. Even without coffee and an aspirin. Even with a head as large as Las Vegas. He'd show her. If he could just remember how to walk.

Chapter Five

"How much farther before we get some food and rest, ah, for the animals?" Brock asked behind Shana.

Shana hid her smile by not turning around as she led the single-file pack train up the steep mountain trail. "Another hour or so," she called back to him. "They're still pretty fresh."

"Oh," came the subdued reply.

Shana had no doubts who Brock really wanted to feed and rest. She had almost laughed out loud when she'd seen how clumsy he'd been saddling his horse and putting a lead on Roseblush. He'd nearly fallen off the buckskin when he'd tried to mount him.

Actually, Shana was surprised he had managed at all. She knew Brock must have been feeling like hell.

But despite the additional beating his body had taken over the past few hours as they climbed the rough terrain, she'd heard no word of complaint. Grudgingly, she had to give the tinsel-town tenderfoot his due.

"You ever camped in a wilderness before?" Shana called over her shoulder.

"No. Matter of fact, first time I was ever in one was when I followed you the day you rescued Lady Blue from Fire Magic."

Shana smiled to herself. This was better than she thought. Not only hadn't he been on a wild-horse roundup before, but he didn't even know about wildernesses! And she was along to confuse him more. Brock Trulock didn't have a prayer of catching Fire Magic.

Shana's comforting gloat dissolved instantly as a deafening shotgun blast broke into the air. She stiffened in the saddle, listening intently for the next shot. As soon as it came she pinpointed its direction and nudged Mickey Finn into a trot. The single-line pack train behind her was forced to pick up its pace, too. But not for long. Soon she reined Mickey in, jumped off his back and rushed into the underbrush, hoping against hope she wouldn't be too late. When she emerged into the clearing, the sight that met her eyes sent a knife through her heart.

She swallowed many angry words, carefully controlling her voice. "Good morning, boys. Into some target practice, I see."

Three youngsters twisted in her direction, two dark-haired boys probably about twelve and a taller, auburn-haired boy who looked a little older. Surprise was evident on all their faces. The auburn-haired one with the shotgun lowered it to his side. "Where did you come from?"

Shana stepped more fully into the clearing, letting them get a good view of her uniform. She drove a small smile into her face. "I'm Shana O'Shea. I work out of the Tonopah Forest Ranger Station."

The auburn-haired boy spoke again. He was obviously their leader. "I'm Dan Duvall. That's my younger brother, Jerry. He's Neal Folsom. Neal lives near us back at our place in Vegas."

Shana gave each of the boys a nod, acknowledging their introductions. "I see from your backpacks on the ground there that you've hiked here. Are your folks at a designated campsite?"

"Yeah," Dan snickered. "With barbecue pits and showers. We've been hiking on our own since sunup. Living off the land."

Shana heard the pride in his voice and cautioned herself to cool down. It wasn't going to be easy. She counted to ten very slowly as she circled their make-shift camp. "There are a large number of wild animals that must live off the land, too, Dan. This wilderness is their home. Are you aware that it's against the law to shoot game here?"

Shana could tell from Dan's expression that the thought had never crossed his mind. She would have loved to have gotten her hands around the neck of the adult who gave these youngsters a loaded gun.

When the quiet stretched uncomfortably, Dan's brother Jerry yelled into it, "He didn't hit nothing, anyway. He's a real rotten shot."

"Ah, shut up," Dan growled as he whacked his younger brother in the shoulder.

Shana walked over to the empty cans of spaghetti that the boys had tied to a short, bushy, multistemmed and malformed tree. Buckshot riddled both the cans and the bark of the tree. She took a deep breath as she carefully untied the strings that fastened the cans to the tree. Then she turned back to the boys. "Do you know what kind of a tree this is?"

Three heads slowly shook.

"It's called a Bristlecone Pine. It's nature's oldest living thing. Bristlecone Pine survive because they possess the remarkable ability to grow in favorable years and almost stop their growth during adverse years. But it's a hard fight for their lives and not many make it. There are only a few left. This one is five feet tall, which means it's fought life's battle for seven hundred and fifty years—two centuries longer than the Roman Empire.''

Shana turned back to the tree and ran a hand lovingly across its gnarled bark. She looked at the boys. "And you were shooting buckshot into its valiant heart."

Two pairs of eyes hit their shoes. Dan Duvall bit his lip. "We didn't know. Nobody told us."

"Someone has now," Shana said calmly and evenly. "Bristlecone Pine are protected by the U.S. Forest Service. What you have done is against the law."

The boys eyes glanced toward the charred ground and then they looked at one another nervously.

Shana stepped toward them. "Give me the gun, Dan."

Dan tested the look in Shana's eye before he held out the gun to her. "My dad's going to be real sore about your taking it. He just gave it to me last week for my birthday."

Shana kept her voice as even as she could. "If your dad has any problem with my taking your gun, tell him I'll be happy to discuss it next week at the Tonopah Ranger Station where he may come by to reclaim it."

"My dad didn't say I couldn't build a campfire or shoot my gun," Dan protested.

"A man doesn't rely on others to teach him what he should know, Dan. Now put your packs on and head back to your parents' camp. Take every scrap of your trash with you, stay on the designated trail and do not bother the wildlife or step on the plants. Do you understand?''

Shana felt the sharp tightness in her voice. The three boys responded to it, scrambling to pick up their gear. She watched them all but running back down the well-marked trail. She stared at their retreating dust until all sound of them had ceased.

"Don't you think you were a little rough on them?" Brock said from behind her. "They're just kids."

Shana turned to see him leading the pack train into the clearing. His presumption that he had a right to question the way she handled the boys scraped across her already-raw nerves and released the anger she had been containing.

"Rough with them? I was far more tolerant than I had any right to be. The Toiyabe wilderness areas are being destroyed by kids and their parents who come up here and wantonly burn precious wood like this in their campfires."

Shana looked down at the charred remains and sank dejectedly to her knees. "Damn. Even the rotting pieces they picked up off the ground were decomposing and replenishing the soil with nutrients. And they hacked green branches off the piñon and single-cone pines, too."

Shana grabbed a handful of the black earth and clenched it in her fist. "I hate these infernal campfires that not only burn the precious forest wood but scar and sterilize the soil. I just hate them!"

BROCK WAS AMAZED at the vehemence in her tone. But now he was beginning to see the anger that seethed within her at the kids' careless acts—the anger she had kept from them but not herself. She cared for this wilderness very deeply, and each wound in it seemed to cause a corresponding wound in her.

He couldn't find such feeling for the dense, scrubby landscape they'd been traveling through, but her pain reached inside him and pressed uncomfortably against his chest like a heavy weight.

He dropped the lead line, walked over to her and sank to his knees next to her in the dust. He raised a hand to touch her to offer some comfort, but then let it fall.

"I guess you weren't so hard on the boys, after all."

She sighed. "I know it's their parents' fault really. But youngsters have got to learn that their parents may not always be setting the best example. They've got to learn to think for themselves and be responsible."

He studied her face, glad to see her ability to override the lingering hurt. "You want the kids to be better at saving the planet then their parents have been."

"They've got to be. If it's to be saved."

"You're right."

She glanced sideways at him—a quick, casual look. Yet he felt it none too casually as its message of appreciation for his understanding worked its way through him.

"Since you graciously fixed dinner last night, seems only right I should make our lunch."

He saw her appreciative expression turn wary. "What's on the menu—hemlock?"

He chuckled and felt it rumble nicely inside his throat. "Sorry, didn't include any in my provisions. Although if I had known what this morning's ride was going to be like, I not only would have packed some, I probably would have drunk it before we left."

A twinkle of appreciation lit her eyes. She had liked hearing him admit his discomfort. And it felt good to make her a present of such knowledge.

He rested a companionable hand on her shoulder now, one that had decided on its own where it wanted to be. "Just give me some time to get the stock watered and fed and to wash up, Shana. Then I'll be back to whip you up an omelet."

His hand fell away from her shoulder as she quickly got to her feet and snatched up the lead line. "I'll take care of watering the horses and mules. There's a clear stream two hundred feet off to the right, up the rise there. It's safe for the stock to drink and for you to gather water from it for washing, but stand a hundred feet away from the stream when disposing of your gray water, and don't drink from the stream."

He cocked a dark blond eyebrow at her as he rose to his feet. He was disappointed her quick movement had brushed his hand away. And he was disappointed to see the twinkle in her eye was gone. He hid both with a smile. "Can't drink the water? Pollution even up here?"

"Not the kind you're probably thinking of. Giardiasis is an extremely uncomfortable intestinal disorder caused by a microscopic organism that can be present in a mountain stream. Best to be on the safe side."

"Thanks for the warning. After the beating my body has taken from Tommy's cactus juice this morning, I don't need anything else attacking it."

The amusement was back in her eyes, the icy shield once again lowered. He took a measured step forward. "Although I wouldn't fight back if a certain black-haired, golden-eyed forest ranger wanted to try."

He smiled at her then. A blinding, flashing smile that he instantly knew had caught her entirely off guard. She stepped back, quickly turned her head away and busied herself with caring for the animals, but she couldn't hide the faint flush on her cheeks.

She might still want to dismiss him, but he'd bet she was having a harder and harder time doing it. This campaign was going even more smoothly than he thought. Suddenly, aspirin or no, the hangover felt as though it was lifting. Brock whistled as he picked up a plastic bucket, slapped his bathing towel over his shoulder and headed toward the stream.

"THAT WAS A GOOD OMELET," Shana confessed as she put her plate down and lay against her saddle, using it as a convenient backrest as she eyed the man across from her.

"The best gourmet freeze-dried product on the shelves," he answered as he held up the empty packet to illustrate.

He looked red eyed, disheveled, the beginnings of a thick sandy beard glinting across his chin and up his cheeks. In short, like a sexy hunk with a hell of a hangover. Her stomach tightened. These all-too-regular involuntary physical reactions to him were making her more than uneasy.

He gave her one of his charming smiles, but this one she kept intently at bay.

His last one had slipped through her defenses. She knew it was the unexpectedness of him that kept knocking her off balance. That moment of gentleness when he knelt next to her. The raised hand that had almost touched her but then had been drawn back.

Strangely, it had been because he drew it back that it had given her such comfort.

Damn, but that stuntman did have more than his fair share of charm.

"How long do you intend to rest the animals?"

She gave herself an emotional shake and leaned forward to answer his question. "They've had a good long drink and a half a feed bag. We probably should let them be until two-thirty."

"Aren't we going to lose Fire Magic's trail if we delay too long?"

Shana frowned. She'd almost forgotten this man was after the red stallion. Her red stallion. The reminder straightened her back. "Not really. We aren't following Fire Magic's trail."

Brock leaned forward, a sudden suspicion lighting his eyes. "What do you mean, we aren't following Fire Magic's trail?"

Shana leaned back again. Leisurely. "Tommy discovered Fire Magic headed for the dense underbrush this time. If we had followed with a pack train the size of ours, we would have trampled much of the unspoiled natural growth. Besides, it takes tremendous physical and emotional endurance to travel in the dense brush."

Irritation laced Brock's words as the volume of his voice rose. "Which one of us did you think wasn't up to it?"

She saw the glint of anger in his eyes and felt a small warning sparking along her nerves. It had a deliciously dangerous feel. She supposed she could string him along awhile longer, but decided against pressing her luck. Something about those gleaming gray eyes told her that this was not an entirely domesticated male.

"I know where Fire Magic's heading. It wasn't necessary for us to track him the long way around. Actually, by taking the established trail we'll reach his range far more quickly and safely."

"But he'll still be there far in advance of us."

"That was never a factor under our control. He had a considerable head start."

Brock didn't look as if he quite believed her. "You say you know where his range is. If that's the case, why did you need to look for his tracks in the first place?"

Shana glanced away from his probing eyes to look over at the tethered horses and mules tied to the high picket line she had carefully prepared to diminish their impact on the clearing. "His range is far and wide and varies from winter to summer. If John and Tommy hadn't determined his direction, we might have ridden for days before we caught a recent sign of him and could determine in what part of his range we were likely to find him. As it is, his tracks have only given us an approximation of where he'll be."

"You can't be more precise than that?"

He still sounded suspicious. But she knew both Fire Magic and this wilderness and he did not. She'd fool him. "Finding wild horses is not an exact science, Trulock. You read the signs and do your best. But if you aren't satisfied with the way I'm handling this hunt, please feel free to find someone else."

She looked at him then, smug and secure in her position. He had no one else to go to, and they both knew it. She was the only ranger in this wilderness.

Brock got up slowly, walked around the portable camp stove separating them and then lowered himself next to Shana like some purposeful predator leisurely circling an easy prey. He was not smiling. The way his eyes stared into hers sent a slight quiver of unease down Shana's spine. All her smugness and security faded.

"You aren't playing a little game with me, are you, Shana?"

Shana felt as if she were sitting beside a mountain, a suspicious, slightly perturbed mountain. She could feel the heat from his body and the look that sought hers and suddenly sensed that this mountain could explode into an angry volcano any second.

She swallowed hard, glanced away at nothing, carefully avoiding those penetrating gray eyes. "I don't know what you mean."

"Is that right? Then why won't you look at me?"

She knew she must meet his eyes, his challenge. She reached down deep for her icy control and held on tight as she swung her head in his direction. "All right, Trulock. I'm looking at you."

And he was looking at her, filling her with his questioning eyes. She clutched at the discarded plate lying beside her leg, trying to hold on to something solid, faced with the liquid gray scrutiny that was threatening to drown her in its deluge.

Then his expression of purposeful inquiry began to change. His eyes roamed to her forehead, then her cheeks, then her mouth. Slowly, sensually they caressed her face. His voice sank low and silky. "And I'm looking at you. But I'm still wondering."

Alarms started to blare loudly inside Shana's head as his right index finger raised, found her sensitive neck, rubbed it with a feather-light stroke. His touch sent warming ripples of unexpected and unwanted pleasure shimmying into her shoulders and chest.

Quickly, she leaned away. Her voice felt scratchy. "Wondering about what?"

Her movement was too late. His hand had already dropped to her back, tracing circular little patterns, sending waves of excitement up and down her spine.

She opened her mouth to protest, but his silky voice interrupted her. "Wondering what rules you're playing by, if any. You know, Shana, if you really want to play games with me, there are several far more pleasant ones I can suggest."

His hand dropped to her waist and angled enticingly up her side, his fingertips expertly feathering her breast through her cotton shirt, leaving hungry sensations gnawing deep inside her. Shana had never dreamed a mere touch of a hand could be so exciting. Her surprised intake of breath was quickly silenced as in one swift movement, Brock's lips slipped over hers, an arm locking around her waist as the other circled the back of her neck.

She could have immediately pulled away. The warning had been sufficient and her reflexes were excellent. But a mixture of heat from his touch and a growing curiosity kept her still. She tensed, expecting an elaborate, sophisticated technique. Instead she felt only the softest brush of a warm tentative tongue that slid like syrup between her lips. And rushed like liquid fire through her body.

Shana couldn't have been more astonished. Or aroused. Her whole body shivered beneath that slight movement of his tongue. She felt as if a key had just been inserted deep inside her into some hidden lock that she had not even been aware of. With an intense moan, her mouth opened eagerly beneath his.

Immediately his mouth fused hard with hers. His hand kneaded her waist and the other stroked the sensitive skin at the nape of her neck. He wasn't kissing her, he was branding her. He tasted like hot lava as he set her lips to burning.

She felt his name singeing her flesh inside and out as her very bones melted into him from the delicious, delirious heat. Her head swam with the power of her arousal, and her body vibrated with its promise, yearning and eager for more.

And now he was urging her into his own private corral for total possession. She felt the shifting of the air as he let out a smug sigh of satisfaction when his arm circled her unresisting body like a final lasso.

That smug sigh of satisfaction struck at Shana's very core, cleaving her mind clear and free from her hot, quivering body. What was she doing? She was nothing to this man but a conquest, a vessel to be used and discarded. The person she was could never, ever let herself be used this way. The disciplined clarity of that thought tightened her muscles, hardened her resolve, sharpened every survival instinct she possessed. She stiffened against Brock's urging arm, tore her lips from his branding kiss, yanked her body away from his skillful hands.

The next instant she was on her feet, looking down at him, shaking from the ice shooting up her veins, where an instant before, fire blazed. "Don't you ever put your hands on me again!"

Brock blinked up at her in surprise. For a long moment he just sat looking at her as though she were some unfathomable desert chameleon that had changed shape, color and form right before his eyes. Then he had the gall to smile as he eased his large frame to his feet in one powerful, fluid movement.

Shana's lungs squeezed tight as he looked down at her, a knowing gleam in his eyes. In it she read his knowledge of her body's amazing response to him. The man knew exactly what he had made her feel. "Your protest comes a bit too late, Shana. I know you don't mean it."

Shana's rage built beneath the blanketing smugness of his smile until she felt she was suffocating. Damn. How could her body have betrayed her so? In fury and frustration, she grabbed for her rifle lying beside her saddle and pointed the business end directly at Brock's chest. "I mean exactly what I say. Don't ever put your hands on me again."

Shana watched all amusement drain out of Brock's face as a very dark and deadly flash settled within his eyes. His fists clenched by his sides as he stared at the barrel of the gun she pointed at him. For one unbelievable moment, Shana was seized with the horrifying certainty that he was going to grab it from her and smash it in his hands the way he had the striking snake.

But he didn't. Still, when he finally spoke, it was in a voice so cold that it sent a shiver down her spine. "Don't ever point that rifle at me. For any reason. And as for putting my hands on you, you don't have to worry, Shana. Before I'd do it again, you'd have to beg me."

He swung away from her and stomped across the clearing, past the tethered animals, into the wild underbrush where the Toiyabe National Forest quickly swallowed him.

Shana watched his trailing dust with a faint thumping in her chest. She shuddered as she lowered the rifle. Letting out a sigh as deep as her soul, she dropped it and herself to the ground, her legs far too weak to support her another second.

Damn, why did she feel so rotten? She had been the injured party here—the would-be victim of the consummate seducer. She was within her rights to use whatever was necessary to repel his advances.

Whatever was necessary. That was the crux of the matter, of course. Even she knew the rifle had not been necessary. Brock would have taken no for an answer. Of course, she doubted he'd ever heard it before.

She sighed heavily. Well, he'd heard it now. Punctuated by a loaded weapon.

She looked at the rifle lying in the dust. She'd never pointed her gun at a human being before in her life. Shame poked at her like a prickly cactus.

BROCK SCRAMBLED through the brush, trying to work off his anger as he kept to the shady sides of the piñon pines and junipers.

Damn the woman. Threatening him with a rifle, no less! What kind of a man did she think he was, anyway?

The answer brought a deep frown to his brow. She must have believed him to be pretty low if she thought he'd force himself on her. An uncomfortable knot tied itself in Brock's gut as anger faded into irritation. How had she gotten such a low opinion of him? What had he done?

Okay, so he'd kissed her. But he could have sworn he gave her warning and plenty of time to move away. While still in the throes of hangover hell, he hadn't exactly planned on seducing her this afternoon.

Even kissing her had been a spur-of-the-moment thing. He was only looking into her eyes for the truth. Except suddenly he'd found the only truth he could concentrate on was that he wanted to taste her. Badly.

Still, that's all he'd intended to do. He hadn't planned on even deepening the kiss.

That was her doing. He'd never forget that incredible hungry sound she made when he touched her, how her lips had opened under his with an irresistible demand, how she had at once filled him with all the warmth, taste, texture and scent of her. Never before in his life had a woman's kiss so totally and instantly seduced him. And then what does she do when he responds accordingly, but jump up and pull a gun on him!

The image of her standing before him with that rifle nestled in her arms, her eyes shooting icy daggers at him and that glacial shield back in place flashed through his mind. He laughed suddenly at the absurdity of it all and the scrubby brush along the hills seemed to vibrate with him before the beige-white dust swallowed the sound. Damn but this was one exciting woman!

His appreciative smile disappeared as new concerns rose. He had to win her trust before he could claim her. He could see that now. He had to let her feel safe with him. Before he proved she wasn't.

Still, in his pique at having the gun pointed at him, he'd given her a promise he wouldn't lay his hands on her again. On reflection in this cooler frame of mind, he was beginning to thoroughly regret that rash promise.

Hands could be such effective persuaders.

Still, he'd given his word. The only way he'd be able to put his hands on her again was if she begged, so he'd just have to get her to come to him. A pretty tall order, considering that feisty forest ranger, but he'd fill it. He had to. He wanted Shana O'Shea now more than ever.

He checked his wristwatch. Two-twenty. Good. Just enough time to saddle the horses before they left. He headed back toward the clearing. He needed the quiet of this afternoon's ride to make his plans. He had some fences to mend with the lady, and while he mended them, he'd be distracting her from the one he was building around her.

"WE'LL CAMP HERE for the night," Shana called over her shoulder.

It was the first thing she had said to him during the long afternoon and evening ride.

She slipped off Mickey Finn's back feeling pretty tired. Part of it she knew came from battling the palatable tension pressing between herself and Brock.

She reached for the heavy twine in her saddlebag and strung a high picket line between two sturdy pines about fifteen feet apart. She tied one end with a bowline knot and then used a Dutchman knot on the other end to tighten the high line. She was also careful to protect each tree with a padded cinch so as not to injure the bark with the restraining rope.

"Need any help?"

She whirled around. Brock stood there with the lead ropes in his hands, the horses and mules already unburdened of their loads. Her answer shot out. "No."

Memory of their previous emotion-charged scene and the all too uncomfortably quiet afternoon ride had her bracing herself as they finally came face-to-face. She wasn't sure what she was expecting, but it certainly wasn't the easygoing smile on his lips.

"Feels good to walk around after such a long ride, doesn't it?"

"Y-yes."

"You sit a horse well, Shana. I couldn't help noticing. Where did you learn to ride?"

"John taught me."

"I thought as much. He mentioned last night you spent a lot of time with him. Since you were four, I think he said. Was he a friend of your father's?"

Shana didn't normally discuss private matters, but the man had once again caught her off balance with his friendly treatment after their blowup. Conversation was better than the silent tension she had ridden with that afternoon. "No. My mother's. She was busy with a lot of archaeological expeditions into the Toquima and Arc Dome wilderness. When I got too heavy to carry along in her backpack, she left me with John and his wife and kids."

"She must have trusted him a great deal."

Brock's powerful hands were casually stoking Rose-blush. Shana saw the animal's hide quiver and felt a corresponding and very irritating quiver inside herself. "They're very close friends."

"Where is she now?"

"Back at the Smithsonian for the past two years, cataloging three decades of discoveries she made in these hills for their early-Indian archives. I expect she'll be there awhile."

"And your father?"

Shana gave herself a mental kick. This was pretty personal stuff. Why was she discussing it? "I'd rather not talk about him."

Once again he surprised her by having the sensitivity not to pursue the matter further. "Is that creek where we just watered the horses the best place to use to wash up before dinner?"

She nodded. "The only place within walking distance."

His eyes followed the trail they had just used. "Three hundred yards back. A bit of a walk. We always seem to be camping a considerable distance from the nearest natural water source. I assume that's so our campsite won't inadvertently add pollution to the water?''

"Yes. I look for ground that is already denuded of plants and at least two hundred feet away from water.''

He looked around at the denser trees on the periphery of her chosen campsite. "It's a little cooler at this higher elevation. Feels good.''

"It is generally cooler up here. But it can get hot, too. It's hard to know what kind of weather to prepare for, so you just have to prepare for any kind.''

He stroked his Arabian mare. She in turn positioned her dainty muzzle so that she could blow on his chest affectionately.

Shana appreciated someone who admired horses. She found her wary, icy shield thawing a bit. "Have you had her long?''

"About a year. She's smart as well as beautiful. Learns tricks easily. I've toyed with the idea of giving her some screen experience so she can have some fun before settling down to becoming a mother. Would you like that, Roseblush?''

Roseblush nuzzled his neck, clearly willing to do anything he asked. Shana bit her lip. Were even female horses putty in this man's hands?

"You talk about her as though she's almost human.''

He smiled. "I suppose I think of her as almost human. She has the sweetest disposition.''

Shana didn't know if he was packing any additional meaning into his words, but she saw the contrast between her disposition that day and that of Roseblush and decided she came out on the short end.

She extended her hand for the lead rope that he was still holding.

"No, Shana. Let me take care of the horses and mules. You look tired. Take your turn washing up first. I'll wait until you return so you can have some privacy."

Shana stared at him for almost a full minute before she lowered her hand. Brock Trulock offering to give her some privacy? What was this man up to now? She turned quietly toward her saddlebags for her towel, soap and bucket with a glance every now and then toward her back. Amazingly, each time she found Brock not even looking her way, but tending dutifully to the stock as promised.

Still, she made her way warily to the water, keeping an ear tuned for any sound of a step behind her. She didn't know what she was expecting, but she was determined to be ready. Her every instinct told her that Brock Trulock was not the kind of man who would be giving up so easily. She was almost to the small creek when she heard it.

Only it wasn't a step. It was a soft, plaintive cry.

Shana whirled around, her eyes darting to locate the source. But everything was quiet now except the thudding sounds of her heartbeat in her ears. She willed her heart to quiet so she could hear the next cry when it came.

It seemed an eternity, standing there in the hush of the warm evening, straining with every fiber of her being toward the faintest sign of motion or vibration. Then finally, thankfully, it came, and Shana took off for the rocky rise on the other side of the creek.

She dropped her bucket, soap and towel at its base and climbed the black lava boulders hand over hand.

Halfway up, she heard the plaintive cry again and increased her speed. As she reached the top, her eyes quickly searched the brush on the other side. And searched again.

Then she saw it. A lone mule deer, pacing over a steep ravine on the other side, agitation rippling through her sleek brown hide in quivering waves. Shana looked for a pursuer and then frowned in confusion. There was no tracking animal. The doe didn't appear to be in danger at all. Then Shana heard the cry again, saw the doe's ears bow front and down and realized it had not come from her at all but from something in the deep ravine below her. And suddenly Shana knew what it was.

She was down the rocky face on the other side with little regard for scrapes or bruises. The doe heard her noisy descent and bounded several feet away, skittish, undecided—self-preservation vying with motherly love. When she held her ground as Shana approached, Shana knew that motherly love had won out.

Shana turned her attention to the ravine. It went straight down, a deep, narrow rocky cleft in the earth that seemed to be bottomless. About ten feet below, huddled on a jetting ledge, was a tiny speckled fawn.

Actually, it had been lucky. Had it missed the ledge when it had fallen, that deep ravine would have swallowed it up for good. Now the trick for Shana was to get down there and get the fawn out without letting the ravine swallow *her* up for good.

It shouldn't be difficult. As long as she was careful. She planned to be as she cautiously braced herself against either side of the steep ravine. Slowly she lowered herself. The rock was hard, sharp, biting into her palms, cutting through the thick twill of her ranger pants. Pain brought her up short. Until she heard the plaintive, helpless call of the fawn again.

She gritted her teeth, ignored her pain, concentrated on the fawn and the placement of each knee and thigh and shoulder and hand. She descended, inch by painful inch.

The ravine narrowed to only a foot wider than her shoulders. She grew more careful, picking her handholds with deliberation.

The moment her foot felt the solid rock of that ledge, she exhaled a sigh of relief. She leaned down carefully in the close quarters, gathered the fawn in her arms, running her fingers gently over his back and spindly legs. He couldn't be more than a week old and shook like a leaf, but he felt solid and sturdy and nothing seemed to be broken.

She stroked his little speckled back with reassuring fingers and laughed into his large black eyes. "Well, little man, you've had yourself quite an adventure. But I think it's about time we got you back to Mom, don't you?"

His responding sound seemed far more hungry now than scared. Shana gave the bridge of his little black nose a final rub and then lifted his thin body across the back of her neck, dangling his legs over her shoulders.

She'd be climbing this time and she'd need the full movement of her arms.

The fawn didn't weigh much, but even he felt like a ton as she struggled up the rocky surface. Down hadn't been easy. Up was twice as hard. But she was going to do it. She didn't have any choice.

Her muscles had begun to ache from the strain of keeping her weight suspended across the deep chasm. It was slow work bracing and balancing herself anew with each fresh hand- and foothold. Perspiration gathered on her palms, making them slippery.

She braced herself with her legs, wiped her wet hands across the relative dryness of her shirt. Then she saw the bloody cuts on her palms. She took a deep steadying breath and reminded herself it wasn't much farther to the top. Only a couple of feet.

She pulled herself up. Her head popped out of the chasm. She had made it!

Or she would have if the previously docile fawn, wrapped around her shoulders, hadn't decided to suddenly bolt.

With several determined lurches, the fawn somehow righted itself while still on Shana's back and shoulders and then jumped for the ledge, whacking Shana in the chin with an unintentional kick from one of his sharp little hooves.

He scampered safely toward the doe. But Shana did not see. The impact of his kick had knocked her unconscious and she was falling.

Chapter Six

"Shana! Shana!"

Brock waited for a response to his call but was once again greeted with silence as he made his way in the direction where she had disappeared.

After a few minutes he found the creek. But as he looked up and down the rocky soil with the blades of grass giving way to healthier-looking trees this close to water, he couldn't make out any impressions of her boots.

If this had been Hollywood and one of his lady friends had told him she was going to wash up, he'd expect her to be gone for an hour. But this was the Toiyabe wilderness and it was Shana who had gone to wash up, and he knew that took a maximum of five minutes. So what had she been doing for the other fifty-five?

Brock looked at his watch for the hundredth time. Eight-thirty. It would be dark soon. Worry and frustration tore at him. He peered through the dense, prickly brush, looking in vain for a sign of her. He ran alongside the creek, searching for a footprint. "Damn it, Shana O'Shea, answer me!"

But his own angry call and the pops from the bubbling creek were the only sounds echoing back to his ears.

With grim determination he retraced his steps, looking for any sign of her, angry at his slowness, at the difficulty of seeing in the dimming twilight, at his lack of forethought to bring along a flashlight.

He was just about ready to go back to camp to get one when he finally heard her. But it took several moments before he could make himself believe what he heard. She was singing!

"The first time I met him was early last spring,
He was riding a bronco, a high-headed thing.
He tipped me a wink as he gaily did go,
For he wished me to notice his bucking bronco."

Brock ran for the rocky rise as the next stanza rang clearly through the still desert air. He gave her discarded bucket, towel and soap a quick glance, noting them as a mark of her trail.

"The next time I saw him was early last fall.
He was swinging the ladies at Tomlinson's ball.
We laughed and we talked as we danced to and fro,
And he promised he'd never ride another bronco."

By the time she started the next stanza, Brock had slid down the other side of the rocky hill.

"He made me some presents, among them a ring.
The return that I made him was a far better thing.
'Twas a young maiden's heart I would have you all know,

He had won it by riding his bucking bronco.''

Brock paused, looking in vain for a sign of her. He was sure the singing had come from here. And then his eyes took in the deep black ravine. He scrambled over to its edge as she finished her song.

"Now listen young maidens, where e'er you reside,
Don't listen to the cowboy who swings his rawhide.
He'll court you and pet you and leave you and go
Up the trail in the spring on his bucking bronco.''

The echo of her voice played along the nerves at his back as he saw her perched precariously on a jutting ledge, ten feet down in what looked like a bottomless pit.

She looked up at him and almost smiled.

Overwhelming relief drove his words like a jackhammer. "What in the hell are you doing down there?''

Even in the dim light he could see the flashing gold specks as her eyes narrowed dangerously, belying the blandness in her voice. "I was trying out the acoustics to see if they might help my singing career.''

He exhaled a heavy breath. Like nothing else could, that wonderful sarcasm told him she was all right.

"Why the song? Why didn't you just yell for help?''

"Because predatory animals understand the desperation in a cry for help. But singing has more of a tendency to drive them away. Particularly my singing.''

Actually, she had a lovely voice, clear and clean and nicely on key. Not that he felt inclined to tell her so at the moment. He focused his mind on the task at hand. "I assume if you could climb out, you would have?"

"You assume correct. As a matter of fact, I did climb out once, but when the fawn kicked me in the head, I fell back in and my right foot got caught in the tight crevice just to the side of this ledge I'm perched on."

Things seemed to be going a little too fast for Brock. "A fawn kicked you?"

"Well, not intentionally, of course. It just got a little excited when I rescued it off this ledge. Whacked me one while it was scurrying off to rejoin its mom."

Brock could barely believe his ears. "You're down there because you were rescuing a fawn?"

She squinted up at him. "We've already gone over that part. Now we're to the part where you lower me a rope and I pull myself free."

Brock shook his head. Damn this woman, anyway. She goes rescuing some stupid fawn and gets herself caught in a dangerous ravine out in the middle of the wilderness, scaring him to death, and she calmly sings away just waiting for him to find her. And when he does she has the nerve not to act the least bit afraid. What was a man going to do with a woman like this?

He exhaled heavily again. "Oh, what the hell. One rope coming up. I'll be back in a couple of minutes."

SHANA WAS enormously relieved as she heard Brock returning only minutes later. Almost as relieved as she'd been when he finally appeared after she'd sung herself hoarse, hoping against hope that he'd come looking for her. Now she wrapped and tied the rope he lowered around her waist and got ready to climb.

"Take it easy, Shana. I have Hamlet here to pull you up."

"Hamlet?"

"My buckskin. Just hold on to the rope and enjoy the ride. He's a professional. He's done it a hundred times before."

Shana nodded in appreciation. Using the horse would certainly save her aching muscles.

She heard Brock giving Hamlet a gentle command and then the slack rope tightened. Shana threw her weight onto the rope but after a painful yank brought the process to a halt.

"Hold it!"

Immediately the pulling stopped.

"What's wrong?" Brock called from the top of the ledge.

It was getting so dark that she could barely see the outline of his head and shoulders. "My foot isn't budging. It's wedged too tight. Looks like pulling it free isn't an option, after all. I'll have to think of something else."

She had kept her voice even and controlled. It was a harder job to keep her emotions that calm. But years of training and discipline kicked in, and she reminded herself that giving in to the panic would only make things worse. She had to think this through. There had to be a solution.

"I have an idea," Brock called from the ledge above. "I'm coming down."

"No, don't! It's very narrow in parts. And you won't be able to see. You'll get stuck."

"Don't worry about me, Shana. Just keep that rope wrapped around your middle and hang on."

She listened to the scuffling on the ledge. What was he doing up there? It was getting harder to see by the minute. And her arms were gathering goose bumps from the rapidly cooling air.

She peered intently at the edge, waiting, trying to be patient. Then suddenly to her horror she saw him sliding toward her, sideways, no less, and face first!

She jammed her eyes shut and screamed. "No!"

"No what? What are you yelling about, Shana?"

His voice was so close. She opened her eyes in disbelief. Somehow, miraculously, he had stopped his fall, hung suspended no more than a foot above her face. She gulped. "How are you doing that? How are you just hanging there?"

"I've got a rope tied to my feet. Now, no more time for questions. Take this flashlight and shine it on the rock around where your foot is caught."

There was a commanding note to his tone and a confidence in it that had Shana taking the flashlight and shining it on her trapped foot.

"There. Hold the beam steady right there," he commanded. "And hold yourself steady, too. Do not move. Not one hair. No matter how much you might want to."

Shana held steady, watching the beam of light. She did not know what was coming, but she went on faith, on what she read in the deep voice now coming at her out of total darkness.

When she suddenly saw the ax flashing into the light, her heart jumped into her throat. But through force of will alone, she kept still. The sharp blade sliced into the rock within an inch of her foot. She felt the strong vibration from the blow rattle deep into the bones of her toes.

Next she heard the sound of the struck rocks falling down the deep ravine. And then, amazingly, she wiggled her foot and found it was free. Brock had widened the crevice where she had been trapped.

"It worked. I can move my foot. I'm no longer trapped."

She didn't have to see his face to picture his smile. It was there in every inflection of his voice. "You had doubts, Shana?"

For once she didn't begrudge him his victory. After all, it was her victory, too. And her life. "Good job, Trulock. Now let's get out of here."

"Just a moment. First shine the flashlight on your face."

By now Shana had gotten used to responding to his directions and complied. Only a second later did she begin to question the wisdom of her easy acquiescence when she suddenly felt his warm lips brushing hers.

This was quite a different kiss from the first. Quick and warm and spicy and full of the promise of many more to come.

Shana was amazed that Brock could convey all that in such a quick kiss while hanging by his feet sideways into a narrow crevice. This was one hell of a stuntman.

She quickly directed the flashlight away from her rapidly reddening face, wondering how he always managed to find a way to get her off balance. Even when he was literally off balance. "Was that absolutely necessary?"

He sounded very sure and pleased with himself. "Absolutely. And you have to admit I did it without touching you, so my promise is still intact. Although if you'd like to release me from my promise, I'll be happy to try it again with hands."

"No. No. I'd like to get out of here."

If he was disappointed, his voice didn't show it. "I'll have Hamlet pull me up first and then you. Sit tight."

"THANK YOU," Shana said.

Brock watched her over the stove light. An hour had gone by since he'd pulled her off of that ledge—an hour in which they had both had a chance to wash and eat and feel as if they had rejoined the other members of the human race. He knew she was thanking him for rescuing her. The clear and simple gratitude in her eyes made him feel a bit strange.

He looked away. "No problem."

But of course it was a problem. Since the instant he'd laid eyes on her, Brock had visualized himself in the role of Shana's lover—not rescuer.

He knew how to stir a woman's passion, and getting past Shana's icy shield to all that delectable passion imprisoned within her was something he'd eagerly looked forward to. But this unexpected casting as a hero left an uncomfortable feeling in his gut. Almost as though he was being pressured to rise above his baser desires and fulfill some better image of manhood.

He didn't want to rise above baser desires. He wanted the woman sitting across from him stripped nude and lying beneath him, eager for everything he wanted to give her.

The silence between them and the new look in her eye was becoming intolerable. He had to break it. He recognized the irritation in his voice and knew precisely from where it came. "Whatever possessed you to go down that dangerous ravine after a fawn?"

She looked at him blankly. "I don't understand."

"Sure you do. You were the one that made the speech last night all about how humankind shouldn't intervene with nature taking its course. Remember, you said you wouldn't interfere between prey and predator?''

"The fawn was not the prey of another animal.''

"Maybe not at the time you came upon it. But it had trapped itself on that ledge.''

"Are you saying I should have let it die? That you could have walked away and ignored its cries for help?''

"Maybe I wouldn't have walked away. Maybe I would have gotten it off that ledge and had it for dinner.''

Her look definitely told him his heroic wings were slipping. "A helpless fawn? A baby just starting out its life? You could have killed and eaten it?''

Brock felt a curious disappointment at the sound of her voice. He was finding that falling off that heroic pedestal could leave a bruise or two. He looked away into the dark night, wondering what in the hell was wrong with him.

"I don't know what I would have done. You satisfied?''

When he glanced back at her a moment later, she did indeed look satisfied. Not a good sign.

"So was that a sample of the kind of stunts you do?'' she asked.

Brock detected a genuine interest in the question and was afraid it had only surfaced along with her gratitude. Damn, it wasn't gratitude he wanted from her.

He leaned back against the horn of his saddle, feeling it dig a hole in his back, wishing for what less than twelve hours before he'd vowed he'd never want again— another bottle of Tommy's cactus juice. "I've never tried that particular stunt before. But I have hung upside down after stretching a rope between myself and a horse. As a matter of fact, that's one of the stunts I choreographed for the Excalibur jousting tournament."

"You were involved in putting together that entertainment?"

"Yes. Several years ago. Coming to Vegas to set up the stunts was the first time I saw the picture of Fire Magic. Once I saw him in the flesh, I knew he was the sire I'd been looking for. He's a walking, breathing dream come true. The perfect horse to begin my breeding stables."

He heard the immediate change in her tone. "Wait a minute. To *begin* your breeding stables? Are you saying that you don't yet have a breeding ranch?"

He smiled at her surprise. "I have Roseblush. And soon I'll have Fire Magic and his colts and fillies. Everybody has to start somewhere."

"Roseblush is your only mare?"

"My only mare? Do you know how much an Arabian mare of her bloodlines costs?"

"Wiped out your savings account?"

"Damn close. Still, she's all I need until I get Fire Magic and his progeny. Then I'll select the right piece of land—"

"Land? You don't even have a location for this breeding ranch?"

His smile expanded. Now, this challenging, doubting Shana he recognized. He began to relax. "Worried about me again?"

"Worried nothing, it's just that I—"

"I know what I'm doing," he deliberately interrupted. "I'm a worldly man from the vile and wicked Los Angeles motion picture industry, remember?"

He watched her looking at him as though she couldn't make up her mind about many things. The dancing gold flecks in her brown eyes had stilled, as they always seemed to do when she was confused.

"Will you still be a Hollywood stuntman after you get this breeding ranch going?"

"No. I believe in doing one thing at a time and doing it to the best of my ability. I never do anything halfway. Besides, being a stuntman doesn't have the draw it used to."

She raised her hands to her hair, undoing the clasp that fastened the braids to her head. "Why?"

"Oh, the people are nice enough, but the work has changed. Used to be a stuntman performed all the falling off horses, jumping off buildings and dunking into raging rapids. Now a studio can put together special effects using computers that are so good that real-life stuntmen are often not needed."

The thick braids lowered to her chest, and she began to unravel them, beginning with the right. "So computers are phasing out even stuntmen?"

She was freeing her thick, black hair from the restricting braids—a gesture Brock suddenly found both incredibly erotic and inviting, although he very much doubted engendering either of those reactions within him was what she had in mind.

Despite the cold air, his hands began to perspire. "Yes, computers are taking over more and more. I spent nearly twelve years figuring out how to turn some scriptwriter's dream into reality. I'm glad I had the experience, but now I think it's time I concentrated on turning my own dream into reality."

She shook out the hair from the braid she had freed and it fell across her breast like a silky veil. "Fire Magic and the breeding ranch."

Brock swallowed, feeling himself becoming as aroused as if she were performing a striptease. "Those are the ingredients dreams are made of. At least, my dreams." He was getting flashes of other images now. Erotic ones that all revolved around the woman sitting across from him.

She was frowning as she unraveled the second braid. "But if you didn't catch Fire Magic, there would always be other stallions."

"Not as far as I'm concerned. Not now when I know he exists. He's one of a kind. From the first moment I saw him I knew. No other horse will do." *And no other woman will do, either.* "I won't give up until he's mine." *And I won't give up until you are mine, Shana.*

Of course she had no idea where his thoughts were taking him. He could tell hers were diametrically opposed. It was written clearly in the troubled, even angry, look she flashed back at him.

"You're pretty sure of yourself," she spat out.

"Why don't you want him caught?" he couldn't stop himself from asking.

Her hand casually shook out the hair released from her second braid. "What are you talking about?"

Her freed hair moved like black ice against her face, across her shoulder, coming to rest over her other breast. The golden flecks in her eyes glowed at him across the stove light. He was struck with the totally wild, primeval beauty of her.

Without conscious volition, he scooted around the stove and was by her side, leaning toward her, feeling her scent surround him. They had to get this business settled between them. It and so much more.

"I know, Shana. There's no use denying it. You hate the idea of anyone getting a rope around that red stallion's neck. For any reason. But he's going to be tamed. And I'm the one who's going to do it. Best you accept that now.''

Her eyes widened as he spoke. Then her chin came up in defiance. Whatever gratitude she may have originally felt for him when this conversation started had thoroughly vanished. ''I don't have to accept anything you say, Trulock.''

She sat there and defied him with every fiber of her being. He could feel that defiance as if it were tangible, trying to hold him at bay. Instead, it stoked his desire for her even more. His hands ached to touch her and the feeling traveled deep inside him and tore into his gut like a burning poker. It took all his willpower to keep his hands by his sides as he leaned in closer, letting his breath fall across her cheek.

''Shana, it's going to happen. And it's the best thing for Fire Magic. Hell, I'm offering him a life of pampering and protection and his pick of the best mares I can find. What's so bad about that?''

''He won't be free.''

Her simple statement gave him pause. ''Shana, I don't understand. You've caught other wild horses before. Tamed them. Look at Mickey Finn. Does he have such a bad life?''

The gold in her eyes coalesced into daggers that shot out at him. ''Mickey Finn can accept the life I have made for him. He can adapt to captivity. He was never a master stallion.''

''Are you trying to tell me Fire Magic won't?''

''I...he can't.''

He could see that the words were causing her pain, as though until she had said them, even she hadn't recognized their truth. So now he understood. She didn't want Fire Magic caught because she thought he would be unhappy in captivity. Well, maybe he wouldn't be completely content. His happiness or lack of it didn't change anything for Brock.

"Look, if I don't capture him, sooner or later some angry rancher or breeder will get a bead on him and put a bullet through him. At least with me he has a chance to survive. Do you understand what I'm saying?"

Of course she did. Even her ramrod-straight defiance couldn't hide the fierce sadness that crossed her face, settled in her eyes, muddying their liquid gold. Brock felt an overwhelming impulse to remove that sadness somehow.

He closed the distance between their lips. She let out a small startled murmur, but did not move away. Her skin was cool and silky. His breath grew faster as she sighed beneath the featherlike touch of his lips. His cheek rubbed against hers, and he luxuriated in the softness of her skin as his lips planted new, gentle kisses on the sides of her face and on the down-soft lobes of her ears.

He greedily drank in her alluring natural scent, his body vibrating as tenderness melted and desire mounted and engulfed him.

Then before he knew it, she had slipped out from beneath him and rolled to her feet. "It's late. I'm going to bed. Good night, Trulock."

And with that she whirled around, marched toward her tent, unzipped the flap and zipped it closed behind her before he had a chance to raise his dropped jaw.

He rolled over in the dust, trying to put out the fire raging in his body, and groaned. Damn. She'd gotten away again.

"WHAT IS IT that you spray on the horses and mules each morning?"

Shana turned around and tried not to look at the gleaming gray eyes she had felt watching her so closely. She held the nonaerosol can up for Brock to see. "It's a bug spray. I use it, too. Matter of fact, I have to, otherwise the insects up here who gather around the water sources would eat me alive."

His eyes dropped from hers to read the can's directions. "It doesn't say anything about being for horses."

"No, but I don't see why they should suffer, do you?"

He smiled down at her as he shook his head, a warm approving smile. "Strange, insects don't seem to bother me."

"I'm not surprised. I've read about the phenomenon. Nature wasn't fair when it came to odor. Something in the natural smell of many men repels insects."

Unfortunately, Shana found it wasn't repelling her. She inhaled the clean, masculine scent of him, noticing that he'd included a shave with his early-morning wash. He'd changed clothes, too. Today he wore snug-fitting black jeans and a matching open vest that seemed to accentuate every movement of every sinewy muscle. The sun shone on his bronze skin and light hair as though proud of one of its favorite specimens.

Damn, he's so sexy. And he looks perfectly rested. The bags under my eyes are probably sagging to my knees after a night tossing and turning. And all because of those deceptively tender kisses that suddenly turned so hot.

Who was this man? The exciting rescuer who had swept her off that ledge last night, or the uncaring seducer who only wanted to add another notch to his belt?

Heaven help me, I think he's both.

She sighed and hoped it hadn't been audible. Oh, hell, nature wasn't fair when it came to a lot of things.

"So where do we go today?" he asked, looking so innocent that she wanted to kick him.

"Up that mountain."

Brock followed the direction of her pointing finger. The sudden, disbelieving look that flashed through his eyes brought vengeful gladness to her heart.

"Looks like a forty-five-degree climb."

She hummed as she put the cap back on the insect repellent spray and returned it to her saddlebag. "Yes. We'll have to walk the animals. It will probably take a couple of days to get to the top."

She didn't have to see his face to understand the suspicion there. "Fire Magic drove Lady Blue up this mountain?"

Shana concentrated on untangling a twig caught in Mickey's mane. "She's a strong mare. And he would have rested her frequently. There's an alpine meadow at the top that he frequently uses to graze his herd. I've seen evidence of them many times, and I've even chased him across it once."

The suspicion still stuck in his tone. "Are you telling me that there's no easier trail up to that alpine meadow?"

Shana lifted her arms in a leisurely stretch as she sent the twig twirling into the dust. "Look for yourself. Do you see an easier climb?"

Of course he didn't. She had him pointing up the south face of that rise. He saw just what she wanted him to see and nothing more.

"Then let's get to it, Shana."

He sounded too eager for her liking. She'd hoped for more reluctance. Well, she'd see how eager he was after the altitude got to him. They were approaching eight thousand feet. For someone used to physical activity at sea level, this was going to be a climb he'd never forget.

As she put her energy into a brisk pace, she was finding she couldn't forget their conversation of the night before about Fire Magic. For the first time in her life, she'd admitted she didn't want the stallion caught—not just to Brock, but to herself. And now that she had admitted it, she was surprised she had not realized it before. Because she knew with absolute certainty why Fire Magic mustn't be caught. And she also knew she would fight to keep him free.

"I'm glad we're walking the horses for a change," he said a few moments later as he moved alongside her. "Gives us a chance to talk."

Talk? Shana was having trouble just sucking in enough oxygen to handle the physical demands of climbing and leading the animals. Why wasn't Brock out of breath?

"What do you want to talk about?" she tried to ask without wheezing too loudly.

"Well, you could start off by telling me what it is about this particular piece of the earth that seems to be so special to you."

"Why do you ask?"

"No special reason, Shana. I'd just like to know."

She concentrated on several deep breaths before responding. "I'm not sure I can explain it."

"You could try."

She shrugged. Guess there wasn't any harm in it. And she did like to talk about the Toiyabe wilderness.

"When I was a youngster, I remember John walking with me through these mountains. He asked me how I was going to become who I wanted to be. I told him that I would listen to my teachers and learn from them. He pointed to dust at our feet, to the cactus and sagebrush, the animals, the mountains, the streams, the sky above us, and told me that of all my teachers, this wilderness would be my most important. He was right."

"You're saying this wilderness has made you who you are?"

"Yes."

"But you don't live here."

"No. One of the things I've learned from this wilderness is that when humans live here, the balance of nature is upset. Plants and animals are destroyed. I travel through this land, giving it the respect it deserves, leaving no traces of my passage."

"So where do you live?"

"I have a small house in Tonopah."

"Do anything there besides perform as a ranger?"

"I teach singing at the local high school, strange as that may seem."

"I don't think it seems strange at all. You've got a good voice."

There was a sincere note to his words that once again caught Shana off guard. "It is fun," she admitted. "Tonopah only has a few thousand people and the kids are loaded with talent and enthusiasm. Couldn't ask for more."

"So you're satisfied dividing your time between Tonopah and the wilderness?"

"Very satisfied."

"Even though there isn't much to do?"

"I find lots of things to do. And the scenery is spectacular. I went to the university at Las Vegas for a couple of years. But staying in a big city like that never tempted me."

"Why?"

"Cities contain too much car exhaust and people who think the strangest things give them pleasure."

"Like what?"

"Smoking, drinking, gambling, making money."

"You try any of these pleasures firsthand?"

She looked at him, attempting to judge whether he asked out of real interest or just for conversation. There was more than a spark of interest in his clear gray eyes. "On a very limited scale," she admitted. "Just to see what all the shouting was about."

"I take it none of those things made *you* shout."

"None came even close. It's as my mother taught me when I was very young. Everything comes from within me. Pleasure, pain, happiness or unhappiness—it's all inside just waiting for me to tap in to it."

Brock looked at the expression on her face. It had that self-contained quality that he'd noticed the first time he met her. He thought he was beginning to understand. She tapped in to that core of identity she'd found within herself. This was a lady who did not need others to approve of her. She approved of herself.

The knowledge should have removed her mystery. It didn't. Rather, it seemed to create more. A lot more. Brock found himself irresistibly drawn to that self-contained, often defiant core of hers. She was so sure of herself. Not a doubt about what was right or wrong. Maybe that's why she seemed to be so fearless. He had an overwhelming desire to challenge her. The very idea of her enticed him as nothing else ever had.

"But if happiness is all inside you, then you should be happy anywhere you choose. Why are you in the wilderness?"

"I love to sing with the kids, but after a while even their demands on my time can interfere with my seeing clearly who I am. But out here, walking the soft dry earth, surrounded by the plants and animals struggling to survive, paradoxically it is here my struggle ends. It is here I find myself again."

"So the wilderness is important to you because of the way it makes you feel?"

"Yes. Everything in my life gains its importance from the depth of the emotion I let it generate within me."

"You *let* it generate within you? Are you that controlled, Shana?"

She shook her shoulders. "I don't know of anyone who is. Except maybe John. But it's a goal to strive for. Don't you strive for any goals?"

"A lot of them. Every new stunt I face is a challenge. The more difficult the challenge, the more I like it and the better I feel after meeting it."

"You sound as if meeting those challenges is at the heart of your satisfaction with yourself. Surely even computers can't replace all stunts. Perhaps you should rethink this breeding-ranch business. You might miss being a stuntman too much."

"No, I won't. Lately it hasn't been giving me the kick it used to. A certain repetition has begun to creep in with my work and the people I know. Both have begun to feel rather plastic, unconnected with real life." Brock hadn't consciously considered the words until he spoke them. He recognized the depth of their truth.

"So you decided that breeding horses would help you to reconnect with life?"

Her question reclaimed his attention. "Yes, I suppose that's the crux of it."

"But why horse breeding?"

"I've always been drawn to the power and beauty of horses. They've been a part of my life since I was small."

"You didn't grow up in Los Angeles?"

"Yes, but every summer my parents sent my sister and me to my uncle's ranch in Montana. My parents are both part of production crews in the movie business. Since they both worked, they needed to keep us occupied when school got out. It was on that ranch that I learned how to ride and train horses."

Brock grew silent as he found himself lost in the past. He was beginning to realize that the memories from those happy summer days probably had planted the seeds for his current quest.

"When did you start to use horses in stunts?"

"While I was on my uncle's ranch. First few summers I was too young to do much but wash, groom, feed and ride them. But as I spent time with horses and learned how smart they were, it became a challenge for me to teach them. I found with patience and effort, there wasn't a horse I couldn't tame."

"And that led you into using horses for movie stunts?"

"Yes. I used the horses I had already worked with on my uncle's ranch for my first job. After that, lots of offers started coming my way."

"But you don't just do stunts with horses?"

"No, that was just my introduction to the stunt role. It expanded from there. I take on whatever needs to be done. Of course, I still work with horses, but now I also drive cars off cliffs, bounce between railroad cars on a fast-moving train, fall out of airplanes, jump off tall bridges—"

"And medium-size ravines to rescue stranded forest rangers," Shana finished.

Brock looked over at her, enjoying her small smile.

"Do you like living in LA?"

"It has its pluses." Brock looked up. "Although I have to admit, the sky is never this blue."

He took several very deep breaths, hoping his lungs remembered what to do with air full of oxygen.

Hamlet nickered softly behind Brock as though he, too, was enjoying the change in scenery. All around them the silver patterns of the limber pine gracefully and languidly rose from a lazy earth. Tiny white, red and pink wildflowers shoved their faces toward the yellow sun. The air was cool and scented with their subtle scents, each new and different. Peace and quiet reigned.

At this higher elevation, with its healthier-looking vegetation, Brock had to admit this wilderness of Shana O'Shea's did possess a certain charm.

"What are those?" he asked.

Shana's eyes followed his pointing finger to the herd of animals grazing beneath a rocky plateau several hundred feet below and to the left. "Pronghorn."

"They look like African gazelle from here."

"You have a good eye. Anthropologists believe that the gazelle, like humans and other species, came over to the New World on the land bridge that once connected Alaska with Asia and Africa via the Bering Strait. Pronghorn are the descendants of those early gazelles."

Brock nodded. "They're delicate, graceful."

An unusual quality underlined her next words. "Yes. But don't get too attached to any one of them."

He glanced over at her face, read the look of determined, quiet acceptance, and wondered what she was accepting with such determination.

His wondering stopped the moment a terrified screech pierced the air and right before his very eyes a mountain lion leaped from an overhang onto the back of one of the delicate, graceful antelope he had just been admiring.

The herd bolted, leaving the unfortunate pronghorn to his fate within the jaws of its predator. Brock stared transfixed. He had seen such scenes before on wildlife programs. But this was raw and savage and very real.

"We can't stop here," Shana said, her voice breaking into his preoccupation with the scene taking place before his eyes. "The horses can smell the mountain lion."

Brock snatched his gaze away from predator and prey. He didn't even realize he had stopped his climbing. One glance at Hamlet and Roseblush and he knew that Shana was right. Their ears were back. The tension quivered through them in palpable waves.

Quickly, he resumed his pace, patting and talking to them both in comforting tones. They were up the next rise before he spoke again. "You saw the mountain lion. You knew what was coming."

"Yes."

She had responded evenly, quietly, with a strength that surprised him. She could have raised her rifle. She could have shot into the air and warned the pronghorn. She had not.

She had learned the lessons of this wild, primitive land.

"We need to rest the animals," Shana said in a breathy voice beside him after what seemed like only a few minutes.

Brock gave his wristwatch a quick glance, more than surprised to see that two hours had already passed since they'd begun this climb. He looked behind him, pleased to see the considerable distance they'd already covered.

Shana led Mickey Finn and the pack animals toward a small cleared terrace on the side of the mountain. Brock looked over at her and for the first time realized that she was perspiring heavily through her shirt.

He moved to her side. "You all right?"

A flicker of irritation entered her eyes. "Just a little warm and tired. We have been climbing straight up for the past two hours. Or hadn't you noticed?"

He smiled. "Just before coming to Vegas I was involved with a three-month shoot of a picture on location in the Andes Mountains. I got acclimatized to the higher altitudes there."

His explanation didn't seem to sit well with her. Not at all. He understood then that she had wanted him to suffer some from this climb. If she only knew the suffering he'd gone through last night when she left him so abruptly, she'd probably be smiling ear to ear.

Still, he'd be damned if he'd let on. She was already batting a thousand in repulsing his advances. No sense giving her more to cheer about.

She removed her leather gloves, and he instantly saw the pink-stained gauze wrapped around her palms.

The worry came through in his voice before he could even think about controlling it. "You hurt yourself."

She shrugged. "Just a few scratches from rescuing the fawn yesterday. Comes with the territory. That's why I carry a first-aid kit."

Just a few scratches. Sure. He'd seen how shredded her pants were after Hamlet pulled her from that ledge. No doubt she had scraped a lot of skin off her legs as well as her hands. Maybe that's why she looked a little tired today. Couldn't have been too comfortable sleeping.

Still, he knew she wouldn't welcome any offer he'd make to help. She was damn tough and frustrating. His eyes stared at the outline of her breasts against the front of her short-sleeved ranger shirt, then lowered to the other half of her ranger clothes—faded, form-fitting green slacks that hugged the gentle curve of her hips. Every inch of her was damn seductive without even trying to be.

He took a very deep breath and forced his eyes away. "How long should we rest?"

"Just a few minutes. But we won't travel as long as we did yesterday. Make it an early night."

His eyes traveled back to her, hoping for some sign of an innuendo. Of course there wasn't one. She yawned right in front of him and stretched in a totally sensuous catlike movement that pushed out her chest and bottom and had him gulping for air. Then she just straightened again and went to see to the pack animals, leaving him drenched in a cold sweat.

Chapter Seven

"We'll cross here at the top of this narrow rocky ledge," Shana said. "The stream is only a couple of feet deep at this point."

"How deep is it at the drop-off point there?"

Shana followed his pointing finger to where the water rushed down the five- or six-foot waterfall into the wider streambed beneath the trail. "Could easily be six or seven feet deep this late in the spring. The snow is melting off the mountaintop, and this gushing icy stream is the result."

Brock stepped beside her, brushing against her ever so slightly as he held Hamlet's reins. Shana felt the rapidly cooling afternoon air warming considerably in the very small space now separating their bodies. She quickly squelched a totally insane urge to lean closer for more of his warmth.

He turned to her and smiled as though he had just read her thoughts. "Why did you decide to make this a shorter day? Are you tired?"

Shana deliberately took a step away. "It's the water sources that restrict us. The horses and mules have to have ten to fifteen gallons of fresh water every day. The next source of water that affords that kind of quantity is a full day's ride.''

"So we go from water hole to water hole. Just like the mustangs. Any bands up here other than Fire Magic's?"

"Maybe one or two stallions with two or three mares each."

"How many mares would you say Fire Magic has?"

"That's hard to estimate. Judging from the grass his herd devours, I wouldn't be surprised if he had close to thirty."

Brock smiled. "That many females at his beck and call. Not a bad arrangement."

Shana sent him a look at the purposeful innuendo he'd managed to slip into his words. He seemed as fresh and rested as he had first thing that morning. On the other hand, she felt as spent and limp as a worn-out dish mop.

"Well, if we're going to cross this stream, let's do it," he said brightly. He paused by Roseblush to give her an affectionate pat before swinging around his buckskin gelding and mounting in one strong, swift, sure movement.

Shana sighed. Damn. Nobody had a right to be that cheerful at this time of day. Or to look that good.

The pack mules bayed, eager to get to the water and have a good drink.

Ignoring a body tired from a day's walk uphill and a long night's lack of sleep, Shana swung into her saddle, grabbed a firm hold of the lead rope for the pack mules, and clicked her tongue, nudging Mickey Finn forward.

Mickey didn't budge. Instead he settled his two front feet into the moist earth three feet from the flowing stream, both ears ahead, his body tense, his head high, his eyes concentrating hard.

Shana sighed again. Mickey wasn't a big fan of water. From the first time she'd tried to get him to cross a stream, she'd found that out. This was going to take some coaxing.

She leaned forward in her saddle, stroked his neck and whispered in his ear. "It's not very deep, Mickey. And I've saved some special oats that you can have when you make it across. What do you say?"

Mickey's ears turned back to listen to Shana's voice. That was a good sign. A horse scared of something ahead generally kept his ears ahead.

She straightened in the saddle and was just about to nudge him again when suddenly she felt Mickey being bumped. She looked back just in time to see the impatient lead pack mule taking a bite out of Mickey's behind.

Well, she had to admit it got Mickey moving. He let out a squeal and leaped into the stream with a lurch that took her completely by surprise. It took Mickey by surprise, too. He immediately stumbled, nearly pitching Shana over his head.

But her reflexes had her grabbing his shaggy mane just at the last moment, and she saved herself from falling into the water. Unfortunately she couldn't save the pouch from flying over her head and falling into the fast-moving stream.

The instant Mickey righted himself, Shana went into action. She wrapped the lead rope around Mickey's saddle horn, tore the boots from her feet and sailed them back to shore. A male yelp or two followed her volleys, but she ignored them. She had something else very much on her mind.

It wasn't much of a dive she made from Mickey's back, more like a belly flop, but then again, she didn't have much time to worry about form. With every precious second the pouch was quickly being taken downstream where it would be lost forever.

Shana was not going to lose that pouch.

She hit the icy water and barely went under before she struck out in swift, sure strokes. She was a good swimmer. Her mother had taught her at a very young age in a stream just about as cold as this one.

She kept her eye on the bobbing pouch as the swift current sailed it along. But the current was carrying her along, too, and so were the well-tuned muscles of her arms and legs. With every strong kick and carefully executed swipe into the water she gained a few feet.

But there was another rocky waterfall coming up. Soon. With a sixty-foot drop. She didn't like the idea of going over it.

Blood beat in her ears, drowning out the sounds of the rushing water. She would have been chilled to the bone by the icy water if she'd let herself think about it. She concentrated on one thing and one thing only. The pouch.

She closed the distance relentlessly, resolutely. Then the other sounds started to intrude and she realized that they were from the second waterfall crashing onto the rocky bed of the stream below. It was coming up quickly—directly ahead. With renewed vigor she drove herself forward toward the pouch, grasped it in her hand and then swung toward the shore.

She battled the swift current now, but her jubilance at having the pouch back in her possession gave her tired muscles new strength. She kicked and stroked her way with every ounce of her resolve. She reached out and grabbed at a shore rock. Her hand slipped and she plunged back into the icy stream. She raised her head and fought again to find a rocky anchor, strained and stretched with all her might, this time securing a better grip. She took a quick breath and then dragged herself up onto the bank, her wet clothing weighing her down like an anchor. Then she collapsed on top of the soft springy green sprouts of grass lining the bank and gulped in air.

That was all she concentrated on for nearly thirty seconds. Then something big and wet suddenly surfaced out of the water in front of her like an angry sea monster and brought her to an uncomfortable, full-sitting attention.

Brock heaved himself up on the slimy bank, wet and cold and furious as hell for the damn fright she'd just given him. He'd jumped in the water almost immediately after she had, but soon found there was no catching her. She was as fast and sleek as a seal.

And now that he'd satisfied himself that she hadn't drowned, he had a couple of bones to pick with the lady.

"Just what in the hell do you think you were doing throwing your boots at me and then jumping like an idiot into that stream?"

She was still having a great deal of trouble getting her breath but she managed to hold up the rescued pouch.

"I thought that's what I saw fall in when your horse stumbled. Let me have that damn pouch," he said, grabbing it out of her hands. "And I'm warning you right now that if there isn't at least a knuckle-size emerald or diamond inside it, you're in trouble."

He ignored her surprised cry of protest, still breathy as her lungs labored to catch up with air deprivation. He was breathing fairly hard, too, but he ignored that, also.

Curiously, the pouch felt almost dry in his hands. He could think of only one material that was that water resistant. Deerskin. He could see that it had been sealed somehow with a sticky substance that also appeared to repel moisture. Ruthlessly, over her strong protests, he dug a fingernail through the seal, opening the pouch to expose what was inside.

When he saw what it contained, he blinked in surprise. He didn't really know what he was expecting, but this wasn't it. His surprise was soon replaced by incredulity. "A feather? You dived into that damn icy stream to rescue a feather?"

She snatched the pouch out of his hands and hugged its precious contents to her. "It's not just a feather. It's an eagle's feather."

Brock threw up his hands, totally exasperated. "Oh, well, then that explains everything."

Her voice was stronger now, less gaspy as she got back her breath. "Of course it doesn't explain everything. But I can. John gave me this feather. It's very important to me. One of my most prized possessions. Oh, why am I wasting my breath? You couldn't possibly understand."

He watched her bowed head, still dripping water as she tried in vain to close the pouch. He felt the cold chill of the air like knives of ice stabbing through his wet clothes. Within minutes, they'd both be numb if they didn't hurry to get back to the pack train, dry off and change into something warm and dry. This was not the time to go into any more explanations. However, he had a feeling that this was something she wanted him to understand, even if she didn't think he would.

He stayed seated on the wet grass. "Why is this eagle feather so important?"

She looked up at him, the gold in her eyes glinting behind the streaming water that still trickled from her wet braids. He could tell she had registered the change in his tone and his look. Still, she examined him a moment more before responding.

"John Cloud studied medicine when he was drafted into the military service as a young man. He went on to get his medical degree. But he is not what you might call a conventional doctor because he also uses the wisdom of Indian medicine. He is a very important man of the Numa, his people—their *Poo ha gum*."

"What does *Poo ha gum* mean?"

"It's the Numa word for healer. John understands the tradition of his people and uses many different things from nature along with modern medicine in his healing rites. The rattles from snakes, the feathers from eagles, different herbs."

Brock's voice expressed disbelief. "You took the rattles from the snake and gave them to John so he could use them in some healing rite?"

She sighed, as though the disbelief in his voice were a weight she had trouble lifting. "Do you consider everything crazy that you don't understand?"

Brock gestured to the pouch. "Am I to understand that John Cloud healed you at some time by waving this feather?"

Shana shook her head, twirling a hefty spray of water in all directions with the action. "A feather cannot heal. But faith can work miracles. And there are people gifted with the power to instill faith in others. John has such a gift.''

He watched her stare at the fast-moving stream before them, but he knew it was something else she saw. Her voice drifted into his ears like music. ''I was seven when I was badly stung by a deadly scorpion. There was no antidote. I was dying. John put this eagle feather in my hand and told me to become one with the spirit of the eagle, to fly with him high above the craggy mountains and give my sick body time to heal.''

Brock looked past the wet, flushed skin of her face to the gold-flecked shine in her eyes. He was already shivering with the cold, but she was still and calm. Once again she had found that quiet center of hers.

She smiled—not at him but at something beautiful inside herself. ''Whatever it is that makes me who I am departed my body and became one with a magnificent eagle who took me on a soaring flight in a bright blue, windswept sky away from pain and away from death. When I awoke the next day, the poison was gone.''

Brock continued to stare transfixed at that shining face.

Her eyes turned to his face. ''This feather reminds me of what I can do, what any of us can do if we only have faith in who we are.''

Brock realized it wasn't only passion he had glimpsed behind that shield of unattainability she wore. There was magic there, too. The magic of the little girl whose belief in the power of an eagle feather had saved her life. The magic that was her life.

Strange things were happening to his insides. He moved toward her, wondering how he might catch the dancing golden light in her eyes. ''Shana?''

Her eyes looked into his—fully, clearly—but only for a second before they looked away.

She got to her feet and slung the pouch around her neck. A new look entered her eyes. "I realize I left the pack train rather abruptly, but I wish you hadn't abandoned them. They might be wandering off."

Brock got to his stocking feet, disappointed that she had avoided facing whatever it was he had felt they had been moving toward, while at the same time feeling relieved. The mood she had just broken possessed a dangerous as well as an irresistible pull. He felt almost disoriented in its wake. He grabbed at irritation—a more familiar, comfortable emotion. "You wish *I* hadn't abandoned the pack train?"

She ignored his pointed emphasis. "Mickey will stay in the vicinity, and he has the lead rope tied to his saddle horn, so I suppose they're all right. But you were taking an unnecessary chance. What could you have been thinking of—diving in after me like that?"

Brock sucked in an exasperated breath. "I was thinking of trying to prevent you from being hurt."

He watched his admission disconcert her. She looked as uncomfortable casting him as a hero now as he had felt at being cast as one the night before.

He watched her square her wet shoulders and flash him an irritated frown. "It's not like I asked for or needed your help. I knew what I was doing."

She turned from him then and began climbing up the green bank, following the curve of the stream up to where they had left the pack train, her bare feet skimming across the sharp rocks without any show of discomfort.

Brock had no idea what to say to such an infuriating woman. He decided nothing was probably the safest thing after several rather colorful curse words crossed his mind.

But as he followed her up the steep bank of the stream, he concentrated on admiring the view of her well-shaped bottom outlined so definitively in her wet green slacks. He found it a welcome distraction.

"SO WHAT SHOULD I COOK for you tonight?"

Shana looked up, a little surprised to find Brock waiting for her outside her tent when she emerged an hour and a half later, after getting herself dry and putting on some warm clothes.

"I already put some quinoa on to cook about twenty minutes ago. Takes a lot longer to get things to boil at this altitude, but it will probably be done in another ten minutes or so."

He looked at her from eyes turned midnight blue by the color of the warm, bulky turtleneck sweater he wore and matching corduroy pants. As always he looked rugged, sexy and very male.

The setting sun glinted off his fair hair and turned his bronze skin into gold and her stomach muscles into mush. Damn, how many times did she have to remind herself? This was no knight in shining armor standing before her.

"What's that you're cooking?"

Shana gave herself a swift emotional kick as she looked away. "It's one of these ancient supergrains from Bolivia or Peru. It's actually spelled Q-U-I-N-O-A but pronounced *kee-wa*. Supposed to contain all the amino acids for a complete protein. Getting sufficient protein while engaged in vigorous exercise is important. That's why I always pack some for a trip like this."

"What's it taste like?"

"Pretty bland, like most things good for you, but I have some spices that should liven it up."

His gray eyes gleamed at her hungrily, but he made it very evident it wasn't for quinoa. "All right. Let me consult the saddlebag pantry and see what freeze-dried delicacy I can mix with some boiling water to make something to complement a grain dish. You have two burners on the cookstove, so we can prepare our culinary delights side by side and then share them. How's that sound?"

Shana felt herself automatically taking a step back as he took a step toward her. "I don't think—"

"Surely you don't think that I expected you to fix my meal, too? Do I look like a male chauvinist?"

What he looked like was something she was trying valiantly to forget and what she expected and hoped was that she'd fix her own meal tonight. Very far apart from those bulging muscles and charming smiles.

She took a deep, labored breath, feeling as if she were still marching uphill. "All right. I'll go stir the quinoa."

He was by her side in less than a minute with some kind of freeze-dried stew. It didn't smell too bad once he added water to it and it began to cook, but Shana was too distracted by Brock's scent to be the best judge. He used no cologne. And it seemed to Shana that wherever she went lately, even in her own tent, his scent surrounded her.

Damn it, but she didn't seem to be getting over these irritating physical responses to his presence. On the contrary. They seemed to be getting steadily worse day by day. A sudden vision of tightening rawhide flashed across her eyes.

"Looks done."

"Hmm?"

"The quinoa. It looks done."

Shana snapped out of her far too distracted thoughts. It looked done, all right. All the water had been absorbed into the grain. Another minute and it would have burned. She quickly removed it from the heat and started stirring in the salt, pepper, garlic, onion and tomato powder she'd brought along.

And all the while she was acutely aware of him crouched next to her—his heat, his scent, his size—surrounding her, warming the air between them and every inch of skin on her body.

His stew tasted good. So did the quinoa. Shana sat back enjoying an after-dinner cup of licorice-spiced herbal tea. "Things just always seem to smell and taste so much better out here under the stars."

She saw Brock lean back against the blanket she had spread on the ground next to the cookstove and gazed up into the night sky. "Damn, there are a lot of stars up there. I forgot how beautiful a sky full of stars could look."

"Come, lie down beside me, Shana. We'll play a game. Try to see how many constellations we can name."

"Does that line actually work, Trulock?"

His eyes shifted to hers as his lips stretched into a smile. "Yes, it works. Every time a woman used it on me, I succumbed within minutes."

She laughed in spite of herself. He made it so hard to resist him when he smiled at her like that. But of course that was all part of the package of a smooth seducer. She just had to keep remembering who this man was.

"Shana, lie down and let's stare up at the stars together. The moon's rising. It'll be full tonight. Very romantic. You can't tell me a red-blooded American woman like you can resist a full moon? You'll be perfectly safe. No hands, remember? I won't do a single thing you don't want me to do.''

"Yeah, I'll bet. Last time I heard that one I was eighteen. Trulock, you need to update your material ''

He fell back against the blanket, his forearm over his face in feigned despair. ''I'm getting desperate. I haven't even needed to use a line since I was sixteen. You're a hard case, O'Shea ''

Shana squelched a smile. "Get up, Trulock. I'm not going to wash your dishes, too.''

He groaned as though in pain and rolled over to get leadenly to his knees. "Sex deprivation and now dishwater hands. What other fiendish tortures do you have in store for me?''

"Just stick around and see,'' she said, unable to hold back the smile this time.

His eyes continued to follow her as he took the cooking utensils from her hands. He was careful not to brush her skin with his fingers, but still there was an intimacy in the exchange that left her feeling breathless and shaky inside.

"We talked about my dreams today, but we never got to yours. What do you dream about, Shana?''

Shana turned back to the pail of water that had been heated over the stove to wash their dishes. The previous light banter had suddenly skipped onto dangerous ground.

"My dreams are private. I don't feel comfortable discussing them.''

"Why? Are they that X-rated?''

The look she flashed over her shoulder would have frozen a lesser man. Brock just returned a smile.

"Come on, Shana. Talk to me. What are you afraid of?"

She tried to put some primness in her tone, but she was having a hard time feeling prim with him standing so close. "It isn't a question of fear. It's a question of privacy. I'd like to maintain mine, thank you."

He moved in a step closer, and his voice dropped into that silky whisper she now knew so well and that melted her spine so quickly. "All right. Since you won't tell me what your dreams are, why don't I tell *you* about one of them?"

"You can't possibly know what I dream."

He leaned very close to her as he dropped his dish into the water. "Can't I? Shall we make a wager on it?"

She released the dish she was washing in the pail and turned toward him, planting her feet firmly where she stood, fighting down a small quiver. "What do we wager?"

"You tell me what you want from me, and I'll tell you what I want from you."

Exciting possibilities flashed through her. He was giving her an opportunity she couldn't pass up. Her hands found her hips. "I want you to stop this search for Fire Magic. Tear up the adoption papers. Go back to LA."

His eyes bored into hers as he hesitated. She could see he didn't like the stakes. Not one bit.

Still, this was her chance. She wasn't going to let it slip by. She made her tone as taunting as she could. "So you don't want to bet, after all. Your bragging was just that?"

Shana could see the silver lightning flash through his eyes at her challenge and felt an excited shiver shoot up her spine. As she had glimpsed before, cool steel hid behind that easy charm.

"All right, Shana. If I lose, I leave without Fire Magic. And now I'll tell you what I want if you lose."

She tensed. Every fiber of her being.

Her thoughts must have shown clearly on her face because he smiled that knowing smile of his. "Not that. I wouldn't want a woman who came to me just because of a lost wager. No, I'll wait until you decide to take the handcuffs off."

She tasted a surprising disappointment along with a lot of annoyance at the irritating tone of inevitability with which he had imbued his last words. With great difficulty she pushed both reactions aside and concentrated on the matter at hand. "Then what do you want, Trulock?"

"If I guess one of your dreams, I want you to stand still and let me kiss you. Really kiss you."

"No hands?"

"No hands."

Her eyes narrowed. "And I'm the sole determiner of your having guessed right?"

An easy smile. "I'll trust you."

Shana felt the frown on her forehead. She took a moment to go over every possible escape clause in her mind that he might try to use when he lost. She could find none. Still—

"So you're afraid to take me on, is that it?"

His taunt bristled against her pride. Her chin rose. "On the contrary. It's a bet. Go ahead. Tell me one of my dreams."

He crossed his massive arms across his chest and smiled. "Like you once soared with an eagle, I think you dream of running with Fire Magic. And I think you know how to make your dream come true. Every night while we mere mortals lie asleep, I think you are racing through the wilderness on his swift legs, using his powerful lungs, jumping thirty-foot chasms, outfoxing every man who chases you as you live the freedom of the truly wild and untamed.''

Shana felt her mouth open in shock. How had he done this? How had he read her deepest dream?

He stepped forward, and she saw the triumph in his eyes. He did not have to ask. He read her expression and knew his guess was right.

''And now for that kiss.''

His mouth claimed hers with undisguised relish. If Shana had had time to think and plan her response, she probably would have broken the kiss off within a few seconds and still felt she had lived up to the terms of her lost wager. But he gave her no time to think or plan. One instant the cool desert night surrounded her and the next the heat from Brock Trulock had taken its place.

His very experienced lips and tongue had her mouth opening to him without even token resistance as he hurled a spear of desire through her to expose and excite every nerve ending. He filled her with his taste and scent and spun her thoughts into a blinding sandstorm of desire. Small sounds were coming from her throat and reverberating through her body in deep, delicious waves of sensation.

Yet it was only his mouth that touched her. Somewhere that thought helped to clear her swirling perceptions, to steady them. He was keeping himself in check. As promised.

That very restraint was a lure calling to her. Shana's body answered as she brushed lightly against him. She felt the pounding of his heart as the hardness of his chest wall met the softness of her breasts and instantly brought her nipples to hard attention. His thighs were thick and hot, and she felt the full length of his arousal in surprise and alarm.

He stood straight and still, the only exploration of her coming from his very expert mouth as he deepened the kiss with a groan of raw hunger that vibrated through her.

She fought to hold on to her wits, to her own control, as aching desire cut through her. Carefully, tentatively, she laced her hands around the back of his neck, letting her fingers explore the surprising cool softness of his hair as her mouth burned with the hot flavors and textures of his mouth.

He spoke her name into his kiss and she nearly lost it again as she shook with the intensity of the need she felt in its sound.

This huge mountain of a man wanted her for all he was worth and he was controlling it. Nothing in her whole life had ever excited her more. A sharp sensation of playing with fire lit her from within. He had given her a promise not to touch her with his hands. She could torture him with her touch, and he would just have to stand there and take it.

If he did just stand there and take it. How far could she push him? By stroking him with her body, could she drive him beyond his control?

It would be such a delicious experiment. Dared she conduct it? On the other hand, as a red-blooded American female, how could she pass it up?

She leaned into the full length of his hungry hardness, molding herself against him, shaking with the overwhelming sensations such boldness brought. She tasted flames licking through him as well as her. Danger threatened—precariously close and imminent—whipping her excitement to new heights.

Shana was finding that playing with fire could be one hell of a thrill.

And then suddenly his lips released her and he drew back his head.

The cold night air swirled around her. She opened her eyes, only then aware she had closed them. His were staring into hers with a raw, savage need and intensity that sent new shivers through her. She barely recognized the ragged voice as his. "Take off the handcuffs, Shana."

He was so much man. And she wanted him. Oh, how she wanted him.

But she wanted something else even more.

She stepped back, remembered who he was and, more important, who she was. Her body still hummed from the heat of their encounter, but a coolness of purpose had also returned to superimpose itself over all else. "No."

"No?"

His voice was hoarse with incredulity. "Shana, I want you with a desire I can barely control."

"But you will control it."

He stepped forward, brushed her body with the rock-hard muscles of his. "Why should I? We both know you want me just as badly as I want you."

His heat immediately engulfed her. Yes, heaven help her, she did want him. She stepped back, shivering as she left the warmth of his orbit and the evening air cloaked her once again. "I'm not your nightly entertainment on this wild-horse hunt, Trulock. I'm here against my will. I'm not planning on doing anything else against my will."

If ever Shana had seen a look that could kill, the one Brock now gave her was it. Every single muscle in his body seemed to flex all at once. She sucked in an involuntary breath.

"Against your will? Whose will was it that had your lips returning my kiss and your body rubbing against mine and your fingers raking through my hair?"

Damn the man for reminding her. Her chin went up defensively. "You were the one who introduced the game, Trulock. I was just learning the moves."

The look he flashed her now was worse than the one before. Shana stood up to it, not knowing how she did. And then suddenly the leashed violence simply dissolved into something that looked very much like a smile and he laughed raggedly. "I'd say you'd mastered those moves quite well. Too well."

She would have believed the laugh if it hadn't been for the clenched hands at his sides and the bright glitter that remained in his gray eyes.

She couldn't seem to keep the taunt out of her voice as she asked far too sweetly, "Have any more games you wanted to teach me?"

His fists flexed, sending a new tremble through her. Something she couldn't explain kept her facing him and goading him and becoming more excited by the moment because of it.

"I think, Shana O'Shea, that you've got your technical knockout for the moment. But I wouldn't advise kicking a man when he's down. Sometimes that brings him back to his feet and makes him forget insignificant things like promises."

She read the gleam of new challenge in his eyes and decided that the moment had come for a quick retreat.

She turned toward the washing pail. "I'll do the dishes tonight. You can do them tomorrow."

She bent down to collect the rest of the utensils, but the lingering passion in her made her clumsy and it took awhile. He was very quiet behind her. As she put the rest of their dishes into the washing pail, she thought he might have actually left. A couple of minutes later she was scrubbing the pot when a sudden sharpness in his voice brought her stock-still.

"Did you hear that?"

Shana's eyes flew to Brock's face. He was standing a few feet behind her, very tense, still, listening.

"Hear what?"

He held his hand up for silence and remained still. Shana listened, too. She heard the shuffle of hooves as the horses and mules paced and tried to get comfortable for the night. Off in the distance the echoes of the splashing water from the fast-moving stream washed by as a distinct whoosh. An insect buzzed near her ear, then flew off. A minute stretched into two. She was just about to tell Brock he must be hearing things, when a sound low and feral and barely audible drifted into her ears on the still cold air and brought a million goose bumps up her spine.

"Do you recognize it?" Brock asked.

Shana dropped the pot she'd been cleaning back into the pail and shot to her feet. "It sounds like an animal in pain. And close by. Next to the stream, maybe."

Automatically, she headed toward her saddle and the rifle. She felt Brock come up behind her. "What are you doing?"

"I have to go see. If it's hurt—"

"And if it's a mountain lion with its fresh kill, Shana? You prepared to risk getting clawed or worse?"

Shana considered the image that had risen far too quickly at Brock's words. "That's why I'm taking the rifle."

"It's too dark. You could easily trip."

Shana had already dropped to her knees and straightened up with a battery-operated lantern in her hand. "I'll have this."

"But if you're carrying the lantern, it will interfere with your ability to shoot if you need to."

A valid point that gave Shana pause. Brock stepped closer and held out his hand. "You hold the lantern. I'll carry the gun. We can bring along the kid's shotgun, too, if you like."

Shana eyed him for a second. When she nodded her head, however, it wasn't the gun she handed him. "I'll welcome your company, but as light bearer only. I don't trust anyone but myself with a loaded gun in this wilderness. I know when to fire and at what. I'm not sure you do."

He hesitated before taking the lantern. "Shana, I don't—"

"Look, if you don't want to come along, I understand. But I'm carrying the gun and I'm going, with you or without you. Make up your mind."

It wasn't a choice Brock was happy with. She could see that clearly in the lantern light that played against the sharp lines and planes of his scowl. But in the end, he took the lantern from her outstretched hand with a surprising smile. "Okay, my wilderness woman. Lead the way."

Shana moved into the brush away from the light of their camp very cautiously with the rifle in the ready position. She had a funny feeling in her stomach. She wasn't sure why it was there, but she knew it had something to do with being called his woman.

She yanked her thoughts back to the serious business at hand. Brock was right behind her, holding the lantern up high so that it lit the ground immediately in front of her. She quickly found it didn't make for a very bright light.

His presence and warmth were reassuring. Many predatory animals in these ranges were nocturnal. And whereas they generally avoided a human campsite, they might not be so squeamish about avoiding a lone human on foot venturing into their hunting range.

Shana was guessing at the direction from where the plaintive sound they heard had come. She made directly for the stream she'd dived into that afternoon after the pouch. It was about two hundred and fifty feet straight ahead. It didn't take long before they had reached its bank.

She stopped at its edge and turned to listen, trying to hear over the rushing water. Brock was as stock-still as she, standing close beside her, holding the lamp. She felt the tension in his body, the wariness. He was on full alert.

Shana couldn't tell how long they stood there like that, straining for the sound that would give them the direction they needed. Wondering if it even would come. But then finally, at long last, the eerie moan pierced the night.

"Over there," Brock whispered in her ear at the instant she was turning in the same direction.

They moved as one downstream and then arrowed into the nearby brush. As they got closer to where they judged the noise had come from, Shana moved even more slowly, carefully. This was an animal in pain they were approaching, and one who would probably feel scared and cornered by their presence.

Her heart had begun to thud sickeningly in her ears when she finally eased aside the last tree branch in their way with the barrel of her rifle. The sight revealed by Brock's raised lantern stopped her dead in her tracks.

Chapter Eight

"It's a mustang mare," Brock said as he moved beside Shana. He frowned as he held the lantern out. He didn't like the way the mare stayed on her back. She must have heard them approach.

"She's getting ready to foal," Shana replied. "That's why she's left her herd and is out here all alone. Quick, Brock. We've got to get out of here. A wild mare needs seclusion to foal. With us here she'll run off and maybe hurt herself and the unborn foal."

Shana stepped back, but Brock moved closer. "This mare isn't going to be running off anywhere, Shana. She's in trouble."

Brock took the lantern and squatted beside the mare's head where she lay on her side in the tall grasses. Her breath was coming out in painful gasps. As he knelt beside her, her eye went almost white and she kicked out as though trying to stand. Then she moaned with that awful painful sound that had brought them. She was so weak that she barely had the strength to lift her head, much less run away, as she obviously wanted to do. Gently, Brock ran a hand across her hot hide, feeling the thick sweat.

"What's wrong, Brock?"

"She's been in labor a long time. Too long. Something's wrong. I'm going to have to take a look. Come here and hold the lantern."

She obeyed him now as silently and efficiently as when he gave her the necessary orders to rescue her from that ledge. He liked seeing that response of reasonableness in her. The way she sensed the seriousness of a situation without it having to be spelled out to her. Her instincts in that regard were excellent, her reactions reliable.

Brock examined the mare quickly.

"I can see the foal's legs, but it's not coming out on his own. Looks like she's been straining at it for quite some time. I'm going to have to try to see if I can find out what's wrong. I've got to wash up first. Stay with her."

He didn't take the lantern with him. The sound of the rushing water would be all he needed to get him back to the stream. Once there he removed his sweater and his shirt beneath it. He tied his sweater arms around his waist and, bare chested, he plunged his arms up to his biceps into the icy stream and rubbed them briskly with the cleansing water. When he finished, he dunked his cotton shirt into the stream and made sure it was good and wet. Then he made his way back to the clearing.

He found Shana cradling the mare's head in her lap, stroking it and crooning to it with soft, melodious nonsense.

He dropped down to his knees and handed her his wet shirt. "Wipe her neck with that. It will help to cool her off and may distract her from the examination I'm about to perform."

"You won't be hurting her?"

"No. But she's a wild mustang and I very much doubt she's going to appreciate the, ah, attention."

Shana nodded. "I know. The only reason she hasn't kicked us silly yet is because she's too exhausted. And we can't be sure she won't be getting a second wind any second now."

Once again he found himself appreciating her very down-to-earth understanding of the situation. Even in his wildest imagination he couldn't picture any of his LA lady friends coming anywhere near this sweaty, dangerous mare, much less trying to offer it comfort.

The foal's forelegs were visible. Right at the opening. Where they should be. So far, so good. Slowly, carefully, he slid his hand along the top of the foal's forelegs to try to feel the foal's muzzle. When he had inserted his hand up to his wrist and still had not located it, he knew what was wrong.

"The foal's head is turned back. Unless it's forward in a diving position, he can't be born."

"Are you saying if we don't do anything he'll die?"

"They'll probably both die."

"How can they be saved?"

"The foal's head has to be turned forward."

"Can you turn it forward?"

It was an amazing question for her to be asking him so nonchalantly.

"I'm not a vet, Shana."

"You seem to know what you're doing."

Damn, she sure expected a lot of him. He looked into her steady eyes and found a faith that both surprised and scared him. And steadied his hands. He took a deep breath. "Hold her head. Very firmly. I don't know if this is going to hurt her."

By the time Brock felt the foal's head, he was covered in sweat and wondered why he had ever thought he could do this. But he was doing it. And through feel alone he gently and steadily turned the foal's head in its narrow confinement.

"I don't think she's got the strength for any more contractions. I'm going to have to pull the foal out. Keep her as steady as you can."

Shana said nothing, just curled her arm more securely around the mare's neck.

Brock pulled, finding this a job that took all his strength and concentration. He hoped that the mare's moans and very few halfhearted kicks made at him during the next very long and agonizing minutes were a sign of her getting her strength back and trying to help with this birthing process, rather than her reaction to his clumsiness.

He paused to rub his bare shoulder against his face, trying to get the dripping sweat from his forehead out of his eyes, feeling the weariness in his muscles. Then he took firm hold, keeping the foal's head down, and began to pull again.

"Come on, Sunshine. You can do it," Shana crooned to the mare, as she gently wiped the sweat from the mare's neck with Brock's shirt.

"Sunshine?" Brock echoed.

"She has the pale hide of a palomino," Shana crooned in the same voice she'd used for the mare.

Brock let out a silent curse as he just barely dodged a kick from the mare he could have sworn had been directed right at his face. "Perhaps you shouldn't have named her until we see whether she survives this ordeal or not."

"Come on, Sunshine, you can do this," Shana continued to croon, ignoring his pessimism. "You're a Nevada mustang. The hardiest breed of all. Come on, mare, bear down. Let's get that baby born."

Almost as though the mare had heard Shana's encouragement, Brock suddenly felt a responding contraction. Then another.

He couldn't help the excitement that laced through his voice. "It's coming, Shana. The foal's coming."

Brock tugged in rhythm with the mare's continuing contractions, watching as the lantern light exposed the chest and shoulders. The foal slid out onto the soft green grass as the mare sighed in what Brock was sure was a relief only marginally bigger than his own.

Brock cupped his hand under the foal's eye to prevent it from being injured by the sharp blades of grass. Then he got up and moved away.

"Shana. Come. Stand with me here. The rest is up to them now."

Carefully she rested the mare's head back onto the grass and got to her feet, bringing Brock's shirt and the lantern with her. They stood together as the foal went through its last struggles to kick its hind legs free from the mare.

For the next several minutes they watched in silence. Finally, the mare shakily but resolutely got to her feet and dropped her head over the foal, nickering to it softly before beginning to lick it dry. Within only a few more minutes the foal responded to its mother's encouragement and stood.

"It's a little filly," Brock said, feeling a strange kind of pride and accomplishment.

Shana's voice drifted to him full of light and wonder. "She's a darker palomino than her mother. Let's call her Moonbeam."

He smiled at her complete acceptance of this small miracle and squelched a strong impulse to wrap an arm around her and draw her to him. He concentrated on watching mother and daughter getting to know each other. "Sunshine and Moonbeam. A pair of lovely ladies."

Shana's voice dropped lower, softer, but the wonder remained. "You saved them, Brock."

His eyes drew to her face. She looked up at him, her face glowing in the full moonlight, a thoroughly approving look in the golden flecks glinting in her eyes. That look shook him at depths he never knew existed. He just stared at her, speechless.

If even days ago someone had told him the quiet and sincere approval of a woman—any woman—could have shaken him so thoroughly, he would have laughed.

His voice came out raw and unsteady. He was surprised it made any sound at all. "We didn't exactly follow that noninterference-with-nature dictum tonight."

Her smile was small and self-possessed as her gaze returned to the mustang mare and her foal. "I can live with it. They need privacy now. We should wash up at the stream."

Then she turned to lead the way.

He followed her, silently cursing her calm. How could she act so unaffected when so many feelings were rocketing through him?

"How did you know what to do?" Shana asked as she washed out his shirt in the icy stream after rinsing off her hands.

"We had a mare on my uncle's ranch that went through something similar," he said from beside her. "My uncle called in the vet when the labor became protracted. The vet explained everything he was doing and why."

"And he saved them as you saved the mustang and her foal tonight?"

"Not exactly. He managed to turn the foal's head, but it was too late."

Shana was amazed at what Brock had done. She looked at his strong capable hands and remembered how gently they had held the newborn foal's head. She watched him wash off his smooth bronze skin with those same hands, and felt transfixed by their beauty flashing beneath the moonlight.

So much strength. So much gentleness. So much man.

He glanced over at her, as though he felt her eyes, and caught her staring.

Shana knew he saw right through her. She looked quickly away, focused on wringing out his shirt. "I, ah, wanted to thank you for what you did. It was really wonderful."

He moved closer to her, and she felt his heat rushing in to warm several key parts of her body that were already far too aware of his half-naked status. "Their survival had a lot more to do with their own hardiness than anything I did, Shana."

Oh, damn. He was being modest, too. Where was the arrogant stuntman when she needed him? Something seemed to be constricting around her chest. She could have sworn it was drying rawhide. She took a deep breath and stared at the wet shirt in her hands. "Even the hardiest sometimes need a helping hand to survive. You were that helping hand tonight."

He said nothing in response. The silence grew between them like a tangible thing. His closeness was far too compelling, drawing her. Shana wrung out his shirt but couldn't seem to get herself to hand it to him or go back to the camp.

"Is that all you wanted to say, Shana?"

The sudden, deep silkiness of his voice set off all her alarms. She stood suddenly, finding her legs shaky. "What more is there to say?"

He rose beside her, keeping her as still as if his hands had reached out for her and held her in place. She found herself looking at his massive bare chest, wanting to touch it to see if it could possibly feel as hard and smooth as it looked.

His voice slid down her spine. "You may have nothing to say, but I have much to say."

She swallowed, battling her racing pulse, trying to find her icy composure. "What?"

His head leaned closer. "I want to take down your braids and free them, Shana, rubbing the black satin of your hair through my palms. Then I want to take off all your clothes slowly, touching you fully, thoroughly, kissing every inch of your sweet flesh. Your lips, your breasts, your—"

Shana found herself jumping backward away from that damn silky voice that was so quickly reducing her to a quivering piece of jelly. But she couldn't jump back very far. Behind her was the icy stream. And in front of her was Brock Trulock, wearing a very intense and determined look that cut into her like a sharp ache.

Brock immediately reduced the distance between them to a simple sliver of moonlight as his voice resolutely continued. "Then I'm going back over every succulent morsel of your skin and..."

Shana closed her eyes and swallowed, praying for sanity, praying for his voice to stop putting so many libidinous images into her head and so many anticipating ripples down her back.

Brock leaned down to her neck, rolling his hot tongue across its sensitive skin, sending hungry fire through her. Shana felt the panic swarm over her as deeply as the passion. Dear heaven, she'd had no idea he could do this to her simply with his voice and the strategic placement of his tongue. If she didn't do something and soon, she knew she was going to be begging for those hands of his and a lot more.

He spoke near her ear now, his hot breath burning her every nerve ending to a crisp. "Then I'm going to take you in my arms and teach you what ecstasy and joy really are—over and over again. Beginning with now."

His teeth scraped against her earlobe as his hot tongue thrust into her ear. Shana moaned as her whole body shook with lustful yearning.

Shana felt her sanity teetering on the brink of some deep and dangerous precipice. Any second she was going over the edge. Only this time there would be no rescue. This time it was him sending her over that edge. In one last desperate move to reclaim her reason, she deliberately stepped back and let herself fall into the icy stream.

"GOOD MORNING," Shana said far too brightly as she approached the cookstove where Brock had already prepared the coffee and was flipping over a pancake.

He didn't have to look up to see her. He'd been watching for any movement from her tent since dawn and had seen her leave it. It irked him that she could not only sleep so soundly, but even oversleep an hour. He, on the other hand, hadn't slept even one of the past nine hours since she'd thrown herself into an icy stream rather than let him make love to her.

Damn, she acted like making love with him were a fate worse than death, or at least worse than falling into an icy stream on a cold night. That attitude even more than her refusal to have him had grated on his pride. With all the passion and tenderness and so much more he felt for her, how in the hell could this woman continue to refuse him?

Still, that wasn't the only question lingering in his mind this morning. A night awake had left him with a lot of time to think things over, and several things were not going over well at all.

Brock tried to dig deep for some largess of character to return her sunny greeting, but found he was fresh out. He growled a response beneath his breath.

She ignored his tone. "Coffee smells good."

She helped herself to some. He muttered again.

Her braids were down today, resting on those lovely soft shoulders he shouldn't have been thinking about. She wore a clean uniform, the pants of which hugged her slim curves far too well for his already-overtaxed control. Again the memory of how she had once again eluded him made him wild with frustration. Next time he'd back her into a solid rock wall if he had to. And it was beginning to look as if he had to.

"Pancakes smell good, too. You're not a bad cook."

She sounded so cheerful that he could have strangled her.

"I'm making enough for two."

"No, thanks. I'm going to go check on Sunshine and Moonbeam." Cup of coffee and all, she turned and headed toward the stream.

"They're gone," Brock called after her.

She turned back, surprise all over her face. "When?"

"A little before sunrise."

"You were up then?"

"I thought someone should keep an eye on them. In case a hungry mountain lion came along."

She gave him one of those looks that made him feel good and noble and irritated and aching for her.

He exhaled a heavy breath. He didn't like wanting a woman like this. He didn't like it a lot. "I was up anyway. No big deal. Sit down, Shana. We've got some things to discuss."

She came back very slowly, hesitantly. He flipped the pancakes out of the pan and onto two plates, then slit open a packet of syrup and poured it over both servings. He handed one to her.

"No, thanks. I really..." she began.

"Eat it," he said and he knew the tone of his voice got through when she picked up a fork and carved off a slice and obediently shoved it into her mouth. As he watched her every movement, he recognized he had just one real hunger inside him, but he ate the pancakes and washed them down with coffee anyway, because he knew that up against this woman he was going to need every ounce of his strength.

"Where is Fire Magic?" he asked when she'd finished her plateful.

She put the plate down slowly with carefully measured movements. "What kind of a question is that?"

"A straight one. And I expect a straight answer."

She dropped her eyes, buried her nose in her cup of coffee. "As I've told you before, I'm taking you to his range."

"If we were in his range, that mare last night would have given birth to his foal. That was not his foal."

Her head came up. "How do you know that wasn't Fire Magic's foal?"

"I was there, remember? I saw it. Delivered it, as a matter of fact. It was a typical mustang foal. Shaped like its mother. If it had been Fire Magic's, it would have had his distinctive stamp."

She put her coffee cup down. "You're only assuming it would have, Trulock."

Brock couldn't keep the bitterness out of his tone. "So we're back to Trulock, now. Last night it was Brock."

Unease flashed in her eyes. Her voice was defensive. "You don't know that Fire Magic is breeding true. This idea you have about him being a new breed of horse is just that. An idea. Now, I tell you we are going to his range. And we should be there tonight."

"It wasn't his foal."

Her lips came together tight. Her voice and manner were all defiance. "What makes you so sure, Trulock?"

He leaned forward. "Well, if it was, then you've been leading me in the wrong direction for the last day, because both Sunshine and Moonbeam headed down the mountain this morning to rejoin their stallion."

Just for an instant, he watched her eyes widen as the news made its impact. Then she was quickly back in control. "All right, maybe it wasn't Fire Magic's foal. I did tell you that Fire Magic wasn't the only wild stallion who has come through here. And his main range is still a day's ride away."

She jumped to her feet. "And now it's getting late and I've yet to water or feed the stock."

"It's done," he said quietly, watching her growing agitation.

"Well, then, we need to break camp and get on the trail. I'll go take down the tents and start packing up the mules while you do the dishes."

And off she went, as if someone had set fire to her enticing little tail. Brock frowned. She was lying about Fire Magic. He had suspected it from the first. He knew it for certain now. He downed the coffee from his cup and wondered what the hell he was going to do about it. And what the hell he was going to do about her.

"WE'RE HERE," Shana called over her shoulder as she slid thankfully from Mickey's saddle and immediately loosened the cinch around his stomach.

Brock drew Hamlet beside her and dismounted, also releasing his cinch as he looked briefly at the black-and-red lava rock terrace she had selected for a campsite.

"It feels like it's eighty degrees. I thought this was an alpine range."

"It's on the fringes of an alpine range. But the entire wilderness is probably experiencing this hot spell. If it's eighty here, it's probably ninety-five to a hundred at the lower elevations."

"I thought John said it was going to rain. I don't see a cloud in the sky."

"John said we'd have rain by the end of the week. It isn't the end of the week until the day after tomorrow."

"Doesn't look like it's rained on this dry ground or rock for a year. Amazing to find flowers blooming. What are these red flowers, Shana, the ones that look like small flags?"

"They're ocotillo. They bloom in the desert each spring. This is the season for many flowers."

"Yes, I've noticed. Amazing how the need to impregnate even these arid regions is so powerful, isn't it?"

Shana knew better than to touch that question with any kind of a response.

Brock didn't seem to expect her to. "It's quite a view from here, looking down at all those rolling foothills covered with all that piñon pine, juniper and sagebrush as far as the eye can see. And then up to the jagged mountain peaks, covered in snow."

Shana glanced around her shoulder and halted in her unsaddling of Mickey. Her sigh was appreciative as she let her eyes drink it in. "Yes, the view is spectacular. Like being at the top of a quiet, beautiful world. I never tire of it. It's worth the climb all by itself."

"All by itself?" Brock echoed.

Shana redirected her attention to unpacking the animals without responding. She couldn't remember the last time she'd felt so weary. A string of nights without adequate sleep coupled with days of hard climbing were taking their toll. And today she'd pushed herself, Brock and the animals far harder than she knew she should have in the increasing heat.

But he'd scared her with his questions about Fire Magic. He was too suspicious. She wanted to get him as far away from where she suspected Fire Magic might be as fast as she could. Except, after a few days up here without catching a sign of the red stallion, how much more suspicious would he become? And what would he do then?

Shana sighed. There were some things she wasn't ready to let herself think about. Not until she had a good night's rest.

"Where is the meadow you mentioned you chased Fire Magic across?"

"It's nestled in a canyon on the other side of the mountain. Just a couple of miles. I'll take you there tomorrow."

After the stock had been seen to, she got out the portable cookstove and looked for the easiest and quickest thing to prepare from her stock of freeze-dried selections. It was chicken-noodle soup. When she dumped its contents into a pot of water and brought it to the stove to heat, she was surprised to see a nearly identical pot full of chicken-noodle soup on the other burner.

"Tired minds running in the same rut?" Brock offered as he, too, noted the similarities of their selections.

Shana deliberately scooted to the other side of the burner, sitting across from him. She glanced at his face, noticing for the first time the lines of fatigue and remembering his admission that he hadn't slept the night before. Comforting to see he was mortal, too.

Like two zombies, they stirred their respective pots of soup. Then they both ate, not even bothering to put it in a dish.

It tasted hot and good, but the food didn't lift Shana's fatigue. She knew nothing could now but a good night's rest.

"So when was the last time you saw Fire Magic in this range?" Brock asked in a voice that sounded full of distrust.

Shana rubbed her eyes. She felt too tired to care how he felt.

"I saw Fire Magic here several months ago."

"That would have put him here during the winter. Don't wild horses have separate ranges for summer and winter?"

Damn. For someone out of his element, he caught on pretty quickly. But tired or not, he wasn't going to get her to make any mistakes. "You heard John. Fire Magic isn't like other wild stallions. He's totally unpredictable. There is no way to second-guess anything he might do."

"And when he doesn't show up here, Shana? Is that the excuse you're planning to use on me?"

Shana met his accusing eyes across the cookstove and felt a shudder at the anger she read in them. She held on, trying to convince herself that he was only guessing, that he couldn't possibly be certain.

"If you don't think I'm taking you where you want to go, Trulock, then fine. Pack up your stuff and ride down the mountain we've just climbed."

Of course he wouldn't. She knew it and he did, too. It was obvious in the continued glare he shot at her that could have etched steel.

She looked away from his anger, deciding she'd spent all the strength she could afford to face it. She knew she should get up and clean her dishes and put up her tent, but she just didn't have the energy. She leaned back against the saddle on the outside of the blanket she'd laid out in front of the cookstove and closed her eyes. Just for a minute.

BROCK HADN'T PLANNED on falling asleep. Certainly he didn't think he'd be able to, full of anger, frustration, and desire for the lady lying across from him. But he found the sudden, deep, rhythmic breathing coming from Shana's direction mixing with the heat of the afternoon and the warmth of the welcome food in his stomach and his weariness. The irresistible inducements quickly claimed him.

But the sound of the pounding hooves brought him instantly awake and upright. His head shot around as he strove to overcome his disorientation of where he was and what had wakened him.

And then every one of his nerves was on alert as he saw dancing beneath the moon's silvery light, right before his startled eyes, bigger than life and twice as impressive, the magnificent red stallion known as Fire Magic.

Brock's pulse raced as he battled a disbelief nearly as deep as his admiration for the splendid stallion. Was he dreaming? No. This was no dream.

Fire Magic reared on his hind legs, pawed the night air with his silver hooves catching the moonlight and let out a shrill powerful call that left no doubt of his challenge to any living thing within hearing.

Brock felt a primitive jolt coursing through him, urging him to rise and accept that wild challenge. But reason dictated that he stay where he was. This was no time to face that powerful animal and begin its taming. If he was to be successful with this magnificent stallion, he would have to pick a time and place for their eventual confrontation.

Fire Magic snorted and raced toward the tethered horses. He approached Roseblush head-on with a confident swagger, his head and tail arched high and proud as he sounded his mating call. Brock watched Rose-blush's ears perk up with attention.

Fire Magic lifted his head high. Cautiously now, he rubbed noses with her, bumping aside the mules and geldings. She struck out at him with a foreleg and he deftly avoided the sharp hoof. He circled her now, nickering to her gently, nipping playfully at her flanks.

From her kick and Fire Magic's cautious circling, Brock knew that Roseblush wasn't yet ready to accept him. But she was interested. Still, when Fire Magic made to dash off and called to her to join him, all she could do was strain at her rope and nicker softly in return. She was tied fast.

Fire Magic snorted and squealed in frustration as he called to Roseblush and again she twisted and strained at the rope.

Brock began to get concerned that the mare might injure herself as she continued to pull against the rope and decided to call this night's courtship ritual to a halt. He walked over to Roseblush and gently put a hand over her neck and on her cheek.

"Steady, girl. I want him for you, too. But let's not let him have the bait before the trap is set, shall we?"

Fire Magic snorted in frustration as he flipped his tail and raced off into the night.

Roseblush nickered. Brock smiled as he stroked her. "Don't worry, girl. He knows he's got a few days of teasing you yet before you're completely ready to accept him. He'll be back. You've got plenty of time."

Roseblush's ears pricked forward, as though she was listening for any possibility of Fire Magic's returning hooves.

Brock let his hand drop from her neck. "I, on the other hand, don't think I'd better let much more time go by before I offer my sincerest apology to that lovely, and surprisingly truthful, guide of ours.''

Brock turned back to where he'd left Shana asleep on the blanket in front of the cookstove. But she wasn't asleep. She was standing at the edge of the campsite, looking in the direction where Fire Magic had disappeared only seconds before, her face clearly reflected in moonlight. And she wore a look of absolute astonishment.

Seeing that look, Brock knew he need offer no apology.

Chapter Nine

"So why do you still want to go look at the meadow?" Shana asked Brock as she saddled Mickey in the lingering chill of the next morning. She didn't even try to keep the irritation out of her voice.

"To see if Fire Magic's herd is there, of course. I'm surprised you have to ask, Shana. It was you who told me the meadow was where the red stallion would take them, wasn't it?"

Shana counted to ten. He was goading her, of course. He knew Fire Magic's appearance of the night before had come as much as a surprise to her as it had to him. She'd never forget waking to his shrill stallion call, opening her eyes to see him standing not ten feet away, a magnificent vision in moonlight as he reared over both Brock and her, challenging their right to be anywhere near his range.

Dejectedly, she raised herself onto Mickey's back. "Just because he showed up at the camp last night, that doesn't mean his herd is nearby. He may have sensed Roseblush from a long way off."

Brock shrugged as he mounted Hamlet in one easy, powerful movement. Shana couldn't help notice that with the arrival of Fire Magic, he looked remarkably more rested and his charming smiles were back in abundance.

He was bursting with one at that very moment. "Well, it is spring and that stallion's nose is probably more acute than most. I suppose you could be right about *that*."

She clenched her teeth. He was rubbing it in again. Reminding her she had stumbled into Fire Magic, despite all her efforts to the contrary. Like it or not.

And she certainly didn't like it. Why was Fire Magic here, hundreds of miles away from where his tracks told John, Tommy and her he was going?

She gave Mickey a nudge forward. The answer seemed pretty clear now. Fire Magic had fooled them, of course. He had laid a false trail. And like many times before, he expected her to follow it. Only this time she had purposely not wanted to find him so she'd gone in the opposite direction. And found him. Damn. What absolutely rotten luck.

Brock moved Hamlet alongside. "So how do we approach the canyon so that we don't spook the horses?"

"You're assuming we're going to find some horses."

Another charming smile was in evidence. "Well, I just figured since you didn't think we would anymore, there might be a very good chance."

She sent him an icy glare, but he just laughed it aside.

"Come on, Shana. His capture is inevitable. Let's make it as easy on ourselves as I plan to make it on him. What do you say?"

What she really wanted to say she didn't. "I say we shouldn't approach the meadow at all, but look at it from that high rise over there. Then if there are any horses grazing in it, they probably won't catch our scent since we'll be downwind."

"All right. My instincts tell me I probably should do exactly the opposite, but considering how poorly you've been doing lately at sabotaging this outing, I'll follow your advice. See you up there."

And with that, he nudged Hamlet forward and took the lead. Shana rode dejectedly behind. She had no heart for this chase that put such a gleam in her companion's eyes. When she finally reached the top of the rise to join Brock, she was perversely glad to see that he frowned as he surveyed the meadow below with his binoculars.

She glanced quickly across it. "Empty, huh?"

He surprised her by slipping the strap of the binoculars from around his neck and handing them to her. He pointed at a deep green spot at the edge of water in the northern section. "There. Among the grasses."

Shana looked through the binoculars and felt her heart drop in disbelief at the flash of red coat. There, grazing all alone and without any apparent concern, was Fire Magic.

"I know he saw me when I rode up," Brock said from beside her. "I watched his head come up and I could have sworn he looked right at me. But then he just resumed grazing like he couldn't care less."

Shana lowered the binoculars. "He probably couldn't. He's perfectly safe and he knows it. If we were to rush him, he'd just outrun us. With ease. And lose us in one of the rocky canyons surrounding this meadow. Still, I've never known him to stick around humans for any length of time for any reason."

Brock's head turned, and she could feel his eyes on her profile.

"He's caught Roseblush's scent, Shana. He won't leave this territory without her now. He plans to make her his. And I plan to let him have her. As soon as I have him fenced in."

He sounded so sure of himself. So damn sure.

Shana raised her chin as her head angled toward him. "You still haven't caught him."

She could feel his eyes like soft caresses exploring her face. Little excited goose bumps rose up her arms. "I will, Shana. I'll capture everything I've set out to on this journey. Everything."

Shana saw the challenging gleam in his eye and knew exactly what he meant by that "everything." His unflinching claim on her sent a delicious fire through her blood, followed immediately by an icy wave of irritation at his cocky assurance.

"In your dreams, Trulock," she retorted as she turned Mickey back toward camp.

His words followed her, dropping like promises in her ears. "Yes, Shana. In my dreams. But I'm a man who makes his dreams come true."

"WHAT IS ALL THIS STUFF you've been having the mules carry?" Brock heard Shana ask with the kind of questioning intensity that had built up over the past few hours as she had silently watched him roll out the material he had brought along.

"It's a canvas corral. When I get finished stringing it around these piñon pines, it will create a corral about fifty feet in diameter."

She studied his handiwork more closely, seeing the line he was laying out around the trees. "You expect Fire Magic to walk into a corral?"

"Not one he can see. But he won't be able to see this one until it's too late."

The curiosity in her eyes overcame her unease. "How does it work?"

"Well, I'll separate Roseblush from the mules and other horses tonight. Tether her in the center there between those trees to draw Fire Magic to her."

"And?"

"And I'll have this canvas strung on the circle of piñon pines surrounding her."

She came over to him and picked up the heavy twine he'd been wrapping the canvas around. "It looks like rolled-up newspaper. A line of rolled-up canvas around the trees isn't going to fool Fire Magic into thinking he's been caught in a corral."

"No. But when he enters the circle to get Roseblush, I'll pull on this second piece of twine and it will make the canvas unroll to the ground. Before Fire Magic knows what's happening, he'll be surrounded by an eight-foot-high wall."

She squinted as she looked again at the circle. "He won't be fooled."

"Yes, he will, Shana. Horses respond to something they can't see through as though it's a solid wall. Believe me, I took a few very unpleasant falls in setting up some stunts before I learned my lesson about that one."

She bit her lip. "He won't like it. He'll fight to get out."

"Yes, finding himself suddenly corralled will probably enrage Fire Magic, but he won't try to run against the canvas because he'll think it's solid. And if he kicks it savagely in his anger, he'll do no harm either to himself or the canvas."

Her frown of worry was gratifying. Clearly she was thinking it might work. Then the look in her gold-flecked eyes changed. She seemed suddenly far away from him, captured in dark thoughts.

Brock could feel that look like a heavy hand pressed against his chest. He put down the thick canvas and twine he'd been working with and scooted closer toward her where she knelt on the white desert dust.

Her skin glowed in the sunlight. She smelled like the warm spring air, fresh and sweet. His hand raised to touch her, then dropped when he remembered he couldn't. His quick temper had gotten him into trouble before, but never had it goaded him into making such a stupid promise. He was beginning to think he'd rue it for the rest of his days.

"Shana, don't worry. I'll take Fire Magic without hurting him."

Her eyes flashed up to his like golden fire, hot and accusing. "You think taking away his freedom won't hurt him?"

"I know he won't like it, but—"

"You don't know a thing about him! All you can think about is the money you can make with him as your sire."

The gibe hurt. "Money? You think this is about money?"

Her response was a huff. "What else?"

"You're wrong, Shana. Fire magic is a magnificent, unique creature whose presence in this world of the commonplace is nothing short of a miracle. His very existence thrills and excites the imagination. I want him and his progeny to flourish, not perish out here barely eking out an existence on scrubby bunchgrass and white sage. He was made for better things. I want to give him his chance at them."

She looked away as the hard golden flecks began to liquefy in her remarkable eyes. "You don't understand. He's not a pyramid, a thing of stone, created by humans for their use. He's a living creature. And he was born wild and free. He must remain that in order to survive."

"Shana, I'll be good to him. He'll have the best."

Her eyes flashed anger. "The best? As human beings we always think we know what is the best for other creatures." Her voice broke. "I was eighteen when I thought I knew what was best for another master stallion in these mountains."

Brock sat back on his ankles and waited, seeing the pain on her face, knowing he had no power to remove it.

She sighed and her shoulders slumped. "He was a big sorrel. The Indians called him Blaze because of the white blaze on his face. When I told John I meant to try to catch him, John did his best to talk me out of it. I didn't listen.

"I kept him in a large, fenced meadow with water and grass. I even turned two mares out with him. Within twenty-four hours, he'd battered down a part of the fence, and escaped, taking the mares with him.

"I had to get the mares back. They weren't mine, and I wanted Blaze back. John rode with me and others from the tribe came, too. When we got the mares, John wanted me to turn back, to forget the stallion. I wouldn't. He was with me when I cornered Blaze on a rocky ledge. There was nowhere for the stallion to go. We were in front of him. On the other side of him was a drop of several hundred feet. I got out my rope. I knew I had him. He knew I had him. He turned and jumped off that rocky ledge."

Her hands were fists by her sides as she battled to remain calm and hold on to her control. "He was a master stallion. He knew freedom as we will never know it."

Brock wanted to reach out and gather her in his arms. Now he understood so much more about her fight to keep Fire Magic free. She had convinced herself that captivity would kill him.

He moved closer. "I'm sorry about the sorrel. I can see you feel responsible in some way for its death. But, Shana, you can't know for certain that the sorrel jumped because he'd rather die than be captured. Just as you can't predict that same fate for Fire Magic."

The pain in the look she gave him twisted in his heart. "I know."

Every fiber of his being ached to take her in his arms, to tell her it would be all right.

But he couldn't. And it wasn't just because of his promise not to touch her. It was because it wasn't going to be all right. He was still going to catch Fire Magic.

He deliberately tore himself away from those beautiful eyes and went back to fashioning his canvas corral. But his fingers were sweaty and unsteady and the heavy hand that had pressed against his chest was now a hard fist that clenched in his gut.

For no matter how gently he captured the red stallion or how good he was to him afterward, the moment Fire Magic became his he suspected Shana O'Shea would be lost to him forever.

"I OPENED A BIG CAN of chili, Shana. Can't possibly eat it all. Won't you join me?"

Shana ignored his offer as she had all of his overtures ever since he had so doggedly completed the canvas corral. Now it was in place around Roseblush, and the trap was ready to be sprung.

Shana paced the campsite, restless and edgy. Even though it was almost nine at night, she didn't feel hungry.

She felt angry.

"Shana, will you at least sit down and talk to me?"

"About what?" she snapped.

"About anything you'd like to talk about. You could start off by calling me all those names you want to."

Her eyes flashed over to him. His charming smile was in evidence. But so was the worry in his eyes. It was the worry that gave her pause. He held all the cards now. He seemed to care about what she thought. But not enough to change his mind.

She sighed, feeling the anger ebb. Deep down she knew that Brock was not a man who willingly injured any creature. She remembered clearly his strong gentle hands with the mustang mare and her foal.

That was the hardest part, of course. Heaven help her, but she liked the man she found him to be. And she knew he sincerely believed what he was doing was right. That he could provide Fire Magic with a better life. That he wasn't going to be ensuring his death.

"Come on, Shana. Share some of this chili with me. It's my sister's own special recipe."

Shana dropped next to Brock on the blanket. "Is your family close?"

Brock dished out some of the chili into a bowl and handed it to her. "Yes. Mom and Dad still work on the production crew of pictures and my sister has broken into the ranks of the previously all-male domain of the cameraperson, so we bump into each other a lot."

"What do they think of your plan to get out of stunts and breed horses?"

"I have no idea."

Shana brought a spoonful of the chili to her lips. "You mean you didn't ask them?"

His gray eyes sought hers. "Do you ask others what they think of your dreams?"

"I..." She faltered.

"No, of course not. You don't even discuss your dreams with anyone." He paused for a moment until her eyes met his. Then his voice took on a very different tone. "You could tell them all to me."

Shana found herself momentarily mesmerized by those gleaming gray eyes. She remembered vividly how he had described the dream of hers. And what had shortly followed. Suddenly she started to become aware of other things that her previous anger had been blocking from her consciousness.

The glint of stove light catching his hair and the stubble on his chin. His powerful bare arms casually resting on his black denims. His black vest open all the way to his flat stomach, exposing all those well-defined smooth muscles of his bronze chest. And finally, his look of undisguised hunger that raked over her even now.

Quickly, she looked away.

His voice followed her, a bit lower, a bit more husky. "You enjoy the chili?"

Shana looked down to see the empty bowl in her lap with surprise. "Yes. It was very good. Best I've ever tasted, as a matter of fact."

He moved closer. "My sister will be pleased."

At least that was what his words said, but the tone of his voice was saying something quite different, as was the heat from his body. Shana started to get up but suddenly felt his body all around her as his hands shot out to grip the saddle behind her.

She had nowhere to go. Behind her was the saddle. In front of her was Brock Trulock. With that damn gleam in his eyes.

His voice was that silky caress that was so familiar and mind melting. "Don't run away from me, Shana. You have nothing to fear. The handcuffs are on, remember?"

Shana prided herself on not making the same mistake twice. "Yes, and I also remember what you've been able to do without them."

He chuckled low and deep and the sound vibrated dangerously throughout her body, setting her nerves to humming.

"Have I excited you by telling you all the things I want to do to your body? Shall I tell you about them again?"

"No. Please."

She knew her response had come too quickly, too desperately. But she was feeling desperate this close to him.

He bent his elbows and moved a smidgen closer. She could feel his breath against her cheek, and a million mutinous sensations racking her body. "All right. I don't want to do anything you wouldn't like, Shana. But I think you might like a kiss. A soft, gentle kiss?"

Oh, she'd have liked it, all right. And a whole lot more. Shana looked away from those gray eyes so close to hers and stared at the horses and mules, tethered away from Roseblush, as she tried to fight down the delicious heat of expectation creeping through her veins.

With a discipline that was getting harder and harder to summon, she started to form the word no on her lips, when suddenly a distinctive flash of red caught her eye.

Shana's heart beat hastily in her ears as she tore her eyes away from the horses and looked directly into the gleaming gray eyes hovering above her. Deliberately, she laced her hands about Brock's neck, slipping them through his hair, and then raised her head to press her mouth firmly to his.

BROCK HAD HOPED to show Shana all the tenderness he was feeling for her, and all the restraint, but he was quickly finding the passion she returned was far from restrained. Her lips met, engaged and conquered his in an instant. Her body arched up to brush tantalizingly against his as her hands dived beneath the open collar of his shirt, greedily exploring his shoulders as they pressed him closer.

Within less than an instant she had aroused him fully. His arms braced his body above her as her kiss that had begun none too tenderly became bruising and spread fire through him. His lips devoured hers in return, with the unmistakable message of his fevered and insistent need.

Her tongue danced with his, hot and moist as the pressure from her hands urged him closer. His breath broke from him as he ended the kiss to stroke his tongue down her neck, nibbling, sucking at her earlobes, feeling her pulse beat wildly. His tongue slid down to her collarbones, nibbling each in turn. She moaned and sighed and writhed beneath him.

He eased himself on top of her with the full length of his need and she melted beneath him. In one glorious, mind-blowing moment, he knew she would be his. Now.

Except he forgot he wasn't the only one out courting that night. A shrill stallion mating call suddenly pierced the air with a tardy reminder. Brock's head flew up to see a red blur leap over the blanket where he lay with Shana and race full speed toward Roseblush.

Shana immediately stiffened beneath him in a way that had nothing to do with passion. And then in a blinding flash he understood. Her response to him had been a deliberate distraction. She had tried to get his attention in order to save the stallion from being caught.

In all his life he had never tasted a more bitter flavor of disappointment than what he now swallowed.

Without a look in her direction, he jumped to his feet and raced toward the twine that would bring down the canvas wall into place. He reached it just as Fire Magic was circling Roseblush, sniffing her, nipping her, whipping up her excitement so that she would willingly join him.

Then Brock froze in absolute amazement as the red stallion went to the rope that held Roseblush in place, took it within his teeth and with one powerful snap of his jaws severed it in two, freeing the mare.

If he hadn't seen it with his own eyes, he knew he wouldn't have believed it. Horses weren't supposed to be able to bite through ropes like that. With an effort, Brock gave himself a shake. He had no time to indulge his surprise. He had a horse to catch.

With lightning-fast reflexes, Brock pulled on the twine and within an instant the eight-foot-high canvas corral whooshed perfectly into place around the two horses at its center.

Brock exhaled a sigh of relief. He had just come far too close to losing not only Fire Magic but Roseblush.

He couldn't see over the eight-foot canvas, but he could hear Fire Magic racing around inside, neighing in anger. It didn't bother him. He knew Fire Magic couldn't be hurt. The horse was reacting as Brock had expected. Everything was going as expected.

Except then the red stallion did what Brock had never expected. One second he was venting his rage at being trapped, and the next he was sailing over his eight-foot trap as though it was nothing but a small inconvenience in his way.

SHANA'S DESPAIRING spirits soared as she watched Fire Magic fly over the walls of his very temporary prison with all the power and ease and beauty that thrilled her to her core. He landed with a grace and control that implied had the canvas been higher, he still would have leaped it with ease.

His magnificent neck arched and his tail flew up as he pranced in a proud circle of defiance around its perimeter, snorting in disdain, his red coat iridescent fire. Even now as he was free of the canvas corral's paltry restraint, he didn't run away, but rather called brazenly to Roseblush still inside, urging her to join him in freedom.

Shana stood transfixed, waiting to find out what Roseblush would do.

But from the corner of her eye, she could see that Brock had no intention of just waiting. He scooped up two thick ropes to circle about his shoulders and ducked beneath the canvas corral to secure the mare. Shana heard intermittent cajoling followed by bouts of cursing as the mare's hooves pounded the earth within the canvas corral.

It seemed Roseblush had her heart set on Fire Magic.

Shana laughed. But it wasn't just a laugh of mirth. It was a laugh of relief. Brock's trap had proved no trap at all. She had worried for nothing.

She stared at the stallion as he danced beneath the moonlight and continued to call to the mare—a wild, powerful, tenacious lover who had no intention of being denied. And she knew that even if she got a good sleep tonight, she very much doubted if Brock Trulock would.

Hell, he'd be afraid to close his eyes. Afraid that if he did, that very determined stallion might just chew off Roseblush's restraints and whisk her away.

She laughed again and the stallion's call seemed to mix with her laughter in a joyous echo. Then with a shake of his glowing mane and a twirl of his fiery tail, he turned and ran into the night.

"IF WE LEFT NOW, we could be back at the stream where we found Sunshine and Moonbeam by nightfall," Shana taunted Brock at breakfast the next morning.

He took in her rested face and smug smile and thought what a difference a day made. This time the day before, he had been the one wearing the smug smile and she the worried frown.

"You think I give up that easily, Shana?"

"I think you should. Unless you want to risk losing Roseblush."

"I'm not going to lose her."

"But your trap didn't work. You don't have a prayer of catching Fire Magic."

"I'm going to get him, Shana. It will take me all day, but I'm fixing the canvas enclosure to make it twelve feet high. No horse, not even Fire Magic, can jump twelve feet."

He watched the news create a crease in her previously smooth brow. "You don't have enough canvas."

"It's double-sheeted. All I need to do is slit it apart, rework the ends together, and I've got more than enough. It will be a bit thin when I get through with it, but it will still present a barrier the stallion can't see through."

The crease in her brow deepened, belying her tone. "He probably won't even come back. He knows that Roseblush can't jump the canvas corral."

"Oh, he'll come back, all right, Shana."

"How can you be so sure?"

"Because we're alike, he and I. We've seen the female we want and we're going to have her—whatever it takes."

Something—he couldn't tell whether it was panic or excitement or both—flashed in her eyes.

Her chin went up. "Seems to me you were more interested in capturing Fire Magic last night than in what I had to offer."

He waited until her eyes met his and then he held her gaze. "If you had been serious last night, Shana, nothing—not even the chance to capture Fire Magic—could have dragged me from you."

He saw his words hit her. Hard. He'd meant them to.

Their import had already hit him far harder than he wanted to even think about. But he had thought about it. Nearly all night as he stationed himself right next to Roseblush in case Fire Magic returned.

She tore her glance away and got up to leave.

"Are you running away again?"

"I'm going to wash my breakfast dishes."

"You haven't drunk all of your coffee."

"I've been drinking too much coffee anyway."

"That isn't what's been keeping you from sleeping."

"You know nothing about my sleeping, or lack of it."

"I know you lie awake every night thinking of making love with me. Wondering if the reality could be even half as good as your imagination."

She looked back at him, sudden anger solidifying the golden flecks in her eyes. "Look, Trulock. I know who I am and I will allow neither you nor anyone else to redefine me into a one-night stand."

"Is that what you think I want to do?"

"Isn't it?"

She stood before him, all challenge and spirit and beauty, and he ached for her as he never had for anything or anyone before in his life. "Not even from the first instant I saw you did I consider you a one-night stand, Shana."

Her tone was flip, but there was something else in it, too. Something Brock had come to associate with her taunts. "Oh, you mean because we're alone in this wilderness together and there aren't any other women around, I'll do for a few nights."

Brock got to his feet, frustrated in more ways than he thought possible. "No, that isn't what I mean. You're not just another woman to me. Shana, you could never be. You're... Damn it, take the handcuffs off me, and I'll show you what you are to me."

Purposely she walked up to him until they were only a foot apart. He could see the anger in her eyes, but he also read the excitement there, and that defiance. "You mean you won't prepare your trap for Fire Magic today if we make love? Or were you planning on just getting in a quickie before you started to fix the canvas?"

Brock's hands clenched at his sides as he battled two competing emotions. One was to put his hands around

that lovely long neck and strangle her, and the other was
to crush her to him and take her with or without her
consent, and to hell with promises.

Grabbing a rope of control that seemed to be fraying
more by the minute, he ignored both temptations. "I
don't like being treated as less than I am any more than
you do, Shana. Remember that."

He turned sharply and stalked away.

"IT'S NEARLY MIDNIGHT and he hasn't shown. I told
you. He knows Roseblush can't jump the canvas corral. He's not coming." Shana hoped her voice carried
some conviction, but she was afraid it didn't.

"You don't have to wait up, Shana. I'm not stopping you from going to bed."

No, he wasn't. But still she paced around their
campsite, nearly stumbling over a large rock as one of
several plump clouds that had moved in over the past
hour chose that moment to cover the full moon.

"Why don't you sit down? You're wasting a lot of
energy for nothing. Your pacing isn't going to discourage him."

"You know that for certain, right?"

He had the nerve to smile. "I know it's not discour-
aging me."

She felt his eyes all over her and quickly sat down and
sought to change the subject as the ovenlike night air
plastered her clothes to her skin, making it shine with
perspiration.

All day long his words of that morning churned
through her. *"If you had been serious last night, Shana,
nothing—not even the chance to capture Fire Magic—
could have dragged me from you."*

Those words thrilled her to the very marrow of her bones. Still, her mind fought against taking them seriously, warned her not to be taken in by what was just probably another smooth line. But was it?

Nervously she searched her mind for a neutral subject that would divert both their thoughts. "The Alta Toquima village is not a very steep climb from here. It's over on the western margin of Mount Jefferson. Probably no more than a day's trek."

"Is that an Indian settlement?"

Shana's fidgety hands brushed an imaginary speck of dust from the blanket. "Not now. The village is at a little over eleven thousand feet and was probably settled about A.D. 500. Then later abandoned. My mother found dozens of prehistoric hunting blinds in the area along with a lot of artifacts. Some date back at least seven thousand years. You might want to see it, since you've come this far."

"Ancient artifacts don't do much for me, Shana. I'm here for just two things. Fire Magic and you."

Shana got to her feet again and resumed her pacing, fighting as always the conflicting emotions his staking claim of her generated. This damn stuntman was as brazen and bold as the stallion he pursued. And, heaven help her, just as exciting.

"Do you share your mother's interest in archaeology?"

Shana wrapped her arms around herself, finding she was eager to discuss just about any subject other than the one that kept popping up. "Not really. Oh, I learned a lot from her, but I was always more interested in survival in present-day terms. But she knew how to travel through the wilderness with respect for it. My initial love of the land came from her."

"And what did you learn from your father?"

"He wasn't around long enough for me to learn much."

"You sound still angry at him for that."

"Let's just say I don't have much use for a man who can't make a commitment and keep it."

"Is that why you haven't married Donner when he's asked you?"

Surprise at his question brought Shana's eyes to Brock's face. She was even more shocked at the genuine interest she saw there.

"How do you know Donner has asked me to marry him?"

"It didn't take a genius. Are you worried about him not being able to live up to the commitment?"

"Look, this is getting a bit personal. Shall we change the subject?"

"I don't want to. Is his lack of dependability the reason you haven't married Donner?"

"No. Not that it's any of your business, but I don't love him."

He smiled at her then in a way that Shana didn't remember seeing before. "So, my wild wilderness woman does think in terms of falling in love."

Shana's stomach did an irritating somersault. "I'm not your wild wilderness woman."

"Whose are you, then?"

"I'm not anybody's. And I don't think in terms of falling in love."

"I don't believe you. Everyone thinks of falling in love, Shana."

"Well, there you're wrong. Love isn't something you fall into like a ravine. I think love is like a mountain—

something you rise up to—an emotion that can lift you to heights you haven't known before."

"So you've experienced it?"

"Not ... exactly."

"It's something you've only imagined?"

"It will come. When I'm ready for it."

His voice sounded suddenly bitter. "Ah, yes. I remember now. When you *decide* to let it touch you. Such control. You must snicker at us mere mortals."

She was puzzled by his tone. She looked down at his face, but it was surprisingly shuttered. She found herself curious. "I suppose you fall in love against your will."

He smiled, but curiously with no real mirth. "It's been known to happen."

"Probably every week."

A glitter in his eyes joined his mirthless smile. "You think so? The reality might surprise you, Shana."

"I doubt it. I know your type, Trulock."

The glitter in his eyes turned hard and sent a small shiver up Shana's spine. "My *type?*"

"Yes, your type. You've probably been in love at least a hundred times."

His smile remained. "Not quite. Only ninety-nine."

His admission brought a sad little ache to her heart, and she was all too afraid she knew why. So he'd been in love with many women. Well, it's what she expected, wasn't it?

"Something spread that thin can't go very deep."

She didn't know what made her say it, but she could tell from the flash of anger across his face that he wasn't too pleased with her analysis. He continued to watch her as he stretched out leisurely on the ground in front of her. "You want to try seeing how deep it can go, Shana?"

More than irritation was evident in her voice now. "Well, if that's what you think is love, Trulock, then I'm surprised you only found it ninety-nine times. I would have guessed much closer to nine hundred and ninety-nine!"

She turned and stalked off, angry at the stupid conversation he'd roped her into. She felt incredibly agitated and unsettled, but with no clear idea why. All she was really clear about was that she wanted to put as much distance between Brock Trulock and herself as possible.

His voice instantly followed her, insistent and demanding. "Where are you going?"

"None of your damn business," she snapped over her shoulder.

She heard a mumbled oath behind her as she plunged into the heavy moonlit brush and headed directly for the mountain stream four hundred feet away. Her skin felt so hot and irritated that she could barely stand it.

The moment she reached the stream, she yanked off every stitch of clothing and dropped it on the grassy bank before wading into the icy water. It wasn't very deep. She got to the deepest spot and lay on her back, letting the water close over every inch of her. Relief rushed in as it encased her in its cool cocoon and soothed her overheated body. Her head popped to the surface, and she let out a sigh of pure pleasure.

Gradually all tension just slipped out of her body into the dark water and still night. She knew she should have been cold, but she felt warm and relaxed and at peace as only this wilderness could make her feel.

She looked up at the night clouds, watching the full moon light them with its silvery torch as they slowly stretched across the sky. The desert was absolutely still and silent around her except for the slight rippling sound of the icy water lapping over her body as she floated.

"Shana."

Her eyes flashed to the shore where the moon lit him like a spotlight. She hadn't heard him approach. But she could see him now next to her discarded clothes on the bank, staring at her.

Shana's sudden violent quivering had nothing to do with the icy water she was lying in but everything to do with the unmistakable look on his face.

He tore off his vest and threw it to the ground. Then he tore off his boots. He waded into the stream directly toward her and Shana knew that no promise Brock Trulock had made to her was going to stop him this time.

Chapter Ten

Brock knew he would follow her the moment she left. He argued with himself for several minutes against it, but it did no good. In the end he gave Roseblush's restraints a final check and went after Shana.

Then he saw her. She floated naked in the silver stream, her arms above her head, her breasts and legs shimmering, her lovely face turned up at the adoring moon.

His heart stopped. She was so incredibly, wildly beautiful that he could not believe she was real. But she was as real as this wilderness she loved so much. She was one with it. And he knew that to possess her would be to possess a piece of its very soul.

He didn't realize he'd said her name until he heard its sound vibrating in his ears. Then the pounding of his need for her overtook all other sound.

She looked at him with eyes as dark as the waters beneath her—full of passion—eyes he would drown in if he didn't look away.

He didn't look away.

He didn't think about the promises he'd made. He didn't think about the clothes he discarded, or the icy water he waded through. He thought only of her.

Getting to her.

Then Fire Magic's shrill mating call shattered the air.

For one very long instant in time, Brock froze in the icy stream above Shana.

Suspicion pierced him like a dagger. Had she staged this seduction to once again lure him away from Fire Magic? Was this yet another deliberate tease? Was all the passion in the eyes gazing up at him merely a desert mirage he was trying so hard to believe in?

Roseblush returned Fire Magic's call.

Brock twisted back to the shore and grabbed his boots and vest and ran as fast as he could toward the campsite, telling himself that he'd just made the right choice. But his body and his heart ached in protest.

He reached the clearing just in time to see Fire Magic chewing through the last of the three ropes that had secured Roseblush.

Brock dived into the dirt for the twine and yanked for all he was worth. When the canvas corral came tumbling down around the two horses, trapping them inside, he gave a hoot of triumph.

The captured stallion kicked wildly at the flexible canvas. Suddenly, the bottom of the canvas was kicked so high that Brock could see inside the enclosure.

Brock didn't have a good feeling about this. He quickly ran over to his saddlebags for more rope. He was just returning with a ready lasso when suddenly the stallion kicked the bottom of the canvas into the air and out from beneath it ran Roseblush. Instantly on her heels, giving her bottom a gentle bite to move her along, galloped Fire Magic.

Brock twirled the rope and let it sail at the stallion's head. But at the last second, as though he had seen the rope coming, Fire Magic dropped his head and the lasso flapped harmlessly against his neck.

In a cloud of dust and a call full of thunder, Fire Magic made off with his new prize.

Brock didn't waste time on self-recrimination for letting the stallion outthink his trap or his lasso. Even before Fire Magic had chased Roseblush out of the clearing and into the black night, Brock was on the run toward Hamlet. It took him less than a minute to saddle his horse. He heard Shana move up behind him.

"You can't go after them. Not in the dark. It's crazy."

He didn't trust himself to turn around to look at her. "I'm not just going to lie back and let him have her, Shana."

"But you won't be able to see. If your horse trips, you could take a nasty spill. Damn it, Brock, be sensible!"

He turned to look at her. Her shirt and pants were back on, but she was barefoot and her braids were streaming wet, soaking her shirt and emphasizing her lack of a bra. He looked away quickly before she sidetracked him any more tonight than she already had. "Save your breath. I'm going."

"Then I'm going with you."

Brock swung into the saddle. "No."

He nudged Hamlet and took off into the brush, hearing her call after him. A mile later, although he knew it was physically impossible, her voice still echoed in his ears.

SHANA WATCHED Brock ride back into camp just after dawn. She got to her feet, her muscles strained and achy after a long night of waiting.

"Any luck?"

His features were controlled, his voice cool and distant. "They've gone into the canyon up ahead. He didn't take her far away from our camp in the dark. Obviously, he planned to move her out this morning. I waited at that rise above the meadow and saw them take off at first light. Now that I know what direction they took, I can follow them. I just came back for one of the pack mules to carry my supplies."

"That was...a smart thing to do," Shana admitted, feeling a sad little prick in her heart at his distant manner. She knew what it meant. Just as she knew why he'd left her in that stream the night before. He believed she had lured him out there so he'd lose his chance at capturing Fire Magic. And she also knew nothing she could say would convince him otherwise.

"You realize your chances of tracking them over this rocky terrain are nil?"

His tone was so cold that it gave Shana a chill. "You trying to convince me to forget it?"

"I'm trying to give you the facts."

"You mean the way you gave me the facts about how he knew what to do so he couldn't be lassoed?"

She gritted her teeth. "If we head back to the ranger station, maybe I'll be able to spot them by helicopter."

"The ranger station is days away. You know trying to locate them by helicopter after all that time passed would be a waste. Stop trying to talk me out of it, Shana. I'm going after them."

He was so pigheaded. Still, it was better this way. If he stayed angry at her, he'd keep his distance. And that's what she really wanted him to do, wasn't it?

"I've made some coffee. Would you like some before we start?"

He stayed mounted on Hamlet and just stared at her for a moment. "*We*, Shana?"

"All right, I'm not going to pretend. I'm happy you didn't catch Fire Magic. But I know how valuable Roseblush is to you. And how much you care about her. If you're fool enough to go off after her in a wilderness you know nothing about, I guess I'm fool enough to go along and try to help you get her back."

His eyes stayed cold and fixed on her face for several long seconds before he spoke. "I'm not just going after Roseblush. I'm going after Fire Magic. You still want to come along?"

Damn the man, but he had a one-track mind. At least, now. She took a deep breath at the pain that knowledge caused her. "Yes."

"Because you don't think I can catch him? Or because you hope to sabotage all my efforts to try?"

Shana swallowed the bitterness of those words, knowing she had no defense against them. "Look, I'm offering to try to help you get Roseblush back. Are you going to take me up on my offer or not?"

He studied her a moment more, then dismounted. "All right. Let's have some of that coffee."

"There's some oatmeal on the stove, too. Help yourself and I'll put a feed bag on Hamlet and get the mules ready."

She had everything packed in record time and added the portable cookstove to a saddlebag as soon as Brock had finished his hasty breakfast.

"I'll lead the way," Brock said as he mounted Hamlet in one swift swing. "I hope you have a lot of trail mix handy, because I'm not planning on making many stops."

And with that he gave Hamlet a good nudge and the buckskin took off at a fast clip. Shana urged Mickey forward, pulling the pack train behind her, silently cursing stuntmen who were far too hardheaded for their own good.

It was a long, tiring climb up the steep canyon into the mountains above.

Brock led the way between the sharp rocks in silence. A few times they stopped to rest the horses and mules and Shana got a glimpse of his profile; she couldn't miss the hard set of his jaw or the determination in his eyes.

As morning turned into afternoon, the clouds clumped and the air stilled. When Brock dismounted and began to lead Hamlet up a nearly perpendicular rocky rise, Shana flinched through her perspiration-soaked clothes and dismounted from Mickey's back with no inclination to follow. But of course, she did. It took nearly an hour to reach the top of the baked lava rock, and nearly all of Shana's breath. Even Mickey and the pack mules were heaving.

When she reached the flat plateau that Brock had led them to, she found him standing with the binoculars to his eyes, searching the numerous canyons and rocky rises all around them.

She dropped her weary body onto a flat rock and got out her canteen for a much-needed drink. She was just enjoying the trace of cool liquid down her parched throat when he yelled.

''There! See them?''

Shana jumped to her feet and rushed to his side. She put her hand over her eyes to shade them from the sun and peered out in the distance where one of his hands was pointing as the other held the binoculars.

It took her a moment but soon she could make out two specks on the landscape, heading into a V-shaped canyon.

"You can see them better with these," Brock said as he handed her the binoculars.

Shana took them and confirmed her impression. It was Fire Magic carefully making his way over the rocks as he entered the canyon with Roseblush. She watched for the next couple of seconds until the rocky face of the canyon swallowed them from view. Then she lowered the binoculars.

She turned to find Brock still beside her, having just taken a gulp of water from his canteen. "So how long will it take for us to get to the entrance of that canyon?" he asked.

"Probably the rest of the afternoon."

"It doesn't look that far."

"Distances in the desert can be deceiving. It's that far."

"You ever been in that canyon before?"

"Not that I can recall. But I've flown over it. If memory serves me, it's a box canyon with just that one entry. Seems kind of strange that Fire Magic would lead Roseblush inside it."

"Maybe he makes mistakes, too. I want to go straight toward the canyon, Shana. No circuitous routes. I want to keep it in sight at all times just in case Fire Magic has gotten himself confused and when he realizes he's boxed in, comes galloping out of there."

"All right. There's a trail just over that slope there. It's steep and we'll have to go more slowly so the horses don't stumble, but using it will let us keep the mouth of the canyon in sight the whole time."

"Let's get moving, then," Brock said as he took hold of Hamlet's reins with grim determination.

Shana turned toward Mickey, battling distinct disappointment. She never thought she would, but she missed Brock Trulock's charming smiles. Very much.

"DAMN. Where in the hell did Fire Magic and Roseblush go?"

Brock knew all the frustration he was feeling underlined his words, but at the moment he was just too upset to care as he stared at the sheer rock rising all around him.

"We had the mouth of the canyon in sight the entire afternoon," Shana said from behind him. "If Fire Magic had led Roseblush out of the canyon, we would have seen them. We didn't."

"So you tell me where they are."

"I can't."

Brock picked up a red rock and threw it against the wall of the canyon. It pinged against the rock face, making a ghostly echo across the steep canyon cage.

They'd been walking the horses for the past couple of hours to save their strength over the snaking and treacherous terrain. Under the unrelenting heat of the hot desert sun and after too many nights without any real rest, Brock had only the hope of capturing Fire Magic and Roseblush to keep himself going.

And that hope had just gotten dashed against these rocks.

But even this disappointment wasn't as deep as the one he'd endured since last night. He glanced back at Shana's perspiring and weary face as she stroked Mickey's neck, and wished to hell he'd met her before she'd ever seen that damn red stallion and given her heart to it.

"We need to get to higher ground," she said as she gazed into the cloud-filled sky. "And soon, or we could get caught in a flash flood."

"You think John's storm is coming?"

As though in answer to his question, lightning streaked through the air, causing Hamlet to rear in sudden fright. Brock held tightly to his reins and brought him back to all fours. "Steady, boy."

"Storm's coming fast," Shana warned.

Brock looked up and had to admit that the dark clouds were massing with incredible speed into thunderheads. "Where do you suggest we head?"

"I don't think we've got time to get out of the canyon. Our only choice is to try to find a trail up one of the sides."

"A trail?"

"An old animal trail through the rocks. Anything that we can lead the horses and mules up. And we've got to hurry."

"Lead the way," Brock replied.

They had gone but a few steps when the rain started. Brock welcomed it at first. Anything seemed better than the heat. But as the heavy rain beat down on the dry earth, suddenly he found himself walking in mud. The next thing he knew, Hamlet had tripped and plowed into him.

About fourteen hundred pounds of horse giving him a shove in the already-slippery mud was all it took to get Brock to lose his own footing. One minute he was walking beside Hamlet and the next he found himself sitting in the mud with a new cloudburst breaking overhead.

Within just a few seconds, Shana had sloshed to his side. She shouted over the sound of the pounding rain. "You okay?"

He shouted back. "Fine. Looks like Hamlet and I haven't gotten our desert sea legs yet."

"I've spotted a pretty good-size ledge with a rocky overhang about a hundred feet up over there. It will give us and the animals some shelter. Come on, I'll help you up."

But as she tugged on his arm and Brock tried to get to his feet, they both lost their footing in the slippery mud and the next instant Brock was on his back and Shana had landed on her behind next to him, wearing a shocked look on her mud-splattered face.

It was the shocked look and all that mud that got past the disappointment and weariness and the wet to tickle Brock's funny bone. He started to laugh and soon was falling over into the mud as the laughter took him over. It had claimed him so completely that it was several minutes before he realized that Shana was laughing, too. And just about as hard as he was.

The gold in her eyes danced before him. His laughter faded at the glorious sight of just watching her. She must have felt his eyes on her because suddenly she brought her laughter under control, too.

Brock no longer heard the sound of the rain as the look in her eyes had his heart drumming in his ears. He raised his hand to brush the mud from her cheek, but stopped an inch from it when he once again remembered his promise. She turned her head away and shakily but resolutely got to her feet.

"We'd best get up to that ledge with the overhang."

Brock rose successfully this time. With each step forward, his boots seemed to be sinking deeper into the mud of the canyon floor. As Shana led the way up the circuitous and precarious rocky trail along the side of the mountain, the muddy surface turned to a rocky one as slippery as glass. More than once Hamlet or one of the mules lost their footing and had to be helped back to their feet. Only Mickey seemed surefooted enough to handle the slippery terrain.

And still the rain poured.

After what seemed like hours but was probably no more than twenty minutes, Shana called back over her shoulder. "Right around this bend."

After Brock turned around the rocky facing, he saw it, too. And not just a clearing with a rocky ledge, but a black hole that signaled the entrance to a cave. Shana was already ducking inside to take a look, with the rifle nestled in the crook of her arm.

She came out a moment later with a big smile. "We're in luck. This cave's empty and mostly dry. It's even got a skylight. Come on, let's unload the animals. They'll be fine out here under the ledge until the storm passes. Meanwhile we can get dry and changed inside."

She was already uncinching Mickey, and Brock joined her in making the animals comfortable. Then he helped her drag the saddlebags into the cave.

It proved to be unexpectedly large, about eight by ten with a ceiling high enough for even Brock to stand. As Shana had promised, in the far top corner a hole about two feet in diameter let in the subdued light from the storm-ridden sky. It also let in a stream of steady rain. Fortunately the water cascaded down a rock-worn rivet that drained off the corner downslope of the cave floor and out over the side of the cave opening, leaving the rest of the floor dry.

Brock shrugged as he put all but the saddlebag containing his dry clothes down. "Well, it's not exactly LA's Bonaventure, but it does seem to have running water."

Shana was busy going through the saddlebags she had brought in, and drew out a couple of blankets and some dry clothes of her own. "I hope there's enough water to wash the mud off. When this stuff dries, scraping it off generally takes some skin, too."

She looked up at him then and smiled. Brock felt her smile shining right through him like a warm summer sun. His eyes traveled over her kneeling form on the stone floor—her boots, her pants, her shirt—all wet and covered in mud. Her braids had come undone from their circle about her head, flopped across her shoulders in tangled, muddy ropes. Her face was splattered in mud. It covered her cheeks, her forehead, even the tip of her nose.

He said the words because they demanded to be said and he couldn't keep quiet any longer. "You're beautiful, Shana."

Her smile faded. Slowly she got to her feet. She headed directly for the opening in the ceiling of the cave where the water dripped in a steady stream. She stepped directly under it, just as she might step under a shower. She lifted her face to the falling water and ran her hands over her skin to wash away the mud. But her eyes never left his.

And their look started the blood hammering through his veins so hard that he could barely breathe. He knew he could not speak.

She undid her braids one by one and let the water wash the mud from her hair, fanning the wet, clean strands across her shoulders. Then slowly, with her eyes still fully on him, she began to unbutton her blouse.

Brock swallowed as he dropped the saddlebag in his hands. He stared immobile as button by button the blouse came undone and then slid to the floor of the cave. Then she undid her bra and it, too, dropped to the floor.

He stared at her luscious firm breasts glistening beneath the cascading water and found he couldn't breathe. She had him riveted to the cave floor. And she wasn't done yet.

She unzipped her pants and eased them over the swell of her hips, stepping out of them one leg at a time. Then she slipped her panties down and stepped out of them, too.

His heart stopped.

She stood before him more naked than he thought a woman could ever look. The water slipped over her supple shoulders, across her erect nipples, down her compact belly, and eddied over the glistening dark triangle between her legs, forming rivulets down her shimmering firm thighs.

His eyes went back to hers, and the message he found in them was unmistakable. Brock was out of his clothes before he was even conscious that had been his intent.

He tried to hang on to his sanity as he moved toward Shana, stepped beneath the watery spray, only a raindrop away from that mind-boggling body.

She raised a hand, slid it over his cheek, washing the mud from his face, sending intense shudders of pleasure through him. Her beautiful eyes liquefied into melted gold that turned those shudders into hot knives of need. He closed his eyes and fought for the control she was so expertly stripping away from him.

"Shana." His voice was barely a hoarse whisper. God, he had never begged before, but he knew he was about to.

Then he felt her hands grasping his, bringing them to her breasts, rubbing his knuckles against her nipples. He groaned in exquisite pain as the last shreds of his sanity slipped away.

He crushed her into his body, all the luscious suppleness of her naked female flesh. And she came to him with a wild, happy laugh. He silenced that laugh and everything else as the scorching demand of his lips fused her to him. Her passion ripened sweet and lusty under the heat of his kiss, and she slowly wrapped her legs around him.

He wanted to be patient, tender, but his hands roamed her body with a greed beyond any he'd ever known. Denied for so long, he had to touch her, every inch of her. The downy softness of her cheek. The wet satin of her long black hair. The firm flesh of her shoulders. The slender curve of her back. The sleek globes of her bottom. He filled his hands with their softness and picked her up.

Her hands tangled into his hair as a gasp ripped through her throat into his.

Instantly he tore his mouth from hers. "Shana, I'm sorry. I—"

"Sorry? Are you crazy? It's heaven!"

She laughed and threw her head back, her cheeks flushed with passion. He didn't know how, but the intensity of her enjoyment drove his desire even deeper. He pressed his lips against her neck and licked his way down to her breasts, sucking the mist between them and then the wet hot nipples that rose eagerly to greet him.

She moaned and cried out, again and again, as his tongue devoured her flesh, but it was not enough for him.

She cried out in deep pleasure and reached for him, but he moved out of reach and kept up his delicious torture.

"Brock," she called, her breathing raspy and broken.

Her uninhibited sensuality shook him, drove him blind with the violence of his need for her. He rolled over on his back and brought her with him, setting her on top of him, joining their bodies with one powerful thrust.

Her warmth opened to him and swallowed him completely as she fell against him. He closed his eyes, marveling at the unbelievable feeling of being so fully inside her.

His hands worshiped the lean, silky length of her legs wrapped around him. He raised one, shaking with his desire to caress her erect nipples. She leaned eagerly into his touch.

Her unrestrained response to his intimate touches nearly made him lose it, but he gritted his teeth and held on. For her. Just for her.

With each wave of pleasure that he brought her, Brock felt his own raw male potency blaze through him, until it finally burgeoned and burst inside her.

SHANA LAY NAKED against Brock's massive chest with a small, satisfied smile. Her imaginings of making love to him had been spectacular but didn't even begin to approach the real thing.

She had found a depth of passion in herself that she knew was possible only with him, and the knowledge filled her with awe. And now, curled up against that powerful body, surrounded by his clean masculine scent, feeling his firm hands gently caressing her back and legs, sending warm delectable ripples everywhere, she was finding out something else about herself that was even more astounding.

She was weightless, floating, above the highest mountain in the world. And she could see now that it had been her real destination for days. She was in love.

And what did this man she loved feel for her? Surely something special. His look was certainly something special when he told her that her bedraggled and mud-splattered body was beautiful. She sighed with the pure pleasure of that golden memory.

No, she mustn't let herself dwell on these things or expect too much in case disappointment was around the bend.

"Shana?"

She felt the sound of his voice as it vibrated through his chest and sent a new wave of warmth through her. She tried to snuggle closer. "Sorry. Three times in an hour appears to be my limit."

He laughed, a wonderful rumble rising against her nestled cheek. "I'm immensely happy to hear it, since that also appears to be mine. Shana, I just wanted to tell you that you make me feel alive. More alive than I've ever felt before."

She curled her leg around him. "I'm feeling rather . . . special at the moment myself."

He kissed the top of her head then turned her face up to his, cupping her chin with one of his hands.

This time she could feel his smile circling her heart in a perfect lasso. She rested her head back against his chest and heaved a luxuriant sigh. His warm arms wrapped around her and held her to him. She felt as though he'd never let her go as the sounds of the rain fell all around them like a rustling curtain against their Edenic cave.

She was drifting off to a happy sleep several moments later when his voice rumbled through her again. "Shana, what does that look like to you?"

She opened her eyes and turned so she could see his face. "Where?"

His eyes flashed to her face. He gave her a smile that lit every one of her nerve cells, and then looked back toward the far wall. "Over there."

Shana turned onto her other side so she could follow the direction of his gaze. She squinted in the dull light of the cave. There did seem to be something on the wall. Some kind of carvings in the stone. Her curiosity aroused, she rolled to her feet and walked over to get a better look.

She immediately felt Brock move up behind her, his body bringing all his wonderful warmth as his arm circled her waist. She leaned back into him as she studied the wall. Then she suddenly realized what she was looking at.

Her voice rose excitedly. "Brock, these are petroglyphs."

"Petroglyphs?"

"Line drawings in the stone. Prehistoric ones!"

"Prehistoric? How can you tell?"

"Suffice it to say that after being around a mother who settled snapshots of similar stone drawings on her lap every night instead of crochet needles, I recognize the patterns. But these are so much more extensive and detailed than in her snapshots."

"Are you saying no archaeologist has seen these?"

"I'm sure none have or there would have been a concerted effort to have them preserved."

"Isn't it pretty strange that they haven't been found before?"

Shana couldn't keep her eyes off the exciting find. "Not really. The cave wasn't visible from the canyon floor. You can't even see it unless you're right in front of it. I only led us up here because I saw the rock overhang and hoped it would give us sufficient protection from the storm and any possible flash-flooding through the canyon. Finding this cave was just luck. Incredible luck. Oh, Brock, Mom will be so pleased when I tell her!"

She looked up to see him smiling at her. His free hand raised to lightly stroke her hair and the look on his face sent her stomach into a dozen flip-flops.

"Why did prehistoric people in this area make petroglyphs?" he asked.

Shana turned back to the wall, knowing that if she continued to look at him, she wouldn't be able to say a coherent thing. "As landmarks to find game mostly. This one seems to be telling such a story."

Brock's arms circled around her as he kissed the top of her head. "Tell me about it."

"Well, those human figures represent the hunting party. See the skins of animals they're wearing and the spears in their raised hands? They are walking along a rocky path. Looks like four of them. No, wait, four and a half. Hmm. That's strange."

"What?"

"Well, see this fourth figure in front of the others? You can only see the back of his head, neck and shoulders and only one of his arms and legs. Someone drew a wall in front of him, like the wall was swallowing him."

"A wall?"

"It appears to be a wall. See the vertical lines all close together? Oh, and look on the other side of the wall. The figures of the animals with the curled horns. Those are bighorn sheep eating grass in some kind of a meadow. That's consistent with what my mother has told me about these primitive people. They were hunters of the bighorns. Looks like this is an extensive petroglyph showing these prehistoric hunters following a trail to hunt the bighorn sheep they found on the other side of this wall."

"Shana."

She turned at the odd tone suddenly in Brock's voice. She was equally startled by the look she saw on his face. "What is it?"

"Look over here. Behind the figures of the hunters. See what's carved into the stone? It's the rocky overhang. And the cave. The cave we're in, Shana."

Shana's eyes followed Brock's pointing fingers. "Yes, you're right. They've drawn the canyon floor and the trail up to the overhang and this cave that we followed. This petroglyph is a map of where we are!"

"So prehistoric hunters carved this stone to let others who would follow know that bighorn sheep could be found farther up on this trail."

Shana's eyes darted back toward the human figures and concentrated on the partial hunter who walked into the wall as a new idea started to form. Carefully she studied the carvings, running her fingers over and over them before she finally answered.

"Brock, I think these prehistoric artists were trying to tell other hunters of the tribe that in order to get the bighorn sheep, they were going to have to pass through a canyon wall farther up this trail."

Brock's fingers reached over to trace the petroglyph, as though he needed to feel its substance. "Shana, a canyon wall? An opening where animals can slip out of one canyon into another without being seen? Do you know what this means?"

Shana nodded, her words coming out in a whoosh of held breath. "Yes. Fire Magic and Roseblush could have used this trail. It would explain why we didn't see them leaving this canyon."

She watched as his gray eyes gleamed with the possibilities and felt an ominous premonition as his eyes returned to her face. "You say you've flown a helicopter over this canyon. What did you see farther up—in that direction where the carving shows the sheep?"

"Nothing that I can recall clearly. A lot of trees, I think."

"Yes, that's got to be it. Shana, don't you see? A hidden plateau between canyons. Covered by trees that would mean a source of water. And that would mean a perfect hiding place for Fire Magic and his herd."

Yes, she saw, all right, long before he'd said the words. Inside her chest, excitement and dread both battled around her uneasy heart.

But she could see only excitement on her companion's face. "Let's get dressed, Shana. We've got some climbing to do."

"It's still raining."

He left her side and headed for his clothes. She felt a cold draft of air in the absence of his warmth and tried to assure herself it was just temporary.

Brock's voice was deep with purpose. "It's down to a trickle and will be stopping any minute. Come on, we've still got several hours of daylight left."

He was already in a dry pair of jeans and reaching for his socks and boots when Shana's hand slowly stretched into her saddlebag for some dry clothes. She sighed as she watched him, eager to pursue his chase of Fire Magic and Roseblush, everything else obviously pushed aside.

So much for all that first careless rapture of their joining.

Of course, what they had shared together might not mean a thing to him.

No, she wouldn't accept that. His every look and touch told her he cared. If she hadn't been sure of that caring, she never would have made love with him. Now the only question that remained was, how *much* did he care?

Chapter Eleven

"Sure you haven't seen anything unusual?" Brock called back over his shoulder for the twentieth time in the past two hours.

"No. Nothing."

Even in his eagerness to find the break in the canyon wall and locate the plateau he was sure Fire Magic had escaped into, Brock was aware of how subdued Shana had become since their interpretation of the cave carvings.

He knew what had generated her unhappiness, and for the life of him he didn't know what he was going to do about it. The only thing he could think of was to capture Fire Magic and prove to her that the stallion could adapt to living in benevolent captivity. If the horse she loved accepted the future Brock had planned for him, surely Shana would. Wouldn't she?

For the first time in his life, Brock felt a twinge of uncertainty. He had never backed down from a challenge, but this one carried with it a terrible penalty for failure. He pressed on, aware the dream he chased could be just ahead but was also riding quietly behind him, and somehow he had to merge them to make them whole.

The air had stilled and become hot again now that the storm had faded from the afternoon sky. Stratus clouds remained, with thin wispy tails. The canyon ledge they traveled was steep and narrow and rocky. Brock could feel the heat radiating from it and from Hamlet behind him as he lead the way on foot.

Then suddenly Brock felt an almost undetectable shaft of cooler, pine-tinged air that seemed to come out of nowhere. He halted in mid-stride. Waited. There it was again. Unmistakable.

Squinting from the sun's glare, Brock studied the face of the canyon wall. It took a moment before he saw it. He called back over his shoulder, but in a softer voice now, not knowing how the sound might travel.

"Shana. Up ahead. Just a few more feet. There's a fissure in the rock."

Brock led Hamlet carefully through the narrow gap between the canyon walls, just big enough for a horse to go through. Both sides of the passage were smooth rock walls, as though an ancient lava flow had once melted off any hard edges. Beneath his feet was stone washed equally smooth. Up ahead he saw only more stone as the canyon walls looked as if they curved into each other.

But the cooler air was coming from somewhere. Somewhere up ahead.

He moved through the long passage quickly, his excitement growing. After about twenty feet, he found it curved to the right. When he turned the bend, the air became even cooler, fresher, and he saw the light of the passage's end. He hurried forward.

But even his expectations couldn't compete with what he saw when he stepped out of the passage.

Nearly fifty feet below on a tableland, nestled beneath the copious canopy of pines and munching at the new spring grass glistening in the afternoon sun, were horses of every size, shape and description as far as the eye could see.

It was a full minute later before he heard Shana speak beside him, her tone full of wonder. "There must be close to a hundred horses down there. I thought he'd have maybe thirty, but a hundred! Fire Magic must have stolen most of the wild mares in the Toiyabe!"

Brock quickly reached for his binoculars as something else caught his eye. He exhaled in satisfaction.

"And look up at that rise on the far side. The outcropping of rock there to the right. Here, take my binoculars so you can see."

"I don't need the binoculars, Brock. I can see his red coat flashing in the sun. It's Fire Magic. Positioned so he can keep an eye on his herd. And I bet when a helicopter goes over, he signals them to get beneath the trees and runs beneath one himself. No wonder I never saw a horse up here!"

Brock laughed at the good-natured chagrin in her voice. He raised the binoculars to his eyes again and took a closer look at the horses grazing quietly across the tree-dotted meadow.

"He must not be able to see us up here on this rocky ledge," Shana continued. "Good thing the breeze is coming from his direction and not ours or he'd already know we were here."

Brock answered, preoccupied. "Hmm."

Shana went on. "I don't see any other way in or out of this plateau other than the rocky climb we're on. I wonder if Fire Magic has a hidden escape route stored away in his crafty brain? I'll bet he does. He's too smart to box himself in.''

Brock didn't even try to hide the satisfaction in his voice. ''I don't know about any hidden exit route, but Fire Magic isn't the only red-coated horse out here. I've just counted ten more red iridescent coats and I'm just getting started.''

Her voice rose. ''Ten more?''

''Colts and fillies,'' Brock said with a smile.

He could see her catch on immediately. ''You mean Fire Magic's progeny? They have his color? Quick, let me see.''

Brock laughed again as she all but tore the binoculars out of his hands. After a moment, her response came out all in a rush. ''Brock, they're beautiful! And so big! Can some of them be only a month or so old? Yes, they must be. Look there, that one's dam is one of Amy's Thoroughbred mares. And there's Roseblush. And there's another one of Amy's mares with a red foal. Do you suppose all of his foals are red? Do you suppose that will be one of the characteristics he passes on?''

Brock wrapped his arm around her shoulders and hugged her to him, as excited and full of wonder as she. ''I wouldn't be a bit surprised. And that's not all. Did you notice their short backs, long legs, high rumps?''

Shana still had the binoculars up to her eyes. She exhaled a breath of wonder. ''You're right! Even the ones with mustang dams. I can't believe it. His genetic stamp is unmistakable. Fire Magic *is* a new breed of horse!''

He loved the sound of her excitement, finding it giving him more pleasure than even his own. To have her with him sharing this moment felt so good. So right.

Brock eased the binoculars away from her eyes, hugged her to him, kissed her forehead, her nose, her lips, full of the joy of discovery. But it was more than finding Fire Magic and verifying his undeniable stamp on his progeny. Much more. It was the discovery of who she was and who he was with her.

"Brock, he's so magnificent. I've often dreamed of seeing him like this, standing stately above his herd, in all his regal splendor—lord and master of all he surveys. He's a true king in his wild world."

He took her lips again with his. He tasted the love in her, as sweet and hot as it had been when he joined with her in body and soul only hours before. He wanted always to feel her in his arms this way.

But he knew other things had to be said and done first. Reluctantly, he released her mouth and leaned back to see her face. She looked up at him, her eyes dancing specks of golden mirrors, reflecting all the emotion he was feeling.

His voice sounded husky and hoarse as he tore the words from his heart. "Shana, you know what I've come here to do. But before I do anything, there's something else you must know. I love you. With all the love a man can feel for a woman."

He watched her smile light her incredible eyes and felt his heart swell. Then those eyes narrowed into catlike scrutiny as she said, "For the hundredth time?"

His arms crushed her to him, with a fierceness that surprised even him. He was in no mood for any light-hearted jokes. This was deadly serious stuff. "I've never loved anyone but you, Shana O'Shea. I only told you I'd been in love ninety-nine times before because you goaded me into it and you know it. Or if you don't, you should."

He kissed her then with all the wild want and need that pulsed inside him, and all the desperation and fear that told him after he followed this dream to its inevitable end, she might never let him near her again.

He felt her own need and desperation being returned in her kiss and it panicked him even more. Because she, too, knew the stakes.

"Well, well, well. Looks like I'm interrupting something."

Brock jumped back from Shana as the harsh male voice sliced through the air between them.

Shana lunged for the rifle in her saddlebag as Victor Badham's unmistakable voice registered in her ears. But she froze as she saw the ready rifle in his hands waving at her in warning as he sat astride a well-muscled, enormous black stallion. "Hold it right there, O'Shea. I'll shoot if I have to."

Shana was just wondering if she should take a chance and rush Badham when she saw his bodyguard, Jebb, also wielding a rifle, ride up behind his boss on a large gray stallion. She decided prudence, not heroics, would have to do for the moment.

Jebb reached into the sheath across her saddle and removed her rifle, then the boy's confiscated shotgun, off the pack of one of the mules. Shana turned to Badham. "What are you doing here?"

"Why, following you, of course. Although I must say that you do take the long way around things. Why didn't you scale your mountain the easy way?"

"She wanted to show me the scenic route," Shana heard Brock say as he moved in front of her, deliberately getting between her and the rifle. "Why should Ms. O'Shea's itinerary interest you so much?"

"Ah, stepping in to rescue the lady, huh, Trulock? You hoping for star billing this time, instead of just a stuntman credit?"

Shana heard the chill in Brock's words. "How do you know who I am?"

"I make it my business to know who people are. And what they're up to. And I know that Ms. O'Shea has been leading you to that red stallion overlooking his herd down there."

Shana stepped around Brock. She had no intention of letting him shield her from a bullet by taking it himself. Besides, she needed an answer. "Phil Hudson told you?"

"No, not Phil. Whatever you threatened him with did the trick. He was as closemouthed as a clam. But the guys at the BLM were talkative. Real talkative. Told me all about how the famous Hollywood stuntman Brock Trulock had filed adoption papers on Fire Magic—a horse that had defied their numerous attempts to capture. They've even got a betting pool going. Want to know what odds they've got against you?"

"Not particularly," Brock said as he folded his arms across his chest. "But I would be interested in knowing why you've decided to make this business yours."

Badham's smile made Shana's skin crawl. "Because I intend to have the horse, of course."

"What for?" Shana demanded.

"He's a bucker, O'Shea. One hell of a bucker. I don't have to tell you that. You photographed him bucking that mountain lion off his back. I got copies of all your pictures from the newspaper."

"What could you possibly want with a bucking horse?"

"Why, to sell him to a rodeo, of course. Real bucking horses are rare. Very rare since these stupid laws about protecting the wild mustangs got on the books. Do you know how much I can get for one with spirit?"

"Badham, you've got more money than you'll ever spend in your lifetime. You don't need to do this."

"Don't need to do this? O'Shea, I never realized you were so naive. Money is power. The more money a man has, the more powerful he is. And even you must understand, a man can never be too powerful."

Shana felt the anger shimmer through her body, tightening her muscles. "No, I'll never understand the chase after that kind of power. But you better understand this. Fire Magic is not yours to take or sell anywhere. And that's the end of it."

"Ah, but this rifle in my hands says otherwise, O'Shea. I'm taking that red stallion out of here and then I'm coming back for the rest of his herd. And what a herd. Damn, nearly a hundred head! Never seen so many wild mustangs in one place at a time. Who knows? I might find a few others with bucking spirit."

Shana lunged forward, forgetting the rifle pointed at her, as the anger that seethed through her put only one thing on her mind—and that was to get her hands around Victor Badham's throat. But before she took a step, Brock's strong hands shot out to grab her shoulders and bring her to a unceremonious, and probably life-saving, halt.

Badham laughed. "Too bad you aren't a horse, O'Shea. I could get a lot for one with a spirit like yours."

She fought back the anger to get out her words. "I'll see you in the federal pen. They'll be so many charges against you that they'll lock your prison door and throw away the key."

"No, O'Shea. You won't be seeing a whole lot of anything much longer. It seems as though you and Trulock are going to have a fatal accident up here in the wilderness. A real tragedy. They probably won't even find your bodies for weeks."

Shana felt Brock's hands tighten on her arms and experienced a corresponding tightening in her chest.

"Tie them up, Jebb. We'll decide how to arrange for their little accident later when we have more time to get creative."

Brock released her then, but Shana could feel the tensing of his body. Jebb dismounted, placing his weapon and those he had confiscated from Shana's saddlebags on the ground as he got some thick rope out of his own saddlebags.

Shana kept an eye on his movements and on the barrel of Badham's gun pointed at her and Brock. She couldn't be sure, but she felt Brock's sudden tensing meant he was readying himself for action. Surely this was the time for it, while their arms and legs were still free. Without being able to anticipate what he might do, she knew she should keep alert and be ready to do her part.

Casually, very casually, she stepped away from Brock, toward the discarded weapons on the ground, as Jebb readied his ropes. Her nerves stretched with each passing second.

Then Jebb walked up to Brock. "Turn around and put your hands behind your back. Now."

Brock stood his ground. "And if I don't?"

Jebb's fist came out to hit Brock's jaw, but it never reached its target. In a move so quick that all Shana saw was a blur, Brock ducked and landed a kick into Jebb's leg and a chop across the back of his neck as he doubled over from the kick. Before Jebb hit the ground Shana had dived for her rifle. But even before she had gotten her hands on it, the deadly voice slammed in her ears.

"Don't even touch it, O'Shea. Or I'll put a bullet through Trulock's brain. Right now."

Shana lay in the dust and looked up to see Brock standing immobile not two feet from Badham's rifle, its barrel pointing right at his face, as Badham's turquoise-ringed finger twitched on the trigger. For an instant her mind raced ahead, judging how fast she would have to be to grab, raise, aim and fire the rifle. Her heart sank as she realized there wasn't a gambler in the world who would have taken the astronomical odds that she could beat Badham's trigger finger.

Slowly, feeling the defeat creeping into her, she got to her feet and walked away from the rifle.

Badham's voice was nasty as he directed his words to the man in the dirt. "Let's do it right this time, Jebb."

Jebb dragged himself to his feet with a sour look. He poked Shana in the back and then shoved Brock forward until they reached a rocky outcropping a few feet away. Shana watched for an opening, any opening. But Jebb was on guard now and careful not to get between Badham and the barrel of the gun that followed Brock's head.

Then one by one Jebb tied them to the opposite sides of the jagged rock with a thick, cutting rope. As he tightened the rope around her and it bit into her ankles and wrists, Shana concentrated away from the pain. When he had finished tying Brock, she winced as she heard him using his fists to take his revenge against Brock, now that he was tied and couldn't fight back.

Digging deep for her icy control, Shana gritted her teeth against the sounds of fist connecting with flesh and bone. She knew she had to stay cool if she was going to survive this. Finally, relief poured through her as the punching stopped and Jebb circled around the rock, an evil, satisfied smirk on his face.

"You'll never get a rope around Fire Magic, Badham," Shana called as Jebb remounted his gray stallion. "He won't let you."

"Oh, I don't intend to rope him, O'Shea. All Jebb and I need to do is get close enough to shoot him."

Shana felt her heart slipping into her socks. "Shoot him?"

"With a tranquilizer dart. I've got the helicopter ready two canyons away. While he's tranquilized, I'll have him lifted and taken to his new owners. Much less messy that way. I wouldn't want to injure such valuable property. You see, I'm a careful man. And considerate. I'm going to let you watch before you die."

He laughed, a low and ugly sound, as he spurred his mount down the canyon trail leading to the meadow below and Fire Magic and his herd. Jebb followed like the mindless sheep he had always been.

"Brock, are you all right?" Shana asked as soon as the men rode out of hearing.

His words came back to her from where he lay out of sight on the other side of the rock. "Not to worry, Shana. I know how to take a punch or two."

Shana sighed in tremendous relief at the warm evenness of Brock's tone. The awful hollow space in her chest refilled with air as her mind wrenched to other things. She twisted at her wrist bonds. "We've got to get loose."

"I'm working on it."

"Can you get your hands loose?"

"Not exactly."

She heard him whistle and watched Hamlet's head perk up. "Come on, boy. Over here."

Obediently the buckskin loped over. "The rope, Hamlet. Let's get to it, boy."

Hamlet nickered as he lowered his head.

"He can chew through it?" Shana asked hopefully.

"He's not Fire Magic," Brock answered. "But I taught him how to untie knots. Ouch!"

"What's wrong?"

"Hamlet just mistook a finger for part of the rope."

"Oh, Brock!"

"It's all right. He's got it straight now. That's right, boy. Come on. You're doing it."

"Is he?"

"Part of any horse's training is encouragement, Shana. I'm being encouraging."

A few quiet seconds passed as Shana strained to hear the progress that was being made on the other side of the rock.

Then Shana sat bolt upright, her attention claimed by the distinctive and angry shrill stallion challenge. She whipped her head around toward the meadow, her eyes immediately flying to where Fire Magic had been on his overlooking ledge. But he wasn't there anymore.

She had anticipated he would outrun his pursuers as soon as he detected them. Her only real concern was if he'd be able to get far enough away fast enough to outrun the tranquilizer dart. But what he was doing she was not prepared for at all. With her heart in her throat she watched in absolute amazement as Fire Magic raced at full speed toward the two mounted men approaching him. And then suddenly everything became deadly clear.

Her voice was a shrill cry. "The stallions! Badham and Jebb are riding stallions! Fire Magic will never run away while other stallions are anywhere near his herd! Brock, he won't even try for freedom. They're going to shoot him!"

"Hang on, Shana. The rope feels like it's loosening. Just a few more minutes."

But a few more minutes were too many. Shana watched in dread as Fire Magic plunged forward, scattering his mares, yearlings and foals to the edge of the meadow, sounding again and again his shrill challenge, his majestic fiery mane and tail flying high in fervid rage at the invasion of his territory by the two stallions.

Jebb's stallion was in the lead as Jebb aimed his tranquilizer rifle, but the red stallion's continuing shrill, angry calls proved too much for the gray stallion's courage. Jebb's mount balked at his rider's spurring and drew to a screeching halt in the face of Fire Magic's charge just as the rifle fired. The tranquilizer dart went wild.

Fire Magic plunged forward, rammed chest first into Jebb's gray stallion, and toppled him and Jebb like cardboard figures. Jebb flew out of the saddle and landed on his backside, yelling several loud oaths as Fire Magic screeched by and headed for the black stallion.

Badham's big black stallion, unlike Jebb's gray, had maintained his forward momentum, ears pulled back, shouting his own challenge for leadership of the herd. But not for long. Fire Magic met Badham's stallion head-on, rearing up and slashing its neck with a sharp, searing stone-hard hoof at the last second before they collided. The black stallion stumbled and fell, pitching Badham into the dust.

Shana would have clapped if her hands had been free. She watched Jebb pick himself up off the ground and then his tranquilizer rifle from where it had tumbled beside him. Then he stomped over to his fallen gray stallion to pull it back to its feet as Fire Magic turned and got ready to charge again.

Badham was on his feet next to his fallen horse. "Shoot him! Shoot him, you fool!"

Jebb jumped back into the saddle of the now-erect gray stallion and aimed the tranquilizer gun at Fire Magic just when the red stallion charged again. Jebb got his shot off this time, and the dart pierced the magnificent red chest. But it did not even slow him down.

Fire Magic descended on the gray stallion like a fire-breathing red devil from hell. The gray stallion reared, bucked Jebb off in sheer desperation, turned and fled. Jebb just managed to roll out of Fire Magic's way as his thunderous hooves pounded by, reminding Shana of a lowly tumbleweed trying to get out of the path of a raging tornado.

Badham's black stallion had had enough. He wasn't waiting around for Fire Magic to come back after him. He scrambled to his feet and took off as fast as his legs could carry him away from the wrath of that red stallion.

For an instant Shana felt like laughing. Fire Magic was defeating his puny enemies with no need of any help from her.

But her relief was short-lived as she saw Badham lifting his rifle and taking aim at Fire Magic, who was still chasing the gray at the far end of the meadow.

Shana could almost see the anger on his face. This was no tranquilizer gun he held. This was a weapon to kill.

She screamed. "No!"

The gun exploded with a dreadful sound.

Shana's heart stopped.

The awful explosion from Badham's rifle reverberated around the canyon walls, echoing back in thunderous roars. Shana watched in horror as shrilling, frightened horses reared and ran between the trees and around the canyon wall in a frenzied stampede.

Charging horseflesh blurred before her eyes. One moment Badham and Jebb stood in the clearing Fire Magic had created with his charge. The next instant a mass of stampeding horse flesh overran the clearing and Jebb and Badham just disappeared beneath thousands of pounds of pounding hooves. The sounds of primitive animal fear and terror echoed and echoed in her ears until she knew she was deaf with it.

After what seemed like an unendurable eternity, the horses finally slowed their mindless stampede that had taken them in circles around the closed-off meadow. The hush was so deep it beat against Shana's ears with a force equal to the loud terror.

"Shana?"

Brock's voice sounded so far away. She was barely aware of his gentle hands undoing her bonds. "I'm sorry it took so long. Hamlet's a little rusty."

The words were coming closer. She could feel her hands being freed. Then her feet. She raised her head. His hands cupped her face and brought her eyes to his. He was there. His voice was so gentle that she felt her heart squeeze. "Shana?"

She looked at his loving gray eyes, at the open cut on his forehead and cheek, to where the swelling had started on his lip. His gentleness after all the violence he had endured and she had just witnessed brought the tears to her eyes. She raised her hand and caressed his cut lip. "He hurt you."

Brock folded her in his arms and held her so tightly that Shana could barely breathe. When he spoke next to her ear, it was in a ragged voice. "Shana, I'm fine. Please, don't cry."

She leaned back and took a deep steadying breath, pushing back the tears, studying his wonderful, smiling face. "I'm all right now."

He took her hands in his and kissed them. Then he helped her to her feet. "We'll need to get mounted."

She nodded as she turned toward where Mickey waited patiently. "Yes. I know. We have to go...see."

But when they rode down into the meadow, what was left of Badham and his bodyguard after the horses' stampede made Shana turn her head away.

"THE HERD seems to be all right," Brock heard Shana call nearly twenty minutes later as she rode up on Mickey. "I've corralled all of Amy's mares and their red foals. And I see you have Roseblush."

Brock gave his mare an affectionate pat. "Yes, she's in good shape. Her estrus is over, so I'm sure she and Fire Magic mated. With luck, we've got another red foal on the way."

"I'm glad she's not hurt."

Brock took a deep breath as he watched her face. "None the worse for wear. Which is more than I can say for you. Come, sit down. I unsaddled the mules and left them by the stream. Everything else is...taken care of."

He could see Shana understood what he meant by "everything else." Her eyes flicked over at the bulges beneath the two blankets Brock had wrapped securely and placed a distance from them near the rocky face.

They had not talked about the death of the two men. Brock didn't know if they ever would. The shock of its sheer violence had numbed them both. There was a fierce, deadly justice in the wild. He had glimpsed it before, but never had it been as raw or savage as he had seen that afternoon.

Shana dismounted, but she didn't sit as he had suggested. Instead she came to stand next to him. "I can't find Fire Magic. Or any... sign of him."

"I didn't find any sign of the gray or black stallions, either. Since they didn't go back up the trail we came in on, you must be right about there being another way out of this meadow. Perhaps into an adjoining canyon. If they found it, they are no doubt halfway home by now. I'll mount up in a minute and go have a look."

Her voice tightened. "You're going to go after him, aren't you?"

Brock looked away from the expression on Shana's face as he slipped the halter over Roseblush's ears and tied her to a nearby tree. "Yes."

"I'm going, too."

He couldn't look at her. "Shana, I really wish you wouldn't. Not this time. Please."

"I'm going with you."

Brock knew there wasn't anything more to say. He grabbed Badham's rifle and mounted Hamlet with one powerful movement.

Shana remounted Mickey, but she held him up when Brock started to ride out of the clearing without Roseblush. "You're not taking her along to lure Fire Magic out of hiding?"

Brock pulled on Hamlet's reins to halt his progress and looked back at Shana. "Fire Magic isn't in hiding, Shana. He was shot. I saw him fall."

He watched his words hit. "No. If he had been hit and fallen, he would have been crushed in the stampede. I told you, I found no trace of him."

"I know. He must have had enough strength to get to his feet one last time and stagger off before the herd plowed over him. Please, face this now—he's out there somewhere, dying."

Shana's eyes flew to the rifle across Brock's saddle as though its significance was only just sinking in. Her eyes flashed back to his with alarm. "No."

"It's the humane thing to do, Shana."

She shook her head. "You're wrong, Brock."

Brock exhaled a heavy breath as he turned Hamlet and headed for where he had last seen Fire Magic running after the gray stallion. Seconds later, Shana galloped by without a word. An ache began to grow in the pit of his stomach as he realized she had joined the search and what the outcome would be. He knew he'd do anything to keep her from the pain of what they would discover. But he also knew he could do nothing to keep her from it. With grim determination, his eyes raked the canyon walls surrounding the high meadow.

But it was Shana's sharp eyes that found it first. "There. Up that eastern rise. That dark slit. See how the setting sun puts it in dark relief?"

Brock pulled Hamlet up beside her and nodded. "We'll have to walk the horses. It's too steep to climb mounted."

Shana was already off Mickey's back. She took the lead again, scurrying up the rough trail like a surefooted sheep with Mickey clambering behind.

Minutes later Brock drew alongside Shana as the fissure in the rocky wall led through a short narrow passage that dead-ended fifty feet up on a wide rock ledge. Directly below was a chasm many hundreds of feet deep. But an easy three-foot jump separated the wide rocky ledge from another narrower ledge across the chasm that connected to a flat mountaintop.

For Fire Magic, a horse used to jumping thirty feet, a jump of three feet would be nothing.

But Fire Magic had not made the jump. He lay on the wide rocky ledge, his great chest heaving as his breath came out in painful gasps.

As Shana cried out and raced to the magnificent downed horse, Brock's heart twisted in his chest. He watched her circle carefully around the stallion's stiff, jerking legs to his magnificent head. She knelt down next to him and slowly and carefully lifted his muzzle into her lap. With reverence she smoothed the thick, magnificent mane away from his sweating jaw and crooned to him, until his legs stopped their jerky movements and his large dark eye looked at her. And she smiled.

Brock watched as all his worst fears crowded in. He was going to have to shoot that magnificent animal. With a sigh as deep as his soul, he raised the rifle.

"Shana. Get up. Step away from him. Please."

Her head came up and she stared at Brock and the raised rifle. "What are you doing?"

"Shana, you must understand. It has to be done. You hear him. He's suffering."

And then to Brock's absolute amazement and abject horror, Shana broke into a laugh. "No, Brock. You don't understand. He wasn't shot by the bullet. He was shot by the tranquilizer dart! He's not bleeding! He's not dying! He's tranquilized!"

"What?"

"Look for yourself. He has no wound. The tranquilizer must have started to take effect while he was running after the gray stallion. That's what made him stumble. Maybe that's why Badham's shot missed him. When the stampede started, he must have climbed up here before he completely collapsed. Brock, the tranquilizer shot will wear off. He's going to be all right!"

Brock let his eyes roam over the stallion's body. Again and again. No bleeding. His muscles blazed in all their blatant glory. His beautiful iridescent coat shone with health. Yes, his heavy breathing had to be because of his fight against the tranquilizer. He was going to be all right. The rifle dropped down to Brock's side.

Relief and all the exciting possibilities instantly drove every other thought from his head. Right before his eyes lay his life's dream. He need only reach out to claim him.

"If I tie his legs before the tranquilizer wears off, I've got him, Shana. The most magnificent stud in probably the entire history of horse breeding. And I'll have him whole and unhurt. To father a generation of the most spectacular horses the world has even known. Shana, do you realize what I'm saying?"

Brock looked at her face. Oh, she realized, all right. The sadness was like nothing he'd ever seen before. He felt its weight anchor his very soul.

And it was at that moment Brock also realized something else. Something suddenly far more important than owning Fire Magic.

"Shana, it's all right. I won't be tying him. Fire Magic will remain free. As he was meant to be."

Slowly and gently Shana laid Fire Magic's head back onto the rocky ledge. She got up and moved around his imposing body, her eyes focused on Brock's face.

As she approached, Brock watched all the pink and purple and red and gold streaking across the late-afternoon sky mixing with her skin and shining in her hair. She looked like a present the desert was wrapping for him—an exquisite, priceless jewel.

Humbly he took her in his arms and held her. "It's all so clear now that *you* are my real dream. John Cloud told me that all a man's growth and discovery of himself depends on what he's willing to give to the woman he loves. I don't know why it took me so long to understand."

She looked up at him. "I love you, Brock. With all the love a woman can feel for a man, I love you."

"Shana."

It was all he could say before his mouth claimed hers and tasted all the sweet, hot, strong promise of her love. When he finally released her several minutes later, his voice was husky. "You think Tonopah could squeeze in a horse-breeding ranch?"

Her tone rose in surprise. "You're going to go ahead with the breeding program?"

"I have Fire Magic's foals from Amy Edel's stock. I'll apply to the BLM adoption program for his foals from the mustang mares. It will take a bit longer without a stallion of breeding age, but I can be patient." He smiled. "With you by my side, Shana, I can be anything."

"But, Brock, are you really serious about Tonopah?"

His arms tightened around her. "Pretty hard to get much of a marriage going between us with me in LA and you here, don't you think?"

"Marriage?"

He kissed the pink softness of earlobe, delighted at her continued surprise at what had been obvious to him now for days. "And kids, too, Shana. I'm a man who doesn't like to do things halfway, remember. Will you marry me, Shana?"

She smiled as she wrapped her arms about his waist, and Brock thrilled to see the happiness glowing on her face. Her tone held that delightful taunt he now knew so well. "You sure you know what you're getting yourself into, Trulock? Tonopah can be pretty dull to a man who's used to the excitement of Hollywood."

He laughed. "Shana, compared to the excitement of my woman and her wild wilderness, Hollywood pales into insignificance."

He kissed her then with the pledge of his love and felt her response, returned with equal strength and potency. She was a part of him now. His best part.

THEY STAYED near Fire Magic until the tranquilizer wore off. When he regained his feet an hour later, they stood all the way down the trail and watched from that safe distance.

Shana sighed with admiration and relief as she watched Fire Magic snort and toss his magnificent head as his silver hooves pawed at the desert dust, his iridescent coat flickering in the subdued rays of the setting sun. With each second she could see he was regaining his strength.

Brock's voice vibrated beside her. "Shana, is it possible someone else might be able to find and capture him now that his hideout is known?"

She leaned into Brock, gathering his warmth, knowing he would always be there to give it. "No. Now that this stronghold of his has been discovered, he'll know better than to come back to it. I don't think he'll ever let himself be found by humans again. I think he'll gather mustang mares on his way to the most remote part of this wilderness where no one will ever even see him again."

Fire Magic began to prance around now, his neck and tail arched in all their fiery luster and defiance.

Shana knew this would be the last time she would ever see the magnificent red stallion. She didn't even know she was crying until she felt the tears.

Brock's arms tightened around her, and she knew he understood even before his words confirmed it. "We'll have his foals, Shana. He'll live on through them. And we'll know in our hearts he's out there. Wild and free. As you always knew he has to be."

She turned to look up at Brock's face. He filled her heart with so much joy by his act of pure unselfish love. "I know that there will be many times in our lives together that I will be proud to stand by your side, Brock. But at no time will I ever be prouder than at this moment."

He folded her into his warm, strong arms. She melted against his chest, listening to the strong, steady beat of his heart.

Then her head rose as the stallion called to her for the last time.

Fire Magic reared up on his powerful hind legs and pawed the air, in freedom, in triumph. And then he turned and leaped across the chasm and raced away, his fiery mane and flying tail disappearing forever into the red skies of the desert sunset.

Fifty red-blooded, white-hot, true-blue hunks from every State in the Union!

Beginning in May, look for MEN MADE IN AMERICA! Written by some of our most popular authors, these stories feature fifty of the strongest, sexiest men, each from a different state in the union!

Two titles available every other month at your favorite retail outlet.

In July, look for:

CALL IT DESTINY by Jayne Ann Krentz (Arizona)
ANOTHER KIND OF LOVE by Mary Lynn Baxter (Arkansas)

In September, look for:

DECEPTIONS by Annette Broadrick (California)
STORMWALKER by Dallas Schulze (Colorado)

You won't be able to resist MEN MADE IN AMERICA!

"Robin!"

Robin flinched

Elizabeth hurr

looking for you

"Are you feeling OK? You look

so white!"

"I'm just tired," Robin whispered.

"I'm taking you to the nurse's office," Elizabeth said, taking Robin's arm.

"No!" Robin shook her head vehemently. "I'm really OK, Liz. I'm just—"

Robin broke off as a flood of tears threatened to overcome her. She wanted so badly to tell someone how frightened she was. But how could she? It was too awful to admit that she was afraid her boyfriend was cheating on her. And it was too embarrassing to admit that she was afraid her diet had gotten way out of control.

"I'm under a lot of pressure, that's all."

It was all Robin could do to convince Elizabeth that she was fine. As soon as Elizabeth walked away Robin stepped into the girls' room. She had to sit down again and pull herself together. Her world was quickly coming apart at the seams.

Bantam Books in the Sweet Valley High Series
Ask your bookseller for the books you have missed

SWEET VALLEY HIGH

THE PERFECT GIRL

Written by
Kate William

Created by
FRANCINE PASCAL

BANTAM BOOKS
NEW YORK · TORONTO · LONDON · SYDNEY · AUCKLAND

RL 6, IL age 12 and up

THE PERFECT GIRL
A Bantam Book / April 1991

Sweet Valley High is a registered trademark of Francine Pascal

Conceived by Francine Pascal

Produced by Daniel Weiss Associates, Inc.
33 West 17th Street
New York, NY 10011

Cover art by James Mathewuse

ISBN 0-553-28901-2

Published simultaneously in the United States and Canada

Bantam Books are published by Bantam Books, a division of Bantam Doubleday Dell Publishing Group, Inc. Its trademark, consisting of the words "Bantam Books" and the portrayal of a rooster, is Registered in U.S. Patent and Trademark Office and in other countries. Marca Registrada. Bantam Books, 666 Fifth Avenue, New York, New York 10103.

PRINTED IN THE UNITED STATES OF AMERICA

OPM   0 9 8 7 6 5 4 3 2

SWEET VALLEY HIGH

THE PERFECT GIRL

One

"We're doomed!" Jessica sighed dramatically and flung herself into a chair at the lunch table.

Unfortunately, not one of her fellow cheerleaders seemed to notice her. But Jessica knew how to get their attention. "There's a really cute new boy out in the hall," she said.

"What?" several of her friends said at the same time and craned their necks toward the cafeteria door.

"You guys are hopeless." Jessica popped open a can of diet soda and helped herself to one of Cara Walker's grapes.

"OK, Jess," Maria Santelli said, laughing. "Why are we doomed, and how can we save ourselves?"

That was more like it. As cocaptain of the

cheerleading squad, Jessica was used to being in the limelight. She was naturally flamboyant and craved attention and excitement. Jessica always managed to be right in the center of whatever was most interesting. She always dated the cutest boys, wore the hottest clothes, and knew the latest scandal. The nickname "Hurricane Jessica" suited her perfectly.

Jessica's love of turmoil came as a surprise to people who only knew her twin sister, Elizabeth. Elizabeth was quiet and hard-working and enjoyed spending time with her boyfriend, Todd. Her ambition was to be a professional writer, and she was a regular contributor to the school newspaper, *The Oracle*. People naturally gravitated to Elizabeth for sympathy and friendship, just as they gravitated to Jessica for adventure and excitement. Jessica was as impulsive as Elizabeth was thoughtful. To those who knew them well, Jessica and Elizabeth were like night and day. Except for their looks, that is. The Wakefield twins were identical, both as beautiful as a golden afternoon, with sun-kissed blond hair that brushed their shoulders, and eyes the color of the nearby Pacific. They were both tanned from the California sun, and their size-six figures looked great in any style of clothes. And if they happened to dress alike, the most reliable way to tell them apart was to see which one was wearing a wristwatch. Elizabeth liked to be on time. Jessica had a much more relaxed attitude, and punctuality was not one of her strong points.

Being the only identical twins in Sweet Valley High's junior class lent the Wakefields a certain distinction. And Jessica thought that was just the way it should be.

"Here's the story," she explained. "I was just at the gym, and the coach said that the whole gym floor has to be redone. Totally."

There was an expectant silence. Jessica's cocaptain, Robin Wilson, was the first to speak.

"And we're doomed because . . ."

"Because it'll cost a megafortune." Jessica looked around eagerly. "Unless we help."

"Another fund-raiser?" Sandra Bacon groaned, and Annie Whitman rolled her eyes.

"I refuse to do another rocking chair marathon," Cara said. "I was rocking in my dreams for two nights after that event."

"How about a bake sale?" Amy Sutton suggested.

There was an immediate chorus of "no ways." Nobody wanted to have a bake sale or a car wash or anything typical. The Sweet Valley cheerleaders had a reputation for putting together exciting fund-raisers. Whatever they did now would have to be special.

"How about trying to set a *Guinness Book* world record?" Robin suggested. "We could sell tickets to it."

"Brilliant idea," Jessica said enthusiastically. "What kind of a record?"

Robin laughed. "I don't know! I can only be brilliant a little bit at a time."

"There's Liz," Cara said. "She's brilliant all the time. She's the smart twin."

Jessica smirked at her friend. But she had to admit that it was always good to have Elizabeth around for brainstorming sessions. Jessica stood up and waved. "Liz! Over here!"

In a moment Elizabeth joined the group. "What's up?" she asked.

"We need to break a world record," Amy stated.

"A particular world record?" Elizabeth asked politely. "Or just any old world record?" The sparkle in her eyes revealed her amusement.

"We want to raise money for a new gym floor," Jessica explained. "Trying to break some kind of record and selling tickets to the event is all we've come up with so far."

"I think it should have something to do with food," Annie said as she popped a french fry in her mouth. "World's biggest pizza. Yummmm."

"That's all she can think about," Robin said with a moan. "FOOD!"

Everyone laughed, and Elizabeth nodded. "Annie's got a good idea. But maybe not a pizza."

"Biggest tuna fish sandwich?" Cara giggled.

"Greasiest hamburger." Jessica's face clearly

showed her distaste. "This cafeteria would win automatically."

Robin laughed. "OK, then, how about the world's biggest ice-cream sundae?"

Jessica's eyes widened. "Yes!" she gasped. "That's it!"

"Really? I was kidding."

"Why not?" Elizabeth leaned forward with an excited smile. "You could get donations of ice cream from all the ice-cream places in town, donations of plastic bowls and spoons, make a huge sundae, and sell people tickets for a serving."

Jessica's mind was racing. She could just picture an enormous mountain of ice cream with chocolate sauce cascading down the sides and whipped cream billowing around the summit like clouds. She giggled at the thought: Mt. Everest of the Ice-Cream Range.

She knew it was a great idea. The only annoying thing was that it wasn't her idea. Even more annoying was that it was *Robin's* idea. Jessica and Robin were cocaptains of the cheerleading team, but that didn't make them friends. There was a gut-level rivalry between them that never really died down. But Jessica had to admit that Robin had come up with a real winner this time.

"We could make the sundae in a swimming pool," Amy suggested with a grin. "And then Robin could dive into it!"

Everyone laughed. Robin was on the local

diving team; so far, she had only dived into water.

"No, thanks," Robin said, waving her hands and grinning. "Get me in a pool full of ice cream and I'll never come out again!"

"What a way to go." Cara sighed.

"OK, Robin doesn't have to dive in," Jessica said. "But I still think we should make the world's biggest ice-cream sundae."

Elizabeth looked at Maria. "Do you think your dad would want to be the honorary chairman? It's a good cause, and we'd get a lot more publicity if the mayor was involved."

"You're right, Liz. I'll ask him tonight. I'm sure he'll do it."

"And if you put it together on a Sunday, you could call the event Super Sundae, you know, as in the Superbowl."

"OK! OK!" Cara said. "Enough brilliant ideas for one day, Liz."

"Sorry." Elizabeth grinned.

"This is great," Jessica said with energy, already thinking about how she could take credit for the project. "Now all we have to do is put Operation Super Sundae into gear."

"And *Guinness Book*, look out." Robin raised her fist in the air. "Here come the Sweet Valley High cheerleaders!"

Walking toward the bus stop that afternoon, Robin thought over the lunchtime planning session. It was typical for Jessica to announce a problem and for Elizabeth to solve it. The Wakefields were always at the center of everything at Sweet Valley High. Being pretty and popular opened doors for Elizabeth and Jessica wherever they went.

Of course, Robin was very attractive and popular, too. But unlike the twins, Robin had not always been so pretty. Until the beginning of her junior year, Robin had been overweight. "Tubby" was one of the nicest of the names she used to be called; "buffalo butt" was one of the worst. Being overweight had meant being picked last in team games, ignored at dances, and teased relentlessly.

In fact, it had been partly due to Jessica and Elizabeth that Robin had changed. The twins were members of Pi Beta Alpha, the sorority Robin had decided to pledge. Elizabeth had stuck by her all the way, but Jessica had made it clear she did not want any "chubbies" in *her* sorority.

So Robin had decided to lose weight, not so that she would be accepted by the sorority, but so that she could snub the group when she was finally Pi Beta Alpha material. It had taken strict dieting and a tough workout program, but Robin had shed the pounds and revealed the trim, athletic girl underneath.

From then on, her life had really changed. Robin had joined the cheerleading squad, started competitive diving, and found a wonderful boy-friend. Still, it bothered Robin that so much in life seemed to depend on physical beauty. It shouldn't be that way, she knew, but that was the real world.

And her own experience proved just how real it was. Over and over Robin reminded her-self that having a boyfriend didn't make her a better person than she was before. But there was no denying the fact that George made her feel special. And it had all happened because she was slim. Robin had no doubt that her life would change for the worse if she ever became overweight again.

But she would *never* be fat again. That was a promise Robin had made to herself, and one she intended to keep.

It was strange, though, that she still thought of herself as a fat person. Years and years of being called tubby had left quite a mark. It didn't take much to make Robin feel self-conscious and unhappy about her looks. When that happened, she had to remind herself that things were different now. And usually a look in the mirror set her back on an even keel.

A honking horn startled Robin out of her reverie.

"Hey, gorgeous. Want a lift home?"

Robin hid a smile and sauntered over to the light blue GTO parked at the curb. "Maybe," she drawled. "Maybe not." Then she grinned and leaned into the car to kiss her boyfriend. "Hi. I didn't know you were coming." George Warren had just transferred to UCLA, where he was a freshman, and he couldn't always get to Sweet Valley during the week. It was a wonderful surprise to see him there.

"I have some really good news," George said as Robin got into the car.

"What is it?" she asked, smiling. "You won a million dollars?"

"Not quite. Promise you won't think this is crazy, but I've decided to start a new flying course."

Robin's eyebrows shot up. "You have?"

Flying was what had brought them together. While he was still dating Enid Rollins, George had met Robin in a flying class. Spending so much time together under intense conditions, and sharing exhilarating hours in the air, had led them to fall in love. Months ago, while he had been agonizing over how to break up with Enid, he had taken her for a plane ride. The small craft had malfunctioned in the air, and they had crashed. Enid had suffered temporary paralysis from the accident, and George had suffered permanent guilt. He had sworn he would never fly again.

Robin waited for him to explain his decision. She was surprised, but hopeful, too. Maybe this was a sign that George's conscience was beginning to clear.

"See, I was talking to a friend the other day," George said. "He just finished a flying program he said was really fantastic. And I got to thinking about it and . . ."

"And you realized you still want to fly," Robin finished for him.

He smiled sheepishly. "I really think if I could just get back into a plane, I could put all that stuff about the accident behind me. Then maybe I could finally stop feeling so guilty. Do you know what I mean?"

Robin looked at George's strong profile and smiled tenderly. "I think so."

"But here's the catch."

"Great. There's always a catch," Robin teased.

He grinned and touched her cheek with one finger. "Yeah. Well, it's an intensive program. Between the course and school, I'm going to be incredibly busy."

"I guess so. Which means . . ."

"Which means, I'm not going to be able to come see you so often, at least for a while. I'm sorry."

By now they had reached Robin's home, and George turned off the engine.

Robin leaned over to kiss him. "That's OK. I know how important this is to you. I'll just suffer quietly," she added with a twinkle in her eye.

George laughed and put his arms around her. "I knew you'd understand. I love you, you know that?"

"I know. Because I'm so nice and sympathetic."

"No, because you've got great legs," George said in a growly voice.

Robin winced. She knew he was just teasing, but for some reason it rankled. There was always a nagging doubt in her mind that George would never have noticed her if she had been fat. Lately this thought had been occurring to her more frequently. Robin had no real reason to feel so insecure, but she couldn't help it. And along with that doubt came an even more disturbing question: Would George continue to love her if she gained weight again?

Of course he would, she told herself firmly. Those strong arms around her meant he loved *her*, the whole Robin Wilson. With a breathless laugh she pulled away and looked into his face.

"You're going to crush me," she scolded.

"Not a chance," George said and pulled her close again.

Two

"So what are you and George doing this week-end?" Elizabeth asked as she and Robin walked to their seventh period class on Friday afternoon.

Robin smiled regretfully. "*We* aren't doing anything. George is starting a new flying course, so he can't come home this weekend."

"So what are *you* going to do?" Elizabeth asked with a playful grin.

"Probably nothing." Robin hugged her books and shrugged. She didn't want Elizabeth to think she couldn't handle a weekend alone without George. But she couldn't think of anything she really wanted to do. "Homework, I guess."

Elizabeth stopped in her tracks. "Robin, you sound pathetic!" she teased. "Why don't you come to the beach with me and Todd this after-noon? We'll be there until dinnertime."

"Oh, thanks, Liz."

The girls walked on a few steps. Suddenly Robin had a vivid memory of a double date that Elizabeth and Todd had arranged for her back in her fat days. It had been so humiliating and awkward. She knew her friends had meant well, but the date had made her feel terrible. Robin's heart ached for the lonely girl she used to be. Just remembering what her life had been like brought on a wave of sadness and embarrassment. Suddenly Robin felt fat again.

"I don't know if I can." She looked down and felt a bit of relief at the sight of her long, slim legs. She was *not* that lonely, fat girl anymore.

"Besides, two's company, three's a crowd, right?" she added.

"Robin!" Elizabeth shook her head. "We're good enough friends for you not to worry about that, aren't we? Just come."

Robin gave Elizabeth an absent smile. "Well, maybe. I have to go to diving practice for a while after school. Maybe I'll stop by the beach after that."

"Great. We'll see you later, then. Bye." Elizabeth waved and ducked into a classroom.

Robin paused in the hallway. She was glad George was enrolled in the flying course. But she was going to miss having a boyfriend around. It meant going places alone, or with other girls. It meant always wondering what other people were thinking about her. Why is she alone? What is wrong with her? Doesn't she have a good personality? *Why doesn't she have a boyfriend?*

Robin shook her head. She knew better than to worry about silly, superficial things like that. But at the same time she knew she was going to be spending more time at home while George was busy. She just didn't want to go through that kind of scrutiny from other people. With a sigh, she headed on to her class.

After school, Robin took the bus to the community pool. Her coach, Dina Taylor, was already talking to the rest of the diving team. She waved at Robin to hurry up.

"Sorry," Robin said when she had changed and joined the group.

She smoothed the sleek nylon of her tank suit around her waist and glanced around. A slim young girl from the junior high was standing next to her. Robin felt enormous next to her, and she surreptitiously inched her suit down on her hips.

"I want everyone to work on legs today," Dina was saying. "Concentrate on your legs: perfect alignment, pointed toes. Just swan dives and jackknives to start with."

Everyone nodded and began to stretch out. Robin stood by the side of the pool and gazed down into the water. As her reflection stared back up at her, a wavelet distorted her image, and Robin had a sudden vision of herself as a short, fat blob. Startled, she stepped back from the edge and shook her head.

I don't look like that, Robin told herself anxiously. She found to her surprise that her heart was beating hard. Why was she so upset over seeing a distorted reflection? It was ridiculous.

"Come on, Robin," Dina called.

Nodding, Robin went to the springboard and stepped up onto it. With her teammates watching her, Robin felt a self-conscious twinge. Robin shook off her uneasiness and prepared to dive. She was in shape now and would stay that way.

No doubt about it.

Elizabeth screamed as Todd dumped her into the surf. She went under and came up sputtering.

"You die, Wilkins!" Elizabeth lunged to catch him and got knocked off-balance by another wave.

Todd reached out to help her up. "Sorry," he said, his eyes dancing with laughter.

"I've had enough. I'm getting clobbered!" Elizabeth strode through the water and up onto the beach. Todd followed her, and they both collapsed onto their beach blankets.

"Do you want some ice cream?" Todd asked as he toweled himself off.

Elizabeth closed her eyes against the sun. "Mmm. Sounds great."

"I'll be right back."

15

Todd's shadow passed across Elizabeth's face as she lay on her back. The sound of the waves crashing against the beach was pleasantly monotonous. Elizabeth sighed. She was completely relaxed.

"Are you awake?"

Elizabeth opened her eyes. "Hey, Robin. You made it. Have a seat."

"Thanks." Robin smiled as she sat down and stripped off her sweatshirt.

Elizabeth could not help but admire Robin's figure. She really looked fantastic in a bathing suit.

"You could be in a swimsuit ad, Robin," Elizabeth said sincerely.

"Yeah, sure." Robin's cheeks grew slightly pink and she fidgeted with the straps of her bathing suit.

"I mean it."

Robin just smiled and looked out at the ocean. Elizabeth bit her lip. She wondered if she had hurt Robin's feelings somehow. Elizabeth knew how sensitive Robin used to be about her weight. Her own sister had been one of Robin's worst tormentors. But Elizabeth had assumed that all that uneasiness was in the past.

Maybe it wasn't.

"I didn't mean to embarrass you," she said quietly. "I was just—"

"That's OK, Liz," Robin said cheerfully.

"Hey, Robin," Todd said as he rejoined them. "How was diving?"

"Fine." Robin reached for her sweatshirt, pulled it on again, and stretched it way down over her tucked-up knees.

"I'll get you an ice-cream cone if you'd like," Todd said, handing Elizabeth her cone.

Robin shook her head quickly. "No, thanks. I never touch it."

"Are you one of those constantly-on-a-diet girls?" Todd laughed.

Elizabeth shot him a warning glance, but Todd didn't seem to notice. Even though she had never had to go on a diet, Elizabeth was always aware of her weight. Some girls dieted religiously, and some girls were almost obsessed with the way their bodies looked. It was hard not to be conscious of it to *some* extent. Elizabeth just hoped her friends used common sense. She knew it had taken some pretty drastic measures for Robin to lose so much weight in such a short period of time.

"Speaking of ice cream, I think this whole Super Sundae idea is really great," Elizabeth said.

Robin nodded. "The most important part will be getting a lot of publicity. If we don't have enough people buying tickets, we won't raise very much money."

"And you'll have all that ice cream to get rid of." Todd grinned. His ice-cream cone was dripping in the hot sun, and he licked it carefully.

"No problem. We just have to make sure we

17

bring along at least three boys from the junior class," Elizabeth said. "I've seen the way you guys can eat."

Todd looked insulted. "Hey. We're all growing boys, you know. We need our vitamins."

"Vitamins in ice cream?" Elizabeth retorted. "Sure."

"Vitamin C, for chocolate," Todd said, nudging her with his toe.

Elizabeth giggled and looked back to Robin. "So when are you cheerleaders putting this master plan to work?"

"Next week," Robin answered flatly. "After cheerleading practice."

To Elizabeth, Robin seemed moody and preoccupied. She remembered what her friend had said earlier about three being a crowd. That might be what was bothering her. If it was, there was nothing Elizabeth could do about it, but she was sorry Robin didn't feel comfortable with them.

"Listen, I have some homework to do," Robin said abruptly as she stood up. "See you around."

Elizabeth felt a pang of regret. "Do you want to go to a movie with us this weekend?" she asked hastily.

Robin glanced at Todd and then at Elizabeth and smiled. "Maybe some other time." She shouldered her bag and strode off across the sand.

"What's wrong with her?" Todd asked.

Elizabeth frowned. "I don't know. I guess she just misses George."

But Elizabeth wondered if perhaps there was more to it than that.

"Hi, Mom!" Robin called as she walked through the back door later that afternoon.

After getting no answer, Robin went to the refrigerator for a glass of orange juice. She spotted a postcard propped up on the kitchen counter.

Paris is wet and dismal. People are more concerned with the weather than with looking at paintings. I leave for Athens tomorrow.
Hugs from Fiona.

Robin frowned and put the postcard down. Aunt Fiona Maxwell was her mother's older sister. Her artwork sold all over the world for thousands of dollars, and she seemed to think her fame gave her a license to be bossy and domineering. Recently, she had tried to pressure Robin into going to Sarah Lawrence College, her alma mater, to which Robin had been accepted in the early admissions program.

The problem with that offer had been the same problem with all of Aunt Fiona's offers. Taking her presents usually meant giving up something important. The glamorous Ms. Maxwell thought diving was a waste of time and had wanted Robin to give up the chance of a good computer department and a diving scholarship at a west coast school for full tuition at Sarah Lawrence. "All expenses paid" was something Robin's family really couldn't afford to turn down. It had taken a lot of willpower to stand up to Aunt Fiona, and to her mother, but in the end Robin had succeeded.

Winning had been a mixed blessing, though. Every time her mother mentioned college financing, or when Robin devoted extra time to her own interests, Robin felt a bit guilty. Sometimes she felt that she had to prove something to her family to make up for the turmoil she had put them through. It didn't seem fair.

Just being reminded of that tense, unhappy period in her life made Robin cringe. She yanked open the refrigerator and looked inside. A plate of gooey-looking brownies sat on the top shelf. Her mouth watered at the sight, and she automatically reached for one.

Then she stopped herself. Fudge brownies didn't go with the skin-hugging jeans Robin had just bought.

Grumbling silently about Aunt Fiona, Robin poured herself a glass of juice. When the telephone rang, she hurried to answer it, eager to be distracted from her thoughts.

"It's me!" George sounded as if he had been walking on air, or at least flying in it.

"Hi." Robin sank into a chair and cradled the

phone against her ear. Her spirits instantly lifted. "How's it going?"

"Great! I had my first class today. I just got back and I had to tell you all about it. It was so fantastic!"

Robin smiled at his enthusiasm. "Tell me everything. How big is the class?"

"There are twelve students," he said. "Some are college students, but most are older. They're so interesting, too. One guy has his own business restoring classic planes, and another used to be a diplomat. Can you believe it? And then there's this girl Vicky. She's incredible!"

"Oh, yeah?" Robin laughed. "What's so incredible about her?"

"Well, she's in college, too. She's an oceanography major, and she does all the calculations on air speed and altitude and stuff in her head, faster than I can do them on a calculator."

Robin pictured a human calculator: short, boxy, and covered with lots of buttons. She grinned.

"What else is so incredible about Vicky?" Robin asked, trying to keep the amusement out of her voice.

"Oh, she's funny, too," George went on. "And she's already a pretty experienced pilot. I told her all about you, and she really wants to meet you."

"I'd like to meet her, too." But Robin doubted they ever would meet. After all, it wasn't likely that George would bring a classmate with him to visit his girlfriend.

George continued to ramble on about his class. "And when we were studying these maps—"

"George?" Robin cut in softly. She wanted to be sure he really did miss her. With the way he was carrying on, it didn't sound as if he did.

"What?"

"When do you think you might have a chance to come up?"

"Soon. I promise," he said in a tender voice. "I can't wait to see you."

Robin suppressed a sigh. Suddenly she felt even lonelier than she had before George called. From soaring high, her spirits did a crash dive. She really wished she could be with him, sharing the excitement of the flying class.

"Call me, OK? Even if it's late. I miss you."

"Me, too," George said warmly.

After Robin hung up the phone, she sat and stared out the kitchen window for a few minutes, lost in thought. She was glad George was taking up flying again. She knew it was important to him.

But she would be glad when the course was over. Without George, Robin felt more than alone. She felt unattractive. It was going to be a long, lonely time without him.

Three

Robin reviewed her mental checklist. They had run through all the new cheers three times and the squad was finished for the day. She glanced over at Jessica, who was helping Cara practice a handstand. The "co" in *cocaptain* was something Robin took seriously, even if Jessica didn't. She always tried to get along with Jessica during cheerleading practice.

"Is that it, Jessica?" Robin called out.

"Yep! Now we do the fun stuff," Jessica replied. "Super Sundae!"

The rest of the cheerleaders grabbed their towels and sat in a circle on the grass. "What should we do first?" Annie asked the group. "Publicity?"

"I think first we should make sure we've got

everything we need," Robin said, shaking her head. "If we find out we can't get enough ice cream, for example, then all the publicity has to be undone."

"Liz can handle the publicity," Jessica put in. "She'll write an article for *The Oracle*, and she knows someone at the city paper."

"And we can make posters," Sandra said. "We can use the art department's supplies because our project is for the school."

"Great." Robin reached into her book bag for a notebook and pen and began to jot down notes. "What else do we need to take care of right away?"

"Donations of plastic bowls, spoons, and paper napkins," Jean West said. "There's a place in town called Party Warehouse. We could try there."

Writing busily, Robin let her mind race ahead, trying to anticipate all the problems that could ruin the fund-raiser. Now that they were committed to the project, she wanted everything to be perfect. "How are we going to get these people to give us the ice cream and other stuff for free?"

"We'll call them sponsors," Cara suggested. "We'll put their names in the school paper and on the posters. They can think of it as advertising, right?"

"Hey, I just thought of something," Amy put in. "We still don't know what we're making this ice-cream sundae *in*. Or where we're going to make it."

There was a short silence. Robin scribbled "Location" in her notebook and looked around. "Any ideas?"

"Plastic kiddie pools?" Annie suggested. "We could put a bunch of them together in a pyramid shape and fill up each one."

"We're going to need an awful lot of donations," Jessica said skeptically. "I hope everyone smiles a lot when asking for all this stuff."

Maria grinned. "Don't forget, my father said he'd be honorary chairman. If we promise people they'll get to meet the mayor, I'm sure they'll give us whatever we want. People always want a chance to talk in person to the mayor about their gripes."

"OK, great." Robin nodded. "And we can probably make the sundae either here at school on the football field, or at the park."

"The most important thing is the ice cream," Jessica pointed out. "We need major supplies of ice cream if we're going to make a giant sundae."

"Then that's what we should get first." Robin looked around at the other cheerleaders. "Who wants to start asking around? I will. Who else?"

Jessica flopped onto her back and waved her arms in the air. "I will! I will!"

"She just wants free samples." Amy rolled her eyes.

"Me, too," Cara said with a laugh. "I admit it! I *love* ice cream!"

Robin grinned. "OK. Let's start right now."

Everyone stood up and started to collect gym bags. Jessica looked at Cara and Robin. "If we go in my car, you two will have to double up."

Cara reached out to strangle Jessica. "Why do you have a two-seater?" she growled.

"Don't hurt her," Robin said mildly. "We need her to drive."

"Thanks a lot, you guys," Jessica grumbled. "Come on."

The three girls squeezed into the red Fiat Spider convertible that Jessica shared with her twin sister. Robin knew *sharing* meant that Jessica got the car and that Elizabeth found another way to get around. But now she was glad Jessica usually had the car. It would make organizing the Super Sundae that much easier. Even if it meant putting up with Jessica's ego for a little while, she knew she could handle it.

"Where should we go first?" Cara asked above the rush of the wind.

"How about one of the Izzy's Incredible Ice Cream shops?" Jessica suggested. "They've got stores all over town."

Robin sat back and enjoyed the ride as much as she could with Cara sitting on her lap. Being in charge of a big project like this was fun. She liked planning and figuring things out.

"Who's going to do the talking?" Cara asked when they reached Izzy's Incredible. She looked from Jessica to Robin. "Not me, I can tell you that. I'm just here to give you moral support."

Jessica glanced at Robin and raised her eyebrows. "Well? I don't mind."

"I'll do it," Robin said with a casual shrug. She knew Jessica liked being in charge as much as she did. Sometimes their rivalry really escalated. Particularly when it came to the cheerleading team. Once Jessica had rescheduled the appointment for the squad's yearbook picture and told everyone but Robin. Luckily, Robin had found out just in time to change into her uniform and join the others. Jessica had apologized profusely, of course, but Robin hadn't believed a word of it. Jessica just couldn't stand sharing *anything*.

"I really don't mind at all," Jessica said breezily. She smiled at Cara. "You know me. Pushy."

Robin suppressed the urge to roll her eyes. It was obvious that Jessica wanted to do *all* the talking. And it was too early to start wrestling for control. She knew Jessica would probably blow off her responsibilities later, and then Robin would take over and follow through to the end.

"OK," she said. "Fine with me."

"Great." There was a triumphant note in Jessica's voice. "Come on."

Jessica led the way into the store. "Is the

27

manager here?'' she asked the woman at the counter.

"I'm the manager. I'm Mrs. Loman. What can I do for you girls?''

Jessica took a deep breath and smiled her most winning smile. "We're Sweet Valley High cheerleaders, and we're organizing a huge fund-raising event for the athletic department. We thought your store might like to be a sponsor.''

"Well, I'd have to hear more about this event,'' Mrs. Loman said slowly.

Jessica smiled even wider. "I knew you would. See, we're making the world's biggest ice-cream sundae. Well, it may not be the *world's* biggest, but it'll definitely be *Sweet Valley's* biggest ice-cream sundae. And that's where you come in. You see, we need a *lot* of ice cream.''

"Just how much is a lot? And do you want it all from me?''

Robin laughed. "No. We're asking all the ice-cream sellers in town to donate what they can. If every store contributes at least several gallons, we'll have plenty.''

"But the stores who donate the *most* will be our special sponsors,'' Jessica added.

"With their names in our publicity,'' Cara said.

"And everyone who participates will get to meet the mayor.'' Robin knew that would impress Mrs. Loman.

"My goodness. This really is going to be a big

deal, isn't it? All right. I'll talk to the regional manager of Izzy's Incredible Ice Cream. I'm sure the company will be glad to help out Sweet Valley High. Maybe we can provide all the ice cream you'll need."

Robin, Jessica, and Cara grinned excitedly. "That's great!" Jessica gushed. "You won't be sorry. Everyone in Sweet Valley will get a taste of Izzy's Incredible Ice Cream. And then they'll all come to the store for more."

"I get the picture." Mrs. Loman shook her head and laughed.

Robin relaxed. The first major hurdle was passed. "Is it all right if I call you in a few days to see if everything's set?" she asked.

"Sure. Now, how about some ice cream for you girls?"

"Great!" Cara eagerly began to review the flavors.

Robin looked into the tubs of ice cream lined up below the glass counter. The whole store was filled with the sweet scent of sugar and vanilla and chocolate. Just breathing deeply for a few minutes was enough to satisfy any sweet tooth. Even though Robin usually avoided ice cream, she thought she should be polite and accept Mrs. Loman's offer.

Then the bell over the door tinkled. A very heavy woman walked in, leading two chubby boys by the hand. Robin suddenly changed her mind.

29

"No, thanks. I'm, uh, allergic to milk."

"Oh, that's too bad," Mrs. Loman replied sympathetically.

Jessica and Cara each gave Robin a funny look, but she ignored them. At that moment she was more interested in getting out of the store and away from the overweight family than anything else. Seeing fat people always brought back her most painful memories of loneliness and shame. Lately those memories had been bothering her more and more. She didn't know why, and right now she didn't care.

"I'll wait for you outside," she said to her friends.

Without any further explanation, she slipped out the door.

"OK, this is what you should write," Jessica said, leaning over Elizabeth's shoulder. The girls were taking advantage of their lunch hour the next day to work on the Super Sundae event.

Elizabeth looked up at her twin. "Do you want me to write it, or do you want to write it yourself?" she asked dryly.

"I want *you* to write it, Liz," Jessica said in a soothingly sweet voice. "You're so good at this kind of thing."

"I feel like I'm getting a snow job here." Elizabeth shook her head.

The cheerleaders had drafted Elizabeth to write

a story on Super Sundae for the school paper. Elizabeth was glad to do it, but with Jessica breathing down her neck it was a little hard to concentrate.

"Just give me all the facts, Jess, and I'll figure out the best way to write the article, OK?"

Jessica dropped into a chair and crossed her arms. "I was only trying to help."

The look on her twin's face was so mournful that Elizabeth had to laugh. "OK. OK! I give up. Tell me what to write."

"Good." Jessica smiled, leaned forward, and took on a look of inspiration. "The Sweet Valley High cheerleaders, led by Jessica Wakefield, are planning the world's biggest—"

"Whoa," Elizabeth said. "I don't take shorthand, you know."

"Just as long as you get that bit about me being in charge, Liz."

"Yeah, right," Elizabeth said. "Should I add that you're the most wonderful person in the world, or does everyone already know that?"

"Ha, ha." Jessica smirked at her.

"Just curious, but were you expecting me to write anything about your cocaptain? Even though I'm sure Robin has absolutely *nothing* to do with this," she said sarcastically.

Elizabeth knew how her twin felt about Robin. Jessica's feelings were totally illogical, but that did not make any difference to Jessica. It irked Elizabeth that Jessica could be so careless about someone whom she herself liked. Well, Elizabeth would be very sure to give Robin as much credit as she deserved. After all, the ice-cream sundae had been *Robin's* idea.

"Whatever," Jessica said dismissively.

Jessica propped her chin up in her hand and looked across the cafeteria. She made a face. "Look at Lois. If I were that fat, I'd live in isolation."

"Jessica!" Elizabeth followed Jessica's gaze and saw Lois Waller sitting down at a table with her boyfriend, Gene White. Lois wasn't really fat, but she was definitely chubby. She had always been a bit overweight, even back when they were all in middle school.

But Lois's weight had not spoiled her good nature. She didn't exactly take teasing in stride, but she knew it was inevitable. Most of the time Lois seemed to be pretty contented with her life. She and Gene laughed together over something and then began to share a big plate of french fries.

"No wonder she's so fat. Look what she's eating," Jessica noted fastidiously.

Elizabeth shook her head in exasperation. "I've noticed you eating french fries once or twice."

"Yeah, but I'm not *fat*," Jessica retorted. "How can she stand it?"

"She seems to stand it just fine. Lois obviously isn't bothered by her weight. So why should it bother you?"

"It doesn't bother me."

"You could have fooled me!"

"It's just that it's not *healthy*. That's all I'm saying."

"Lois gets perfect attendance awards every year!" Elizabeth pointed out. "She keeps up in gym, she always looks full of life, *and* she's in love. What's not healthy about that?"

Jessica looked at the ceiling and sighed. "Let's just drop it, OK?"

"Fine with me," Elizabeth muttered, picking up her pen again.

But she glanced over at Lois one more time. Lois would never be a fashion model, but she clearly had a great relationship with Gene, and her outlook on life was completely optimistic.

So what difference did it make if she couldn't wear size-six jeans?

None at all, Elizabeth told herself confidently. None at all.

Four

On the Wednesday of the second week of George's flying class, George called Robin from school. "I'm coming home on Friday," he said. "It'll be great to see you."

Robin's pulse raced at the sound of his voice. "Oh, it will be great to see you," she said earnestly. "I've been thinking about you."

"Me, too. Listen, I'm going to ask you something, and you can say no if you want." George paused. "How would it be if I brought Vicky along? She really wants to meet you. I'll call a friend and we can all go dancing. Would that be OK with you?"

Robin's first reaction was to say "NO!" loud and clear. She wanted George all to herself. She wanted a chance to get back the confidence that

34

had been slipping away. But she didn't want to introduce a sour note into the conversation, and besides, it was clear that George was really counting on inviting his friend.

George probably felt sorry for Vicky, and inviting her to spend the evening with them was his way of being friendly.

"That's fine," she said pleasantly.

"Great. So, what have you been up to?"

Robin toyed with the phone cord. "Not much. Mostly making plans for this fund-raising event at school."

"Hey, just because I can't come up that often for a while doesn't mean you can't have fun, you know," George said in a cajoling voice.

"I know." Robin laughed. "But I miss you."

"I'll see you on Friday, OK?" he said tenderly. "Try not to be *too* lonely and pitiful until then."

"I promise. Bye."

After she hung up, Robin thought about what George had said. She knew it was ridiculous for her to sit at home feeling sorry for herself. She should be using her extra free time to her advantage—catching up on schoolwork and getting in more diving practice. But instead, she had been spending the time missing George.

Robin shook her head as if to clear away the reproaches. At least Friday night would be fun. She could hardly wait.

Thursday and Friday dragged by. Though Robin was busy with school and diving practice, her mind was set on Friday night. The only thing that captured her attention was typing out her notes on the Super Sundae. Just seeing them so neat in black and white made her feel that she had everything under control.

Finally it was Friday evening. Robin put on her new skinny jeans and a light blue silk blouse. She didn't know how Vicky might dress, and she didn't want to take the chance of making George's friend feel frumpy. When she heard George's car in the driveway, she ran down to open the door.

"Hi!" she called out as soon as the driver's door opened.

"Hey, Rob!" George called. He said something to the person in the passenger seat and then got out. Robin ran down the walk to hug him.

"Robin, this is Vicky Carter."

Robin looked over George's shoulder and gaped.

Vicky was tall and slim, with a cap of pale blond hair. Her bangs accentuated her huge dark eyes and made provocative wisps against her high cheekbones. Vicky was gorgeous.

"Hi," Robin said, her heart pounding from the surprise.

"It's really great to meet you, Robin." Vicky smiled. "George talks about you all the time."

Robin turned and looked vacantly at George. "Where's . . . ?"

"It turned out Hal couldn't make it," George explained hastily. "So it's just the three of us."

Robin swallowed. "Great," she said, trying to force a smile to her lips.

Standing there in front of her house with George and Vicky, Robin could not remember what had convinced her that George's friend was a shy little mouse. Robin cursed herself for thinking that just because a girl was a whiz at math she was unattractive. It was the worst kind of sexist stereotyping, and Robin felt terrible for having fallen into it.

And she also felt terrible about the way she was dressed. Compared to Vicky's stylishly short skirt and beige linen safari jacket, *Robin* was the one who felt like a frump.

"Ready to go?" George asked.

"Sure," Robin replied without enthusiasm.

"It's so nice of you to invite me along," Vicky said cheerfully. "I feel like I know you already, Robin."

As they got back into the car Robin felt a twinge of aggravation. She certainly didn't feel as if she knew Vicky. In fact, George had managed to leave out the most vital information about her, such as the fact that she looked as if she had just stepped out of the pages of *Ingenue*.

Was George's behavior typical of guys his age, or was it deliberate? Robin glanced nervously at George, trying to find some trace of secrecy in his expression. But he looked the way he always did: handsome, cheerful, and self-confident.

"I love dancing," Vicky said from the backseat. "I hardly ever have time to go, though, so I'm really psyched about tonight. I think you're terrific not minding my coming, Robin."

"No problem." To Robin's ears her own voice sounded cold. If Vicky was someone George cared about, Robin knew she should try to be friendly. She didn't want George to be upset with her. She turned around and tried to smile.

"I hear you're a real math whiz," she said, sounding slightly sarcastic without meaning to.

Vicky rolled her eyes. "Yeah. It really comes in handy when you're figuring out the tip in a restaurant."

"I'll bet!" George laughed loudly.

Robin shot him a look. Vicky's response wasn't all *that* funny.

"What are you majoring in, Vicky?" Robin forced a smile to her face.

"Oceanography. That's one of the reasons I took up flying. It really helps if you can fly over areas of the ocean you're studying."

"Oh, really?" Robin began. "I—"

"Did you ever take Professor Richardson's

class?" George cut in, glancing at Vicky in the rearview mirror.

Robin stared straight ahead. George didn't seem to know she was there. She listened mutely while George and Vicky talked about their classes. By the time they arrived at the Beach Disco, Robin was well on her way to a terrible mood.

The Beach Disco threw long rectangles of light onto the sand, and rhythmic music drifted from its windows. George parked the car and held both of his elbows out to the girls.

"Ladies?"

Vicky laughed and took one arm. Robin possessively hugged the other. She remained silent as they headed for the building, while George and Vicky chattered on about their flying class.

How much time was George actually spending with Vicky? Robin began to wonder. From the tone of their conversation, Robin could tell they already considered themselves good friends. She felt a sting of resentment. George was obviously having a great time without her, both at flight school and here with Vicky.

"You two go ahead and dance," Robin said as soon as they entered the disco. "I don't really feel like it right now."

Vicky's dark eyes widened. "Are you sure?"

"We'll be back soon." George and Vicky hurried to the dance floor.

Robin slumped into a chair and frowned. From where she sat she could watch George and Vicky as they danced. Vicky was nearly George's height, and she danced beautifully. More than one boy on the dance floor stopped to look at her. And Vicky was talking and laughing with George as though she found him the most fascinating person in the world. George seemed to be enjoying the attention.

It seemed clear to her now that Vicky's "so glad to meet you" act was just a way of winning George's favor. Why would a college girl like Vicky want to meet Robin? No, Robin decided, Vicky must really be interested in George.

And how interested was George in Vicky? Robin knew perfectly well how strong emotions could arise when two people worked together in an involving, intense project. Their own relationship had started that way while Robin and George were first learning to fly. Though George had still been dating Enid at the time, he had fallen head over heels in love with Robin.

A cold fist closed around Robin's heart. And who was to say it couldn't happen again? If George had been capable of cheating on Enid, didn't that mean he was capable of cheating on Robin?

The loud dance music was beginning to give Robin a headache. She twisted one of the buttons on her shirt and tried not to give in to her awful suspicions.

"Hey, Robin!" Jessica bounced over and sat down next to her. "Who's that girl with George?" Her blue eyes were alive with curiosity.

One thing Robin had learned a long time ago was never to tell Jessica anything important. Jessica was prone to dramatizing the truth until the wildest rumors were flying around school. Now it was best to downplay Vicky's presence as much as possible.

"Nobody. Just a friend of his from his flying class. Her date had to cancel, so we said she could come with us." That was the truth, Robin told herself, but with a slant that didn't make Robin look like such an idiot.

And she felt like an idiot. Only an idiot would let her boyfriend get stolen right out from under her.

"She's very pretty," Jessica said, watching Robin like a hawk.

Robin smiled as casually as she could. "Yeah, I guess she is."

When Robin didn't say anything more, Jessica shrugged and bounced away again. Robin's headache was getting worse.

"Hi."

Robin turned and saw a cute boy smiling at her. Instantly she felt flustered and awkward. She didn't know what to say.

"Do you want to dance?" he asked.

"No, I—uh—uh," Robin mumbled. She turned away and felt a fiery blush overtake her face.

The truth was, Robin had never gotten used to attention from boys or to dating. Not long after having lost the weight, she had met George, and she had been with him ever since. In fact, aside from George, she didn't have much experience at all with boys. The cute boy gave her a sorry look and walked away. Robin felt stupid and clumsy.

"That was great!" Vicky gasped as she returned to their table and sat down. She beamed a dazzling smile at Robin and pushed the hair off her forehead. "I must have looked like the worst klutz out there, though. I haven't danced in such a long time."

"No way!" George scoffed.

Robin returned Vicky's smile coldly. *Klutz* was the last thing anyone would call Vicky. In fact, Vicky was so elegant and poised in her stylish clothes that Robin felt positively drab. Were her jeans just a little too tight? Was the color of her shirt a little too flashy? She shifted uncomfortably in her chair. She hadn't felt so insecure about her looks since—since she was fat.

"I'll get us some sodas," George said.

"Oh, thanks!" Vicky smiled again.

Robin didn't say anything. She stared out absently at the dancers.

"George talks about you all the time, Robin," Vicky said when he had gone. "He's just crazy about you. He said you were really great in that flying class you took together."

"Really? That's what he says about you." Robin's tone made it plain how displeased she was with the comparison.

"And that's just what I say about him." Vicky laughed. "He *really* loves flying, doesn't he?"

It bothered Robin to hear Vicky discussing George's innermost feelings. She turned away and nodded. "Yeah, he does."

Her cold snubs finally got through to Vicky. She blinked in surprise and looked around uncomfortably. "Oh, here comes George."

Robin noticed the great relief in Vicky's voice. Robin tried to send George a message with her eyes, but he didn't seem to notice that she desperately wanted to leave.

"How about dancing, Rob?" he asked. "I can't sit still."

"You go ahead, Vicky," Robin said dismally. "I really don't feel like it."

George gave Robin a questioning look, and when she smiled weakly, he shrugged and walked toward the dance floor with Vicky.

After two miserable hours, Robin couldn't stand it anymore. When Vicky went to the ladies' room, Robin told George that she wanted to go home. George agreed reluctantly.

"We were thinking about leaving pretty soon," George said when Vicky came back to the table.

"Sure, no problem."

Robin stood up and headed for the door.

"Where did you get that blouse, Robin?" Vicky asked on the way home. "I've been admiring it all night."

"Just some store. I forget."

"It's a great color. I couldn't wear it. But it looks really nice on you."

"Thanks," Robin muttered. Talking about her looks always made her feel uncomfortable, as if she were being examined under a microscope.

George sent her another puzzled glance. He was obviously bothered by Robin's unfriendly attitude. They drove in silence the rest of the way home.

"You have such a cute house," Vicky said when they got to the Wilsons. "Would it be OK if I came in and used the bathroom?"

"Sure." Robin slammed the car door shut and strode up the walkway.

George hurried to catch up with her. "Are you feeling OK?" he asked in a whisper.

"I'm fine," she replied shortly.

When they were inside, Vicky stopped in front of a small watercolor by Fiona Maxwell and gasped. "This is wonderful!" she said. "I've heard of this artist. She's quite well known."

"Yeah." Why did Vicky have to find the one thing in the house that would make her feel lousy? "She's my aunt."

"No kidding! That's fantastic! You must be

really proud to have someone like Fiona Maxwell in your family."

Robin didn't feel proud at all. If Vicky only knew what Robin had been through with her aunt, she wouldn't have said that. Suddenly Robin felt as if everything were slipping out of her grasp. She wished that Vicky, and George, would just go away.

"Who's this?" Vicky held up a small framed photograph of Robin that had been taken two years earlier. "Is she a cousin?"

Robin snatched it out of her hands. "No. That's me."

"You? Robin, you've lost *so* much weight! I'm really impressed," Vicky said sincerely.

"Gee, thanks. I know I used to be *fat*, Vicky."

There was a tense silence in the room. George stared at Robin in complete surprise, and Vicky looked very uncomfortable. Finally she spoke.

"Well, if I could use the bathroom?"

"Down the hall, first door on the left."

When Robin and George were alone, he turned to look at her. "Robin? What's wrong with you tonight?"

"Nothing." Robin dropped into a chair and stared at the floor.

He frowned. "Listen, I have to drop Vicky off at her friend's house, where she's staying for the weekend. But I'll come over first thing in the morning, OK?"

Robin shrugged and sank lower into her chair. "Fine. Bye."

"It was really nice meeting you, Robin," Vicky said when she rejoined them. "Maybe I'll see you again."

"Great," Robin said, near tears.

After George and Vicky left, Robin leaned back against the door. She was so relieved they were finally gone.

This was the longest night of my life, Robin said to herself. *The longest and the worst.*

Five

Robin was picking at her breakfast the next morning when George came over. He chatted politely with Mrs. Wilson and sat down with them at the kitchen table.

"I'll leave you two alone," Mrs. Wilson said after a few minutes as she tactfully got up from her chair.

When her mother had gone, Robin continued to stare at her untouched bowl of cereal. She waited for George to speak.

"Well?"

"Well what?" Robin replied. She looked up to meet George's eyes and set her chin at a stubborn angle.

"What happened last night?" he asked. He sounded hurt. "I was really embarrassed, Robin. You acted so strange."

47

Robin fiddled with her spoon. "Strange?"

"Yeah, *strange*." George frowned. "As if you were angry or something."

Robin shrugged. "Maybe you shouldn't have brought another girl on our date."

"But you know what happened. Hal was supposed to come with us, but at the last minute he had to cancel. I couldn't just dump Vicky."

Robin didn't answer. Finding out that the girl George was so enthusiastic about was gorgeous and sophisticated had thrown her off balance. She felt hurt and frightened. People like Vicky never had to suffer the kind of humiliation Robin had to suffer. They were born beautiful and lucky. *And people like me are born to lose, even if things go right for a while.*

"Robin?"

Robin couldn't look at George. The fear of losing him so overwhelmed her that she could not even talk.

"Listen, why won't you say something? I just don't get it," George said, his voice rising angrily. "You were so rude to Vicky last night, when all she was trying to do was be friendly. You practically cut her dead every time she opened her mouth."

"I did not," Robin whispered.

"I really thought you two would get along. I thought you had a lot in common."

Like you, Robin thought.

"Apparently you were wrong." Robin looked

steadily at George, trying to hide her anxiety. "I'm sorry, but I don't like her. I don't pretend to like people. That's all."

George shook his head, perplexed. "But why? What's not to like?"

Robin's stomach rolled over. It was obvious George thought there was *plenty* to like about Vicky. And he was probably right.

"Do I have to have a reason?" Robin said softly. She looked away. It was too painful to look at George, knowing she was losing him.

"I just don't get it." George stood up and walked to the back door. "I have to get back to school. I'll call you."

Robin sat perfectly still until he was gone. She was going to lose George to Vicky. She was sure of it.

She scraped her chair back, stood up, and went over to the counter. Her mother had left out a package of sticky buns, and Robin yanked open a drawer for a knife. But just as she was about to cut into the sweet pastry, she pictured Vicky: slim, elegant, and glamorous.

Robin swallowed the sour taste in her mouth and put the knife away. No wonder George liked Vicky. She probably kept that figure by avoiding anything remotely fattening. Robin let her hands drop to her sides, and she touched her hips. Was it her imagination, or did her legs seem a little chunky?

Frowning, Robin hurried upstairs to the bathroom and pulled the scale to the middle of the floor. She held her breath and stepped onto it.

"Oh, no!" she gasped. "Three pounds!"

No wonder George is beginning to look at other girls!

Robin angrily scolded herself for having gotten so sloppy and careless. Lately she had indulged in french fries, pizza, and chocolate cake. She had gotten out of the habit of weighing each food decision carefully. Now it was clearly time to get back on a real diet.

"No more fattening food," she said out loud in a firm voice.

Robin went into her room and took a sheet of paper from her desk drawer. Starting today she was going to get organized, get a grip on her life. She outlined a strict diet to follow: no breakfast, plain salad for lunch, and a very light dinner. And most importantly, no snacks. She wrote WATER at the top of the page in block capitals. Filling up on water was the best way she knew to hide hunger pangs and lose weight.

To put her plan into action, Robin went back into the bathroom and drank three glasses of tap water. When she was done, she put the glass down and smiled at herself.

"That's it, Wilson," she said. "You're not letting Vicky get George. No way."

*   *   *

Plans for Super Sundae were moving full steam ahead. The cheerleaders met at lunch every day to give their progress reports.

"Party Warehouse is donating a whole case of picnic bowls," Annie said. "You know, they're really for chili. And each case has five hundred bowls."

"Wow!" Jessica cheered. "We could sell five hundred shares of the sundae!"

Robin picked at her salad. The idea of all that ice cream was nauseating. With a grim scowl she speared a cucumber slice with her fork.

"Robin, how can you stand it?" Cara asked. "Salad with no dressing?"

"It tastes fine to me," Robin said lightly. She glanced at the grilled cheese sandwich on the table in front of Cara and did a quick calculation. Cara's lunch probably had a good five or six hundred calories, not to mention about a zillion grams of fat.

"You asked about the plastic spoons, too, didn't you?" Jessica asked Annie.

Annie shook her head. "No, I thought someone else was doing that. Didn't Sandy say she would?"

"I said I'd find out about the kiddie pools," Sandra corrected her.

"No, *I'm* doing that," Jessica said.

Robin straightened up in her chair. "Hey, come on, you guys. We have to be more organized than this. We'll never pull off the Super Sundae if we keep messing up."

Robin opened her notebook to where she'd stapled her typewritten notes on the Super Sundae. She scanned them quickly. "Annie, since you've already talked to the Party Warehouse people, you should go back and ask about the spoons. Sandy, you go with her."

Several heads turned toward her, wearing identical expressions of surprise.

"Yes, sir." Annie saluted.

"I just want to be organized, that's all. *Somebody* has to be."

"OK, OK." Annie didn't want Robin to get any more upset than she already was.

Robin suppressed an irritated sigh. She knew it would be up to her to do the majority of the planning for the fund-raiser. Most of the cheerleaders would be content to leave things to the last minute, and some, like Amy Sutton, seemed completely uninterested.

"I just don't want anything to get screwed up," Robin said for emphasis.

Jessica rolled her eyes. "Fine, Robin. If you want to be the dictator, go right ahead."

As everyone fell back into conversation Robin touched Sandy's arm. "I didn't mean to sound so bossy," she told her quietly.

"That's all right. Forget it. Listen, I'm going to get on line. Want anything? Dessert?"

Robin looked down at the salad on her plate. The word *dessert* sounded like music to her ears. She had been good since starting her diet. And she really was hungry. Her stomach gave a little growl of complaint as if to remind her how little she had eaten in the past couple of days. What difference would a few cookies make?

"Hey, Robin. Have you heard from George lately?"

Robin stared at Jessica. "Why?"

"Just asking," Jessica said breezily. "I wondered how his flying class is going."

The truth was that George hadn't called in days. And the silence was driving Robin crazy. She knew he was spending time with Vicky. Too much time, as far as Robin was concerned.

"Robin?" Sandy repeated. "Do you want anything from the lunch line?"

"No," Robin said through clenched teeth. "I don't want anything. Thanks."

"You're sure?"

"I said, I don't want anything!" she snapped.

"OK, OK, you don't have to bite my head off." Sandy grinned and walked away.

Frowning, Robin put a slice of tomato in her mouth and chewed slowly. The salad was all that she was going to eat until dinnertime, and she wanted to make it last. Still, she knew it wasn't going to fill up her stomach, and it definitely wasn't going to fill up that hollow feeling in her heart.

"How's this?" Elizabeth asked, putting the new issue of The Oracle down in front of Jessica.

Jessica snatched it up excitedly. "Hey, great! Front page!"

The headline read

SVH Cheerleaders Sastisfy Sweet Tooth for New Gym.

The varsity cheerleaders, led by Jessica Wakefield and Robin Wilson, have announced their latest fund-raising event: a record-breaking ice-cream sundae. Tickets for a share of the "Super Sundae" will go on sale next week.

According to Jessica Wakefield, "This ice-cream sundae is the coolest thing we've ever done." All of the ice cream and utensils are being donated by area merchants, most notably Izzy's Incredible. Proceeds will go toward the fund for a new gym floor. To be a part of this record-setting event, buy a share in the Super Sundae. Don't get left out.

"That's fabulous, Liz! I bet everyone in Sweet Valley is going to buy a share. It'll be great."

"I hope so." Elizabeth smiled. "Do you think it's a good article?"

"Good? It's stellar," Jessica proclaimed proudly. "You're the best."

Elizabeth grinned. "And you ain't seen nothing yet. *The Sweet Valley News* got a copy of the article this morning. And Enid's mother showed it to her boyfriend, Richard Cernak."

Jessica's jaw dropped. "He works at the TV station, doesn't he?"

Elizabeth nodded. "He won't promise the Super Sundae will be on the news," Elizabeth explained hastily. "But it might be."

"It's going to be amazing, Liz! I can't wait."

Robin listened to the distant ringing at the other end of the telephone line. There was no answer at George's room. There had been no answer each time she had tried in the past two days. The ringing went on and on while she stared into space. *Twenty-one, twenty-two, twenty-three*, she counted.

With a sick feeling Robin hung up the phone. He was with Vicky. She was sure of it.

"Dinner's ready!" Mrs. Wilson called.

Robin heard her two younger brothers, Troy and Adam, galloping down the stairs. She walked to the kitchen and sat at the table.

"I'm starved," Troy said, grasping his fork for emphasis.

"Me, too," said Adam. "What's for dinner?"

"Roast chicken and potatoes."

Robin ignored her brothers. She crossed her arms and sank further into her gloomy mood. The thought of George and Vicky together drove her crazy, but she just couldn't get them out of her mind. It was infuriating to be so far away from George. She felt helpless to stop whatever was going on. When her mother put a plate of chicken, potatoes, and carrots in front of her, Robin snapped back to reality.

"I don't want this much," she said quickly. She pushed the plate away. No matter how delicious it looked, no matter how hungry she felt, she was not going to eat.

Mrs. Wilson poured her a glass of milk. "Just eat as much as you want, then."

"Do these carrots have butter on them?" Robin asked suspiciously.

"Margarine, yes," her mother replied. "The way I always make them."

Robin shook her head. "I can't eat them. Sorry, Mom."

Robin examined the chicken carefully, picking at it with her knife and fork. The skin was golden brown and crisp, but Robin knew it was mostly fat. She wouldn't touch that. An intense frown of concentration creased her forehead as she segregated the food into different areas on her plate. When she had finished, nearly everything was on the "don't eat" side.

"Aren't you hungry, Robin?" Mrs. Wilson asked in surprise. "You're usually famished by dinnertime."

Robin winced. *Famished* was just another word for *greedy*. It was definitely time to cut back on her food intake.

"I'm on a diet," Robin explained as she handed her glass of milk to Troy. He took it without comment.

"A diet, dear?" Mrs. Wilson frowned. "You look just fine to me."

Robin let out a small gasp of exasperation. "That's what you used to say when I was fat, Mom. No matter how much of a pudge I was, you always said I looked *just fine*."

"But you did," Mrs. Wilson insisted.

"Are you saying you like me fat?" Robin asked in shock. She stared at her mother with growing resentment. "Do you actually want me to get fat again?"

Her mother looked startled. "I didn't say—"

"It's hard enough to diet," Robin went on angrily. "It would be nice if you didn't keep shoving fattening food in front of me."

Nobody spoke. Robin felt her stomach gnawing at her, and the savory smell of the chicken made her mouth water. But she was not going to eat. There was too much on her mind already. She just couldn't add one more worry, like how many pounds this dinner was going to mean. The anxiety she felt about everything else was enough to overpower the hunger.

"I'm not hungry anymore."

Robin stood up, leaving her dinner untouched, and left the room.

Six

Elizabeth grabbed her books and her shoulder bag and ran out the door just as Jessica started beeping the horn.

"Hurry up!" Jessica called out. "We'll be late for school."

"Since when do you worry about being late?" Elizabeth teased as she climbed into the Fiat.

"Oh, Liz. You must be the wittiest person in the world."

"Right." Elizabeth grinned and sank back into the seat. Her sister switched on the radio, and they sang along together for a few minutes.

"Hey," Elizabeth said as she leaned forward and lowered the sound on the radio, "that looks like Robin up ahead."

A lone figure was walking on the side of the road. Jessica slowed the car as they passed.

"Stop. Maybe she needs a ride."

Obediently Jessica stopped the car, and they waited a moment until Robin came abreast of them.

"Hi," Robin said with a faint smile. "You didn't have to stop."

"Do you want a ride to school?" Jessica asked.

Robin shook her head. "No, thanks. I need the exercise."

"Why?" Elizabeth gave an incredulous laugh. "Cheerleading practice and diving isn't enough exercise for you?"

Elizabeth expected Robin to laugh along with her. But to her surprise, Robin looked deadly serious.

"No, it's not."

"But you must be kind of worn out. It's a long walk from your house to school." Elizabeth was beginning to feel a little bit worried. There were faint circles under Robin's eyes, and her mouth had a tired, downturned slant.

"I'm fine, Liz, really," Robin insisted. She gave them both a bright smile. "I don't need a ride."

"OK," Jessica said breezily as she put the car into gear again. "See you later."

When Jessica pulled out into the road, Elizabeth cast an anxious glance back at Robin. She recalled vividly the determined expression Robin had worn when she was still heavy and had started to diet. Robin had run around the track, skipped meals, even jogged up and down the bleachers. She had been absolutely resolved.

And Robin had that same determined expression now. But there was something else, too. There was a look of desperation in her eyes.

"Is Robin on a diet again?"

Jessica shrugged. "I guess so. She's been eating naked salads for lunch. No dressing."

"But why? She's so slim already."

"Who knows?" Jessica obviously wasn't very concerned about Robin. "She wants to be slimmer, that's all."

"Why is everyone in this country so obsessed with being skinny?" Elizabeth said angrily. "It's not right. Girls and women are made to feel they're ugly if they don't look like models or like beauty pageant contestants."

"Well, models and beauty pageant contestants *look good*," Jessica said matter-of-factly.

Elizabeth made a sour face. "Beauty pageants. The whole idea makes me sick. Women being judged on their bodies. It's gross, when you think about it."

"Boy, you sure are getting carried away," Jessica said in surprise. "Don't worry about Robin. It's her business if she wants to lose weight. It doesn't make any difference to me. And it shouldn't make any difference to you."

Nodding absently, Elizabeth looked out the window. It *was* Robin's business. But that didn't settle Elizabeth's worries.

"I can sell tickets door to door in my apartment building," Annie Whitman said at lunchtime. "There are tons of kids who will want to eat ice cream!"

"Think you can sell all five hundred tickets?" Jessica teased.

"Close to it!"

Robin nodded as she wrote in her notebook. "Say something catchy like, 'Turn in this ticket for a bowl and a spoon.' "

The cheerleaders were eating lunch and chatting about the Super Sundae. Elizabeth was sitting with them as an honorary member of the committee. It was her job to find out how big their sundae had to be to set a record, and to continue to direct their publicity.

"How much do we sell the tickets for?" Cara looked inquiringly around the table.

"A dollar," Robin said firmly. "We have to make it worthwhile for us, but not too expensive for everyone who wants a share." She glanced around the table at the other girls. "And I volunteer to handle the money, too."

"Fine with me," Amy said. "I don't want that responsibility."

Robin made a small, satisfied nod. Secretly she didn't trust anyone else with the money. It wasn't that the cheerleaders weren't honest. Robin just didn't think they were very reliable. It was safer for her to take charge from the start.

"I came up with some poster designs, too," Sandy announced as she passed around some sheets of paper.

"This is great! Look, everyone."

Elizabeth held up one of Sandy's designs. It showed a huge ice-cream sundae with the cheerleaders standing on top. THREE CHEERS FOR SUPER SUNDAE the caption read. Below the picture were the details: the where, when, and why of the fund-raiser.

"Fabulous," Jessica said.

"I love it," Robin agreed.

Sandy popped a french fry into her mouth and bowed to everyone. "Thank you, my adoring public."

"Can I have one of your fries?" Cara asked.

"Sure. Here, help yourself." Sandy pushed the plate forward. "Robin?"

Robin jumped as though she'd been pinched. "No! I don't want any."

"Sorry!"

"It's just that I'm trying to stick to a diet." Robin didn't mean to snap at Sandy, but she couldn't help it. Worrying about George was making her very irritable.

Robin sighed and glanced across the table. Elizabeth was watching her steadily. There was an unmistakable question in her eyes, and a look of concern. Robin felt her cheeks flush under Elizabeth's scrutiny. Elizabeth could be very persistent if she thought a friend was upset or in trouble. But Robin didn't want anyone to know what she feared about George. She looked away quickly and gathered her books.

"I'll see you all at practice," she said. Robin stood up and hurried out of the cafeteria. It was getting to the point where she couldn't stand to see other people eat. Her stomach still growled uncomfortably at the smell of food. But she wouldn't let herself give in to her hunger. If she could only get thinner, everything else in her life would get back to normal.

Robin went out into the hall and looked around. She needed a quiet place where she could be alone to think. Robin headed for the library. Once inside, she sat at an isolated table and put her head down on her folded arms. She tried to banish all thoughts of George and Vicky from her head. She felt so tired and unhappy. Robin closed her eyes and tried to relax.

"It's time for class."

Robin jerked awake. "Was I sleeping?" she asked in surprise.

The librarian nodded, her mouth twisted disapprovingly. "You kids stay up too late," she said. "Please don't use my library as a bedroom anymore."

Robin nodded and picked up her books. She shook her head to clear the sleep out of it. She couldn't believe she had actually fallen asleep in the library. Her long morning walks must have tired her out more than she realized. And she was getting an hour less sleep than usual. But Robin knew that she had to make some sacrifices if she wanted to lose weight, and keep George.

Robin left the library and went to her last two classes of the day. After final period, as she was changing for cheerleading practice in the locker room, Robin decided to weigh herself.

The scale told her she had already lost four pounds, and Robin felt a surge of elation. In no time she would be as thin as Vicky.

"OK, let's go," Robin said briskly to the other cheerleaders. "We've got a lot of work to do."

Sandra and Jean looked up at her from where they sat on the benches, tying the laces on their sneakers. "We'll be right there," Jean said.

"Jeez, lighten up, Robin," Jessica muttered as she passed by her. "You're acting like a drill sergeant."

"I am not." Robin laughed self-consciously. "Come on. Let's get that new cheer really perfect today."

By the time the entire cheerleading squad was out on the field, Robin was already stretching out. Keeping active was the best way she knew to stop worrying about George, and the best way to ignore her hunger.

Robin kept up a grueling pace during practice, urging everyone to keep up with her. A lot of dirty looks were directed her way, but Robin didn't let them bother her. After all, she was cocaptain because she was disciplined. It was up to her to keep the group going.

"I'm finished," Jessica said, collapsing onto the ground.

"Me, too," Cara agreed, sinking down next to her.

Robin frowned. "Come on, you guys. We don't really have it down yet."

"Speak for yourself," Amy said irritably. "I know the cheer just fine."

"You're too much of a perfectionist, Robin," Sandra said, exhausted. "I think we've got it down pretty well, too."

Robin looked around at the others for support, but one by one they were sitting on the field and starting to talk.

"Well, I'm not finished," she announced. "I'm going to keep working out."

Annie let out a groan. "What are you, a masochist, Robin? I'm beat. Aren't you?"

"No," Robin lied. She took a deep breath that was almost a yawn. Her muscles felt like water. "I'm going to run some laps, and then work on the gymnastics. Anyone want to join me?"

"NO!" Jessica cried.

Robin glanced coldly at her. "Fine. I'll do it alone."

She stood where she was while the others drifted off. Annie stayed behind for a moment.

"Are you all right, Robin?" she asked. "You look pretty tired."

"I'm fine. See you tomorrow," Robin answered, forcing a smile.

Annie didn't look at all convinced, but she followed the others off the field. Robin looked around the empty playing field and then squared her shoulders. It was time to run some laps. She was going to get back into shape again, no matter what it took.

Later that evening Robin was staring blankly at a homework assignment when the telephone rang. She waited to hear if it would be for her.

"Robin!" Troy yelled. "It's George."

Robin's heart leapt, and she jumped out of her chair.

"Hi, George?" she gasped when she picked up the phone in the hall. "Where've you been? I've tried calling you so many times!"

"Sorry," he said in a tired voice. "I've really been in a crunch. Vicky and I had to study emergency procedures, and then go through an examination. It was murder. But I think we did OK."

"Have you been spending a lot of time with Vicky?" Robin bit her lip, hating herself for asking the question and for sounding so jealous. But she couldn't help herself. All she could see in her mind was George and Vicky, staying up late, laughing, talking, being drawn closer and closer together.

George paused for a moment. "Well, you know, Robin, I have to. She's my partner in class."

"Yeah, I know." Being away from George while he was with Vicky made Robin feel helpless and miserable. In fact, those feelings had been growing stronger and stronger, in spite of her efforts to organize her life. Robin felt as though she were trying to hold on to a big, floppy package. Each time she thought she had a grip on it in one spot, it got away from her somewhere else. She closed her eyes. Somehow she had to get control over her life.

"When can I see you?" she asked in a tiny voice.

"That's what I called about. I just finished this term paper, so I thought I would come up tomorrow night. I've missed you a lot."

"Me, too," Robin whispered. Her throat felt tight, as if she were going to cry. "And I'm sorry about the way I got so upset last weekend . . ."

"No, it's my fault. I overreacted, and that's one of the reasons I didn't call you before now. I've been feeling like such a jerk. But you know what I want to do?" George asked. "I want to take you out to some really fancy restaurant. Like Villa Marino."

Robin smiled. "That sounds great. I can't wait to see you, George."

"And I can't wait to see you," he replied tenderly.

"I love you."

"I love you, too," George echoed.

Robin frowned. She wondered if George's answer was too automatic. Did he still really love her? If only she could be sure!

"Robin? Are you still there?"

"Yes," she said slowly. "So, when will you be here?"

"How about six o'clock?" George suggested. "We'll go out and have a really great time, just the two of us."

"OK. I'll see you tomorrow night."

After she hung up the phone, Robin made a decision. She was going to look absolutely perfect when George arrived tomorrow night. He wouldn't be able to think about Vicky at all.

Seven

Robin stepped out of the shower and toweled herself off briskly. A quick glance in the mirror told her she was definitely getting slimmer. The roundness in her cheeks was beginning to leave. She smiled with relief and stepped onto the scale. She had lost eight pounds in just two weeks. The diet was working.

But there was still a long way to go, she reminded herself. Just because she had lost a few pounds didn't mean she could stop. It wouldn't take much to put the weight right back on.

Robin wrapped the towel around herself tightly and began to put on her makeup, standing back from the mirror once in a while to get the full effect of her efforts. Her eyes looked huge and her cheekbones stood out dramatically.

George won't be able to think about Vicky for a second tonight, Robin told herself happily. George would only have eyes and thoughts for her.

For a moment Robin wondered if George had noticed the weight she had put on in recent months. He was clearly impressed with Vicky, who was very slim. Frowning, Robin hurried into her bedroom and began to look through her wardrobe.

Just the night before, Robin had completely reorganized her closet. All of her clothes were evenly spaced to keep them from wrinkling. The shirts and blouses were hung together next to her skirts, and on the other side of the closet were her dresses. She had even arranged them by color, too. Keeping things neat and organized helped her feel more in control of things and gave her a nice feeling of satisfaction.

First Robin tried on a short white skirt with a white blouse. But she knew that light colors tended to make a person appear heavier. She wasn't at all satisfied with the way she looked in the outfit. Shaking her head, Robin stripped it off and took a black knit tank dress off its hanger.

The dress was better, but the more Robin studied her reflection, the more worried she became. The clingy knit didn't hide a thing. Every little bulge or wobble would show. She bit back an angry mutter and flicked through the hangers for something else.

Finally Robin settled on a forget-me-not blue skirt and a pink V-necked sweater. The colors were fresh and cheerful and brought a sparkle to her eyes. She stepped into a pair of blue sandals and examined herself in the mirror for the last time.

She still thought she looked too heavy. But what she had on was the most flattering outfit she could find. She smoothed the skirt over her hips and frowned. Maybe George wouldn't notice her weight. She would have to make sure he didn't.

"Robin! George is here!" Mrs. Wilson called from downstairs.

"Already?" Robin gasped, checking her watch. She ran a brush through her hair quickly and left the room.

George was waiting at the bottom of the stairs, and he looked up when he heard her footsteps. A warm smile lit his face.

"Hey, gorgeous," he said. "You really look great, you know that?"

Robin felt her stomach flip-flop at the compliment. She ran down and hugged him tight. Her decision to take control of her life was paying off. George was noticing her, now.

"Hi," she breathed. "I'm so glad to see you."

"Me, too," George said, holding her close. "Ready to go?"

She laughed out of sheer relief. "Ready."

As he took her hand and looked into her eyes, Robin knew again that her hunger was worth this attention.

I dare you to think of Vicky tonight, she told him silently.

"Let's go," George said.

As they drove to Villa Marino George talked about the term paper he had just finished for a political science class. Robin relished just being near him. Vicky was far away, and Robin planned on keeping her there. The most important thing was not to talk about the flying class.

"How did that fund-raising thing go?" George asked when they were seated at the restaurant. "Did you make a lot of money?"

Robin was startled. "It hasn't happened yet. It's not for a couple of weeks, still."

"Oh." George looked sheepish. "I guess I thought it was already over."

"I guess you weren't paying very close attention when I was telling you about it," Robin said lightly. But she felt stung. Usually George kept track of everything she was involved in. That was one of the nicest things about him. Now her life seemed to be an unimportant afterthought for him.

He's got other stuff on his mind, she realized unhappily. She didn't want to think about what, or who, might be distracting George from her.

She concentrated on the menu and tried not to let the hurt show.

"You haven't asked me anything about flying yet."

"Oh, you know what?" Robin said, in an attempt to change the subject. "I was reading that book you gave me for my birthday, the science fiction one about nuclear war. It was really intense."

George nodded. "I know. I read it, too. I was telling Vi—"

"What are you going to have?" Robin cut in desperately. "Here's the waiter."

"Ummm . . ." George frowned at the menu. "You go ahead and order."

Robin's mouth watered at the luscious-sounding entrées. She had hardly touched a bite all day, so she felt entitled to a good dinner. Of course, just being with George was enough of a reward, but she *was* really hungry. "I'll have linguine with clam sauce," she decided. "And a Caesar salad."

"And I'll have stuffed mushrooms for an appetizer and lasagna," George said.

When the waiter had gone, Robin picked up her water glass and sipped from it. She had to find a way to keep the conversation from flying and Vicky. "This is pretty nice," she said.

George looked closely at her. "Is something wrong?"

73

"No. What could be wrong?"

"I don't know. Are you worried about this flying class I'm taking?"

Robin's cheeks flushed. "I—"

"Because I'll be totally safe, you know. I'm not going to choke up or freeze or anything like that. I'm getting all that anxiety about the accident completely out of the way."

Unexpectedly, Robin felt angry. He didn't even realize that she might be worried about their relationship. It seemed very insensitive of him. In fact, he had been very insensitive a *lot* lately. She wasn't just being defensive, she was sure of that. George just wasn't considering her feelings the way he used to.

"I'm not at all worried about you crashing again," Robin said firmly.

"Then what is it?" George insisted.

Robin made an effort to smile cheerfully. "Nothing. I'm just hungry, that's all."

"OK." George smiled at her and cleared his throat. "Listen, I have to tell you something. I'm really sorry, but I won't be able to come home next Friday."

Robin's smile faded. "Why not?"

"Well, I promised Vicky I'd drive her to her parents' house. She doesn't have a car, so I offered to take her. She invited you to come along, but I remembered you said you didn't like her very much, so I told Vicky you would be busy."

A sick sensation wobbled through Robin's body. She stared at George without speaking. Her face felt hot.

"I only offered to drive her because she's been such a great partner in class, and she's really helped me a lot," George went on defensively. "I wanted to tell you right away, so you wouldn't be disappointed later. In case you were going to make plans or something."

The waiter chose that moment to bring their first course. Robin stared down at the oily lettuce and grated cheese on her plate and felt a wave of disgust. George popped a steaming mushroom cap into his mouth and chewed it hungrily.

Robin picked up her fork and speared a crouton. But she couldn't bring herself to eat it. Smelling the food, even looking at it, made her feel sick. She put the fork down and pushed her plate away.

"What's wrong with it?" George asked.

"Nothing. I don't want it."

"But you just ordered it." George sounded puzzled and a little bit hurt.

"I don't want it anymore. I changed my mind."

"In five minutes you changed your mind?" George asked, a sarcastic edge to his voice.

"That's right," Robin shot back.

He looked coldly at her, obviously trying hard to stifle a sharp retort. Then he sighed. "Don't eat it, then."

Robin could feel the sparkle rapidly fade out of their evening. She swallowed the rest of her water and looked around for the waiter.

"Is this about Vicky?" George asked suddenly.

Robin's gaze flicked across his face. "That's very perceptive of you."

"Are you upset because I said you wouldn't want to go? Because I assumed you wouldn't?"

"You're right, I wouldn't," Robin replied angrily. "I just wish you wouldn't be so excited about going."

A frown creased George's forehead. "I don't understand why you don't like Vicky. She likes you. And there's absolutely no reason to be jealous of her."

Robin let out a short, dry laugh and looked away.

"Come on! I love *you*, Robin. What could make you think I don't?"

A dozen possibilities raced through Robin's head, but she didn't mention them. The lack of phone calls, the fascination with Vicky, his not remembering her important plans. She pleated the napkin in her lap and tried hard to stay calm.

"Come on," George repeated. "Why don't—"

The waiter returned with their entrées, and George broke off in embarrassment. Before the waiter could put Robin's plate of linguine on the table, she held up her hand.

"I don't want it anymore," she said. "I just want some more water."

The waiter looked surprised. "Was the salad—"

"I just don't want it anymore," Robin said firmly.

There was an awkward silence as the waiter cleared the table of Robin's dishes. George sat staring at his plate of lasagna. His cheeks were flushed.

"That was a nice scene," George whispered hoarsely when the waiter was gone.

Robin closed her eyes. Their whole date was turning into a nightmare. The bickering and sarcasm made her feel physically sick. George said he loved her, but she knew it was only a matter of time before he left her. A few more weeks with Vicky, and Robin would be history.

"Robin," George said pleadingly, "what's *wrong*? Why won't you eat?"

"I'm not hungry," she insisted.

"Are you still upset about Vicky? Because there's *really* nothing to worry about," George continued. "I *love* you, Robin."

Robin raised her head quickly and glared at him. "Well, you sure have a funny way of showing it!"

"Listen," George said angrily, leaning across the table toward her, "just because we're going out doesn't give you the right to run my life, Robin. You know how important this flying class is to me, and if I want to be friends with my partner, I will. I'm going to Vicky's house and that's it."

"Fine," Robin whispered, trying hard to keep her lips from trembling. That awful helpless feeling was flooding back over her, and Robin didn't know what to do or to say.

George began to eat his lasagna in angry silence, and Robin watched him miserably from across the table. After a few minutes of mutual silence, George put down his fork.

"This is crazy. Let's just leave," he muttered.

Robin didn't say a word. George flagged down the waiter and asked for the check. Robin refused to meet George's eyes. She thought she might burst into tears if she did.

By the time they got back to her house, Robin was completely depressed. In spite of all her dieting, her organizing, her efforts to keep things managed and controlled, she was losing George to a beautiful girl. When he stopped the car, Robin opened her door in silence.

"I wish you would trust me more," George said quietly.

Robin just shook her head and got out of the car. George leaned over to shut the door and then drove off.

Sniffling, Robin went inside the house and up to her room. She peeled off her clothes, opened the closet, and let out a gasp. Her mother had put away some newly laundered clothes, and Robin's scheme was all messed up.

"Mom!" Robin called out furiously. "Come here!"

Running footsteps sounded in the hall. Mrs. Wilson hurried into the room. "What?" she asked anxiously. "Are you OK?"

Robin whirled around and glared at her mother. "Look what you did to my closet!" she cried.

"What?"

"You wrecked everything." Robin turned and began to rearrange the hangers. "How could you?"

Mrs. Wilson took a step toward the closet. "I don't know what you're talking about. I just hung up some clothes from the laundry."

"In the future don't, OK? I had everything organized the way I like it, and now I have to completely redo it all."

Her mother stared at her in amazement. "Robin, how can you be so upset about such a trivial thing? I thought you had hurt yourself, but you're snapping at me just because I hung up your clothes."

"You don't understand. Just forget it. I'm sorry I snapped at you."

"Robin—"

"Forget it, Mom," Robin said testily. "I can redo it."

Mrs. Wilson frowned worriedly and then shook her head. "Aren't you feeling well?"

"I'm fine." Robin turned away from the closet. "I'm going to bed now. I'll see you in the morning."

Mrs. Wilson's face betrayed her anxiety, but she left the room. Robin curled up on her bed and stared into space. Her stomach was hollow and empty.

So was her heart.

Eight

When Robin went down to breakfast on Monday morning, she was greeted by the unmistakable smell of pancakes and bacon. Her mother was at the stove.

"Good morning, Robin," Mrs. Wilson said, flipping a pancake with her spatula.

Robin watched her mother suspiciously. "Is that for you and the boys?"

"Yes, but I made some for you, too."

Robin clenched her jaw. "I'm not having any."

Mrs. Wilson turned around and smiled at her daughter. "Oh, come on, honey. Pancakes with real syrup? This used to be your favorite breakfast, remember?"

"No wonder I was so fat!" Robin retorted. "You made me fat by constantly stuffing me full of things like pancakes and bacon."

Her mother blinked rapidly and turned back to the stove. Robin heard her mother sniff, and a heavy feeling of remorse settled on her. She had just woken up from a deep, long sleep, but she still felt as tired as when she had gone to bed. Sighing, Robin pulled out a chair and sat down at the table. She propped her chin on her hand.

"I just don't know what's gotten into you lately," Mrs. Wilson said tearfully. "I never see you eat anything anymore! I'm getting really worried, Robin."

Robin sighed again. "I do eat, Mom. I eat a lot at school. Don't worry about me."

"Are you sure? You eat a big lunch?"

"Sure, Mom," Robin lied.

She picked up the newspaper and pretended to read while her mother went back to the stove and finished the pancakes. Robin poured herself a cup of black coffee and tried to ignore the enticing smell of food. The odors brought with them a wave of nostalgia. Things had not always been unhappy when she was overweight. Robin could remember plenty of warm, cozy Saturday morning breakfasts with her family; she could remember plenty of evenings when she and her mother had sipped hot cocoa with marshmallows and talked about their dreams and hopes.

Even as recently as a year ago, food had been the source of a lot of happiness. Robin could remember her last birthday cake—chocolate with marzipan frosting and raspberry jam filling—as though she had eaten it just yesterday. Her friends had screamed with laughter at her birthday party. Life had seemed so much easier and more comfortable back then. No one made demands on her, no one put pressure on her to achieve this or choose that. It seemed to Robin that she and her mother had both smiled a lot more in the past than they did now.

For a moment Robin considered asking for a very small serving of breakfast. One pancake without butter or syrup, and one small piece of lean bacon wouldn't do that much damage. And her eating would make her mother less anxious.

But then Robin realized she was not even hungry. In the past few days it hadn't been taking all that much willpower to go without eating. And now, this morning, she had no appetite at all. A flicker of fear raced through Robin. She lined up the salt and pepper shakers with the sugar bowl. Somehow, it helped calm her. *I am fine*, she told herself firmly. *I'll start eating again when I've lost enough weight.*

"I have to get to school," she said, standing up.

"You'll have a nice big lunch, won't you?"

Robin nodded. "Sure, Mom."

When she got out on the street, Robin cast a wistful glance at her bus stop. It was so tempting to wait for the bus. Her legs felt as if they were getting heavier, even though she was getting lighter. But Robin made herself turn away and start to walk. Soon she was in the rhythm of her stride. When she arrived at school, she felt surprised. She had been walking in a sort of daze.

A strange, uncomfortable feeling crept over her. It made her nervous that she had spaced out so completely. Frowning, Robin opened her locker and tried to concentrate on what books she needed for her first class.

"Hi, Robin!" a bubbly voice called to her as she stared blankly into her locker.

Robin looked over her shoulder and saw Lois Waller pushing through a crowd of students. Lois's round cheeks were flushed with excitement, and her eyes were sparkling.

"Hi, Lois," Robin said faintly.

"Listen, I know I'm the biggest klutz in gym." Lois rolled her eyes in a gesture of good-humored self-mockery. "But I really like volleyball, and I want to help with the fund-raiser."

Robin nodded. She wasn't really paying attention to what Lois was saying. Looking at Lois was too much like looking in a mirror to the past. She had once been just as chubby as Lois was now, and she hated to be reminded of it.

"I was wondering if I could help sell tickets for the Super Sundae." An impish grin came to her lips. "I could even buy a bunch of them myself. I *love* ice cream!"

Robin looked at Lois and felt completely baffled. How could Lois be so cheerful and enthusiastic? Didn't she worry about her weight? It didn't make any sense at all that Lois could actually joke about eating a lot of ice cream.

You'd think she would be embarrassed about being so fat, Robin told herself.

But Lois didn't seem embarrassed at all. Her face was animated and open. She carefully redid the bow on her ponytail while she waited for Robin's answer.

"Yeah, sure, Lois," Robin replied, looking back into her locker. It bothered her that Lois's hair was so pretty. "It's OK with me. I can give you a roll of tickets at lunch."

"Great. I think the Super Sundae is going to be so much fun! See you at lunch."

As Lois walked away through the crowd Robin absently stroked her own cheek. It felt hollow, nothing like Lois's round cheek would feel. It could be that way if she weren't careful, though. Robin intended to be very careful.

Right before lunch, Robin gave Annie the tickets for Lois. She avoided the cafeteria altogether. Instead, she went to the administration office to talk to the principal about permission to use the football field for the Super Sundae. Mr. Cooper was already enthusiastic about the project, and he pledged his full support to the cheerleaders. Robin left the office feeling satisfied with her work. She knew it was up to her to keep the Super Sundae on track, and she knew she was doing a good job.

"Hey, Jessica!" she called as she saw her cocaptain in the hallway.

Jessica stopped and looked over her shoulder. Her eyebrows went up lazily. "Hi, Robin."

"I just checked with Mr. Cooper about using the football field," Robin said in a businesslike tone. "We're all set for one o'clock. I promised him he'd get to make a speech."

"Oh, great, Robin," Jessica said huffily. "That's all we need to make the Super Sundae a big dud. A big boring speech by 'Chrome Dome.' "

Robin felt a flash of anger but repressed it. She didn't want to argue with Jessica. It was too draining emotionally.

"Well, at least we have the permission we need," she said quietly. "I'm sorry you're so upset about it." Robin turned to walk away.

"Hey, I didn't mean anything!"

Robin stopped and turned back. Jessica looked exasperated.

"That's OK. I'll see you later." Taking the heat for doing a good job was just something she'd have to get used to. But she could handle it. She would just work that much harder to show everyone how easily she could deal with any little problem they threw her way.

After school, Robin took a bus to the community pool for diving practice. She changed into her bathing suit in the locker room and stopped in front of the mirror. Her tank suit was loose. Robin put her hands on her waist. She had already gone down by one size, and that was a good sign. Maybe she could go down another size. Then she would really be in shape. Smiling, Robin went out to the pool for some warm-up dives.

"Robin!" Dina was waiting by the ladder as Robin swam over to the pool's edge. "Can I see you for a minute?"

"Sure, Coach," Robin said, hanging onto the rail.

Dina jerked her head to one side. "Over here, OK?"

Robin knew that Dina was going to ask her about her weight. She didn't want to get out of the pool, but she had no choice. Reluctantly, she pulled herself up the ladder and followed her coach out of earshot of the other divers.

"Robin, I've noticed you've lost a lot of weight lately," Dina began.

"Not a lot, really."

Dina shook her head. "Well, I don't know. But as an athlete in training, you shouldn't be dieting without a doctor's supervision."

"I know."

"*Do* you have a doctor's supervision?"

"I keep meaning to make an appointment," Robin explained hastily. "I will as soon as I can."

Dina looked at her with a steady, insistent gaze. "How many calories a day are you eating?"

"Oh, well, I'm not really counting *that* carefully," Robin said evasively. She hugged herself and tried not to shiver as a cloud crossed the sun.

"All I'm saying is that I hope you're being sensible." Dina frowned. "I hope you're getting adequate nutrition, and enough calories to support you through diving practice and cheerleading."

"No problem, Dina," Robin said with a big smile. She pulled on the nylon of her bathing suit and shrugged. "It's this suit, too. It's old and baggy. You know how the chlorine takes all the stretch out. I'm fine."

"Well, your diving isn't fine. You seem as if you're only about seventy-five percent there. Have you been tired lately?"

"No! I'm just warming up," Robin insisted. "Really. You'll see."

"I'll be watching," Dina said warningly. "And if I think you're not taking care of yourself, I'm coming after you."

Robin smiled again to reassure her coach. She knew Dina was concerned about her, but Robin could take care of herself. She could take care of everything—the Super Sundae, pressure from her family, George, everything. Now she just had to convince Dina of that.

She stepped onto the springboard and readied herself for a jackknife. As she took a deep breath a wave of exhaustion washed over her. Dina was right. She wasn't in top form. But Robin could compensate for that by concentrating harder. She squared her shoulders and strode to the end of the board to dive.

For the next forty-five minutes Robin pushed herself further and further. She knew Dina was keeping a close watch on her, and she didn't want to betray the bone-deep tiredness she felt. She was also beginning to feel terribly cold.

Just push through it, she ordered herself silently.

She waited longer and longer between each dive before climbing out of the pool. Her fingers were beginning to feel numb. Usually she didn't feel chilled, even after a couple of hours in the pool. But today she shivered each time she climbed, dripping, out of the water.

"Robin?" Dina called.

Robin held herself rigid to keep from trembling. "Yeah?"

"Go home," Dina said tersely.

Robin's first reaction was to protest, but she felt overwhelmed by fatigue. Nodding gloomily, she turned and went back to the locker room. As she reached for the lock on her locker, she saw that her hand was shaking violently. She tried to control it but couldn't. Frightened, Robin squeezed both hands together and sat down on the bench.

I need a hot shower, she told herself firmly. *That's all it is. Then I'll be fine.*

After cheerleading practice on Tuesday, Jessica picked up Elizabeth and the two of them drove around the town, putting up posters advertising the Super Sundae.

"We should be calling this the gorgeous gorge yourself gourmet gala." Jessica giggled.

Elizabeth grinned and held a poster up to the telephone pole. "Go ahead and staple," she ordered. "Why can't you be that creative in school?"

"I reserve my talents for more important things, Liz," Jessica replied as she punched a staple through the poster. "Or we could call it General Wilson's Super Organized Sundae," she added sarcastically.

"Oh, come on. Robin isn't being that bossy, is she?" Elizabeth asked seriously.

Jessica rolled her eyes and headed back to the Fiat. "Are you kidding? Today at lunch she was grilling Sandy as if she were conducting the Spanish Inquisition. 'When will the kiddie pools arrive? Who's washing them out to make sure they're clean? What time are the ice-cream trucks coming?' I wish Robin would lighten up!"

"Do you think something's wrong?" Elizabeth asked.

Jessica's description didn't sound like Robin

at all. But Elizabeth knew her sister wasn't exaggerating. Lately a lot of people had noticed how irritable and strange Robin had been acting. And her desire to plan everything down to the most minor detail was driving the cheerleaders crazy.

Robin's obsessiveness was becoming apparent in other areas, too. Todd had told Elizabeth that the day before he had sat in Robin's usual seat in French class. Seats were not assigned, so Todd had really done nothing wrong. But Robin had "thrown a fit," in Todd's words. That didn't sound like the Robin Elizabeth knew.

"I don't know what's wrong with her," Jessica said huffily. "Maybe she got body-snatched and it's really an alien we're dealing with."

Elizabeth smiled, but she didn't think what Jessica had said was very humorous. It sounded too close to the truth. Robin *was* acting like a different person.

"And this dieting thing!" Jessica threw her hands up in a gesture of disgust. "You can hardly eat a carrot stick in her presence without her getting all weird about it."

"Yeah, I noticed." Elizabeth got into the car and waited patiently while Jessica checked her reflection in the rearview mirror.

"And that's not all," Jessica continued as she started the engine. "She doesn't even *look* good! In fact, I think she looks terrible! Did you notice her face? She's got big circles under her eyes and her cheeks are so hollow, it looks as if she's starving."

Elizabeth suddenly felt frightened. The word *starving* had sent a wave of concern through her.

"Do you think she's actually starving herself?"

"Who knows?" Jessica sighed. "All I do know is that Robin Wilson is driving me nuts."

"I wonder if I should talk to her about it," Elizabeth mused. "I mean, if she's not eating anything, she's not dieting. She's fasting."

Jessica shook her head. "Forget it, Liz. You can't say *anything* to her about food."

"That's the whole problem. She won't even admit she's taking this diet thing too far." Elizabeth wished there was some way she could help her friend—before it was too late!

Nine

Robin snapped open her second can of diet soda and took a long swallow. When she put the can down, she looked around the cafeteria. For some reason the lunchtime crowd seemed noisier than usual but, at the same time, harder to hear. Every once in a while Robin became aware of a faint ringing in her ears.

Ignoring a tingle of uneasiness, Robin pulled her math book toward her and opened it. The geometry problems she tried to concentrate on became just a jumble of lines, arcs, angles, and numbers. She was supposed to be calculating the volume of a cone, but she couldn't hang on to the first part of the equation while she grappled with the second part. The Greek letters seemed to squiggle all over the page.

Robin pushed the book away and pressed one hand to her eyes. Then she took another deep swallow of her soda. The bubbles seared a path to her stomach.

"Robin, aren't you having anything to eat?" Elizabeth asked, sitting down beside her.

"No, I'm not hungry." Robin sat back in her chair and took a shaky breath. She felt so tired. All she wanted to do was take a nap. Her muscles ached, too. She moved her shoulders uncomfortably and winced.

Elizabeth watched her worriedly. "Robin, are you sure you're not taking your diet too far? I'm not trying to be nosy. I'm just worried."

"No, I'm . . ." Robin's voice trailed off. She wished Elizabeth would leave her alone. Robin turned her gaze away, hoping Elizabeth would take the hint. She spotted Lois and her boyfriend sitting at a table not far away.

Doesn't it bother him that Lois is heavy? Robin asked herself.

It obviously didn't. Lois showed him something written in her notebook, and they both laughed. To all who saw them, they were the perfect picture of a couple in love.

Robin let her eyes wander and saw Enid Rollins come into the cafeteria. Enid was a very sweet girl, but Robin had never felt comfortable around her. Spending time with Enid always reminded Robin of the way George had deceived her.

And he could be doing the same thing to me right now, she thought unhappily.

History repeated itself. That was a fact of life. All of the pressures that Robin had dealt with in the last year could resurface in an instant.

"I'll see you later." Robin left Elizabeth sitting at the table and hurried out of the cafeteria.

When she was in the hall, she stopped. Her head was swimming. She didn't know if she was just tired or confused. Robin grabbed a door handle to steady herself until the wash of darkness cleared away from her eyes. She felt cold and then hot and then cold again.

A tingle of fear raced up her spine.

This is crazy, she told herself.

She concentrated on putting one foot ahead of the other, and slowly she walked down the corridor to the girls' locker room. Robin went over to the scale and weighed herself. She had lost a few more pounds.

In fact, a few more than she had planned to lose. She caught sight of herself in the mirror. Her clothes hung on her like limp rags, and her face was gaunt and pale.

Robin let her breath out slowly and sat down on a bench.

"Get a grip," she said out loud.

Robin had to take several more deep breaths before she felt strong enough to stand up, but it was difficult to get enough air. There was a deep ache in her chest. Robin fought down a feeling of panic. She had to take charge of the situation. Her diet was as out of control as the rest of her life. There was no use in pretending any longer that there was nothing wrong. It was time to eat something.

Robin made her way back to the cafeteria. She stood on line and breathed shallowly through her mouth. The steaming basins of food behind the counter made her feel sick. Huge mounds of baked ziti in tomato sauce, heaps of peas and corn, row upon row of hamburgers, quivering dishes of Jell-O. It was horrible to look at.

"Can I have a small dish of corn?" Robin said hoarsely to the server.

"That's all?"

Robin pressed her lips together. "And a hamburger."

She watched, mesmerized, while the server spooned the corn onto a plate and plopped a steaming hamburger into a bun.

I can't eat that, Robin realized frantically.

She took the plate like a zombie and walked to the cash register. She couldn't even look at the food she was buying, but she knew that somehow she had to make herself eat it.

"Are you all right?" the cashier asked, giving Robin a suspicious look.

"I'm—I'm just tired." Robin fumbled with her purse, paid, and hurried away.

Across the cafeteria she saw her fellow cheerleaders sitting around a crowded, noisy table.

There was no way she could sit with them while she ate. Lately eating had become an intensely private, personal act. She could not bear the thought of anyone seeing her eat, of anyone talking to her about food, of anyone asking her why she was eating so little.

Feeling like some sort of fugitive, Robin slipped into a chair at an empty table by the wall and put her tray down. The hamburger squatted like a toad in front of her. As she looked at it a wave of nausea rose up in her throat. Robin could feel her body start to tremble.

I have to eat it. Robin closed her eyes and picked up the hamburger. The feel of the bun on her fingertips was strange.

She couldn't put it in her mouth. She just couldn't eat it. She pushed her chair back, stumbled blindly across the cafeteria, and ran out to the girls' bathroom.

She stopped before a sink and gripped it tightly. Her breath was coming in short, ragged gasps, and her ears were buzzing. She didn't know what was happening to her, but she tried desperately to control her fear. Gradually she fought back the nausea and began to breathe more easily. She closed her eyes for a moment, and when she opened them, she stared at her reflection. What she saw was a stranger.

Robin turned on the faucet and splashed some water on her face. The cool water made her feel more alert. She cupped some water in her hand, raised it to her face, and rinsed the sour taste from her mouth. Then she wiped her chin with the back of her hand. Her color was not coming back.

Robin knew that in spite of all her efforts in the past few weeks to take control of her life, everything had gone haywire. While she was trying her hardest to control the forces around her, they were controlling her. Lately Robin had been feeling as if she were chasing something that, in spite of her best efforts, was always just out of reach. Was it love? Robin put her hands to her head. George would fall in love with Vicky. And there was nothing she could do to stop it.

A part of Robin knew that she was making herself sick. And that was just one more reason for George to want out of their relationship. If Robin couldn't do a simple thing like dieting without messing up, she certainly couldn't do anything as complex as survive a long-distance relationship.

Well, if George really didn't want her, there was no point in keeping to the diet. But what had just happened in the cafeteria had terrified her. Just sitting with a hamburger in her hands had been enough to bring on an anxiety attack.

Robin tried to pull herself together. Maybe she ought to go to the nurse. If she told the nurse how sick she felt, maybe she could just go home. The plan gave Robin enough confidence to go back out into the hall.

"Robin!"

Robin flinched and stopped.

Elizabeth hurried up behind her. "I've been looking for you," she said in a low voice. She stepped in front of Robin and looked closely at her face. "Are you feeling OK? You look terrible. You're so white!"

"I'm just tired," Robin whispered.

"I'm taking you to the nurse's office," Elizabeth said, taking Robin's arm.

"No!" Suddenly Robin didn't like the idea at all. She shook her head vehemently. "I'm really OK, Liz. I'm just—"

Robin broke off as a flood of tears threatened to overcome her. She wanted so badly to tell someone how frightened she was. But how could she? It was too awful to admit that she was afraid her boyfriend was cheating on her. And it was too embarrassing to admit that she was afraid her diet had gotten way out of control. Elizabeth was a very sympathetic person, but Robin just couldn't talk about her problems with anyone. How could she when she herself didn't even understand what was happening to her? Her life was shattering into a hundred different pieces.

"Just what?" Elizabeth asked, still holding Robin's arm.

"It's the Super Sundae," Robin explained finally. "It's happening this weekend, and there's still so much to get organized. I'm under a lot of pressure, that's all."

"Really?"

Robin kept her smile fixed in place. "Really. This afternoon the cheerleaders are going to City Hall to have a picture taken with Mayor Santelli for *The Sweet Valley News*. I guess I'm pretty nervous about it."

Elizabeth released Robin's arm. She looked very uneasy. "OK. I'm just worried about you, Robin. You look as if you've lost too much weight."

"Pressure. That's all it is."

It was all Robin could do to convince Elizabeth that she was fine. The effort was exhausting her. As soon as Elizabeth walked away Robin stepped back into the girls' room. She had to sit down again and pull herself together. Her world was quickly coming apart at the seams.

Jessica ran up the steps of City Hall with Cara, Maria, and Amy close behind. The other cheerleaders followed.

Jessica pushed open the big double doors, and the girls filed into the cavernous marble lobby. "This is what I call a photo opportunity! How do I look, Cara?"

Cara grinned. "You look like a Miss America

contestant. Any minute now, I bet you'll break into a baton twirling routine."

"Ha, ha." Jessica smiled sweetly. "You're wearing your uniform, too. So is everyone else."

"Look, here comes the photographer," Sandy whispered.

Jessica looked toward the door. A young man dressed in funky clothes and draped all over with camera equipment was walking toward them.

"Are you from *The Sweet Valley News*?" Jessica asked.

He grinned. "Right. And let me guess. You're the cheerleaders."

"You're so perceptive." Jessica flashed him a flirtatious smile. The guy might have looked a little disheveled, but he was cute. "And I bet you take good pictures, too."

"Pretty good," he agreed as he shifted his equipment from one shoulder to the other.

Jessica stepped closer. "Do you think I might be photogenic? I mean, in your professional opinion?"

"Probably." The photographer winked. "I'll meet you upstairs," he said and walked off.

"What was all that about?" Amy demanded.

Jessica smiled. "You never know. If you want to be a model, you have to have professional pictures. You know, a portfolio. And that's expensive."

"Who said anything about *you* being a model?" Amy rolled her eyes.

"Just a thought." Jessica smiled as if she were in possession of some fabulous secret plan. "Come on, let's get going!"

"We take this elevator," Maria announced, pointing to the left.

Jessica looked with envy at Maria. Jessica wished *her* father had stayed in the race for the mayor's seat. When the mayoral campaign had first gotten under way, Mr. Wakefield had been one of Mr. Santelli's legal advisors. Then a series of malicious rumors forced Mr. Santelli to drop out of the race. Jessica's father had decided to run in his place, but when he discovered that Mr. Santelli had been framed, Mr. Wakefield stepped down so Maria's father could run again. Now Maria was the mayor's daughter, and her picture was often in the paper. It would have been so much fun, Jessica thought wistfully, to be Jessica Wakefield, Mayor Wakefield's daughter.

But she'd be on the front page of tomorrow's morning paper, and that would be a thrill. She knew that one of these days she would make her mark. Just how she was going to make it wasn't so clear yet. But having some professional photographs taken would be a good first step. From there, anything could happen.

"Hey. Where's Robin?" Annie asked.

"She said she was meeting us here, didn't

she?" Sandy looked around the lobby but Robin wasn't there.

Maria looked anxious. "My dad only has a few minutes to spare. He's pretty busy."

Jessica felt irritated. Robin was late, and that would mess up a perfect opportunity for free publicity.

"We'll take the picture without Robin, if we have to," Jessica said firmly. "It's just tough luck for her if she misses it."

"That's not fair," Annie said. "The Super Sundae was Robin's idea."

Jessica glared at Annie. "It was everybody's idea."

"Come on, let's just go up," Maria urged.

Annie folded her arms stubbornly. "No. We have to wait for—"

"Here she comes," Jean said excitedly.

All eyes turned to the door. Robin saw the cheerleaders by the elevator. "Sorry," she gasped as she came up to them. "I forgot what time we were supposed to be here."

"Forget it," Jessica said sharply. She gave Robin a critical look. Her cocaptain's cheerleading uniform looked about three sizes too large for her. "Where did you get that uniform, anyway?"

Robin blushed. "This is my regular uniform." She folded her arms across her chest as though trying to hide or protect herself.

Jessica met Robin's eyes and felt a strange

twisting sensation in her stomach. Robin looked terrible. Part of Jessica was angry that their group photo with the mayor would look lousy because of Robin. But another part of her was really worried. Robin looked as if she were going to drop dead from exhaustion at any moment.

"Robin—" she began.

"Let's just get going." Robin sounded faint and breathless.

The cheerleaders were silent for a moment. Then Maria cleared her throat. "Well, let's go upstairs."

Robin nodded as the elevator doors slid open. "Right. I'll be glad when this whole thing is over with," she muttered.

Jessica bit her lip. She wasn't really sure what Robin had meant by that last statement. But suddenly she had a feeling there was more than just the Super Sundae on Robin's mind.

Ten

After lunch on Sunday, Elizabeth hunted through the piles of books and papers on her desk until she found a small reporter's notebook. "I'm ready!" she called out, slinging her camera over her shoulder.

"I'm not!" Jessica called back.

Elizabeth went to the door of the bathroom that connected their rooms. Jessica was experimenting with hairstyles and was making a ponytail on top of her head.

"That looks really dumb," Elizabeth teased.

Jessica shot her a sour look. "Thanks. That's very supportive of you, Liz."

Elizabeth laughed and reached out to tousle her twin's hair. "It looks great the way you always wear it. Come on. We don't want to be late."

The smile on Jessica's face made Elizabeth laugh again. Jessica always *did* want to be late in order to make a more dramatic entrance.

"Oh, all right." Jessica ran her lip gloss once more around her mouth, blew her reflection a kiss, and then followed Elizabeth downstairs.

"Have fun," Mrs. Wakefield said. "You've got a perfect day for the Super Sundae. We'll be over later to get our ice cream."

Elizabeth and Jessica waved and ran out to the car. On the way to the school football field Jessica chattered on and on about what she would say to the reporters. Elizabeth listened absently. She was thinking about the story she would write about the Super Sundae for *The Oracle.*

"Everyone's here already," Jessica said as she parked the Fiat.

Elizabeth could see the other cheerleaders and several other students already gathered out on the field. She hitched her camera and her bag over her shoulder and hurried out to join them.

"We've got all the pools ready," Sandy announced when the twins were within earshot. "We arranged them in a pyramid, just the way we planned."

Elizabeth took the lens cap off her camera and started to shoot. Jessica put her hands on her hips and looked around. "There aren't any reporters here yet. I thought there would be a TV crew."

"They'll be here soon," Jean assured her from where she was arranging stacks of napkins, spoons, and bowls on a big table. Annie was busy decorating another table with streamers and balloons.

Elizabeth wandered around to watch and take pictures of the preparations. A third table was loaded with extra-large-size containers of chocolate syrup, marshmallow sauce, cherries, and whipped topping. Around her, members of the school board, the principal, and the gym teachers were talking excitedly.

"Mr. Cooper?" Elizabeth said. "Could I get a statement from you about the Super Sundae event?"

Chrome Dome Cooper gave her a proud smile. "Well, Elizabeth, I can honestly say that this varsity cheerleading squad has been one of the most creative, energetic, and school-spirited squads Sweet Valley High has had in a long time. I—" He broke off suddenly.

Elizabeth turned to see what had caught his attention. A TV crew had just parked its van at the edge of the football field. Mr. Cooper was watching eagerly.

"And I think it's a wonderful event. Excuse me, Elizabeth."

Elizabeth smiled wryly as Mr. Cooper rushed away to meet the TV crew. Everyone wanted to be in the spotlight! Jessica was zeroing in on the reporters as fast as Chrome Dome!

"You lost your story?"

Elizabeth turned around and smiled up into Todd's eyes. "Hey, I was wondering when you'd get here."

"I guess school papers just aren't as glamorous as TV news, right?" Todd laughed and kissed her. "You can interview me, if you want."

"Mr. Wilkins, can I have a statement from you about this Super Sundae?" Elizabeth asked, her pencil poised over her notebook.

Todd stood up very straight and cleared his throat. "I would just like to say how very, very proud we all are—" Todd spoke in a perfect imitation of Mr. Cooper. Then he spoiled the effect by bursting into laughter.

"Yeah, yeah." Elizabeth stood on her toes and kissed him.

"Here come Maria and her father," Annie said as she passed Elizabeth and Todd.

Elizabeth looked around at the growing crowd. "I wonder why Robin isn't here yet?"

"I hope she's OK," Annie said quietly, turning around.

Their eyes met. "I'm sure she is," Elizabeth said. She just hoped she was right.

Robin woke up from a heavy sleep. She rolled over groggily to look at her bedside clock, and a jolt of surprise went through her. It was after twelve-thirty! The ice cream was scheduled to arrive at the school at one o'clock.

108

"Mom?" Robin's voice was weak and faint.

With difficulty, Robin raised herself on one elbow. Her head felt two sizes too big, and her chest hurt. Drawing each breath was painful. "Mom?"

She pulled herself up in the bed. The house seemed to be empty. Then she remembered that her mother was taking the boys to a cook-out today. Robin knew her alarm must have gone off, but she had obviously slept right through it. Now she was late for the Super Sundae she had worked so hard to organize.

Standing up brought on a wave of dizziness. Robin hung onto the back of her desk chair and tried to pull herself together. She could see that it was a clear, sunny day, but she felt cold. A violent chill shook her whole body, and her ears began to ring.

"Ohhh," she sighed, closing her eyes. She knew she was sick, but she felt a strong sense of responsibility. All along she had taken charge of the fund-raiser. Now she had to be at the Super Sundae, no matter what.

"What's wrong with me?" she whispered.

Getting dressed was painful and tiring. Even oversleeping hadn't lessened the overpowering exhaustion she felt. Buttoning each button on her blouse took superhuman effort, and running the brush through her hair was almost impossible. Her arms felt like lead. When she was finally dressed, she had to sit down to rest.

Somehow Robin managed to get herself out of the house and down to the corner bus stop. When the city bus stopped to pick her up, she had trouble sorting through her change. She couldn't make herself remember what the coins meant. The bus driver waited impatiently while she counted out enough for the fare. Finally, she collapsed into a seat and sat in a daze until she reached her stop.

By the time she arrived at the football field, a big crowd was already milling around. Little kids chased each other back and forth, and the ticket table was surrounded by people hurrying to buy tickets. Robin tried to focus. The bright, relentless sunlight seemed to cut through her head like a knife. She winced from the pain.

"Robin! Come on, you're so late!" Cara said, running over to her. "We need you at the ticket table."

Robin blinked slowly. "What?"

"Come on," Cara repeated. She grabbed Robin's arm and dragged her along behind her.

While stumbling along, Robin felt another wave of dizziness clouding her vision. She bumped into someone and mumbled an apology. The ticket table was the one thing she could concentrate on. If she could just get there, she knew she would be all right.

"The TV people are here," Cara said excitedly. "They want to get some group shots of us. And when the ice-cream trucks arrive, Maria's dad is going to make a formal announcement."

"OK," Robin whispered.

Suddenly Robin wished George were there. She wanted his strength and his help. But she knew in her heart that she needed something much more than George. She needed her life back again. Right now she felt transparent, weightless, unreal. She wondered for a fleeting moment if she were dying.

"Robin! Where've you been?" Jessica demanded. She shoved a can opener into Robin's hands. "Open the chocolate syrup, will you?"

Robin nodded and grasped the opener. She looked at the rows and rows of cans in front of her. She pulled one close to her and tried to clasp the opener around the lip. Her hand was so weak that she couldn't clamp it shut.

"What's wrong with you?" Jessica asked, grabbing the opener away. "We need all of these open!"

Robin shook her head. "I'm sorry," she whispered. "I can do it."

"Well, hurry up, we—here's the ice cream!" Jessica slapped the opener down on the table and darted away through the crowd.

"Attention, folks!" Mayor Santelli spoke into a microphone. "I see by your excited faces that you're all waiting for something."

The crowd's laughter echoed in Robin's head. She tried to concentrate on opening the chocolate syrup.

"If you're looking forward to this as much as I am," Mayor Santelli continued, "you're *really* hungry for ice cream! Let's remember that this event would not have been possible without the hard work and dedication of the Sweet Valley High cheerleaders. Let's give them a big hand!"

The crowd applauded. Robin stared at the sea of faces all around her. It all seemed unreal. She vaguely saw that the other cheerleaders were converging on two large refrigerator trucks that had pulled up by the kiddie pool pyramid.

I have to open this, Robin told herself grimly. Squeezing her eyes shut, Robin grasped the opener with both hands and punctured the seal on the can. With difficulty she worked the opener around the can. An intense sweetness drifted up into her face, making her feel nauseated.

"Look at all that ice cream!" a little boy yelled. "I never saw so much!"

A babble of excited voices filled the air. People were still buying tickets, and others were exchanging their tickets for bowls and spoons. Jessica, Cara, Annie, Sandy, and Amy were busily dumping ice cream into the kiddie pools. Laughter and shouts of encouragement surrounded them as the mounds of ice cream grew larger and larger.

Robin raised the lid from the can of chocolate syrup. The syrup looked like a dark, sticky well.

Suddenly Robin felt so dizzy that she couldn't see at all. The crowd's attention was so focused on the growing sundae that Robin was left completely alone.

Something's happening to me. She heard her voice as if from very far away.

"Robin?" She heard another faint voice. "Robin?"

A wash of darkness filled Robin's eyes, and she felt herself falling.

Elizabeth shoved Todd toward Robin and dropped her notebook and camera to the ground. "Todd! Catch her!"

Robin fell through Todd's arms like a stone. He knelt by her behind the table and tried to hold up her head.

"Robin?" Elizabeth cried, kneeling by her friend. "Oh, Todd. She looks awful!"

Todd nodded anxiously. "Maybe we should call an ambulance."

By now several people at the edge of the crowd had noticed Robin. Elizabeth stood up and looked at them. "Can somebody call nine-one-one?" she begged. "I think she's really sick!"

She bent over Robin again and took her hand. It was icy cold.

"Todd, she's freezing!" Todd pulled off his shirt and wrapped it around Robin. Their friend was breathing harshly, and her cheeks were deadly white.

"What happened?" Jessica asked as she rushed

113

over. "Oh! What happened to her? She looks as if she's dying!"

"She fainted," Elizabeth said quickly. She looked over at the kiddie pools. The other cheerleaders were still busily piling up ice cream and dumping out entire cans of chocolate syrup, marshmallow sauce, and cherries, but they were aware of the small group huddled on the ground. They knew something was very wrong, but they had a duty to keep the Super Sundae going.

"What should I do?" Jessica asked.

Elizabeth frowned, still watching Robin's ashen face. "Somebody's already calling an ambulance. Just keep the sundae going."

Reluctantly Jessica went back to the crowd. Elizabeth and Todd stayed with Robin and tried to rub some warmth back into her hands. Before long, they heard the wail of a siren, and soon two uniformed emergency medical technicians were taking charge. Curious onlookers were kept at a distance.

"Is she going to be OK?" Elizabeth asked.

One of the paramedics was listening to Robin's lungs with a stethoscope. "I'd say she has pneumonia," the woman said curtly. "She looks malnourished, too."

"Definitely," her partner replied. He raised Robin's eyelids and checked them with a tiny flashlight. "Is she on a diet?"

The question sent a shaft of guilt through Elizabeth. "Yes," she whispered.

She turned to Todd. "I knew she was going too far," she said in an anguished voice. "I should have tried harder to stop her!"

"You didn't know it was this bad." Todd put his arm around her shoulders. "It's not your fault."

The professional attitude and efficient behavior of the paramedics left Elizabeth speechless. She watched silently while they wrapped Robin in a blanket and placed her on a stretcher. Though the entire crowd was now aware of what was happening, people respectfully kept their distance. When Robin was put in the ambulance, a hush fell over the crowd.

"She'll be fine, ladies and gentlemen," Mr. Cooper said into the microphone. "Let's not let the ice cream melt."

When he had finished his announcement, he hurried over to Elizabeth and Todd. "What on earth happened?"

"Robin Wilson fainted," Elizabeth explained.

"Do we know why?"

Elizabeth shook her head. "She hasn't been eating. But I didn't know it was this bad."

"We'd better go call her mother," Mr. Cooper said gently as he took Elizabeth's arm. "You can tell me about it on the way."

Eleven

Robin rose up slowly through unconsciousness before opening her eyes. She had the sensation of being in an unfamiliar place. The bed she was lying on wasn't hers, and there were distant sounds that she couldn't identify. She was so tired that she couldn't remember anything that had happened. At last she lifted her heavy eyelids. She was in a hospital room.

Frowning with pain, she raised her hand to rub her temples. Something held her arm back. She looked down to see a tube attached to it. Under the white surgical tape a needle was delivering an IV drip into her system.

"What?" she murmured.

"Robin!" George whirled around from the window and rushed to the chair at her bedside.

116

"You're awake! I was so worried," he said in a choked voice.

The sight of George's familiar face made Robin feel like crying. She looked at him with wide, shadowed eyes. "Why am I here?"

"You collapsed. You have pneumonia," George explained, taking her free hand. He kissed it gently and held it to his cheek. "How do you feel?"

"I don't know," she replied weakly.

George gulped. "Robin, the doctor says you're really malnourished. Haven't you been eating?"

Robin closed her eyes. She was utterly exhausted. All she wanted to do was sleep. She didn't have the energy to think, let alone talk.

"Robin?" George looked scared and confused. "Why don't you answer me? I mean, don't, if you don't feel well, but I mean—" He stopped and squeezed her hand.

"No," Robin whispered.

"No, what?"

When Robin didn't reply, George drew a deep breath. "Your mother's here. She just went to get a cup of coffee. We've both been here all afternoon. I came as soon as she called me."

You shouldn't have bothered, Robin thought sadly.

"Robin? What's wrong? You're keeping something from me and I don't understand!" George cried desperately. "Why won't you talk to me?"

Robin felt as though a heavy weight were

117

pressing down on her chest. She felt sick and depressed and alone. Her hand lay limply in George's. Just pulling it away would be too difficult.

"Robin?" George seemed about to cry. "What are you doing to yourself? I can't stand to see you like this!"

There were no words Robin could find to tell him how she felt. She knew he was better off with someone like Vicky. Vicky was perfect, beautiful, on top of the world. George wouldn't want to bother with someone as messed up as Robin. He had made it very clear over the past few weeks that he really preferred Vicky.

George sat in miserable silence at Robin's bedside. When the door opened, George looked up, but Robin didn't have the strength to turn her head. Her gaze was fixed on the ceiling.

"Oh, honey!" Mrs. Wilson hurried over to the bed. She leaned over and kissed Robin's cheek.

"Hi, Mom," Robin said in a thin, faint voice.

George sniffed hard and stood up. "She won't talk to me." He sounded as young and hurt as a little boy who had lost his dog.

"Why don't you go walk around a little bit," Mrs. Wilson said kindly. "I'll stay with Robin."

George hesitated and then left the room.

Mrs. Wilson sat down where he had been. "Robin? How do you feel?"

Robin made the effort to swallow and met

her mother's anxious gaze. "Not very good," she said, licking her dry lips.

"What were you thinking of?" Her mother's voice was shaky. "You told me you were eating plenty at school. How could you do this?" Her voice rose in anger and in fear. "Oh, Robin," she whispered, pressing one hand to her mouth.

"I'm sorry. I just don't know how it happened."

Mrs. Wilson kissed her daughter again and smoothed her hair back from her forehead. "Can you eat something? Are you hungry?"

Robin shook her head, and her mother winced.

"I'm really tired, Mom," Robin explained after a moment. "I can't eat right now."

Her mother nodded and tried to smile. "OK. Why don't you just get some more rest. I'll be here when you need me."

As Mrs. Wilson stood up a nurse with a brisk, efficient manner came in and checked Robin's IV bottle. "How do you feel, Robin?"

"Tired." Robin closed her eyes. She wished everyone would stop asking her questions. The effort of keeping her eyes open and talking was wearing her out. Her body felt heavy and solid, as if it were being pressed into the bed by weights.

"The doctor will be by in a little while," the nurse said quietly to Mrs. Wilson. "Robin's going to sleep quite a lot. You have to expect that."

Robin kept her eyes closed until she heard her mother and the nurse leave. She knew she had made herself sick by not eating. She knew she was malnourished. Still, she couldn't imagine ever eating again. She had trained herself into a new, unbreakable habit of *not eating*.

While she lay there, grieving over everything she had lost and what her life had become, she fell back into an exhausted sleep.

When Robin woke up, the curtains on the window were drawn, and she had the feeling that it was night. She turned her head weakly. Surprise coursed through her.

Vicky was sitting on a chair in the corner of the room.

"Robin. Hi." Vicky smiled.

Robin swallowed hard. Her heart was racing painfully. "What are you doing here?"

"I came with George," she explained. "Actually, he came with me. He was so upset that I had to drive his car for him."

Robin was too tired and depressed to voice her skepticism. It didn't surprise her anymore that Vicky would be with George. Of course she would be.

"Listen," Vicky said, pulling the chair closer to the bed. She crossed her long legs and leaned forward. Her face wore an earnest expression. "I think I know what's been going on, and I thought maybe we could talk about it."

Robin turned her head away and stared miserably at the ceiling. "What's there to talk about?"

"You're anorexic," Vicky said quietly. "That's what the doctors told George and your mother. You stopped eating, didn't you?"

"I was on a *diet*."

"No, listen. I understand." Vicky paused as if to gather her thoughts. "You probably didn't like George spending so much time with me. I could tell you didn't like me the first time we met."

Robin didn't answer. She just wished Vicky would leave her alone.

"And you probably thought I was some kind of competition for you," Vicky continued. "But I have to tell you, Robin, you're so wrong. George is crazy about you. You're all he ever talks about. Even if I did want him, I wouldn't stand a chance with you around. Still, even I could tell he was being kind of a jerk about you lately, kind of selfish. I can see how you might have gotten the wrong idea."

Vicky's words didn't mean anything to Robin. They couldn't be true. She ignored them.

Vicky shifted in her chair. "We're just friends, Robin. George hardly even knows I'm a girl."

"Oh, right," Robin said with a gasp. "Vicky, you're beautiful and perfect."

Vicky raised her eyebrows. "You think I'm perfect? That's a laugh. Look, I know you probably wish I would drop dead, or at least go away—"

"Um-hmm," Robin muttered.

121

Vicky dismissed Robin's tone and continued. "—but I want to tell you something. When I was about ten, my parents' marriage started going down the tubes. But they always said they'd wait until I was at least fourteen before they'd split up."

Vicky paused and let out a shaky breath. Even Robin could see she had her own painful memories to deal with.

"You know what that did to me?" Vicky asked. "I was the baby of the family, and it was as if I were some kind of time bomb. As soon as I was old enough, my family would split up. It would be *my* fault. I didn't want that to happen. So you know what I decided to do?"

Robin was curious, in spite of herself. She looked at Vicky and shook her head slightly. "What?"

"I thought that maybe I just wouldn't grow up. If I stayed the baby, my parents would have to stay together. And so I started doing the most crazy, stupid, immature stuff. I started to smoke cigarettes, I stole booze from the liquor cabinet, I smoked pot. And I kept telling myself it was all just for one reason—to keep the family together. I didn't like what I was doing. In fact, after a while, I was pretty miserable."

"So?" Robin felt a growing sense of amazement at hearing Vicky's story. On the surface, Vicky seemed so totally pulled together. But below the surface, there was still a frightened girl whose voice shook when she relived her painful memories.

Vicky stood up and began to pace nervously. "So, I got hooked. I turned into a real dopehead. Instead of *pretending* to get into trouble, I really did. I was completely messed up. I thought I was controlling my parents' lives for the better, but all I was doing was losing control of my own. Trying to keep my family together almost killed me."

Vicky walked over to the window and twitched the curtain aside. Beyond, the sky was a deep, starry blue. Vicky sighed and shook her head.

"But what happened?" Robin asked.

"I got cleaned up. And my folks got divorced." Vicky turned away from the window with a matter-of-fact smile. "I was ruining myself for nothing. I thought I could control what people did and thought and said, but I couldn't. Nobody can stop bad things from happening."

Robin looked down at the IV tube in her arm. She knew why Vicky had told her her story. The past couldn't be an easy thing for Vicky to talk about, but she had shared it with Robin.

"I don't know what I thought I was doing," Robin admitted in a small, puzzled voice. "It's just that, sometimes it seems as if thin people get all the breaks. I know in my mind that it's not true, but in my heart I'm always afraid I'll be fat again. And I'm afraid that if I get fat, I'll lose everything in my life, all that I've worked so hard for."

"Robin," Vicky said, sitting down again by the bed, "George loves *you*. He never talks about how skinny you are, or about what a great figure you have. He talks about how funny and smart and sweet you are, and about how good you are at so many things. God! I was so jealous of *you*! I wish I had a boyfriend who was half as crazy about me as George is about you."

Robin's face flushed, and her heart gave a painful twist. Looking back over the past few weeks, she couldn't quite comprehend what she had done to herself.

"Vicky, is George still here?" she whispered.

"Yes. Do you want me to get him?"

"Yes—no! I can't see him right now. He must think I'm crazy."

Vicky gave her a sad, sympathetic smile. "All he's thinking about right now is how much he loves you, and how much he wishes you would get better."

"Yeah, well . . ." Robin sighed and looked out at the dark sky. "I have to be by myself for a while. But thanks."

She turned to look at Vicky once more. They didn't speak, but Robin felt that something important had passed between them. Vicky smiled and slipped out of the room.

When she was alone again, Robin stared at the ceiling. She had always been scornful of girls who dieted obsessively. How had she started doing it herself? The word *anorexic* came back to her and brought a tingle of fear. She knew that people who suffered from anorexia nervosa often died. She just couldn't believe that it had happened to her.

And what Vicky had told her about George made her see that he did love her, and always had. True, he had been a bit insensitive lately, but because she was feeling so vulnerable, she had blown everything way out of proportion. She wanted to tell George how sorry she was.

She would get better, and maybe they would start all over. More importantly, *she* would start all over. There were a lot of other things in her life that she needed to think about, not just George. For some time now instead of confronting her problems, she had tried to make them vanish through sheer willpower.

But life didn't work that way.

Suddenly Robin realized that getting better meant starting to eat again. A cold shiver went through her at the thought. She wasn't sure that she *could* eat again.

Maybe it was too late to start over.

Twelve

In the morning Robin woke from a refreshing sleep. Her lungs still ached, but the heavy, dull feeling in her head was almost gone.

She glanced at the door as an orderly came in with a breakfast tray.

"Good morning!"

"I'm not—" Robin stopped herself and lay quietly while he arranged the tray on her bed-side table and pulled it close for her. The orderly waved and left.

If she really wanted to get well, she would eat her breakfast, Robin told herself sternly.

Gingerly she lifted the cover from the tray to find two pieces of whole wheat toast, half a grapefruit, and a glass of milk. A pat of margarine peeked out from under the edge of the plate.

"I can eat this," Robin said, drawing a deep breath. She ignored the margarine and picked up one slice of dry toast. Very slowly she brought it to her mouth and took a tiny bite.

Robin chewed carefully, expecting to feel sick. To her surprise, she didn't experience any nausea, but she didn't feel too well, either. She resolutely took another bite and then pushed the tray to the far end of the table.

"Good morning." A red-haired woman in a lab coat walked into the room and pulled a stethoscope from her pocket. "I'm Doctor McCloud. How do you feel this morning, Robin?"

Robin propped herself up higher and nodded. "OK," she admitted. "Better."

"Great." Dr. McCloud listened to Robin's lungs while giving her brief instructions on breathing in and out. After a moment, she snapped the earpieces away from her ears and looked at Robin intently. "You sure don't waste any time when you want to get sick. That pneumonia really grabbed you."

"Oh." Robin felt embarrassed. She knew it was all her fault she was sick.

"That's because you're so weak," the doctor went on matter-of-factly. "And that's because you're anorexic. You know that, don't you?"

Robin nodded. Her cheeks were burning with shame and regret. Everyone must be so disappointed in her, she thought miserably.

"So, what you have to do first is get over the

pneumonia. Then you have to get over the anorexia."

Dr. McCloud gave Robin a sympathetic smile. "And stop blaming yourself. More people than you'd believe have eating disorders. It's nothing to be ashamed of, but then again, you do have to cure yourself of it."

"I know," Robin whispered. "I *want* to eat now. I really do."

Dr. McCloud grinned. "You don't fool me, Robin. I know you don't feel like eating. I know it's not as easy as just saying you want to eat. But you'll have plenty of help."

"From you?"

"From me, from counselors, support groups," Dr. McCloud explained. "You'll need to talk to a therapist about your self-image, and about how to separate self-image from body-image. There's a lot of jargon you'll have to get used to."

Robin was trying to understand Dr. McCloud's approach. She was putting no pressure on Robin. Why?

"Why don't you tell me I have to finish my breakfast?" Robin asked, indicating the tray.

"OK, Robin. Finish your breakfast." Dr. McCloud gave her a challenging look. "Satisfied? I'll leave you alone. I know you'd like some privacy."

Before Robin could think of anything else to say, Dr. McCloud left the room.

Robin looked over at her breakfast tray. She felt that in some way she had been tricked into eating. For a moment she stubbornly decided against touching it again. But then, just as stubbornly, she decided she wanted to show Dr. McCloud that she could be sensible and, above all, determined.

She picked up the toast and munched through it mechanically, ate three sections of grapefruit, and drank half of the milk before her willpower gave out. Her heart was hammering so hard, she could barely swallow the last sip of milk.

But it was the most she had eaten in days, she realized triumphantly. If she took things a little bit at a time, she was sure she would win.

There was a gentle tap on the door, and Robin hastily put the cover over the remains of her meal. "Come in," she said, wiping her mouth.

George opened the door. His expression was so hopeful and nervous that Robin's heart filled with love. She couldn't speak for a moment.

"Robin?" he said in a hesitant voice.

She swallowed hard and gave him a teary smile. "Hi."

It was as though a bright light had just turned on George's face. His smile was brilliant. "Hi!" He sat on the edge of the bed next to her. "How do you feel?"

"Pretty OK." Robin laughed, gripping his hand. "I wanted to tell you I'm sorry I was so stupid."

"Stop." George put a finger on her lips and shook his head. "You weren't stupid. And you're going to be OK. I love you."

"I love you, too. So much!"

As he held her close now Robin tried to really believe that he loved *her*, Robin, the whole person, not just a part of her like a body or a face. But it was hard to readjust her thinking. Robin still didn't feel good enough about herself to believe that anyone else could really feel good about her, too.

"You know what?" she said, pulling away from him with a smile. "Vicky's OK. I like her."

George grinned. "I knew you two would hit it off if you only gave her a chance."

"You were right." Robin looked searchingly into George's face. Being with him was so bittersweet. She knew that coming to grips with her problems was going to be a full-time job.

"Listen," she said in a tired, wistful voice, "I think I'm going to need a lot of time to myself."

"Oh, sure," George said, standing up. "If you're tired, I can—"

"No." Robin shook her head. "I don't mean just now, I mean—from now on."

George stared at her. "I don't understand."

"I mean, I've got a lot of thinking to do. My whole life, my family, my friends, you—I need time to sort everything out. And I have to do it by myself, at least for a while."

"Well . . ." George swallowed hard and looked away. "I guess I deserved that."

"It's not you, George," Robin said pleadingly. "This isn't about you, it's about *me*. Can you understand?"

George nodded and then gave her a brave smile. "I guess so. But I'll always be there when you need me."

Robin smiled at him and squeezed his hand. "Thanks."

Jessica took an enormous bite of pizza and concentrated on breaking the gooey string of mozzarella. "Hot, hot!" she gasped with her mouth full. The cheese didn't want to let go.

"Really classy, Jessica," Cara teased. "Is this your first time eating?"

"Second," Annie said. "I've seen her eat before."

Jessica gave her friends a glare while she chewed. Finally, she swallowed.

"Very funny."

"I thought so. Hey! Here comes Robin!" Amy nodded toward the cafeteria door.

The girls turned to watch Robin walk into the cafeteria. It had been over a week since she had been to school. She was still pale and very thin, but she looked better than the last time they had all seen her, just before she had fainted at the Super Sundae.

"Hi! Come on, have a seat," Annie said with a welcoming smile.

Robin smiled shyly at everyone and sat down. "Thanks. I only came to school so I could get some homework assignments from my teachers," she explained. "I'm not really supposed to be out of bed yet, but I talked my mother into letting me come for an hour. She's waiting for me in Mr. Cooper's office."

"Good going," Jessica said. "Listen, we finally got the money from the Super Sundae added up. Want to know how much we raised?"

Robin gave a small, tired nod. "Sure. How much?"

"With a few extra donations, we made six hundred seventy-three dollars and fifty cents," Jessica said proudly.

"It doesn't seem like very much," Robin replied.

Jessica scowled fiercely. "Well, the building fund people didn't turn it down."

"I know." Robin laughed. "I guess we *did* do a good job, didn't we?"

"A great job," Cara said, waving her hand in a grand gesture. "A superb job. A spectacular job!"

"OK, Walker," Jessica drawled. "We get the point."

"But I'm still dreaming about ice cream," Amy said with a grin. "And I still feel sticky all over."

"Speaking of which," Annie said as she stood up, "who wants an ice-cream sandwich or something from the lunch line? Robin?"

There was a sudden, tense silence at the table. Annie slowly turned red and put one hand over her mouth. "I mean, only if . . ."

Robin gave her friend a warm smile. "Don't worry about it. But no, thanks. Maybe next time."

Jessica met Robin's eyes across the table. She couldn't help but wonder if Robin was back to somewhat normal eating habits. She decided that the only way to find out was to ask.

"Did you already have lunch?" she asked lightly.

"I ate at home," Robin said, not flinching from Jessica's steady gaze. She didn't need to tell Jessica how difficult it had been.

Jessica's face relaxed into a carefree smile. "Good. So, when are you really coming back to school?"

"In a week or so," Robin replied as she stood up. "So, I guess I'll see you all then, OK?"

"Sure," the others replied.

Robin smiled, hitched her bag over her shoulder, and headed toward the cafeteria door. It looked as if the same motivation that had spurred her on to diet was going to help her get back to health. Jessica followed Robin with her eyes for a moment and then spotted Elizabeth and Enid Rollins coming into the cafeteria. "Hey, Liz! Over here," she called.

"Oh, great." Amy rolled her eyes. "Thanks, Jess. Just who I wanted to eat lunch with. Enid Rollins!"

"Thank me in a minute, Amy," Jessica replied as her sister and Enid came up to their table.

"Hi, Jess. What's up?" Elizabeth smiled at the table of cheerleaders.

"Nothing much. I just thought Enid could tell us about her cousin, Jake. You wouldn't mind, would you, Enid?"

"Of course not." Enid grinned and reached into her bag for her wallet.

"What's this about a cousin?" Lila Fowler asked as she joined the group.

"My cousin Jake is coming to spend a weekend with me and my family."

"Oh, is that all? That's really nice, Enid," Lila said condescendingly.

"Yeah. It is nice. I haven't seen him in a while. He's been so busy competing, he hasn't had any time to relax." Enid opened her wallet and removed a photograph from a plastic sleeve.

"What do you mean by competing?" Amy asked, straining to get a glimpse of the photo Enid was holding.

"Jake's a tennis player. And a pretty good one at that. He's won several local championships. . . ."

"Let's see the picture!" Lila snatched the photo from Enid's hand. "Hey! I've seen him on TV."

"Let me see." Amy grabbed the photo from Lila. "Wow! He's really cute."

"Didn't I tell you you'd thank me?" Jessica said with a grin.

"So when is Jake coming to Sweet Valley?"

"And when can we meet him?"

"Yeah, Enid. You can't keep him all to yourself."

Enid laughed at the girls' enthusiasm. "Hey, calm down. Don't worry. I'll keep you posted. I'm sure Jake will be happy to meet each and every one of you."

Enid waved at the group, and she and Elizabeth headed off for an empty table.

"I can't believe that boring Enid Rollins has such an incredible cousin," Lila said, shaking her head.

"Well, he is pretty gorgeous. But I don't know. I still think Tom McKay is cuter." Amy tossed her swingy blond hair and smiled mysteriously.

"That's the second time you've mentioned Tom McKay lately. You know he and Jean West are going out. What's going on, anyway?" Jessica asked.

"Nothing. That is, nothing yet."

Will Amy finally find her true love? Find out in *Sweet Valley High #75*, **AMY'S FIRST LOVE.**

Series
Don't miss any of the Caitlin trilogies
Created by Francine Pascal

There has never been a heroine quite like the raven-haired, unforgettable beauty, Caitlin. Dazzling, charming, rich, and very, very clever Caitlin Ryan seems to have everything. Everything, that is, but the promise of lasting love. The three trilogies follow Caitlin from her family life at Ryan Acres, to Highgate Academy, the exclusive boarding school in the posh horse country of Virginia, through college, and on to a glamorous career in journalism in New York City.

Don't miss Caitlin!

<u>THE LOVE TRILOGY</u>

☐ 24716-6   **LOVING #1** $3.50

☐ 25130-9   **LOVE LOST #2** $3.50

☐ 25295-X   **TRUE LOVE #3** $3.50

☐ 27650	AGAINST THE ODDS #51	$2.95
☐ 27720	WHITE LIES #52	$2.95
☐ 27771	SECOND CHANCE #53	$2.95
☐ 27856	TWO BOY WEEKEND #54	$2.95
☐ 27915	PERFECT SHOT #55	$2.95
☐ 27970	LOST AT SEA #56	$2.95
☐ 28079	TEACHER CRUSH #57	$2.95
☐ 28156	BROKEN HEARTS #58	$2.95
☐ 28193	IN LOVE AGAIN #59	$2.95
☐ 28264	THAT FATAL NIGHT #60	$2.95
☐ 28317	BOY TROUBLE #61	$2.95
☐ 28352	WHO'S WHO #62	$2.95
☐ 28385	THE NEW ELIZABETH #63	$2.95
☐ 28487	THE GHOST OF TRICIA MARTIN #64	$2.95
☐ 28518	TROUBLE AT HOME #65	$2.95
☐ 28555	WHO'S TO BLAME #66	$2.95
☐ 28611	THE PARENT PLOT #67	$2.95
☐ 28618	THE LOVE BET #68	$2.95
☐ 28636	FRIEND AGAINST FRIEND #69	$2.95
☐ 28767	MS. QUARTERBACK #70	$2.95
☐ 28796	STARRING JESSICA #71	$2.95
☐ 28841	ROCK STAR'S GIRL #72	$2.95
☐ 28863	REGINA'S LEGACY #73	$2.95

__ Buy them at your local bookstore or use this page to order. __

Bantam Books, Dept. SVH7, 414 East Golf Road, Des Plaines, IL 60016

Please send me the items I have checked above. I am enclosing $_____
(please add $2.50 to cover postage and handling). Send check or money
order, no cash or C.O.D.s please.

Mr/Ms _____

Address _____

City/State _____ Zip _____

SVH7–4/91

Please allow four to six weeks for delivery.
Prices and availability subject to change without notice.